NIGHTWAL. .

WISH & MERCY

Thank you for reading my book! I hope you enjoy it!

AJ Gala

BUDDY Co

BuddyCo Publishing

SACRAMENTO, CALIFORNIA

BuddyCo Publishing
3458 Ardendale Lane #A
Sacramento, CA 95825
www.aj-gala.com

Publisher's Note: This is a work of fiction. Names, characters, places, and incidents are a product of the author's imagination. Any resemblance to actual people, living or dead, or to businesses, companies, events, institutions, or locales is completely coincidental.

Book Layout © 2017 BookDesignTemplates.com

Edited by Amanda Edens
www.amandaedens.com

Cover art by Kinda Nifty
www.kindanifty.co

Nightwalker: Wish & Mercy/ AJ Gala. -- 1st ed.
ISBN 978-0-578-46598-2

This book is dedicated to my amazing support team: To Bethany, for all our 'Productivity Days'. To Kaley, for every time I've talked her ear off. To the Nightwalker Bookclub, for all the incredible feedback. To my husband Jason, for not going completely crazy! To my friends, family, and co-workers for the time, money, and interest they've given me. To Amanda, my amazing editor for her investment and encouragement.

To my parents for always nurturing my creativity and supporting all of my projects.

And to *myself.*

We did it, brain.

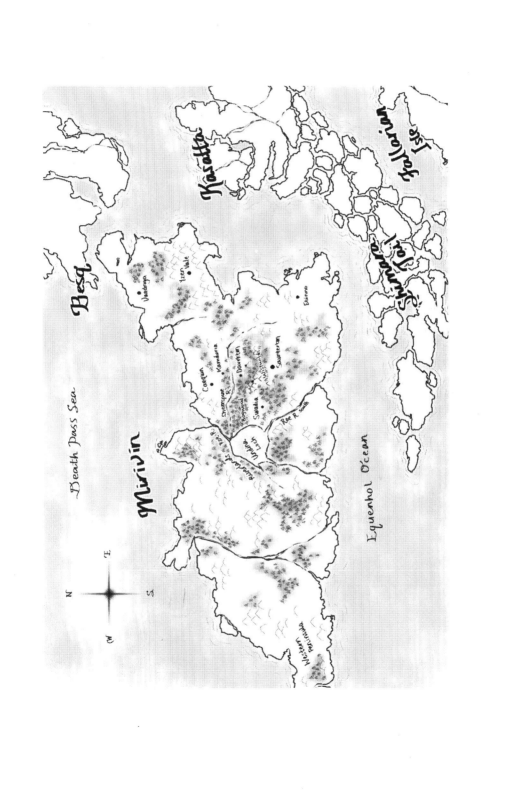

CHAPTER 1

HANGING BY A THREAD

The darkness of the forest pressed against her, bringing a wondrous chill from every angle. There was no better comfort than the damp earth beneath her and the susurration of the wind in the branches. She knew exactly where she was.

Home.

Crickets sang to her as twigs snapped painlessly under her bare feet. The autumn moon was full and bright like a watchful eye and lit up the red colors of the forest. She was still in her town of Suradia, surrounded by the oaks and rowans and elders, but this was a part of the Bogwood that she'd never seen.

She wandered without thought, pulled by her gut every which way through the maze, losing herself deeper amongst the trees. She had never seen such darkness, the branches so thick and twisted into each other that she could barely find the moon above. Her heart raced at the exhilarating possibility of being truly lost, consumed by the woods, never to return again.

But then the trees parted, and she saw a clearing. She found the moon obscured by feathery clouds—had they been there before? She dismissed the thought at once when she noticed others in the distance and stayed behind the tree line, watching in silence.

She watched two figures that were intense, quiet, and none the wiser to her presence. They were both tall, and one of them looked like nothing more than a silhouette of a ragged black cloak in the darkness of night, the torn edges drifting eerily in the breeze. The other was a woman not of this Realm. Her luminous green eyes glowed from afar, and a pair of insect wings were at rest on her bare back. Thin, wispy clothing hung off her dark-skinned body. A faerie.

The longer she stared at them, the more thunderously her heart drummed. The woman gazed at the other one expectantly before conjuring a glowing orb in her hand, and after a long bout of silence, the cloaked figure spoke.

"I can't do it."

"You must." The faerie inspected the energy as it grew in her palm.

"No. I won't!" He bared his teeth when he yelled, showing two elongated incisors. The faerie reached out and gripped his neck with her long nails.

"Yes. You will."

***

Tizzy woke with a start. The midnight forest was gone. Sun beamed into her room through wooly yellow curtains. With a grunt, she rolled onto her back and shielded her eyes, then brushed a mess of curly black hair out of her face. So much for the clouds she had seen. How late had she slept in? She sat up and hung her legs over the edge of the bed, cold with sweat and confusion.

"What was that?" Her forehead throbbed, and she rubbed at the pain. "I can't remember the last time I dreamt. And never like that."

The pain in her head sharpened, but it—unlike the dream—was nothing new. At least she could rely on a good headache to bring routine to her life.

She got to her feet and jumped at the chill on the ground. Stormy, the good mutt that he was, had snuck in and run off with her rug again, leaving behind his chewing rope as an even trade this time. Tizzy fought back a sigh and stretched the sleep from her bones, checking her room for footprints and her boots for mud. Of any evidence of the forest she'd dreamt of. But everything was clear—it had only been a dream.

She pried open the little doors to her wardrobe, deciding if it was the prospect of the dream that was annoying her or if it was just her headache.

"Does it even matter?" she mused, looking over her clothing options. She wasn't sure what would be on the agenda today, but she refused to engage in anything formal and reached for a sensible purple brocade vest to wear with a warm tunic and leather leggings. Just the thought of meeting her siblings downstairs made her head hurt even more.

She dressed and tried to smooth out the sleep in her hair before tying it up in a ponytail. The finishing touch to her ensemble was her Hallenar pendant, a stamped bronze coin on a leather cord. Each of the eight Hallenar children had one, and each bore the symbol of a different bird, chosen for them as infants by their father with his oracle talents. Tizzy's pendant was stamped with a falcon. There were definitely days where she felt like a bird of prey.

She sat at her desk, ignoring the reflection in the mirror. A leather-bound book waited for her, full of pages covered in her jagged handwriting. She stared down at her pencil, at the iridescent black feathers tied to the end, and her stomach filled with dread.

'Rustaumn 27, 1144
No one in Suradia has a cure for my headaches. Not even the
priestesses of the Hesperan Hospices, which is a letdown, to put it
lightly. Why can't they fix this? And if that's a bust, what other
options do I have? I guess I'll have to find a way to search elsewhere
on the Mirivin Mainland.

If only I could get away.

-T'

It was time. She went downstairs, and the fires and sconces flickered brightly as she walked past them. Her chore had already been completed. She wondered if her late start had forced the task into her little brother's hands and didn't imagine it had gone well. She braced herself—it might be a rough morning.

She walked the halls of the needlessly large House Hallenar, critiquing the old masonry in her mind as she did every morning. There was a crack in that corner and a stone fallen from the ancient mortar down that hall, and she didn't even know the faces in half the paintings. She passed the Hallenar banners, pristine in comparison, as they boasted a black eagle against scarlet.

They looked proud, Tizzy thought, to be hanging there in front of no one. After a slow start, she spotted the two people she was searching for. They were already deep in a meeting near the manor's entrance.

Her youngest sister Allanis the Hummingbird—the queen—and her baby brother Athen the Cardinal were the youngest out of eight siblings. When Tizzy approached, rubbing the back of her neck and staring at the ground, she was relieved to hear a pleasant conversation.

"So." She cleared her throat. "What are we doing today?"

"Tizzy! Good morning!" Allanis beamed, strumming her fingers together.

Today the queen didn't plan on meeting with many people. Atop Allanis's head of fluffy dark blonde curls was what she called her 'off duty' crown, though it was only a string of pearls that anyone else would've had the good sense to wear around their neck. Tizzy thought of a snappy remark but decided her sister's effervescence was a good sign and kept it bottled. There was no reason to stir the pot yet.

She glanced up at Athen looming beside her, but he didn't look her in the face. Nothing out of the ordinary. Typically, he radiated a youthful glow, his rust-brown eyes excited and observant, but any time she entered the scene, he shrank away. Today was no different.

"Hey," he greeted her.

She tried not to roll her eyes at the distance in his voice. "Hey."

Allanis shook her hands in the air, rustling all the silver bangles on her wrists. "Alright! Here's the news. I'm having the family get-together soon!"

"Details, Allanis. When is *soon*?" Tizzy arched her brow, waiting for an answer. Athen wouldn't look at either of them, and cutesy guilt smothered Allanis's smile.

"Tomorrow!"

"What? That short of notice?" She rolled her head back and huffed. "Great, so it'll be us and Adeska's creepy family again."

"Not this time! I sent out invites months ago!"

"So you're saying Athen and I are the last to know about this?" Tizzy was glowering.

"Of course not." Allanis waved the thought away nonchalantly. "He's the one who sent the invites. He knows!"

No wonder he wouldn't look her in the eye. As she turned her fury on him, Allanis's bubbly expression dissipated.

"You know…" She started to chew on her lip. "I haven't heard from Lazarus, Rhett, or Rori yet. I wonder if their replies got lost."

Tizzy's agitation grew. Their replies were the whole reason for planning in advance. Without the three of them, the next day's party would be no different from the sorry affair it had been last year. But as she was mulling over Allanis's words, she felt a spark.

"Wait! You mean—" she stopped and swallowed hard, "you mean you heard from—"

"No." Allanis looked away. "No, Tizzy. I'm sorry, I should have been—I should have said—" She sighed. "You know we never hear from him."

"I know." She let the spark die. "I just thought this year might be different."

Allanis clapped a hand on her shoulder. "I have every intention of making it that way, sister. Trust me." There was something so sure and confident in her storm blue eyes that when she squeezed her shoulder, Tizzy could almost believe her.

She looked up at Athen, who stood tall and awkward, and finally he made eye contact.

"Fine," she grumbled. "Fine, let's find these damn letters. Meet me at the door in twenty minutes, Athen." She didn't wait for a reply before heading back to her room. Allanis watched her, rubbing her chin.

"Are you okay here if I go searching with her?" he asked, mussing his short auburn hair.

"Oh sure, I'll be fine. Lora and I are just going to go over the finances for this month. The party is going to be the biggest we've had yet, but I don't think it's making a dent in the Byland funds. That's good," she said, putting her hands on her hips, "because there's a lot of planning and budgeting to do myself for this winter since the last advisor from King Byland's Council is dead."

"Should we appoint more?"

"Like who, Athen?" Allanis watched as Tizzy disappeared behind a corner. "We don't know anyone. Every connection we had died when King Byland did. Don't worry though!" She patted him on his back. "You're doing a great job as my Right Hand! At seventeen, you're just a fountain of wisdom!"

He could sense his sister's sarcasm and would have chuckled, but with Tizzy out of sight, his tone changed. "Does she seem worse than usual to you?"

"Yeah. Look, I know we're not real close with her, but try to listen if she opens up, okay?"

"She acts so weird this time of year."

"I think you'd better get your things and catch up with her. Good luck!"

He waved and left down the empty halls to retrieve his cloak and sword. When he was ready, he found Tizzy on her way to the entrance. It took all his courage to engage her.

"Where are we going?"

Her dry stare was piercing. "The roost. Where letters go."

"I've already checked there. All week, in fact."

"Then where else do you suppose we look?"

He was ready for this question. He had thought about it all morning, trying to prepare for her every possible word. "Maybe they got lost in the Bogwood?"

She threw her head back and groaned. "The Bogwood? Athen, are you sure? This is going to be a long day."

They cut through the humble town of Suradia with precision, starting from House Hallenar at the north and ending at the Eastern Gate into the Bogwood. Four guards stood in their dingy, mismatched armor over black and red tabards, letting people in and out with only a casual glance. When they caught sight of Tizzy and Athen, they grinned amongst each other.

"Well, if it isn't the royal family!"

Tizzy let out a full breath before responding. "If it isn't the ever-vigilant keepers of the Eastern Gate."

One of them stared at her stony expression and raised an eyebrow. "Boy, that would have sounded impressive coming from someone else."

She glared back. "We have business outside the gate. Please open it."

A guard elbowed one of the others and smirked. "Sure thing. Hey, Lady Tizzy, remind us again—how long has it been since King Byland passed away?"

His partner's grin was not friendly. "Yeah, how's the Queen faring? Oh, and didn't Master Elengin die of pneumonia recently? Gods, that's gotta be—"

When the gate had opened just enough for Tizzy and Athen to squeeze through, she grabbed his hand and brushed past them.

"Have a good day. Don't let any murderers in."

Her signature cold formality was the end of it. Any other parting words they may have had for her never reached them. Athen sighed.

"They were only trying to be polite," he said. She glanced at him over her shoulder, shook her head, and looked back to the road.

"No. They were trying to be nosy. 'How long has it been since King Byland passed away?'" She mimicked the question in a bumbling voice. "No one asks that, Athen. They know damn well how long. Thirteen years is not long enough to just forget. They want to see us respond so they can gauge how we're handling things without him."

"So?"

"It's none of their business how we're handling things without him! 'How is the queen faring? I heard Master Elengin died of pneumonia recently!'" She mimicked the other question in a shrill voice. "Good for you! I'm glad you have ears! See, Athen? It's a stupid, nosy question, and we don't need to answer stupid, nosy questions."

"Allanis said she doesn't plan on appointing any new advisors."

Tizzy shook her head again—at this rate, she thought she might shake it right off her shoulders by the end of the day. "I wish she would change her mind. She's only *twenty*; she doesn't know anything about anything. I could help find someone trustworthy, and it would take so much pressure off me to have a new council. And Lora! Poor Lora. I know she stuck herself to Allanis's side by choice, but still."

She found a proper place to step off the road and began the search for her siblings' letters. "Everyone likes to forget Allanis was six when King Byland married her and named her his successor. Lazarus should have stuck around to be her advisor, or at least he could have appointed someone *he* trusted, besides Lora. He knew Frankel Byland was too old to make it much longer than a year. We all did."

"You sound more bitter about it than the rest of us!" Athen laughed.

"Of course I'm bitter!" She could feel herself shaking. "All of our brothers and sisters got to leave and do what they wanted with their lives. But I'm stuck here because I'm the only one left to make sure you two are okay!"

An emotion hit Athen, but he wasn't sure which one it was. He was sure he was supposed to be offended, but there was also a feeling of pity and a tiny bit of astonishment that she was around because she cared. It was a brutal internal fight that left him silent. Tizzy realized too late that she had spoken a bit raw for her baby brother and changed the subject as a breeze swept through the trees.

"Gods, aren't you cold? This place is freezing."

"Not cold," he said. "But I'm a little scared. It's the Bogwood. You're not afraid of this place?"

She looked at him over her shoulder again and gave him a playful smirk. "No."

The next second, a sickening, unearthly screech made them both jump. Tizzy wasted no time searching for the source and darted between the trees, over a clutch of moss-covered boulders, and beneath a wisteria-choked branch reaching across the canopy. It had to be close.

"Over there!" She beckoned and Athen followed.

A man had fallen in the distance, one Tizzy didn't recognize from town. A fully-grown imp hovered above him, beating its leathery wings and sending leaves and feathers flurrying into the air. It was the size of a vicious guard dog, with glistening black teeth as long as Tizzy's fingers.

She identified the man as an accomplished mage right away by his green and silver Academy robes. He was trying to fend the creature off from the ground, but his staff was just out of reach.

Tizzy gripped the hilt of her sword, still in its scabbard. It was now or never.

"Stay back unless it gets ugly."

"Wait, what—"

She unsheathed Wish, her black longsword, and raced forward. Neither the imp nor the man had noticed her coming until she hacked the imp through its middle, sending it into the ground with a splash of violet ichor. It twitched and died in front of her as she caught her breath. The ichor, thick like syrup, dripped down the black blade.

"You okay?" she asked, helping the man to his feet.

He was middle aged and average in just about every regard, with tan skin and graying dark blond hair in a ponytail. Green eyes perused the siblings from behind thin bangs.

"Yes," he said, looking back at the slain imp. "Who are you two?"

"You don't know who we are?" Athen asked.

"I'm not from around here."

Tizzy sheathed Wish, cracking a smile. "Clearly. I'm Tizzy; that's Athen. We're from House Hallenar."

The man's eyes widened, and suddenly he was embarrassed. "House Hallenar? My apologies for troubling you." He bowed his head and retrieved his polished wood staff. Smooth, tumbled amethysts inlaid into a crescent shape at the top started to glimmer at his touch. "My name is Gavin Castillo. I came recently to teach at the Mages Academy. I'm not familiar with these woods, I'm afraid. I lost my footing, dropped my casting tool, and that's when the imp ambushed me."

Athen scratched his head. "Why are you in the Bogwood to begin with?"

"I'm mentoring a young mage. She ran in here looking for a spell ingredient." He eyed the trees warily. "Isa can't handle this place."

"Can you?" Tizzy smirked, folding her arms.

"Of course!" To prove the point, Gavin gripped the staff with both hands, and a ring of magenta flames flourished behind him. They danced for a second, then condensed into one fiery orb that hovered above his head.

"Good." She nodded. "Since we're both here looking for something, let's stick together. You shouldn't do the Bogwood alone." Once again, she didn't wait for an answer and started walking.

Athen followed her. "I hope your student is okay, Gavin."

"Thanks. So do I."

"This place is full of Greenkind!" Tizzy called back to them. "Keep your eyes peeled, Gavin, lest you be ambushed by a goblin next!"

***

They wandered the Bogwood for at least an hour. Tizzy tried to admire the touches of autumn all around, the colors of flame on the leaves and the bite in the air. Gavin's orb wove between trees to help search and periodically returned with no results. Even Athen was beginning to feel hopeless.

Tizzy walked past him and looked up into a tree that still had a cluster of green in its branches. "I can't believe we're looking for letters in a forest."

He sighed, digging through a bush. "Alright, so maybe it wasn't my best idea." He decided there was nothing to find and had started to stand up when something caught his eye.

Forty feet away, someone sat in the dirt between the trees. Athen approached, unsure if he'd been noticed yet, and when he was close, he saw the person was a girl. She couldn't have been more than a couple years younger than him. He didn't think she looked like a mage, at least not like the ones *he'd* seen at the Academy. In place of robes, she wore a short, billowy brown dress and leather leggings. A matching cap sat on her head and two long ponytails of dark blonde hair were draped down her shoulders. Her face was small and round and dark tan, and her large eyes were locked onto a bird at her feet.

"Isa?"

She looked up at him, crinkling the dimple in her chin. "Hm?"

"Are you Isa?"

"Uh-huh."

"Isa!" Gavin raced forward, his roomy sleeves trailing behind him.

Before Tizzy had even taken notice of the girl, she saw the bird on the ground with her. A plump white dove with a tan speck on its wing. "That's Rori's carrier. Is she crazy, sending that thing all the way from Sila'Karia? What is that, four thousand miles? Five?" The bird cooed rapidly, huffing and twitching with panic.

"It looks injured," Isa said, getting to her feet and dusting herself off. She stared up at Athen's eyes for only a second before scurrying to Tizzy. "It was carrying this too." She smiled and dropped a tiny leather tube in her hand. There was an embossed rose on the side that Tizzy recognized at once.

"This is definitely Rori's. Allanis will be relieved."

"One down, one to go!" Athen said, picking up the bird as though he had been picking up birds his entire life. "Assuming Lazarus and Rhett are sending their response together like they usually do."

Isa came up next to him and patted the dove on its head. "It doesn't seem hurt too bad. That one wing is a little roughed up, but with a little bit of care, it should be okay to fly again. Not that I'm an expert, of course!"

"I wonder how long it's been holed up here," Tizzy sighed. "Rori's an idiot." She surveyed the area where they were stopped, taking in the ground they had covered. "We've been everywhere in this damn forest except the actual Bog with no sign of Lazarus and Rhett's carrier."

Gavin chimed in. "If you're looking for letters, why not check the roost at the Academy? It's seen a fair share of unfamiliar carriers recently."

"Guess it's worth a try." She took a moment to get her bearings before starting to lead them back, shaken by a sudden cold wind. Soon they found a line of broken posts and a beaten path. The Eastern Gate waited for them at the end.

"It's the road!" Isa clapped. "I didn't realize how deep in the woods we were."

"Isa Vega!" Gavin's voice turned cross. "If you ever run off like that again, I'm making you translate the entire Tome of Anatanth!"

The student walked beside her mentor, rubbing her arms and staring at the ground. The idea of facing text in the God of Magic's cryptic language was a harrowing one. "Sorry, Gavin. But I found the red cinderflower root!"

With the road going straight back to Suradia, there was no need to continue navigating for them, so Tizzy let the others pass her. She lingered behind, taking a minute to unwind and observe what the changing of the seasons had done to the landscape this year. High winds and a powerful summer storm had changed parts that she once knew like the back of her hand. The tree she used to come out and read under was charred and black.

There was more on her mind today than there had been in years. She'd had a dream. It had been so long, she didn't think she had dreamt in at least ten—

Anxiety seeped into her chest and winded her at the very thought, and she buried it. It didn't matter how long ago it had been. It didn't matter, but her head started pounding the more she repeated it. With a deep breath, she calmed herself, and that's when she saw it.

Movement. From behind the trees. Not the wind or an animal; something else. But then it was gone. Had it been there at all? She scowled.

"I don't have time for this." The others had to be twenty paces ahead of her. She jogged ahead to reach them, ignoring a nagging thought begging her to look back. There was nothing there, and she wouldn't let herself be spooked into believing otherwise.

"Are we all friends now?" Isa asked, looking over as Tizzy rejoined them.

She ducked under a branch. "Acquaintances."

Athen, with cooing bird in hand, stared at her with his jaw hanging open, offended for Isa's sake even though the girl was oblivious. "I'll be your friend, Isa."

Tizzy ignored him.

When they were back within Suradia's walls, the sky had gone from crisp blue to a roaring sea of dark silver clouds. Rain was almost guaranteed, and Tizzy knew by the middle of next month she'd be seeing her breath outside. Gavin and Isa led the siblings to the Mages Academy, which was little more than a fat stone tower standing beside the magical library universally called the Hall of Anatanth. Even it had little to boast.

Once, Tizzy had seen the Mages Academy and Hall of Anatanth in Suradia's neighbor city, Saunterton. Both structures in the city were each at least as big as House Hallenar and garishly decorated inside and out. In comparison, Tizzy thought what Suradia offered was pathetic. She stood in front of the tower's double doors and looked up at the top of the spire, squinting.

"Gavin, can I ask you something?"

He noticed her dubious expression. "Of course."

"Why on Rosamar's Green Earth did you decide to come here?" she asked. "To Suradia?"

He rubbed his chin. "It's a long story, *la dama*." To be polite, he didn't gawk at her attempt to figure out the clue to his origin that he'd dropped, instead gazing up at the spire with her.

"To be honest, I wanted to go somewhere quiet. It's roomier than it looks on the inside, I swear, but we mostly use the Hall of Anatanth. Especially for practices and evaluations. It's just easier. Believe it or not, the Hall in your town has some very rare tomes."

"If you say so, Gavin."

"I can take you to the roost now," Isa announced, "if you'll follow me!"

Tizzy held up the leather tube from the dove and gestured to Athen. "Wonderful. You go do that. I'm going to get Rori's letter to Allanis." She turned away without waiting for an answer, but this time she gave them a parting "Bye."

She was gone. Athen's fists shook.

"Tizzy!"

Isa tugged at Gavin's sleeve. "Hey—"

"I know." He stood quietly as Athen grumbled out his frustrations, then cleared his throat. "Excuse me, Lord Athen. I wanted to ask you something, and please forgive me if this is too much of an intrusion. Do you know there's something off about your sister?"

He looked back at him with a scowl still on his face. "Obviously."

"No, no!" Isa said. "We don't mean her attitude. That's not it. There's something else."

He sighed and rubbed the back of his neck, watching Tizzy grow more and more distant like some kind of terrible metaphor. "I know. My oldest brother and sister are both mages, and they've hinted at it for years, but they've never really come out and told us anything. There's this big gap in time that everyone just ignores, and whenever I get the chance to ask them myself, I lose my nerve."

"I can't put my finger on it," Gavin said, pushing open the doors, "but something is definitely strange about her."

Athen looked up at the magical symbols carved in the doorframe as Gavin led him in.

"Something wrong, even."

***

House Hallenar was a half-hour walk from the Academy. Tizzy climbed the steps to the front terrace, her breath leaving her sometimes in a grunt and sometimes in a sigh as her feet grew heavier and heavier. The ivy was out of control, growing up anything it touched, but Allanis often balked at the thought of hacking it all away. She had told Tizzy a hundred times that she thought the overgrown look was 'charming.'

She arrived at the entrance doors and pushed past them. Of course they weren't barred or locked; Allanis's blissful ignorance wouldn't allow for even a shred of safety. She let them close behind her and leaned on them for a moment. Her headache was getting worse. Fortunately, the day would be over soon, and she could fight it from the comfort of her bed.

Allanis was farther down the entrance hall in a small, dusty throne room. The queen treated it more like her own personal office, especially today. She was sinking into the throne's plush red cushions, a ledger in her lap and twirling a leather-wrapped pencil, deep in thought. When the front doors creaked shut and were followed only by silence, she looked up.

"Tizzy?" She stood up. "What's wrong?"

Tizzy straightened up and walked over to her, placing the leather tube in her hand. "Here. We found Rori's letter."

Allanis took it and raised an eyebrow. "You didn't answer my question."

"It's just a headache."

"Another one? Tizzy, I told you to see the court physician about those! And then I told you if you didn't want to talk to him about it—because I know how you are—at least go to a Hesperan Hospice! You need to get those taken care of!"

"It's nothing."

"But it's every day."

Tizzy watched her pout before walking past her. "Athen is looking for Lazarus and Rhett's letter in the roost at the Mages Academy. I'm going to sleep for a while."

Allanis sighed and opened the tube, unrolling a letter almost too small for the handwriting it bore.

'Hello, Sister!
I am ecstatic to announce that I am en route to House Hallenar, and I will be attending your party!
Love, Rori'

Next to the signature was a sketch of a rose and the Hallenar 'H' in loopy cursive. Allanis wanted to be excited but wasn't.

Tizzy fled to her room and shut the door, then threw herself onto the bed. Grumbling like a child, she rolled on her back and folded her hands over her stomach. Her rust-brown eyes stared at the wood beams above, and flashes of what she'd seen in her sleep came back to her.

"Was that really just a dream?" She searched her memory for the cloaked figure's face, but all she could remember were his fangs. Fangs like bloodkin.

"No. I won't."

The words echoed in her mind before she rolled onto her side.

"Of course it was just a dream."

She was desperate to fall asleep, but there were too many thoughts swimming through her head, and she couldn't make peace with any of them. Instead, she lay on top of the blankets, running from memory after memory as they tried to swallow her whole.

The first one she forced herself to relive was pleasant enough. She was young, maybe eight or nine. Her father was recently deceased. With her mother having died shortly after giving birth to Athen, the death of her father meant that she was in the care of her two oldest siblings, Lazarus and Adeska. This was no easy task for two adults, much less for a sixteen-year-old and a thirteen-year-old, respectively. But as Tizzy recalled, life wasn't so bad despite their grief.

Back then, they were still living on the family farm and there was more than enough work to keep everyone busy and cooperative. Studies, chores, tending the farm, looking after baby Athen, and somehow staying afloat despite not knowing how the world worked.

Their system worked until it didn't have to. In this memory, Tizzy had a large scrap of paper laid out on the wood floor. She couldn't remember how she had come across it, but she remembered what it felt like. The clumps of paper pulp weren't smoothed out, leaving the surface bumpy and toothy. Had Adeska bought something wrapped in it? Details lost to time. All she knew for sure was that she had marked it to hell with a scavenged piece of charcoal. She beamed proudly as she drew what she thought was a fantastic-looking tree.

"Wow! That's so good!"

That's why this memory hurt so bad. She looked at the boy next to her, and chills ran through her body. He looked a lot like she did at that age. Before her hair grew dark, it was auburn just like his, though he hadn't inherited their mother's curls. He looked at her from under scruffy bangs with her same rust-brown eyes. He was stuck to her side in this memory just like in every other.

"Thanks!" she had replied. She could remember how dirty her face felt from the charcoal. "I'm going to sign it just like a famous artist!" She scratched a big 'T' in the bottom right corner of the paper.

"Tizena Hallenar!"

The use of her full name was jarring. Adeska marched in and stood in the doorway with her hands on her hips.

"I thought I told you to stop digging through the hearths! You're a mess, and you're setting a terrible example for the rest of your siblings!"

Only thirteen, and Adeska the Peacock had the heavy-hitting words of a matron. Even back then, she was perfect at being perfect. Clear skin, golden hair, sapphire blue eyes, a sharp mind, and a kind heart.

She was the standard that others would set themselves to, not that it was necessarily Adeska's fault. She was just naturally that way and always had been.

She stared Tizzy down with an angry look that she rarely wore in those years. Tizzy looked back up at her with shame.

"But look at what she made, Adeska!" the boy piped up with a smile.

Adeska took a few more steps into the room to look at the drawing and her face softened. Tizzy had painstakingly drawn the entire farm, including the cramped little farmhouse and barn, the wheat field and the cabbage field, Tizzy's favorite horse, a single flower in a random place, and the whole family of eight.

Adeska gazed at it with a thoughtful smile. "If I get you some real pencils, will you stop using lumps of charcoal?"

Tizzy gasped and cupped her hands together. "Yeah!"

Chuckling, Adeska walked out and peered back at them from behind the doorframe. "Alright, clean up, you two. Lazarus and I are almost done making dinner."

When she left, the boy rolled onto his stomach to inspect the drawing. "Wow, real pencils! What are you going to draw with them?"

They did everything together. She could have drawn any number of adventures. The times they pretended to be pirates and she was the captain, plundering Adeska's things. The times they dug out trenches and raced rocks. Or the one time they'd carved faces on every single potato in the pantry. He had tried to take the blame, but everyone knew she was the one running the show.

She didn't have a waking moment without him.

"I'm going to draw us!"

The memory faded after that. She gripped her pillow till her hands were shaking. A quick nap was all she was asking for. That was it. But her mind fed her another memory instead.

"What happened to you?" she remembered herself saying.

She was older now. Fourteen? Almost fourteen? So much had changed from the last memory, including their living conditions. Four years prior, when Tizzy was ten, Allanis had snuck out to go swimming in the lake at night, and it turned out that the king, seventy-year-old Frankel Byland, had done just the same thing. But the cold night waters treated him much differently than they did young Allanis, and she jumped in to save him from drowning. This feat left the king both impressed and grateful. Frankel Byland's own family had all died of pneumonia almost a decade before, leaving him completely devoid of a successor. Thus, at six years old, Allanis was married, tested for Royal Magic, and made queen.

Frankel himself succumbed to pneumonia less than a year later. The whole family lived comfortably at the newly renamed House Hallenar. Things changed.

Tizzy's hair had grown dark brown with the years. So had the boy's from the last memory. He was standing in front of her, his face bloody and bruised.

"It was Rhett," he finally answered her. His left eye was newly blackened before the right one had time to completely heal, and his nose looked broken. Again.

She would have done anything to avoid this memory, but her mind fought her like a person in its own right. She would see this, and she would feel this no matter what. Instead of the compassionate response she knew she should have given him in hindsight—a response she had always given him when this happened—she remembered her pointless anger and the scathing words that had actually come out of her mouth.

"What is the matter with you? This wouldn't keep happening if you could just stop pissing everyone off!"

"I don't even know what I'm doing wrong!" he cried out. "Nobody even cares that this keeps happening to us! Why don't they care?"

She scoffed. "You're such a liar. You know exactly what you're doing. That's your real problem, isn't it?"

"Tizzy."

The broken look on his face was the last part of the memory she could bear before opening her eyes. She was in tears as she rolled onto her back and stared into the beams.

***

There was commotion in House Hallenar. Tizzy, disoriented from her failed attempt at sleep, came halfway down the grand staircase to observe. Athen was finally back from his expedition into the roost of the Mages Academy and had brought Gavin and Isa back to receive the queen's gratitude.

Lora was there, too, glued to the queen's side. She was a tall, dark, and handsome woman Lazarus adopted into the family ten years ago when he'd made a trip to the arid Besq Mainland. She rubbed Allanis's shoulder fondly while the queen bubbled over with anticipation.

"Well, Your Grace," Gavin began, stealing a glance up at Athen. "It took us awhile, but we managed to find this." He handed over a foul-smelling black leather tube, and Allanis snatched it up. It took her just seconds to read its contents, and then she burst.

"I can't believe it!" She threw her hands into the air, then brought them back to look over the letter again. "Yes! This is amazing! Everyone is coming!" She looked up at Tizzy on the staircase. "Tizzy! Tizzy, they're all going to be here!"

"No they're not!"

Allanis felt her breath leave her. "I—"

"How can you say that?" Tizzy shouted. "You all act like he doesn't even exist!"

"Wait, Tizzy, please. I didn't—"

"You and your stupid parties." She turned and stomped back up the stairs.

Allanis's big eyes looked silvery as they welled up. She bit down on her quivering lip. She worried about Tizzy as usual, but this time, she was wounded for her own sake. For a long, hollow moment, it didn't feel like there was anyone else in the room with her. Then, Isa broke the silence.

"Like who doesn't exist?"

She looked down and fidgeted with her hands. "Aleth." She swallowed hard. "We don't really talk about him anymore." She felt Lora's hand on her shoulder again. "But it's funny. Lazarus used to say that the only people in the whole world who knew Tizzy and Aleth were Tizzy and Aleth."

He hated to be nosy, but Gavin couldn't stop himself. "What happened to him?"

"Athen and I were too young to remember what really happened," she said, sniffling, waving her hand in the air. But she wanted to explain. She wanted to *have* an explanation. "It was just—"

She stopped trying and put a hand over her mouth. There were no words. She stared down at the rough stonework under her satin slippers, feeling all the eyes in the room heavy on her shoulders.

Then she stood up straight and found a smile. "On a different note, is there anything that you or the Academy needs? You two were a great help. I'd love to make some extra contributions."

"I only ask for your continued support, my queen." Gavin bowed deeply, and Allanis continued to fidget.

"If you say so."

"Come on Isa, let's go."

"Good night, Your Grace! And you too, Lord Athen, Lady Lora!" Isa waved and showed her dimply smile. "Oh, and tell Lady Tizzy we said good night!" A moment later, she was gone with Gavin.

With a defeated sigh, Allanis took a few steps into the throne room and crumpled up into the chair. "Athen, bust out the good wine."

He scratched his head. "You mean for tomorrow?"

"No. For tonight. Definitely for tonight."

CHAPTER 2

MY SISTER'S PARTY

RUSTAUMN 28, 1144

It was midnight in the forest again, but this time, she knew exactly where she was. She stood in the middle of a patch of blackened trees that would never grow anything again. She strode through the Bogwood, ducking past the sharp, jagged branches that reached out for her like monsters in the night.

She saw the cloaked figure again, deep in the woods. He was searching for something. In the sky, the moon was full and round and glinted off the black-bladed sword in his hand.

***

Tizzy opened her eyes. It was morning, but no sun greeted her—the colors of sunrise were fighting with a sky full of heavy, dark clouds. Pinks and purples bounced off the sullen gray. She rolled onto her back and tried to sit up, but her body was cold and felt a thousand pounds heavier. With a grunt, she forced herself out and wrapped herself in a blanket.

This morning, she was drawn to the old, ornate mirror on her desk as she recalled the dream. Had she missed something? Was there supposed to be more to it? She approached her reflection slowly, her joints cracking a little with each step.

Once upon a time, the mirror belonged to her mother, but when the woman passed, it was inherited by the oldest sister. Then, some years later, Adeska confessed that having it around her all the time was depressing, and the heirloom went to Tizzy. It was a nice mirror. It looked proper with all the other nice things Tizzy kept on the desk in an effort of feeling like 'royalty.' She had a small lacquered box for jewelry that she never wore next to birthday letters from family members she didn't openly resent. There was even a dried yellow rose from a birthday bouquet—she figured it was Allanis who was leaving it anonymously every year, but the queen wouldn't fess up to it. On the other end of the desk, she kept her favorite books and plays, her diary, and a black feather that lit up with iridescent colors in the right light.

She looked down at everything and got a sour feeling in the pit of her stomach. Her reflection stared back at her.

"I look like hell this morning." For so many years, she had seen herself in the middle of that tarnished bronze frame. She narrowed her eyes and touched the mirror's surface, smearing a fingerprint down the middle. "I'd smash you into a million pieces right now if I wouldn't have to clean it up."

"Tizzy, are you awake?"

She looked back toward the door. "Allanis?" This was another strange morning. Her sister never came for her this early. When she opened the door, the queen stood with a proud smile and a mess of quality black fabric in her hands.

"Good morning!" she sang. She was still wearing the 'off duty' crown, but today she paired it with a fine gown of forest green and ivory silk and a black lace bolero. Pearl accents and jewelry made the perfect queenly touch.

"Good morning," Tizzy replied, leaning on the door. She fought the tiny smile that worked its way onto her lips but gave in. Allanis always woke on a fresh start, too busy buzzing about from project to project to stay angry, and after the tense ending of the night before, Tizzy was grateful.

Allanis brought her shoulders up in excitement. "I got you something for tonight!"

Tizzy winced. The phrase was attached to horrible memories and poor taste in fashion over the years. "Allanis, I don't—"

"*Before* you say no, look at it." She handed over the fabric with a little shove.

Tizzy took it and stepped back into her room, trying to bottle away all her new anxiety. She hated the autumn reunion. The dress made it real. It was happening, just like it did every year. With a shaky exhale, she found the top of the garment, shook it out, and held it against her body.

"I—"

"Yes?"

But this year's dress was different from the ones Allanis had commissioned for her for past events. She would say "Tizzy, you need some color!" or "Tizzy, this shape would look beautiful on you!" before spurring garish patterns, ruffles, lace, *chartreuse*, and other mishaps on her. This dress was not like that. Its main feature was a low-cut bodice constructed with black feathers, and Tizzy tried to hide that it nearly took her breath away. Sheer black silk formed a high-collared neckline to afford her a little modesty. At the neck was a black laurel leaf choker. The gown had delicate black beading under the bust that glittered in the low light coming in through the window, and at the hip, it trailed off into several heavy black skirts. Allanis balled up her tiny fists in anticipation.

"I actually kind of like it," Tizzy told her with a smile.

She let go a sigh of relief. "That means you'll wear it tonight, right?"

In fact, Tizzy couldn't *stop* smiling. She held out the skirt, pretending to be ladylike. "I guess so."

"Great! I've got some—" she coughed with a smile, "—important matters to take care of now, preparations to arrange, you know how it is. Have a good day! I'll see you in a while!" Allanis turned away with a wave and Tizzy closed the door.

She laid the dress out on her bed and smoothed it out. "Maybe this year will be different."

The outlook on the party may have been a bit brighter, but she desperately needed to start her day. There was a whole new set of chores left in her lap now that Athen was on cooking duty and Lora would be accompanying Allanis wherever she went. She threw on some sensible clothes, slipped on her necklace, and headed out.

She made her way to the last fireplace before the grand hall and saw someone waiting for her, curled up into a little ball, wagging his tail.

"Stormy!" The gray-brown mutt leapt up and jumped around her. "Do you want me to make you a fire? Are you cold, boy?" She rubbed the dog's jowls. "Did Athen give you eggs this morning? Hmm? Did he give you eggs?" Stormy barked in excitement, and Tizzy laughed. "Okay, Stormy, okay. I'll get this fire going just for you. It'll be *your* fire. Don't let anybody else sit by it, got that?"

Stormy barked again and followed her outside to a woodshed. Maintaining the fires in cold weather had always been Tizzy's job and her job alone, so stocking the shed with different firewood had become a hobby. It was exciting to find traders with exotic-smelling woods that she could burn for special occasions, and Allanis said to make it festive at the onset of the season. Today, Tizzy had bundles of walnut, maple, and applewood at the ready with a hint of cinnamon bark.

She picked up a bundle for the fireplace in Stormy's belvedere and another for the hearth in the grand hall. Stormy carried the bag of kindling supplies in his mouth, proudly following her inside.

"Such a good boy!" she whispered to him, laughing at the crazy movement of his tail, the way it shook his whole body back and forth.

She lit the fire in the belvedere with ease. The woods she chose were slow burning and wouldn't need attention until much later. She patted Stormy on the head, made some kissing noises, and moved onto the hearth in the grand hall.

It was an unusually good morning, Tizzy thought, striking a spark onto a bed of tinder with her flint. Even the pain in her head was bearable. For a moment, she sat by the growing flames, then started for the woodshed again for supplies for the next fire in the belvedere on the opposite end of the manor. But hushed voices on the other end of the grand hall stopped her in her tracks. She crept behind a corner to watch.

Athen walked Gavin in through the front doors. What was Gavin doing here? She strained to hear what they were saying.

"Did you find out what's wrong with her?" Athen asked.

Gavin looked away. "We did."

"Well?"

There was a long pause before Gavin had decided on what to say. He folded his hands neatly behind him. "Lord Athen, you and Lady Tizzy not only came to my aid yesterday but to Isa's as well. I believe your sister is a good person." He cleared his throat and stared at the ground. "That is why I feel it's better I say nothing. Sometimes, silence is the most helpful information of all. I hope you understand."

"Good morning, Lady Tizzy!"

She nearly jumped out of her skin at Isa's arrival. "It's you." She had been seconds away from tearing into the scene. "Why are you two here?"

Tizzy held her scowl despite Stormy liking the girl enough to leave his private hearth and come over. Isa fidgeted with the lace trim on her pink capelet as the mutt sniffed her boots.

"Well, we—we came because we wanted to tell you something."

Athen grew belligerent. "What do you mean you won't tell me? If you really know something, I will have the queen come out here and demand—"

Gavin didn't flinch. "We've had words already, actually. She was quite understanding of the situation."

Isa took a deep breath. "I don't know how to say this, Tizzy, but I'll do my best. If you ever need anything, come find us. Okay? Gavin and I are here to help. You can't tell them everything." She paused and gestured to Athen. "I get it. You'll just get them all riled up and worried. Sound about right?"

Tizzy clenched her jaw. "You come here thinking that after half a day walking around together, you know something about me? About my family?" The worst part was that Isa had it exactly right. "You think I'm that easy to read, do you?"

Isa watched her and Tizzy could see that the young girl fought the fear that her cold responses evoked. Tizzy told herself to soften, to be kinder, but right then she felt like she was going to come undone.

Isa's face changed again, this time from fearful and intimidated to wondering.

"I feel like I should push you away, but I know you need someone," Isa said.

"Are you serious?" Tizzy narrowed her eyes. "I'm getting your *pity* right now? Isa, what the hell is this? *What's going on?*"

Isa's face screwed up in thought for a second. Then, she draped one of her ponytails across her chest and started working at the soft pink ribbon tied around it.

"Gavin said that where we're from, girls like to share little pins and bows and trinkets with each other to show that they want to be friends." She offered it to Tizzy with a nod. "Here. Just hold onto it, okay?"

"Your ribbon?"

"I don't have much else to offer you, unfortunately, but I think you should have it. You ever get one of those feelings? Maybe try it on! I think pink is your color." When she smiled and didn't see it bleed over to Tizzy, she cleared her throat. "Boy, it looks like Gavin and I better get out of here before your brother turns purple!" She scratched Stormy between the ears and waved goodbye before running to Gavin's side. Athen was furious watching them leave, and Tizzy was too, for a completely different reason.

Was it too much to ask to be left alone? To not have people you were supposed to trust always talking about you? Isa's ribbon shook in her fist.

The rest of the fires could wait. She set off for her room to fume until she was fit for company again, but as she opened the door and crossed the threshold, her head erupted in pain.

It was the worst it had ever been.

Her eyes watered, and she struggled to swallow back the tears. The throbbing in her skull grew sharper and louder with every beat of her heart. The all-consuming agony pushed out all her thoughts. All she could hear was her body and the blood rushing through her veins.

"Just breathe," she told herself. But she could barely see. Her eyes couldn't focus, and everything around her was hazy and dancing and added to the chaos.

"Tizzy?"

Allanis stood in the doorway as Tizzy leaned over her desk.

Tizzy bit her lip. "It's *just* a headache."

The queen came inside and shut the door behind them. "I know you've been having them since the accident."

"Shit, Allanis! I don't want to talk about the accident!"

"What happened, Tizzy? Lazarus won't tell me the whole story, but I know that's when everything changed. Just talk to me, please!"

"Why do you want to know?"

Allanis folded her arms. "Because I need to know how to help you when you get like this!" When Tizzy remained silent, she threw her hands up. "Come on! I have been asking this family forever, and no one ever answers me! What happened twelve years ago? Out with it! I'm tired of this, and I know you are too!"

Tizzy straightened and glared at her. "You really want to know what happened? Fine. I don't know what he told you, but I'm sure there's not much more to it. You've already got the first part down—I was twelve.

"I had just finished my chores, and Lazarus and I were horsing around in the garden before he left for his classes. Remember? That's how it was every day after you became queen. But Lazarus always let me win no matter what game we were playing. I wanted to win for real, so I climbed a tree and waited for him to walk by, and then, when I leapt, the branch beneath me broke, and I missed him entirely. My head was the first thing to hit the ground, right on the rocks at the base of the tree.

"I know you remember all the blood if you think hard enough. Lazarus doesn't like to talk about it because the court physician said I was *dead*, and you know him. He blamed himself. He never stopped. And a day after my Rite of Crossing, just before I was to be entombed, everyone says I just *woke up*. And then everything was different. Everything changed."

The memory of Aleth coming to her after a violent encounter with Rhett was vivid in her mind for a second. *Everything changed*. She sat on the edge of the desk and sighed.

"And then, all the things that happened *after*... there's just no way to explain—" She let the words die in her throat, then threw her hand up. "Now do you understand why we don't talk about it?"

Allanis was frowning. "I suppose." She leaned against the desk beside her. "Do you think, maybe—"

"I don't know why things are the way they are, so drop it, okay?"

"Fine. I put up with an awful lot from you, you know that?"

Tizzy grunted. "I could say the same of you."

"Are you going to be okay tonight?"

"Yes."

"Alright. I believe you."

She left, and Tizzy thought about what Isa had said. Once her headache dulled, she went back to her chores.

***

It was still early in the day when the first guests arrived. Allanis was discussing linens with Lora, who sported a dirty apron with disdain. Athen walked by with a towel and a hot pot, dodging an inquisitive Stormy. Then the doors, unbarred and unlocked as usual, creaked open.

"Hello? We're here!" Adeska walked in with a toddler on her hip and a tall, somber man behind her. "Hey everyone!"

"Adeska!" Allanis tossed her paperwork into the air and ran to her sister's side. Lora picked up after her, trying to remain patient. "Is that a new bodice? It looks nice! And the peacock on your Hallenar necklace is so shiny!"

Adeska chuckled. "Allanis, stop. You know I don't have anything nice to wear. Not after the weight I put on with *this little one!*" She kissed her daughter on the nose—her daughter who didn't resemble anyone in the family at all. And that wasn't the only thing the family said about Mariette when Adeska was out of earshot.

Often, she was lovingly described as creepy. The pale girl stared unblinkingly with heterochromatic eyes—one that was dark blue like her mother's and the other a haunting icy blue. Somehow her gaze, though it met no one, felt as if it were locked onto every soul in the room.

Allanis shook away a sudden chill and moved to give her sister a hug. "You're as beautiful as ever, Adeska!" She batted her eyelashes and then started laughing. "Listen to me say that like I haven't seen you in ages. You were here just the other day!"

"Feels like it's been forever, though!"

Athen started fumbling in front of the kitchen. "Hot, hot! It's hot!"

"I'd better go help him." Adeska handed the child over to her expressionless husband who had not grasped the word *formal* written on the invite. "Here, sweetheart!" He took the girl without a word and watched Adeska scamper off to the kitchen with Athen.

Just like that, Allanis's anchor was gone. She looked up at Centa with a sheepish grin. Sure, he may have been a little disheveled, but it was no mistake why Adeska was first interested in him. His expression, though it was hard, was worn on a handsome, chiseled face that was deep, coppery tan. He left his dark brown hair a tousled mess, always, and seldom locked his dark, mysterious eyes on anyone.

"Hello Centa; hello Mariette!" Allanis cooed, tucking a lock of the toddler's white-blonde hair behind her ear. She liked her sister's family, and it was never *enjoyable* to talk about them in secret, or at least that's what she said to Lora to make herself feel better afterward. And besides, sometimes the children of mages just looked strange, and Adeska was proficient with magic.

"Say hello," Centa told his daughter. Allanis didn't know much about the man but had gathered that he wasn't from the Mirivin Mainland. He had just the faintest remains of an accent, and all Adeska had said regarding his birthplace was that it was "some islands." And the name Centa Anuhea Jinzera didn't help her narrow down which ones.

"Hi."

At last, the girl spoke. Allanis cheered and clapped her hands.

The day was getting back to a fine start once the earlier hiccups had passed. Tizzy spent over an hour getting ready in her new gown.

She hated how vulnerable she felt in it. It wasn't her; she didn't belong in it.

She fixed the problem with a pair of leather leggings and boots underneath. Allanis would never even know.

Before long, Lora came to her room with makeup. The Besqi woman set a silk-covered chest on top of Tizzy's desk, then turned to look her over.

"My, my. Allanis bet it all on black and hit the jackpot."

Tizzy stared at herself in the mirror. "You think so? I don't really feel like myself."

Lora chuckled and opened the chest, taking out a little black pot and a thin brush that came to a point. "That's good. If you stood up straight and glared at everyone like usual, this dress would give you too much power."

She accented Tizzy's eyes with a thin line of black kohl paint, then dabbed a pomegranate-red stain on her lips.

"There." Lora twisted the lid back on the stain. "I don't think I need to fuss with you any more than that. You're fetching, even if you do look like you're going to eat someone alive. The queen will just have to accept that. What do you think?"

Now that she saw herself all done up, Tizzy wasn't sure how she felt. On one hand, she thought she looked ridiculous. Did her body even look right in a dress? But on the other hand, she was downright impressed. The black feather bodice, the glass beads glittering like stars against the fabric—she'd never seen herself in a garment that was so inarguably *her*.

And then Lora left, and she realized it was easy to admire herself from behind a locked door all day, but that would never stand. The queen's big event brought the same dread every year—formal attire she didn't feel comfortable in and distant family that she didn't feel comfortable around.

"Allanis needs me," she mumbled, fighting for the courage to leave her room. "I have to go out there. Allanis needs me to help her with this stupid party." She let out a shaky sigh, running her fingers over her Hallenar necklace. "Breathe, Tizzy."

She left her room and walked the upstairs hallways that looked into the grand hall, sliding her hand along the rails. A massive table had been set up, seating at least fifty, though there would be half that in attendance at best. Lora had almost finished the centerpiece when it came time to help Allanis again, which left Adeska to put in the finishing touches. The oldest sister took pause in the chore to fold a napkin for Mariette, who remained unresponsive.

Centa was setting up a smaller table only a few paces away, arranging wine glasses and House Hallenar's finest collection from vineyards far and wide. He picked a few unique bottles and came over to the main table.

"See the napkin bird, Mariette?" Adeska asked, giggling and waving the napkin. "What noise do birds make?"

Mariette said nothing.

"So." Centa set one of the bottles down and eyed it beside the autumn-inspired centerpiece. "The necromancers are really going to be here?"

Adeska heard his thinly veiled disapproval loud and clear. "Yes, sweetheart. They're my family. And Rhett isn't actually a necromancer, just Lazarus."

"It matters? They both practice Forbidden Arts."

Adeska grumbled and leaned into her hand.

Up above, Tizzy drummed on the rails and whispered to herself. "Of course. The Lord and Lady Perfect are here."

As if on cue, Centa started again. "And what's Tizzy's problem?"

"Hey!" Adeska raised a finger at him. "We are never to bring that up! I told you that!"

Tizzy was gripping the railing so tight, her hands were shaking when she let them loose. Everyone always had something to say when they thought she wasn't there. "So far, this year is looking a lot like the last." Too much alcohol and not enough entertainment, as she recalled. 'Criticize Tizzy' had become the fun game of the evening for the few family members who had bothered to show up.

Then everyone heard soft footsteps. Allanis darted into the grand hall, winded.

"I've got just a minute to check in! I have to start getting myself ready, but everyone should be showing up soon! And wow!" She stood in front of the table, completed at last. "This looks great!"

"Thank you!" Adeska smiled. "Mari and I did alright, but Lora laid some impressive groundwork. I can't take all the credit."

"She is amazing," Allanis swooned. "I just came by to let you all know that I'll be awhile. If you could just check up on Athen in the kitchen every now and then, that would be good. He prefers to cook by himself, but he'll also bite off more than he can chew. Now if I could just find Tizzy."

"I'm here."

Allanis whipped around and gazed at the grand staircase, her jaw agape. "You look fantastic!" She tried to contain her excitement as Tizzy came forward. She couldn't. Beaming, she bobbed up and down, watching as the great vision she'd had bubbled over into her surroundings. "I know you said you liked the dress this morning, but I was still worried you weren't going to go through with it. Look at you!"

Tizzy fought the sudden urge to smile. She kept her composure and didn't meet Allanis's eyes.

The queen shook the last of her jittery enthusiasm out, all her pearl bracelets clinking against one another. "This is perfect! Here's the guest list. You know the drill—if anyone shows up who isn't on this list, can I count on you to handle it?" She grinned.

"Yes, I'll handle it." She took the paper and chewed her lip.

"Okay, see you soon everyone!"

Allanis skipped away, and Tizzy was alone with Adeska and the in-laws. She had no time to avoid her older sister's hug.

"Tizzy!"

"Calm down!" She shrugged her away. "I just saw you a few days ago."

"Sorry!" Adeska blushed and started rubbing at a speck on her bodice that wasn't there. "I just get excited to see family. You know how I am."

Everyone moved to the table, and Centa opened a bottle of wine. He made her nervous, so she turned her attention to her niece while he poured three glasses.

"Hi there, Mariette."

"Hi, Auntie."

"Hello, Tizena."

Tizzy swung her head in Centa's direction and gave him a dry stare. "I told you to stop calling me that. And hello." She rolled her eyes and finally decided to go over the paper Allanis had handed her. "Wait, she said this was a family reunion, didn't she? Why is there a guest list?"

Adeska swirled the wine around in her glass. "She said she wanted it to be really special this year, so the first part of the night is going to be friends and family. Then the friends will leave, and it'll be just us! Like a real party!"

That sounded exhausting, Tizzy thought. "The 'friends' part of the list is just people from your guys' old raiding party."

"Really?" Adeska's sigh was bittersweet and longing. "That's wonderful! Who's coming?"

"Let's see," Tizzy scanned the names. "Lex and Dina are both coming. If I remember them correctly, that's a party in itself."

"You remember correctly." Adeska took a sip. "Ooh, that's tart. Sweetheart, I don't know if I like this one."

"Let it breathe; I just opened it." Centa tried to get comfortable on the padded bench seating, scooting from cushion to cushion until he finally stilled himself. "Who else is going to make it?"

"Someone named Cato."

Mid-sip, Adeska spewed wine all over the table.

"Mommy, there's a mess."

Adeska coughed and blushed as she reached for a napkin. "Yes, honey, there sure is."

"I haven't seen Cato in ages!" Centa was oblivious to the spill, caught up in a reverie that made him smile in a way Tizzy had never seen before. Actually, she wasn't sure that she had ever seen him smile. "After the raids, most of us still stayed pretty close, but Cato, he's always got a lot going on. I feel bad that we drifted apart."

Tizzy had only been half listening when she saw her mistake. "Oops, I was wrong. His name is crossed out. Silly me."

Centa expressed his disappointment in a mumble, then left to look at more wine labels. Adeska sopped up the mess, the red in her face turning deeper with every second. Tizzy smiled inwardly at a job well done.

***

When the sun began to drop in the sky, the next guest arrived. While Adeska and her family had let themselves in, the new arrival slammed the knocker like a proper visitor and waited patiently. Tizzy opened the door and said nothing.

"Hello, sister!"

It was Rori, the Hallenar Dove. The younger, taller sister threw her arms around Tizzy in a genuine hug, showering her with affection and long, blonde curls. She hadn't donned a gown for the party but instead wore several pieces of pearly white armor on her shoulders and hips and a matching ornamental gauntlet. Tizzy thought Allanis would be pleased with the Diamond Knight of Sila'Karia, whenever it was Allanis would finally make her appearance.

Despite the warm greeting, Tizzy couldn't do more than pat Rori's shoulders in return.

"Gods, it's been years!" Rori smiled. "Two of them!"

"Yeah. Two whole years." Tizzy could only think of all the miserable things Rori had done to her in their youth. They were all things that Rhett had convinced her to do, but Tizzy also remembered all the glee in Rori's face as she did them.

"Come in."

"Oh my gods, Rori!" Adeska ran forward as she entered, and they hugged, bringing themselves to tears. There was another round of greeting and hugging once Adeska had fetched Athen from the kitchen and then a long gabbing session when Mariette remembered Rori's name. Tizzy stood away from them, watching, almost wishing she could feel their same connection.

When the buzz died, Rori approached Tizzy with cautious steps. "Um, Tizzy, I brought you something."

"Me?"

The blonde smiled and reached into the small bag around her shoulder. It was embroidered with beads and pearls to create Rori's signature white rose. She fished out a leather folder, then handed her a slip of paper from inside. "It's a pressed sunburst blossom. I picked a yellow one; I know that's your favorite. And I even made the paper myself."

Tizzy took the gift and stared into the dozens of tiny sunrise-colored petals. The sunburst blossom was the flower her family chose at her Rite of Crossing. Tizzy only knew because there were vases of them all over House Hallenar when she unexpectedly came back. One vase in the grand hall had been engraved as a gift to the family for their grieving. *May she be at Peace, Tizena Hallenar the Falcon.* Tizzy had broken it later that year, not entirely on accident.

She came back to the present, her emotions uncertain. "Thank you, Rori."

Rori saw she hadn't hit her mark but smiled warmly and walked back over to the others. Adeska was all too happy to continue catching up, and they were lost in a new conversation. Tizzy was numb.

***

Two more guests arrived as the sky turned purple with the last remnants of dusk. Mischievous laughter rolled into the halls of House Hallenar as the doors creaked open for them. The hooded figures strode into the grand hall, and everyone was quiet. Then, when they dropped their hoods, Adeska cheered.

Rhett the Crane, tallest in the room, looked down a straight nose, his blue eyes bored, slicking back his blond hair. He didn't look at any of his siblings, didn't acknowledge any of the excitement in the room at all. But Lazarus the Owl with his kind, tired smile and thinning auburn hair regarded them all with relief in his rust-brown eyes. Before Adeska could sweep in with her cries of family and reunion, Tizzy bolted forward and jumped into an embrace with the eldest.

"Lazarus! You made it!"

"It's good to see you, Tizzy!"

Adeska's heart swelled to see the first real smile on her sister's face all day. "Did you two have a safe trip from the Fallarian Isle?" she asked Rhett. He looked back at her and yawned.

"It was fine. Where's the wine? Any food yet?"

Tizzy glared at him and swallowed hard.

"Don't worry," Lazarus said. "I've been keeping my eye on him. He's a handful, but we've been alright. It'll be okay."

"Thank you." Tizzy backed away and regained her composure. "And thanks for coming. I know it must have been hard to get away."

"I couldn't miss another year! Good news is that the school disbanded for safety, so we'll be able to stay for a while. As long as we're careful, of course." He looked over his shoulder at Rhett, who already had a full glass of wine in his hand.

"I think the only one you'll have to worry about is Centa. I doubt he cares for any of us, but he especially doesn't like you two."

Lazarus chuckled. "One problem at a time." He gave Tizzy another hug before leaving to greet the others. As expected, he was met sternly by Centa. Tizzy wandered away from the grand hall, putting space between her and a room of complicated history.

She knew she wasn't being fair to everyone. Lazarus had never done anything to hurt her or Aleth, unlike Rhett and Rori, but he hadn't done anything to make it better. Athen and Allanis had been too young to do any harm or to understand what was happening around them, so they couldn't have helped, and Tizzy tried not to blame them for that. But Adeska's screaming and arguing were fresh in her mind. She could remember begging her to help Aleth like it had happened just yesterday. She could remember being cursed at and belittled. And she could remember Lazarus's absence. Whenever they needed his help to escape Rhett and Rori's torment, he was gone.

It wasn't until Aleth left that Lazarus saw how gravely wrong everything was. Tizzy remembered his promise, and his leaving and taking Rhett with him so that she'd be safe. Was that why she didn't resent him? A part of her wanted the resentment anyway. She wanted it for all of them equally because it didn't matter that he took Rhett away.

It never brought Aleth back.

She sighed, and suddenly Stormy was at her side.

"What a good boy you are, Stormy."

***

As the night progressed, Tizzy's post was at the front doors to see guests in. The first to arrive was Centa's best friend from their raiding party. Phiothilus Heywood. She'd met him a few times before, more than the other raiders, and Allanis had even commissioned a few portraits from him once the raids had ended. Tizzy didn't mind his company. He was a short man with a bright, cheerful face, and his very presence mellowed Centa out. Tizzy was glad that someone could distract him from Lazarus and Rhett.

Lex and Dina came together. They were two very chatty, flirtatious, beautiful women from the raiding party. Lex was a Ruby Mage, tall, muscular, and sultry, with long red hair and a long red gown, the scent of roses following her around like a seductive trap. With the vibrancy of her attitude, it was no surprise that her secondary focus was in Fire Magic. She shadowed Dina everywhere.

Dina was a Sea Priestess who was petite in every sense of the word. She wore her black hair braided in an intricate bun, and a pastel gown draped delicately over her dark skin and rippled like waves behind her. She was demure and graceful and the perfect balance to Lex's social aggression.

Rhett kept trying to flirt with both of them, oblivious to the fact they were more into each other. He sauntered up to Lex with a second glass of wine in his hand and put on a charming smile, showing one little dimple in his right cheek.

"Have you tried the red from Havenfold?" He offered her the glass.

She covered her mouth and grinned. "I hate wine."

"Oh."

He walked away confused, and Lex and Dina both burst into a fit of laughter.

Adeska and Centa's original raiding party was a dizzying twelve people large. They were not all in attendance, which was something that made Tizzy sigh inwardly in relief. She would have had a far more hectic party on her hands.

Phio, Lex, and Dina rallied around the table and all started clinking on their wine glasses, red-faced and full of laughter.

"Attention, attention!" Dina's gentle voice seemed to float above them all. "Everyone, I would like to present the Tale of Burshen, as told by the stunning Lex Ivanen!"

Phio took an empty wine bottle and blew over it, producing a hollow note that was anything but melodious.

"Thank you, Phio." Lex gave him the smile of a vixen and he made a few more flat notes. Then she cleared her throat and began to sing. The grand hall filled with her powerful, sultry story, punctuated by Phio's slow, haunting tempo.

"It was six years ago when the man called Ruan of Burshen heard the first whisper. He said to us it was the sound of a muse! But the darkness gathered inside him while we were none the wiser, and with a crack of thunder from Hell, we learned it was a ruse.

"We found one another, each pulled onto each other's paths with Botathora's touch of Fate! We made an oath and became the raiders that chased after Ruan and his Greater Daemon now on the Mortal Plane, but then his hoard of daemons took to Burshen and we were too late.

"A village in ruins, smoke choking the sky. The raiders pursued—no one else could die. Hunting, chasing, slaughtering daemon after daemon, they fought across the land until they tracked down Ruan and the Greater Daemon. The final battle reopened the tear to the Hell Planes, swallowing up them both in a glorious blaze of Hellfire!"

Tizzy wasn't impressed by their song writing, but Lex had an amazing voice. Tizzy knew there was more to the tale than the valiant parts in the song, though. During the fight, the raiders had suffered a casualty, but even before then, as the disaster panned out, many had lost friends and family. Though they all settled down for a normal life afterward, Adeska had never been the same. Tizzy knew she tried hard to go back to her old self, but something about her, beneath the façade, was different. Disturbed and sad.

Adeska's smile betrayed only a sliver of pain, but she clapped at the end of Lex's performance with Centa anyway.

Tizzy observed the guests break away into their own groups after the event. She knew Allanis would want her to make rounds and ensure everyone was having a good time, so with a sigh, she started to wander.

"Do you ever miss the raids?" she overheard Centa asking Phio. They both stood away from the others in their own quiet conversation.

"Gods no!" Phio laughed. "This life that I have now, I like it much better. I don't think I'll ever stop being anxious, but I can enjoy something normal like this, at least for a little while. Why? Do you miss it?"

Centa took a long time to answer, taking a sip of his wine. "I think I do. It feels like my life is missing something. I love Adeska and Mariette, but—"

"It's okay," Phio cut him off. "You don't have to say it. I know what you mean."

"Is it bad?"

"I think it'll make your life a lot harder, but I wouldn't call it bad. Everyone has *some* problem, you know? Just don't let your something get out of control like it is wont to do."

Centa stared down at his hands. "Sometimes every moment feels the same." His voice was almost a whisper. "Every threat feels the same. Every single problem, I treat it the exact same—"

"*Stop.*" Phio's one word stilled the man. "We will get through this, all three of us, okay? But this is not the time to go into it. There's got to be some priest at home that can sort you out."

Tizzy always suspected that Centa had violent tendencies. The overheard conversation was confirmation she didn't want.

All the guests had arrived and were making themselves comfortable. Athen started bringing out hard cheeses and fruit for them to try before the main meal was served. Tizzy scanned the grand hall.

"Where the hell is Allanis?" There was no sign of Lora either. Stormy sat down and wagged his tail. "Come on, let's go find Her Majesty," Tizzy grumbled. No one noticed her stomping out down another hall and up the stairs.

"This is ridiculous." She kept talking to the dutiful mutt. "This is *her* party! Why am I the one stuck making sure everyone is entertained?" Stormy whimpered. "I know! I'm not even entertained! Who's going to entertain me, huh?" By then, she knew she was only complaining for the cathartic effect. It didn't help that the dog listened better than anyone else.

The prettiest needlework tapestry announced Allanis's bedroom door, tacked at the top like a proud sign of her personal territory. It had dainty flowers and a colorful hummingbird, like one might expect, and a cobra. Its mouth wasn't opened menacingly, nor was it poised to attack. Rather, the cobra and the hummingbird shared the scene in peace.

Tizzy rolled her shoulders and banged on the door.

"Go away!"

"Allanis! Open the stupid door!"

The queen tore it open with a scowl, and Tizzy stifled her laughter. Allanis's face was flush red, and her hair was a mess of frizz and tangles.

"What's keeping you?" Tizzy's tone changed completely from the one she had planned on using. She tried to hide a grin behind her hand. "Everyone's here waiting for you!"

Lora cleared her throat from inside the room. "*Her Grace* will not let me finish her hair."

"I-I can't get it right! Any of it!" Allanis cried. "Tonight is supposed to be perfect, Tizzy. *It has to be perfect*!" She was only partially dressed in a beaded ivory slip. The kirtle that went on top was draped over a mannequin.

Tizzy came into the room and shut the door behind them. "It's not just your hair that you're worried about, is it?" she asked, crossing her arms.

Allanis returned to the stool in front of her vanity where Lora was waiting for her and sighed. "No." She slouched over, resting her chin in her hands. "I just feel like something is going to *happen.*"

Lora tended the girl's unruly curls, and Tizzy paced the room. It wasn't until she heard something peculiar coming from outside that she knew what to say. Allanis was too deep in her thoughts to notice it, and Lora was too busy to care. Tizzy went to Allanis's bedroom window and pushed aside the magenta curtains, revealing the stark night outside.

Plink! Patter! Plink!

"Something like that?"

Allanis glanced in her direction. "Huh?"

"Something happened. It's raining. Prophecy fulfilled my queen," Tizzy said with a comically sweeping bow. "So relax. Everyone is excited to see you."

Allanis bit her lip, but the smile still came. "Thank you, Tizzy."

Working a chunk of the queen's hair into a braid, Lora flashed a grateful smile to Tizzy as the older sister left.

Tizzy felt accomplished until she returned to the grand hall. The atmosphere was crushing. Everyone was gathered around the table for a game, save for Mariette, who sat by herself in front of the hearth.

"I guess *I'll* watch your child for you," Tizzy grumbled. She poured herself a glass of wine, slipping past everyone, invisible as always. She scooted a settee over to the fire and slumped down with a sigh, watching the lambent light bounce off Mariette's hair. The night was far from over, but Tizzy could already tell it was just like all the others. It was an improvement on last year, of course, but that didn't count for much.

Then, at long last, the chatter and laughter quieted for Lora as she came down the grand staircase in an elegant red and gold gown. She put her hands together and smiled at the crowd.

"Attention, honored guests! I present to you Her Majesty the Queen Allanis Byland-Hallenar."

The queen moved down the staircase with grace, looking nothing like the girl Tizzy had seen in her room. Allanis was a calm, composed woman wearing the ruby and pearl crown with just enough pride to be charming. Her silky curls framed a grin that knew all eyes were *really* on the dress. The kirtle she wore over the ivory slip was a stunning creation of fabrics cut into maple leaves and layered to make a gradient. Merlot started at her shoulders, then turned into rust, orange, and sunset yellow at her feet. Freshwater pearls adorned her wrists and neck.

"Good evening, everyone! Thank you all for coming!"

In a matter of seconds, she was engulfed by friends and family, and she started a speech that was both genuine and a little rehearsed. Tizzy drank her wine and sank deeper into the cushions, having no courage to enter the fray.

"At least you'll talk to me, right Mariette?"

It was a preposterous thing to say, Tizzy realized. She was a girl of few words.

"He's coming for you."

At first, Tizzy thought she was hearing things. But Mariette was staring right at her.

"What did you say?"

The firelight danced on the girl's face. "The man in the black cloak is coming for you."

Tizzy's heart stopped, and her dream was fresh in her mind. "How do you know about that?"

She turned her attention back to the flames. "The people in the fire told me."

Tizzy forced herself to breathe through the tightness in her chest. The sweat gathering at her temples felt cold. The night was no longer about her pity party. She stood up, trying to stop her hands from shaking by balling them up, and then she made a beeline for Centa.

Dinner was served now that Allanis had finally made her appearance, and guests were hovering around the table. Centa and Phio stood at a distance, waiting for the crowd to disperse.

"Centa!"

"*What?*"

She marched up close and pointed over her shoulder at Mariette. "What are you letting Adeska teach that girl?" she hissed.

She expected a vicious retort, but when he saw his daughter, his eyes went to the floor, and he rubbed his shoulder.

"She's being weird, isn't she?"

"Yes!"

He rubbed his face. "Dammit. Adeska keeps saying it's *fine*, that it's just the same shit she does and Mari's copying her." One second-long glance at Tizzy's face told him that she wasn't buying it. "I know what Mari does isn't normal. She's not even three yet. I know she shouldn't be acting like that, so don't give me that look. What did she say?"

"Nothing!" Tizzy felt her cheeks turn pink. "N-Nothing, but she's been there for hours!"

"I'll take care of it. One of us should have been watching her, anyway. It's probably time to put her to bed."

Tizzy watched him go to his child. She could hear him say something about food, and Mariette only nodded.

"Boy." Phio smiled and shrugged. "The way you came at him just now, I thought for sure he was going to get angry."

"So did I."

She inhaled deep, past all the knots in her chest. The night was still young. She ducked away to the table to make a plate of food for Stormy.

***

As the night went on, so did the rain. It was a pleasing backdrop behind the ruckus of the party. But the guests could tell it was coming down ever harder, and some of them had a long journey home. Little by little, family friends began to depart.

First were a few people from the raiding party that Tizzy never got to know. Adeska and Centa saw them out. Then Lex and Dina stumbled out, drunk as could be.

Adeska held the door open. "Do you need Allanis to have one of her carriages come—oh." She looked into the courtyard. "Nevermind. You two have your own."

"Yeah we do!" Lex cheered, leading Dina outside with swaying hips.

"Did you tell her where we're staying?" Dina giggled.

"The *Luster Lady*! How's that sound for a fancy inn?"

"We're excited. Really excited."

Lex's face was as red as her hair. "It's just big-breasted women in corsets all over the place!"

"Lex!"

"But only other big-breasted women in corsets go there. Does Allanis know that her town has its first lesbian attraction?"

Dina snorted. "Now, we don't know if that's actually what it is—"

"But it certainly seems that way."

Dina had nothing else to argue and started laughing. "Yeah, it does!"

"After party for big-breasted women in corsets at the Luster Lady, leaving now!" Lex hollered. Adeska and Centa waved goodbye, in stitches with laughter.

"I missed those two," Adeska said, wiping away a tear.

Centa cleared his throat. "A party isn't a party without them!"

Phio was the last to leave. Centa stalled him at the front doors for almost half an hour. The others knew the rain was getting worse, so Allanis finally joined them.

"Phio! Are you leaving without a hug?"

"No, of course not!" He exchanged a friendly embrace. "Thank you for inviting me, Allanis. I had a great time!"

"All you have to do to return the favor is make it home safely, okay? Wayward Destrier is an inn just down the road. The carriage driver knows it. When you get there, tell the innkeeper you just came from my party, and he'll bill me for your stay. It's a nice place; take any luxuries you want!"

Centa finally let him leave. When Phio was in the carriage and out of sight, Allanis closed the doors and threw her arms in the air.

"That was the last guest. Now it's just us!"

"What now, sister?" Rori asked, slinging her arm around Allanis's shoulder.

"To the kitchen!"

Tizzy followed behind the others. Athen was a mess from cooking dinner but was still excited to be going back to his work station. Centa was being pulled into the mass of family by his wife. Rhett followed behind Lazarus with his usual disinterest.

"Why are we going back there?" Tizzy asked.

"You'll just have to wait and see!" Allanis was bubbling over with giddiness. She ushered everyone into a spotless kitchen. Tizzy couldn't believe it. Athen and Lora must have been tidying everything up while the party toiled on. Then Tizzy saw the reason they were there. Something familiar sat nestled in a crackling hearth fire.

Nobody was more surprised than Lazarus.

"Alli, is that our old kettle?" he asked, his jaw agape.

"From the farm? Yes it is!" Allanis beamed. The kettle was generations old, unmistakable, with a third handle crudely bolted to the side. As children, it was the only way they had leverage to carry it back and forth.

"I went down to the farm a couple months ago," Allanis explained, grabbing a mug off the stone countertop. "Remember the people who bought it from us all those years ago when we first moved to House

Hallenar? They had a bad summer crop this year and reached out to sell some things to me." She ladled the kettle's contents into the mug. "So I went over there and bought this all by myself so I could surprise everyone!" She handed the mug to Lazarus.

He breathed in the scent. Apple cider. Tizzy could smell it from where she was standing. Cinnamon, maple, cloves. It was tradition. Apple cider had been a part of every family gathering during the fall since her earliest memories. Allanis tried hard to keep traditions alive every year, and when Lazarus took his first sip, his face lit up.

"The old recipe! Alli, *how*? I thought I'd never taste this again."

"While I was getting the kettle, I found Mother's old recipe box too. Surprise! Grab a mug, everyone!"

They huddled around the hearth, pouring themselves generous servings of the Hallenar spiced cider, then relocated back to the table in the grand hall. They picked at table scraps while recalling memories from simpler times. Lora emerged to try the cider she had secretly been collecting the ingredients for before bidding them all goodnight.

Tizzy sat surrounded by her siblings, taking in aromas long forgotten. The red pears and the allspice and the hints of orange rind and ginger, all in a sweet dance with apples and maple syrup and a grip of warming spices. Her anxiety melted away. She didn't engage in any of the conversations, but she took comfort in the nostalgia everyone shared. Athen and Rori teased each other about facial hair and blemishes while Adeska and Lazarus tried to retell a crazy story from their youth for Centa. Rhett had left for the wine table.

Then a hand squeezed Tizzy's shoulder. She looked up.

"Allanis."

"Hey, how's the cider?"

She smiled and took a sip. "You did good, Allanis. And you were right."

"You've got to be kidding! About what?"

"This year was different."

Allanis did everything in her power not to throw her arms around Tizzy right that second. Instead, she sat beside her and shared a plate of food. The next story being told had something to do with an old green rug, but Adeska never got to finish it.

There was a knock at the door.

Allanis pursed her lips. "Who could that be?"

Adeska started for the door. "It's coming down pretty hard out there. Maybe someone's carriage got stuck in the mud, and they walked back for help. I'll get it!"

Tizzy couldn't breathe. She could hear her heart thumping in her ears. Adeska stood in front of the doors, fixed her hair, and pulled one open. She stared up at a rain-drenched figure in a hooded, ragged black cloak.

CHAPTER 3

CATALYST

"Good evening, sir. I'm sorry, but the queen isn't seeing anyone tonight." Adeska kept her composure despite being dwarfed by the figure.

"I need to speak to the queen."

His voice gave away no emotion. Adeska cleared her throat. "I'm sorry, but it's as I said, sir. She isn't seeing anyone else tonight."

"It's urgent."

She didn't make an effort to hide her growing agitation and put her hands on her hips. "I'm not letting you in here." She looked down at his belt to study a sheathed longsword. "And I'm especially not letting you in here with a weapon."

The others mobilized at once at the mention of a weapon. Rori unsheathed the saber in the ornamental scabbard she'd been wearing all night and stood a short distance behind Adeska. Lazarus joined her, materializing a twisted ebony staff that pulsed with black Akashic energy. Several paces behind him was Centa, who had fetched his own sword. Allanis stood back behind all of them, Tizzy guarding her like a statue. Athen froze. He stared at the queen, his eyes wide and confused.

"Fine. Leave your weapons at the door, and you may enter."

The man bolted past her with speed she'd never seen. He skirted past Rori and Lazarus easily, but Centa was ready for him. They stood almost eye-to-eye; the newcomer had an inch over him.

Tizzy couldn't believe what she was seeing. It was him, the same cloaked man she had seen in her dreams. And just like Mariette had said, he was here. She could feel her heart in her throat as she watched Centa swing downward with his sword and miss. Just like that, there was no one between Tizzy and the intruder. She thought she might faint, but as soon as he came close, her adrenaline soared, and she was ready to protect the queen at all costs.

The man slowed when he approached her. She didn't know why, but she didn't care—it was his own damn mistake. With no better plan, she put her hands on his chest and shoved him away as hard as she could. He stumbled back, and Centa was there in a flash to take advantage of the situation, grabbing the man's shoulder and throwing him to the ground. He hovered over him with his sword ready.

The hood fell as the man sat up. Tizzy couldn't breathe as Allanis shoved past her and ran to him.

"Aleth!"

It had been a long time since they'd seen that face. A pallid face full of contempt. His black hair hung in front of rust-brown eyes that were cold as death.

She thought she would never see him again.

"Aleth! You're here!" Allanis dropped to the floor and hugged him. He did nothing except stare through them all. The queen stood and offered him a hand, but he rose on his own.

"I need to speak to you. Alone."

Rori stepped in, balling up her fists. "Hell no! You have to be out of your mind!"

"Shove off, Rori!"

"Guys!" Allanis put her hands up. "Please! It's okay!" She looked up at Aleth. "I know where we can go. Follow me."

Allanis led him away up a narrow staircase and out of sight while the others looked on in disbelief. Then they turned to Tizzy, who hadn't moved. She couldn't say a word, yet they waited for an explanation. Her voice, her breath, everything was gone. Then a weary hiccup came from elsewhere in the grand hall.

"What's going on?" Rhett asked, rising from a chaise with a half-empty glass of wine. Rori rolled her eyes, ignoring his drunken stupor, and ran to Lazarus.

"Are we serious right now? We're really just going to let him go with her? Alone?"

"Rori, stop." Lazarus was tired. It was in his voice and on his face.

"He walked out on us! We don't even know what kind of person he is anymore!"

"He walked out because of what we did to him!" He raised his voice, and Rori backed down. "Did you forget every time you and Rhett ganged up on him? Besides, Alli can handle herself." But he stopped, scratching his beard in thought. "Tizzy, is there still a way you can find out what they're saying?"

She felt like someone had just pulled her out from a frigid lake. Sensation washed over her again, and she came back to the present. "Yeah, I know where she's taking him. I'll be back." She set off for the kitchen, feeling grounded again.

In the pantry, amidst the barrels of grain and baskets of onions and potatoes, a woven rug covered the floor. It was riddled with flour-laden footprints and dead leaves. Tizzy pushed it aside with her foot, revealing a hatch to a cellar.

She had never liked the cellar. It was dark and smelled of rotten fruit from their failed attempts to make wine. And she hated the noises. The late King Frankel Byland was famous for his episodes of acute paranoia, and early in his position on the throne, he contracted a tinner to run pipes inconspicuously throughout the manor. Each one led back to the cellar for convenient eavesdropping.

Besides his spy, the Master of Dusk, the only other person King Frankel had ever divulged the secret to was Allanis, and of course she had told Tizzy. The manor even had a second cellar to throw others off its trail. Tizzy had used the pipes to eavesdrop many times before when Allanis would conduct meetings or talk to people in private. Most of the guests she invited in turned out to be untrustworthy, and now Tizzy would find out whether the same was true of Aleth.

She crept between the barrels and found the fluted end of the pipe she sought. There were already muffled sounds of movement and a door creaking shut.

"Well, here we are!" It was Allanis. "My room! All the privacy you could ask for."

Allanis tucked a curl behind her ear and looked up at him. "I know you said you just came here to tell me something, but you made this night perfect by being here." She quickly brushed away a tear. "I want you to know that. It's been ten years since we've all been together like this!"

"I'm not here to spend time with everyone," he said bitterly.

"We don't want to push you away, Aleth."

"Yeah? Tizzy pushes pretty hard."

Down in the cellar, Tizzy huffed. "Damn straight."

"Allanis, I'm here to warn you." He watched the confusion spread on her face. "The Hunters in Vandroya are preparing an attack on Suradia."

"Wh-*what*? *Why*?"

"I don't know."

"Yes you do! You are still such a bad liar!" More tears rolled down her cheeks, and the tiniest sob escaped her lips.

Aleth said nothing, but his sigh was uneasy. Allanis put her hands in front of her mouth and tried not to bite her knuckles.

"Oh gods, did they find out about Lazarus and Rhett?"

He rubbed his forehead. "Allanis, I've already said too much!"

"No, I can't accept that! Aleth, what am I supposed to do? I've never gone to war. I, I've only ever read about them! I can't do this! What do I do? Help me!"

He rolled his shoulders and looked down, trying not to watch as she cried. "You either take everyone you can, leave House Hallenar, and go into hiding—" he swallowed hard and met her eyes for just a second, "—or you fight."

Tizzy stared at the flat stones beneath her as she listened. *War.*

"I know you can do it," Aleth told her. "You couldn't have become queen if you weren't able to use the Royal Magic. But if you don't think you can do it, *don't.*"

Allanis took off her Hallenar pendant while he spoke. The bronze piece that bore the hummingbird had been set in a diamond-shaped bezel when she was crowned. The blue metal rimmed in silver hummed with Akashic energy and had an inscription that declared her worthy of the Guild of Kings. It showed various symbols of Hanarn, the God of Law, Order, Justice, and Leadership. She ran her thumb over the engraving of the scales. The bezel and pendant together made her casting tool for Royal Magic, but she hadn't used it since she was tested for the ability on her coronation day.

"I mean it," Aleth said. "You take everyone, and you run. If you don't think you can win, you won't. Suradia can't afford your doubt."

She looked up at him. "Something bigger is going on, isn't it?"

"Always is."

"Well, I'm going to fight!" She closed her fist around the bezel. "Fight with me!"

"Allanis, I've *been* fighting for you! You don't see me, but I'm out there. I'm fighting with you."

From the cellar, Tizzy was rife with guilt as he spoke. She leaned into the pipes as Allanis spoke again.

"Do you really think I can do this?"

"I risked my life coming here to tell you all of this!"

Silence.

Aleth turned away from Allanis and looked out her window, shaking his head. "So what do *you* think?"

Allanis fidgeted with her hands. She knew the conversation was coming to a close. "Aleth, all of this, it's—nevermind. I'm glad you came; that's what matters. Will you please stay?"

He looked back at her with narrowed eyes. "You know I can't."

She sighed. "I know. I'll take you back."

Tizzy listened as they left the room. The door shut softly. A thousand thoughts brewed in her mind, and her emotions went to battle.

"This isn't happening." She held her head in her hands. How could he just show up out of nowhere? They didn't even know if he was still alive! Tizzy could feel her breathing grow more erratic. He picked the party *of all nights* to make his appearance, made Allanis cry, threw around the word 'war' and then *left*. She growled and kicked an empty barrel.

"No. Hell no! I'm not letting it happen like this!" She climbed out of the cellar. "He didn't even say anything to me! No hello, no sorry, nothing!"

The kitchen doors were farther away than ever. She hadn't felt such rage boiling up inside of her in years, and it only grew with each step. She clenched her fists and burst out into the grand hall.

"*Where is he?*"

They gawked at her. No one could muster up words until Allanis started to sniffle.

"He just left."

"You're not going after him, are you?" Adeska asked as Tizzy tore past her. "It's pouring out there!"

She didn't say a word and raced down to the front doors. There was nothing to say, even though Adeska's comment infuriated her. How could she not go after him? When would she ever get another chance to talk to him? She pried the doors open to meet the full force of the storm outside and stomped down the terrace steps, anger quaking inside of her. She splashed into the muddy courtyard without hesitation.

She was ready for this. She was glad Allanis's formal standards hadn't broken her of her practicality. She knelt down and ripped away at the skirts of the gown, now soaked with rain and mud, and ran forward.

"Aleth!"

She could see him just ahead of her. He kept walking.

"Hey, stop!"

He continued, unfazed by the relentless rainfall and her yelling.

"Where are you going? Answer me, you asshole!"

He stopped. He turned to her with a smirk and pulled down his hood. "Well, well. I see nothing has changed."

Tizzy closed the distance between them. "What's that supposed to mean?" She narrowed her eyes. He returned the look.

"Exactly what it sounds like."

"How could you just walk back out like that? You hardly told Allanis anything!"

The condescending smirk didn't leave him. "I knew you were listening."

It was all he said as time stood still. Tizzy stared at him, searching his face, still in disbelief that it was him. The last time she'd seen him, they were just kids, but there were only traces of that same boy left in him now. He towered above her, the rain trickling down his face, rolling off his chin and onto the ground.

She clenched her jaw. "What else does she need to know?"

He saw her fist trembling and gave her a flat smile. "It's safer for her that she knows less. Safer for you, too."

"What are you trying to say?"

He sighed, sharp and impatient. "You know you're not like them!"

Tizzy shuddered. They were having a different conversation now.

"You don't even look like them anymore! You changed, just like I did." He bent down enough to look her in the eye. "And you know it, *don't you?*"

"I—"

"Things are happening, Tizzy, and you're a part of them whether you like it or not."

She knew what was coming next, and her stomach lurched with nerves. She should have stayed inside. *She should have stayed inside.*

"So you've got two choices!" he yelled at her, pointing back at House Hallenar. "You can either stay with them, where you don't belong, or—" he could barely say the words, "—or you can come with me."

She swallowed back tears. "You didn't actually come here to talk to Allanis, did you?"

"I did in part." He brushed the rain-drenched hair out of his eyes. "I have to go, so make your decision—"

"You have to go?" She was shaking. "So that's it? You're just going to fucking walk away? *Just like last time?*" She hoped the rain was hiding her tears because she couldn't contain them anymore.

The rain cascaded down his face as he stared at the ground. He wondered if there was even a point in explaining himself. "I didn't leave to hurt you, Tizzy."

"Then *why?*"

"Because I had to!" He looked back at her, and she saw the pain twisted on his face. "They were just as cruel to you as they were to me! But you, *you* could just lock it all away." Tizzy's heart dropped. "I couldn't do that. I wasn't like you! Tizzy, you were the only person in this whole damn world I needed to have my back! But then you finally broke and you deflected all of your pain onto me, and I had *no one.*"

She tried to say something. Anything. It wasn't just raindrops running down his face anymore, and it killed her.

"You have until dawn to make your decision," he said, pulling his hood up. "I'll be at Secret Teller till then. After that? You'll probably never see me again." They were the hardest words he'd ever said; she could hear it in his voice, in the way it was about to break. He turned away and started walking.

"No, wait!" She tried to chase after him, but her body wouldn't move. "Aleth!"

He wasn't turning back. It was over. He was right there in front of her, and now he was gone. She stared ahead at nothing as the rain pelted her without mercy.

The doors to House Hallenar finally opened, and Tizzy came inside. Alone. A trail of water dripped off her clothes and her ponytail as she came into the grand hall without a word.

Rori broke the silence. "Did you find him?"

She ran her tongue over her teeth, trying to keep herself contained. She could feel the makeup that Lora had painstakingly applied running down the corners of her eyes. She knew she looked like a mess. And then she exploded.

"You should all be ashamed of yourselves!"

Rhett had gotten to his feet at last and looked like he had something to say, but Rori put her hand up to stop him. The others just stared.

"Yeah." Tizzy wiped her eyes. "You heard me."

Adeska huffed and put her hands on her hips. "Oh for gods' sake, Tizzy, can we just talk—"

"No! I've had enough! This night is over!"

She didn't care how ridiculous she looked storming out. She couldn't stand to be around them anymore. For long enough, she'd entertained Allanis's idea of a party. When she had made it up the stairs and to her room, her nerves came crashing down, and she couldn't stop trembling. Her room was pitch black, the light from the full moon hidden behind the storm clouds.

She shut the door behind her and lit a single pillar candle on her desk. She tried to keep her mind clear and her hands steady as she peeled the remains of the soaked dress off her body.

"No thoughts," she whispered, shivering as the cold air touched her skin. "Don't think about it. Don't think about anything." She looked at the garment in her grasp. Her hands shook with the chill, then with anger, guilt, and finally unbearable anguish. "Gods dammit!"

She threw the dress against the wall, and it fell to the floor in a puddle. Tizzy couldn't hold it in any longer. She dropped to her knees in front of her bed and cried.

"Why am I like this? Why did I make such a mess?" She could only imagine how she'd made Allanis feel. All her youngest sister ever wanted was to bring everyone together again, and Tizzy realized she made that almost as impossible as Aleth.

"What am I supposed to do now?" She sniffled again and looked up. There was a small break in the clouds, and the moon glowed through the blanket of night. "Allanis needs me. She and Athen are practically children still. What is she going to do if I leave?" The scenario ended in disaster every time she thought about it. "Get some advisors? Listen to them? Yeah right."

She put her head back down, burying it in the rough lavender blankets. "Everyone had to go move away and get on with their lives. I'm the oldest one left." She hated that she was pitying herself. "I have to take care of them."

For over three years, Tizzy had guarded over them like a parent. She didn't have a choice; there was simply no one else left to do it. She told them when their ideas were terrible and naïve, when they wouldn't succeed, and they fought her every step of the way, but she couldn't blame them. When Adeska was still living at House Hallenar, she was full of motherly wisdom that Athen and Allanis were used to thriving on. Tizzy's jaded and cynical approach was never popular, but she couldn't fake what came naturally to Adeska.

"When do I get to move on with my life?" She stared at the falcon on her Hallenar necklace, hanging against her bare skin. Everything felt so out of her control. "Can I ever leave the nest?"

Then the thought struck her as stupid. "Of course I can." She used the blankets to wipe the makeup stains off her face. "If *Rori* can survive on her own, Allanis and Athen will be just fine."

She'd had enough of this life, and she'd used Allanis and Athen as an excuse for continuing to live it for too long. With a deep breath, she got to her feet and opened her wardrobe. She dressed for travel, then balled up the rest of her clothes and shoved them into a shoulder bag. She had no idea how to pack for what she was about to do. How was she supposed to know what she'd need? Did she even own everything she needed? She shoved a small purse of gold coins into one of the bag's pockets to compensate for all the surprises she couldn't prepare for.

When she was finished, the flickering candle drew her back to the desk. There was one last thing she had to do. She opened the drawer underneath the desktop and reached into the back corner until her fingertips found a tiny key, swallowed by the palm of her hand. It opened a compartment to her lacquered jewelry box that had been locked for ten years. She opened it and pulled out its contents, fresh tears stinging her eyes. The Raven Hallenar pendant. She slid it on over her head and tucked it out of sight underneath her tunic. After returning everything to normal, she scrawled a quick note on a piece of paper and blew out the candle.

Allanis, I'm sorry. -T

She picked up Wish and its sheath and fastened it to her belt.

"I have to do this."

And that was the end of it. Stormy was curled up outside her door, waiting patiently despite a wagging tail. She gave him a sad smile.

"It's okay, boy. Lora, Athen, and Allanis are going to take good care of you. Be good." She kissed him on his head and began her journey.

The grand hall was quiet. The fires were out, so it was dark and empty. No one would even know she had left. She was careful to keep her footsteps light and her pace steady, but her heart was racing with anxiety. She could do this. She had to.

The front doors had been locked and barred for the first time in ages. She slid the bar over just enough to open one door, making it look like an accident, and slipped out.

From the shadows of the grand hall, silent like an owl, Lazarus watched her go.

CHAPTER 4

TRUST AND TRUTH

RUSTAUMN 29, 1144

The rain let up just after Tizzy left. Her boots sank into the mud and left footprints across town as she trekked in darkness. Suradia was a ghost town before dawn, but that's when she found she liked it best. Rainbirds skipped around the puddles, anticipating the light of day, while crows came out early to start hunting for worms that had been flooded out of their earthen tunnels.

What she did not find charming, however, was the inn she had been instructed to go to. She stood in front of the Secret Teller with disgust.

"Was he serious?"

It didn't even look like it was in business. All its windows were boarded up, and it sat on a foundation of bloated wooden slats, flooded with six inches of water. Dubious, Tizzy opened the front door to a fully functioning establishment. A short old man—she guessed he was a monkling with his slightly pointed ears and short stature—was asleep on the front desk. Wax from a scattered collection of pillar candles dripped dangerously close to his curly white hair.

"Wayward Destrier is right up the road and way nicer than this place," she mumbled, closing the door behind her. The monkling didn't stir. She cleared her throat. "Sir?"

The front room was frigid and devoid of patrons. Its hearth held no fire but was full of ash and mud. Dead leaves floated in standing water.

Eventually, the monkling came out of his slumber, rubbing his eyes. "Pardon me, my lady, I'm so sorry! How may I—" When he slipped his glasses over his nose, he jumped. "Lady Hallenar?"

She blushed, forgetting her notoriety. "Hello. I'm looking for someone, and could we keep this a secret, please?" She slid a gold coin across the counter to him.

"Of course, My Lady. Tall, a bit lanky, dark hair, black cloak?"

Tizzy tilted her head. "Yes, that's him."

"Upstairs, very last room."

She tried not to sigh. "He's the only one here, isn't he?"

"He is."

Tizzy thanked him for his help and rolled her eyes. "It figures." She climbed up a squeaking staircase to a hallway with three rooms. She tried to think of what she'd say as she approached the last door, but truthfully, she didn't want to say anything. A kick in the shins summed it up perfectly. Swallowing her dread, she raised her knuckles but stopped.

"What am I doing? Am I knocking?" She twisted up her face. "He's the only one here, and the innkeeper is awake now, so—"

She balled up her fist and started banging on the door. "Hey! Open up!"

There was a thump from somewhere and a stream of cursing that grew louder. Finally, the door opened just a crack. Aleth glared out with a blanket and bedhead.

Tizzy folded her arms, and a smug grin crawled across her face. "Good morning."

"*Morning*? Tizzy, what the hell are you doing here?"

"What do you mean? You told me to be here by dawn! Well guess what? It's *by dawn*."

He rubbed his face and looked over his shoulder at a grimy window. "It's almost four hours till sunrise! If I had known you were going to get all nocturnal on me, I would have made you decide on the spot!"

"Are you going to let me in?" she asked, taking a step closer. "Or are we restricting this bullshit to the hallway?"

He grumbled, then opened the door. "Just wait in the corner for a few minutes, okay?"

"You want me to stand in the corner?" She put her hands on her hips and stepped inside as he closed the door. "Are you kidding?"

"No, I'm not! I'm wearing a blanket, Tizzy. Quit being a brat, face the corner, and let me get dressed!"

"Fine." She threw her hands up and shuffled to the corner, looking around at the squalor. She knew better than to expect much after seeing the entrance of the inn, but she still thought there would be more to his room. A table leaned against the wall, warped with water damage and uneven with mismatched legs. A shard of polished glass hung on the wall above it, trying to be a mirror. The bed was hay-stuffed canvas on top of crates.

"I hope you're not paying more than a silver for this," she said, staring at the cobwebs above her head.

"I couldn't even if I wanted to."

Now she felt bad all over again. She scanned the walls, at the cracks in the wood, then started to wander, hoping to catch a glimpse of his personal belongings. There was nothing.

"Sorry for coming so early. I knew I wouldn't be able to sleep."

"I wasn't getting much, either. *Stay in the corner.*"

Tizzy scoffed. "Right, because I've never seen a man's chest before."

"You probably haven't."

Her jaw dropped, and he started laughing.

"That shut you up real quick!"

She hadn't heard his laugh in so long, she thought she'd forgotten it. For a second, it was like no time had passed at all. Then she remembered she was supposed to be defending herself and snapped around, jabbing her finger in his direction.

"Excuse me! How dare you—" She stopped and narrowed her eyes. "What the hell are you doing?"

He stared back at her with the end of a bandage in his mouth, wrapping the other end around his upper arm to cover the bare skin showing under a ripped and worn sleeve. He had already done the same procedure to his other arm, leaving no skin exposed.

"Corner!" he yelled through the bandage, his face red.

She obeyed and took sudden interest in the ground. "Yeah, the corner. While you do that, let's talk. Why do I need to be here, exactly?"

"No." He tied the bandage off. "My questions first."

"What? You think *you* get to ask questions?" She was done with the corner and flung her arms into the air. "You, who already knows everything but can't be assed to tell the rest of us? I don't think so!"

He slipped on leather gloves without fingers, tugging them into place at his elbows. "Why are you here?"

"Why am I here?" The answer felt stuck in her throat. "What the hell kind of question is that?"

"Why did you decide to come here?" He leaned over the table, trying to fix his hair in the looking glass. "And none of this *because I missed you* crap. I know you better than that."

"But I—"

Nothing would come out. She *did* miss him, but once again, there was a feeling just out of reach. She knew why she had walked out of House Hallenar. As much as she cared for Allanis and Athen, she was tired of living her life only for them. But what was the reason she walked into the Secret Teller?

She could see herself in the glass as only a frowning smear. "Aleth, how did you know when to show up?" Her voice sank to almost a whisper. "Was it all just a coincidence, or did you know it was the night of Allanis's party?"

He licked his finger to try and smooth down a cowlick. It resisted, and he gave up. "I knew. I didn't know everyone would be there, but I knew."

"How would you not think everyone would be there? It's the annual family reunion! That implies that everyone is going to be there, doesn't it? If you never show up to them, how can you think—"

"Alright, gods!" He stared into the ceiling, clenching his fists. "Most years, Allanis's invites find me. She has this one damn bird that always knows where I am. I hate that thing. *Sometimes*, I wander close when the night comes so I can see how things are going. I know not everyone shows up. I saw last year." He went back to looking in the glass. "See? I'm not some heartless monster like you all think I am."

Tizzy looked away. "Maybe not. It does make you kind of a creep though, don't you think?"

"Whatever. I went to House Hallenar yesterday knowing I'd make a scene. It was the whole point. Now—" he turned and glared at her, "—why are you here?"

Her heart hurt, and she was tired of talking. She was tired of everything. She could feel her eyes getting glassy, but she didn't have the strength to cry again after last night. "Because." She took off the necklace she had hidden earlier. "You left this behind when you left us. I came to give it back."

She handed it over, and when he took it, she could almost feel the way it crushed him to have it in his hands again. He gazed down at it, and a trembling sigh left his lips.

"My Hallenar pendant." He remembered when he had never wanted to see it again. "I didn't leave it. Rhett took it from me."

"That explains why he was the one who found it when you went missing." She took a step closer to him.

"I still can't believe Father picked a raven for me. I should've been the falcon and *you* the raven. You're the dark, brooding one."

"No." She put her hands on her hips. "Father got it right. Look at you! You are *definitely* a raven, all scruffy with some scary black cloak—and, excuse me, you brood way more! I am definitely a falcon."

"How are you even remotely a falcon?"

She sat on the bed. "Because I'm majestic."

"Majestic? That's not the word I would've used." He sat down on the floor beside her, and the room suddenly went quiet.

Everything felt off, Tizzy thought. She knew he could feel it too. It didn't matter that they could have a moment like old times—there was still a painful gap between them that couldn't be ignored.

She bit her lip, reaching for something to say. "You're taller than I expected."

"I'm taller than I expected," he replied wearily.

She looked down at him and could see the little smile he was trying to force away. Her dream suddenly came to mind, and she knew she had to say something.

"Aleth, I saw something. Gods, how do I say this?" She sighed and scratched her head. "There's no eloquent way to say this, but I think I saw you get your ass handed to you by a faerie."

He hugged his knees and hid his face. "That never happened."

When the relief hit her, she was embarrassed to have mentioned it at all. "Then it was just a dream. Thank gods."

"You saw it in a dream?"

"Pretty stupid, huh?" She smiled. "That must've been the first dream I've had since…" She swallowed hard and realized she had never actually said the next words out loud. "Since you left."

He ran his fingers through his hair and grumbled. "She didn't *hand me my ass*, per se, but I didn't win. What else did you see?"

The other details from the dream made her nervous, and she buried them. "Nothing really." She stood up and clutched the strap of her shoulder bag. "So what's your deal? Why do you want me to come with you? Where are we even going? And most importantly, what does any of this have to do with me—"

"I'll tell you everything when we get somewhere safe." He wouldn't look up at her.

"We are somewhere safe!"

"Tizzy, sit." He put his hand on the ground.

She slid down in front of the bed and sat next to him, frowning. "What?"

With the softest, most careful voice, he told her. "We're not safe."

"Aleth, I want to trust you. More than anything, I want to trust you. But you have to give me *something*! Look at me! Why did you want me to come here? Can you tell me that? Tell me that, and I'll go with you!"

"It's like I said before. House Hallenar is safer without you—"

"Bullshit! Don't act like you care about them!"

"And you're safer without them! That's all I can tell you!"

"Why?"

"No!" he yelled. "I answered your question, now hold up your end of the deal! I'll tell you everything when we get to the safehouse, but you'll just have to wait till then!"

He stopped. She was staring at him, shivering.

"I'm sorry." He took a deep breath. "I would never hurt you, Tizzy. Please tell me you know that."

She clenched her fists and screamed at him. "Did you forget that you were gone for ten years? Because I didn't! How can you have me believe that you're the same as before? That you're still my best friend, that you're still the only person who doesn't feel like a stranger?"

"I—"

"Don't you *ever* leave me again!"

He took her and held her as she sobbed. "Never."

***

Dawn enveloped Suradia at last. The morning was dark and cloudy but carried the refreshing scent of wet earth. Allanis sat up from her mound of pillows and stretched. Lora was still fast asleep beside her, wrapped up in more blankets than Allanis could count. She smiled and climbed out of bed, careful not to wake her.

Despite the party's unforeseen events, unsettling news, and explosive emotions, Allanis found that the night had been a success. She stood in front of her vanity mirror, fluffing her sleep-flattened curls with a grin that couldn't be contained. She had really done it, she thought. They had all been together, in the same place. Not for very long, of course, but a win was a win. She reached for a thick, fluffy robe with satin trim and tied it on. It was going to be a difficult day, but she was riding it on a wave of accomplishment.

The night had been rough for everyone, but Allanis knew the worst of it had fallen on Tizzy. She came down the hallway to her sister's room and hesitated. What was the right thing to do? Of course Tizzy would want to be left alone, she knew that much. But wouldn't it make her feel a little bit better to know that the others were thinking of her?

She knocked gently on the door. "Tizzy? Good morning, sister!" There was no response. She wasn't completely surprised, but at the very least she thought she'd be told to go away. "Tizzy?" She put her ear up to the door and heard nothing.

"Alli."

She gasped and spun around. Lazarus was standing next to her with a weary frown and dark circles under his rust-brown eyes. He hadn't slept.

"Lazarus! I was just, I-I wasn't trying to bother her, I swear—"

"Alli, she's gone. She left hours ago."

"What?"

He put his arm around her shoulder and sighed. "You and I both knew the second Aleth walked through that door that she'd be gone come morning."

Allanis clutched her chest. "No! No, Lazarus, this is bad! What if she's in danger? What if he's done something to her? What am I supposed to do without her?"

"Calm down, Alli." He raised his hand, and Allanis noticed it was bandaged heavily at his palm. Had he hurt himself during the party? She said nothing. "It's time Adeska and I told you something. Meet us in the kitchen and don't wake anyone else up, okay?"

She blinked back tears and hung her head. "Okay."

He walked away, and she was left to process another bombshell. She balled up her fists, grumbling, wiping her cheeks dry. "What's wrong with you two? You're both stupid. You both could have stayed! I needed you to stay."

She wasn't sure she wanted to meet with Lazarus, but Stormy raced up to her with a hungry, expectant look.

"Guess there's no reason to stall. Lead the way, boy."

House Hallenar was cold and quiet, but the kitchen was flooded with warmth. Lazarus had lit a fire in the hearth and was standing by the flames with a mug of last night's cider. Adeska sat at the counter with a bowl, trying to feed Mariette, who was sitting on her chair atop a stack of books.

"There you are, darling. Apple porridge!" Adeska sang. Mariette held onto the wooden spoon and looked at the bowl with her typical empty expression. She didn't touch the porridge.

Allanis put scraps in Stormy's bowl, then took a seat at the counter and plopped her head down in silence. Lazarus came over and exchanged a worried glance with Adeska.

"I told him," Allanis cried. "I told Aleth to stay. I told him we wouldn't push him away. All I've ever wanted was for us to be together again, like a family. The way it's supposed to be."

Adeska reached out and held her hand. "Allanis, honey, Tizzy and Aleth never should have been separated. There's a lot that went wrong all those years ago, and there's a lot that we should've done about it. They may not be right here with us, but they're together, and that's what's important."

Allanis looked up at them, puzzled.

"They're not like the rest of us, Alli."

"I don't understand," she said. "Wait, oh gods, are they bastards? Or adopted?"

"No." Adeska winced. "They're definitely Hallenars."

"Something changed when Tizzy had the accident," Lazarus started. "She wasn't—she shouldn't have woken up. Alli, she was dead."

Adeska stared into the wood grain of the table. "This was around the time your *brother* was getting particularly engrossed in his *studies*." She paused to glare at Lazarus for only a second. "So he noticed it right away that she was dead. The court physician kept trying to assure us that it was a coma, but—"

"It wasn't," Lazarus said. "I can grasp at a few things that might have happened to her, but the reason they don't make sense is because they happened to Aleth too. I don't understand that part."

Allanis remembered the day. Tizzy, back when her hair was red and vibrant, laid lifeless on top of the stone tomb she was to be encased in once the Rite of Crossing was completed. It wasn't a widely practiced ritual anymore, but her parents had always done things The Old Way, and Lazarus was determined to lead the family along the same path. Adeska had fit Tizzy into a delicate white dress and had woven sunburst blossoms into her hair. The physician told them again that morning that it was likely a coma and they should wait a little longer before starting the rite. She remembered Aleth begging Lazarus to listen to him and how cruel she thought it had been for Lazarus to ignore him and conduct the rite anyway. It was one of the clearest memories she had.

"What are you two trying to tell me, exactly?"

"Most people—" Lazarus wet his lips nervously, "—they can sense that something isn't right about the two of them. You, Alli, I don't think you were born with that sense, but maybe that turned out to be a good thing. The rest of us—"

He had to stop. Old memories were fresh in his mind again after burying them for ages. He didn't think he was ready to face them.

"We didn't know *what* was wrong," Adeska said for him. "But subconsciously, we knew that they were *off* somehow, and that warning, that feeling, it made us hostile. That's what happened to us after the accident. It's why we let all those things happen."

Lazarus stared at his muddy reflection in the cider. "We didn't care that we were hurting them. Something was telling us that they weren't like us, that they were *wrong*, that we needed to drive them away. So we didn't care what they were going through. I didn't care." His fists were shaking. "I didn't even try to stop Rhett from beating his little brother mercilessly until it was too late."

He remembered the red on Rhett's hands and Aleth hiding in the courtyard with blood and tears running down his face. And he remembered just how much it hadn't bothered him.

"It's why we didn't do anything when Rhett told Rori to push Tizzy down the stairs. Or when Rori ripped apart all of her drawings and shredded her clothes. We let Rhett turn that girl into someone who literally *poisoned* the two of them!"

"Lazarus!" Adeska squeezed his shoulder. "Lazarus, calm down. It's alright."

"No it's not!" He laid his hand on top of hers. "We have to fix this. Alli—" he turned to her, "—here's what we know: All humans have an innate sense for the Forbidden."

"The what?"

Adeska found herself glaring at Lazarus again in her softly disapproving way. "Things that neither the Gods of Order nor the Gods of Disorder will claim are called Forbidden. Things like, oh, for example, *necromancy*."

"Wait, *that's* what that means?"

"Alli, she was dead! I don't know what happened, but I promise you, it wasn't my magic!"

"We don't know what it was," Adeska said. "But we know that it's bad. Forbidden. Our sense picked it up after the accident." The shame in her voice was haunting. "And then we were the way we were."

Mariette was finally eating, and a glob of porridge hit the counter. Allanis stared at it.

"And you're saying that whatever it was that happened to Tizzy after the accident, that *caused* this Forbidden feeling you all had, you're saying that it happened to both of them?"

She remembered staying by Tizzy's side for hours during the Rite of Crossing, long after the others had said their meaningful speeches and departed from her burial site in the woods. The rite was complete once the dead spent a full day cycle beneath the stars and atop their place of interment, and she remembered being worried about Tizzy laying there all night alone. Rhett left the site first; then Adeska took Athen and Rori. For almost an hour, she waited with Lazarus and Aleth, just standing under a tree beside Tizzy's body, lost in thought. When Lazarus finally left and tried to take her with him, she pleaded to stay just a little longer, and he relented, leaving on his own. Then she saw Aleth shaking with sobs.

"Yes," Lazarus told her. "It happened to both of them."

CHAPTER 5

THE IMPULSE

It was time to leave Suradia, and Tizzy was more nervous than ever. The mountain of emotions she'd been climbing for the past two days was making her daily headaches worse and worse. She stayed several paces behind Aleth, hoping he wouldn't notice, not that she could have kept up with his stride if she'd wanted to.

She thought of home, of Allanis, and the memories made her cold. This was a mistake, she thought. But there was no getting out of it as they slipped out the East Gate back into the Bogwood.

She learned that Aleth was serious about getting from one point to another. Either that, or he wasn't used to company. He didn't say a word as he walked and never noticed her falling behind.

"Could you slow down?" she called. "Maybe you haven't realized it yet, but I don't have damn spider legs like you do."

He stopped and looked over his shoulder. "Sorry, I guess I walk fast."

"I walk fast," she grumbled, hustling over. "But compared to you, I'm also at a disadvantage." The pain in her head was ferocious. She tried not to let it show.

"Are you okay?"

She failed at trying not to let it show.

"I'm fine."

"You're grimacing, though."

"Yeah. It's *you*."

He frowned and started walking again. "Whatever. Have it your way."

That was stupid of her, and she knew it. Why did she say that? Why did she always lash out at anyone showing her an ounce of compassion?

"Are we really heading to Davrkton?" she asked.

"Sort of."

"Thanks for the clarity."

"There's a river that branches off from the Undina Loch. The Sheerspine. We'll be halfway to the safehouse when we get to that river."

The Undina Loch was the river where Allanis had saved King Frankel Byland and earned her crown. Tizzy huffed as they finally stepped off the road and into the twisted woods.

"You said we were 'sort of' going to Davrkton. The Undina Loch is west of Suradia. Davrkton is to the northeast. Sounds to me like we're going not at all to Davrkton."

"You don't trust me!" he said. "I get it! It's okay, Tizzy, you can just come out and say it."

She felt the first raindrop fall, and her mood plummeted. "How can I when everything you say makes no sense?"

He sighed with impatience. "When we *get there*, you'll see it's actually closer to Davrkton than you think. And this is the route we're taking because this is the route I know. Could you please stop acting like this?"

It started to pour almost immediately.

"Like *how*?"

"Like exactly the way you are now! Having a word for it isn't going to make you magically comply, so don't argue for one."

"It sounds like you already know I'm not going to comply, so why should I bother?"

"I swear, the whole trip better not be like this, or I'll—"

"Or you'll *what*?" Tizzy yelled.

They both stopped. Her head was throbbing with white-hot pain. He turned to face her and closed the distance between them, one step at a time. She took a step back without realizing.

"Maybe I went about this the wrong way." He narrowed his eyes. "Tizzy, I'm not like everyone else. I'm not afraid of you."

"I know you've been following me!" she growled. "The other day when Athen and I were out here looking for everyone's letters? I know that was you!"

"Was I supposed to be impressed?"

"Back off, Aleth!" She took another step back. "Just leave me alone!"

The rain was colder than it had been the previous night. She shivered and locked eyes with him. He kept coming closer.

"What is your problem?" he asked. "Please, be specific."

"My problem? How stupid are you?" she screamed. "My feet hurt, my head hurts, there's a hole in the bottom of my boot—what a great day to find that out! It's raining, you're an asshole, and I still have no idea where we're going! That's my problem!"

"I'm sorry, Princess. Let's call a servant to come carry you."

"What the hell did you just call me? Don't you call me a princess! And we don't even have servants! You're an idiot. We've never had servants!"

He came another step closer, and Tizzy felt her back against a tree. She clenched her fists.

"What's that for?" He leaned over her. "Are you gonna hit me? Did you get tired of using your words?"

He was so close she could hear him breathing, but she gritted her teeth and didn't say a word. The pain in her head made it too hard to keep thinking, anyway. He craned his neck down until he was as face-to-face with her as he could get.

"Go on. Do it. I dare you."

She launched her left fist up as fast as she could with all the force she could muster, then gasped. He caught her wrist before it could land, and he squeezed it hard.

"I'm tired of fighting with you!" he yelled. She twisted, but he didn't let go. "Are you listening? Get it out of your system now because I'm done!"

"Let go of me!"

She felt pathetic as he stared down at her. Finally, he released her arm, and she blinked back tears, looking away. He walked on without a word.

They hiked for hours. Tizzy wished for the moment when her whole body would stop aching and go numb. Whether it came because she'd grown used to the pain or because it just up and died didn't matter anymore. The throbbing in her head wouldn't leave, sinking deeper and deeper. She didn't know how much more she could take.

She rubbed her temples to no relief, then stepped on a long, fallen branch hiding in the leaves. Aleth slowed down and looked over his shoulder as she stumbled.

"Do you need a minute?"

"I'm fine!"

"Of course you are. Why do I waste my breath?"

"Wait." She exhaled, her breath sharp and shaking. "I'm sorry."

He came to a full stop and turned around. Something was wrong. "Are you okay?"

"Can we please take a break?" There were tears in her eyes.

"Yeah. Wait here. I'll see if I can find some place dry to camp out for a while."

She choked down a sob. "We're going to stay out here? Aleth, it's cold and wet. Isn't there someplace else?"

"Like an inn? You have to walk to those. I thought you wanted to stop."

"Alright." She shut her eyes tight and rubbed her temples again. "You're right; that's what I said. Out here is fine."

"I'll be right back. Can you gather up some boughs while I'm gone? I think I can find a good spot."

Tizzy nodded. The ground was littered with soggy pine boughs that had fallen in last night's storm, and she picked through them, looking for the driest ones. Aleth couldn't make himself leave. He shuffled a few steps away and paused, watching Tizzy with a pit in his stomach. She leaned over to pick up a branch, but a tree root caught her foot, and she fell straight into the mud with a yelp.

"Tizzy!"

Arms trembling, she pushed herself up, and the searing pain lit up like lightning behind her eyes. She buried her face in her hands. Then with a stream of profanity, she pulled them away, but it was too late—she'd covered her face in mud.

"What the hell is wrong with me?" She sat in the mud, crying. A new low. "Why does this keep happening?"

Aleth crouched down in front of her and tried to wipe away the wet dirt on her cheek. "What's the matter, Tizzy?"

"The headaches. I get them all the time, but the past few days they've been—and this one—this is the worst one yet." He started biting on his knuckle, and she knew it meant he was worried. "What? What is it?"

He almost didn't see it, the faintest red ring around each of her pupils. "You're having your first one. Damn, I thought we'd have more time."

She shook. "My first what?"

"Impulse. Leaving home must have set it off."

She wrapped her arms around herself. Her cloak was soaked through. "Aleth." She couldn't stop shivering. "What are you talking about?"

He never got the chance to answer her. Her scream of pain rang through the trees and shook the Bogwood to its core.

"Hey! Can you still hear me?" He put his hands on her shoulders.

"It's starting to go black."

"Stay with me. You can get through this; I know you can."

Her body was weak and faint as she tried to move, and the tunnel vision tightened until she could barely see a thing. Aleth cursed under his breath and tore off her cloak, tossing it aside. It splashed in the mud. She would have been angry, but she couldn't feel the difference without it. The rain pelted her, and each drop felt like a knife in her skull. Then it stopped. She looked up.

"Wh—yours?" Aleth's cloak was draped around her, and she gripped it tight. "It's dry on the inside."

"It's not pretty, but it's functional." He was already drenched without it. Still crouching, he surveyed the woods around them, adjusting his bearings. "Alright. Here's what you're going to do." He turned his back to her. "Hold tight. I know a place we can go, but it's a hike."

"You are *not* carrying me!"

"Really?" he snapped back at her. "Because if you took even two steps, you'd be eating mud. Again!"

"No!" she cried.

"*Tizzy!*"

Her walls crumbled around her, and she sobbed. She could remember an old part of her, crying in front of him after she'd broken some dumb trinket she used to love. For everyone else, she always fought her tears. She wouldn't be caught dead sobbing in front of any of them.

Thunder rolled in the distance.

"Please stop fighting me, Tizzy. I got you into this mess."

He felt her hands on his shoulders, and he lifted under her knees. Tizzy lost track of the time as she was carried, and then she lost track of where they were. She couldn't remember what landmarks they had passed or the turns they'd taken, not when her head felt like it was splitting in two. And the sound of the rain was anything but soothing. Out of her element, it was terrifying. She found her only comfort was the cloak. It smelled of dirt, pine, and sweat, but it was warm.

The world was slipping away, and she faded further into darkness with each step Aleth took. Looking at the forest was dizzying. She clung to him with weak arms. Her grasp pulled down part of his collar, and the last thing in her vision before she lost consciousness was a scarred-over bite mark on his neck.

***

Allanis looked out her bedroom window at the storm pouring over the town and surrounding woods. It was the first storm of the fall. Half the town would be flooded if it didn't let up soon.

"I hope she's okay out there."

"She'll be fine," Lora replied. She sat on a stool by Allanis's wardrobe with a bevy of sewing supplies, fixing the seams of an old dress hanging on a mannequin. "Do you still like the sleeves on this one, love? I could make changes from some of the other gowns you don't wear anymore."

"Make any changes your heart desires," Allanis told her, pacing. "I know how much you love piecing all that old stuff together."

Lora held up a length of trim she'd scavenged from another garment and laid it over the dress's bodice. "I don't get many opportunities to be creative around here. It's fun."

"Did you want more opportunities?" Like a hummingbird moving from flower to flower, Allanis went wide-eyed and found something new to panic about. "I didn't realize, I'm so sorry Lora. We could redecorate! Or you could take a painting class from Mister Heywood! Or maybe—"

She chuckled. "Allanis, I didn't say I was unhappy. Relax, I'm fine. This is quite enough for me presently." She pinned the trim in place and stared at it for a while. Allanis paced again, and the woman stood. "Come here, Little Bird. How are you?"

The queen heaved a crushing sigh and let Lora's arms envelop her. "There's just so much to think about. I had no idea the party would end up like this."

"Do the others know she's gone?"

"Athen, Rori, and Rhett? No. I haven't said anything yet. I don't think Adeska and Lazarus have any plans to, either. It's just easier to pretend she's trying to avoid all of us."

Lora grinned. "More realistic too. She'll be okay, Allanis, but you need to consider what *he* told you." She stroked Allanis's curls.

She knew Lora was right, but the thought of Aleth's words scared her. "Wait! I've got it!" She looked up and cupped the woman's face. "Anavelia!"

"Oh no."

"She'll know what to do! Saunterton is over three times the size of Suradia! She's got a real army, Lora; she'll have answers! I know it!" She scrambled back to the window. "I know you can't stand her, but she *is* a very good friend. You can't argue that. Whenever I've needed her, she's been there!"

"Yes, but she has never asked for anything in return."

Allanis shrugged. "I don't really think she needs anything."

"When she does, are you going to be able to deliver? Like it or not, Little Bird, she is a friend for the politics."

"That's what you keep telling me." Allanis sighed. "I really hope you're wrong about that. For once."

There was a knock at her door.

"Come in. It's open."

Lazarus, cleaned and fully dressed for a busy day in a thick black tunic, crept in with an armload of books and scrolls, and Allanis's stomach filled with dread. He waved and cleared a spot on the desk by her bed.

"Hello again, Alli. Good morning, Lora."

"Good morning."

"What on Rosamar's Good Grace is this?" Allanis asked, gesturing to his mess. "If you think you can come visit and then make me do studies, you can march right back to the Fallarian Isle."

"It's an island; that's impossible. Have you ever taken a look at these?" he asked. "They came from the King's Vault. You should have taken them out of there years ago."

"What are they?"

"Royal Magic." He thumped on a tome closed with a gold-edged indigo clasp. "You need to start reading, Alli. Your studies are back on. I'm staying with you in Suradia."

The queen groaned and picked up the tome. She knew he was right. "This is really going to happen, isn't it?"

"There's always a chance Aleth was lying," he said, pulling up a chair. "The thought definitely crossed my mind. He's never been good at it, but maybe ten years is enough time to learn. But Hunters coming here—"

He scratched his beard and Allanis thought she could see shame in his eyes. "It just makes too much sense. Even before what Adeska and I told you."

The conversation ran through her like a ghost. "Oh my gods." She hugged the tome close to her chest. "Lazarus, he got her to leave because they're coming for *her*. For both of them."

"Could be. And you need to be prepared for the event where they don't leave us in peace just because they're not here. The Hunters have a reputation. When was the last time you used the Royal Magic?"

"Not since I had to prove I could."

"Alright, that settles it." He slammed his hand on the desk, the bandage from early that morning peeking out from his glove. Allanis thought she had found the nerve to ask about it, but the question died in her chest before she could get it out. "Your lessons start tomorrow."

"Not tomorrow." She set the tome down and strutted back to her window. "I've decided to go to Saunterton and meet with Queen Anavelia Lovell. She has an army, and there's a lot I could learn from her. Lessons will have to wait till I come back."

There was another knock at the door.

"Yes? Come in."

To her surprise, Rori was on the other side of the door when it opened.

"Goodness, there's another party in here. Good morning, everyone!"

"How did you sleep?" Allanis asked her.

"I slept well, all things considered. I just wanted to let you know I'll be out for a bit. Is that okay?"

"Of course! Is everything fine?"

Rori scratched her head as Allanis came to her. "Yeah, everything is okay. I just have some things in town I need to take care of. You know, before the rain gets worse. I'm going to send a carrier to Sila'Karia and request a longer leave too."

"Rori, that's wonderful! I appreciate it. Your dove is still recovering, but you can use one of the bigger birds in our roost to make the flight. I keep a couple of Caevarish geese specifically in case I need to contact you out there. They'll fly right to Sila'Karia! Maybe not back here afterward, but I'll deal with that problem later."

Rori smiled. "Thanks, Allanis. One more thing—is Tizzy okay?"

Allanis faltered for a moment, taking glances from both Lora and Lazarus. "Yeah, she's okay. You know how she is. We'll just have to give her some space, I think."

"Well, if you see her, give her my best. I'll be back in a while."

"Stay safe in the rain!"

Allanis watched her leave. Something didn't feel right. When she closed the door and turned back into the room, she pursed her lips. "Lora."

"I'm already on it, my queen."

The woman went into her own wardrobe and started pulling out a mess of black clothing. Lazarus, having never seen Lora wear anything resembling the garments she was preparing, raised an eyebrow.

"Wait, are you going to follow her?"

"Yes," Lora answered plainly. "And I've got to hurry if I'm going to catch up to her."

"What could she possibly have to do in town when the weather out there is like *that*?" Allanis jabbed her hands to the view outside.

"I don't know," Lazarus said. "But I'm sure it's none of our business, Alli. Let her be."

"Sorry, brother." Allanis grabbed a heavy blue capelet and started fastening it. "Grown-up Allanis can't afford to think like that anymore. That's something Tizzy taught me. Pick out one of those books. I'll start one today."

CHAPTER 6

SHEERSPINE SPIRE

Tizzy's eyes opened. She was on a dirt road in the forest. Again. There was no rain, just a brightly beaming sun. She looked up into the trees, blinking into the harsh light. It was summer? There was no one else in sight.

"Aleth?"

No answer. She walked down the road, spying tiny yellow wild-flowers in the brush on either side of her. This part of the forest didn't look familiar. Was she still unconscious? She had to be dreaming. A breeze sang sweetly through her hair, carrying a pleasant floral note. When she realized what it was, it turned sour.

"Sunburst blossom. Where am I?"

The road continued far into the distance, but then she could see a lightly worn trail branching off to her right. She chose the trail with confidence. It was a prettier hike than the one on the road, not that she'd based her decision on such a detail. There was a little brook bubbling away between glistening stones, too pretty to be real. All of the scenery seemed distantly familiar and somehow wrong.

"Alright, Tizzy." She stepped over a rotten log. "Try to remember. What came before all of this?" There had been rain. Lots of it.

She heard a crack of thunder in the distance, but there was no flash in the sky, no clouds, no anything. She remembered she had been arguing with Aleth damn near since she'd left House Hallenar.

"We weren't really fighting about anything! I just wanted to be mad! I always want to be mad. What the hell is my problem?" She kicked a pinecone. "Maybe he deserves it. I don't know anymore. Maybe—" she kicked a rock, "—if he had just talked to me, I wouldn't have been like this! I am so sick of this secretive *crap*."

She felt a little better. After walking the trail further, the forest opened up. That's when she knew without a doubt that she was in a dream. Aleth sat on a stump in the shade of a proud oak tree. The area he stared into broke away to a view of an open field, a breeze carrying through long, wispy green grasses in a jarring, unnatural change of scenery that made her stomach turn.

"Aleth? What's going on?"

"He can't hear you."

Tizzy jumped. A woman in a dark veil emerged from behind a tree. "Not when he's like that, at least."

"Who the hell are you?"

"Pardon me." Her voice was gentle and low. She held up her delicate hands which were covered in lacy black gloves. "I promise there's no need to be defensive. I'm Talora." Her deeply tanned skin looked sickly and drab. Heavy-lidded almond eyes with long eyelashes studied her. Big cheekbones boasted a smile on a heart-shaped face.

"Where am I?" Tizzy asked her, clenching her fists.

"We're in your head." Talora folded her hands over her stomach. "Your head is a lot easier to get into than his!" She pointed back at Aleth, who was still like stone.

"How do you know my brother?"

"I live at the place he's taking you to. Well, sort of."

"There we go with this *sort of* shit again."

Talora clapped her hands. "Right! I had a point to all of this, Tizena."

"Tizzy."

"I'm sorry. Tizzy it is! I wanted to show you something." She gestured to the open field. "But it looks like I can't." She snapped her fingers, and the field became a hall lined with books.

"That's the Hallenar library. What's that got to do with anything?"

"Absolutely nothing." Talora sighed, snapping her fingers again. It changed to the empty streets of Suradia. "But that thing I wanted to show you? I can't find it in your head. It's in there somewhere but nowhere I can get to."

"Then *get out*," Tizzy said through clenched teeth. "I don't know who or what you are, but I never gave you permission to be here in the first place!" Her eyes flashed to Aleth. "And what is wrong with him?"

"He's thinking, Tizzy." Talora turned to watch him. "He has a lot to think about. Always does. Maybe he'll tell you about everything."

"Fat chance. That asshole hasn't told me anything."

"Then he must have his reasons. Trust him, please. He made the decision to handle things the way he is, with careful consideration. Everything will come together soon."

"Talora, right?" she asked. The woman nodded. "Look, I feel like I can barely trust him, so what makes you think I'm going to trust *you*?"

"I understand." She pulled at the edges of her veil. It was black like her long, wavy hair, but Tizzy could see dark green patterns in the fabric. "I'm here when you need me, Tizzy. I'm a friend, I promise. But be prepared because not all of us will be."

Tizzy saw her dark eyes flash red, and then everything faded away.

***

Aleth shuffled Tizzy's weight around on his back. She was more difficult to carry since losing consciousness, and he'd hiked over a mile already, hunched over to keep her from falling backward and into the mud. Fortunately, the rain had eased up a little.

"Just a bit more," he grunted. "We're almost there, Tizzy."

Not that it would make things any easier, he thought. Up ahead, there was a clearing that terminated at a wisteria-covered cliffside. At the top were two mossy boulders that jutted into the clouds. He had arrived.

"Show me the Sheerspine Spire."

Tizzy's senses started to fade back in as she felt Aleth readjusting her body. When he uttered the words, she heard a peculiar sound. The wisteria vines twisted away just enough to reveal an old wooden door. Aleth kicked at it several times in lieu of a better way to knock, and a woman opened it. Short brown hair framed a mature, round face. Three hazel eyes stared at him, and then she laughed.

"Oh this is good!" It was a deep, melodious laugh with no less than an ounce of malice. "Is this how you're getting the ladies now?"

"Naia! It isn't what it looks like, I swear! I need a room."

"Yeah, that ain't happening." She crossed her arms. They were tough and toned, freed by an old yellow tunic with the sleeves torn off. "You're still banned. For life."

"Can you please make an exception? Just this once?"

She looked at the rain and probably sweat running down his face. "You do sound pretty desperate, but it wouldn't matter if I lifted your ban or not. Kenway's got the rates for your kind high enough to keep you out of here."

"What? Why? Who else has been causing problems?"

"No one," Naia answered, picking at dirt under her nails. "Because they can't afford to."

"I've got fare. Two rooms with amenities."

"Sixty gold. Each."

"Fine!" Aleth snapped. "One room and amenities! Can I just—" he huffed, "—can I just pay you when my arms are free?"

She shrugged. "Whatever. Is that girl going to be okay?" She let him in and closed the door behind him.

"Yeah, I can take care of it."

Naia remained unconvinced. "I'll set you two up in a room upstairs." She smirked.

"I know you don't want me here. You don't have to make me suffer more to get the point across."

Tizzy nodded off again as she was carried upstairs, listening to the two bickering with each other the whole way. The next time she woke, she was alone. The room she'd been taken to was an improvement on Secret Teller. A vast improvement. It was warm with steam coming from someplace she couldn't see. Wood paneling covered the entire room. There was a small hearth with a rack for drying, and Aleth's cloak hung on it. A green woven rug covered most of the floor, and half the room was divided by a green silk tapestry.

She was in a bed, bigger and softer than her bed at home, and she almost decided to go back to sleep. She sat up and sighed.

"Aleth?" There was no response. Of course. At least the pain in her head had subsided for the time being. She got to her feet and started to investigate. Her shoulder bag had been set by the fire, and she decided it was a good call after rummaging through it. Everything in it was soaking wet.

"What is this place?"

Then there was a knock at the door joined by giggles. "Services!"

Tizzy raised an eyebrow. "Services?" She opened the door, and two young women stood in front of her. One was tall and wiry, pale, and with a messy bun of frizzy blonde hair. She looked at Tizzy with a smile of crooked teeth. The other woman was short and soft but looked like she could throw Tizzy halfway down the hall. Her pigtailed dark hair was a cute juxtaposition to the scowl in her big, dark eyes. Both women wore green tunics with white aprons and held woven baskets.

"Yeah, services!" the shorter one repeated. Tizzy squinted at her nametag. *Velana*. The other girl kept giggling, her face turning red. Tizzy looked at her nametag. *Mayriel*.

"Guys." Tizzy slapped her thigh in annoyance. "I don't know what any of this is."

"It's a bathhouse, silly!" Mayriel said.

"Among other things," Velana added. "We do the laundry. Give us your clothes."

"Excuse me?"

"Oh dear." Mayriel tapped her chin, and it was only after another look that Tizzy saw she was using a third arm. She gasped.

"Wh-what is that?"

"It's an arm, stupid."

"Vel, Naia told you to quit talking to patrons like that!"

Both girls revealed they each had four arms. Mayriel smiled. "Ever heard of a quadramanus? That's what we are!"

"No," Tizzy said, feeling out of breath. "I have never, ever heard of that."

"Well, enjoy the culture shock," Velana told her. "This is Sheerspine Spire. It's a haven, magically warded to be hidden from *normal* people. Understand?"

"Some wards. *I'm* a normal person."

"Honey." Velana put one of her hands up. "I don't know who's been feeding you that lie, but it's time to strip to the truth."

Tizzy hated the phrase.

"Clothes!" Mayriel shouted. "This process can't continue until you hand 'em over!" She shoved Tizzy aside with her basket and came into the room. "Hey, is Aleth in here?"

"No."

"Ooh, that means he's in the public bath!" Velana clapped Mayriel's shoulder, and her eyes went wide. "We'll have to go look for him after this!" Mayriel wiggled her shoulders and responded with a whisper, probably something indecent, and they both turned a shade of scarlet that rivaled Suradia's banners.

Tizzy rolled her eyes. "Do I have to give you all of my clothes?"

"Of course you do. You're filthy." Velana snapped her fingers. "Strip. Here's some towels and a robe to preserve your precious modesty." She took them out of her basket, and Tizzy snatched them with a grumble.

"This is weird."

"It gets better!" Mayriel chirped.

"Way better."

Tizzy peeled off her muddy, damp clothes and threw them into Mayriel's basket. Then, covered with the robe, Tizzy set her boots by the fire and surrendered the clothes she'd packed in her bag.

"Now what?"

"You get the special, private bath all to yourself!" Mayriel said, leading her to the green tapestry. "Goodness, you must be important."

"I'm not. He's being ridiculous."

On the other side, a tiled tub was recessed into the floor and steam rose from the water's surface. Tizzy couldn't believe the room could accommodate a five-by-eight-foot bath.

"It's deep in the center, about four-and-a-half feet where the drain is stopped up," Velana told her. "And on the edges, there are benches so you don't drown when you sit."

Tizzy tried to imagine the network of plumbing and the magical and mundane methods it took to maintain such a place.

"Hey, eyes away from the bath for now!" Velana snapped her fingers again. "As I said, you're filthy. If you get dirt in Kenway's mineral tubs, he'll have a fit."

"You're going to clean up in here, first." Mayriel showed her a station with a water pump, a stool, several wooden buckets, and a basket with jars and towels. "Get the dirt off of you before you get in. The boiler is enchanted, so the water will always come out hot. Pump some into the buckets, take a rag and some soapweed pulp, and wash up. This batch of soapweed is scented; you're lucky!"

Tizzy's eyes were wide. "This did get way better."

The girls promised to bring food up soon, then left her in peace, whispering about Aleth and giggling as they ambled down the hall. It felt good to be alone, she thought, but she sorely missed her dog. She missed Allanis and Athen and Lora, too, of course, but the absence of Stormy was a different kind of hurt.

He'd followed her home from the marketplace as a puppy, years ago. She remembered how the breezy spring day had come to its end, how all the people had taken down their stalls at dusk, ignoring the little thing sniffing around and begging for attention. The last sounds in town as she headed home were Stormy's excited little yips trailing behind her. And every day since, he'd been just as happy to see her.

Tizzy couldn't believe she'd just abandoned him. She started to pump hot water into the bucket, and with each splash, she became more and more painfully aware of where she was.

Away from home. So much of the day had passed. Allanis and Athen had rarely spent so much time without her in all her memory. She hoped they were doing okay.

She took a rag, soaked it, and then investigated the soapweed pulp in the jars. "Jasmine!" With a generous amount, she started to wipe away the grime on her skin. What a terrible journey it had been.

"Traveling on foot in the storm. What a stupid idea," she scoffed. Dirt rolled down her cheek along with sudsy water. Each time she wrung the rag out, more dirt collected in the bottom of the bucket. "What was he talking about? What did he call it? An *impulse*?"

She decided it was best not to think about it lest she remind her head to start aching again. It was time for another bucket anyway. She found a drain in the floor and poured the old water out and pumped fresh water in.

Her hair was begging to be washed. Taking it out of its ponytail was no easy task as much of it had tangled around the tie. The mud and rain made it heavy, and her arms ached as she finally set it free. The damp, grit-laden curls tumbled down her shoulders, and she couldn't get her hair in the water fast enough, eager to shake the dirt loose. The soapweed pulp felt amazing as she worked it in.

Suradia was less affluent than most of its neighboring towns and cities, so House Hallenar did without many typical royal luxuries such as steaming hot baths and scented soapweed pulp. After careful preparation, Tizzy thought she had cleaned up quite well. The amount of dirt that piled up in the bottom of the bucket from her hair alone was alarming. She emptied out the water, wrapped up in a new towel, and sank into the murky mineral waters of the bath.

"This is amazing."

She sat on a bench at the edge and tilted her head back onto the edge. Time disappeared. She could've been sitting for an hour or for ten seconds—she had no idea. For the first time in too long, she was relaxed.

Then the door squeaked open.

"Tizzy?"

"Aleth!" Her heart jumped. "Where were you?"

"The public baths downstairs. They're too crowded and honestly kind of gross. I'll wait till you're done and use the one in here."

"Did all the arms come to take your clothes too?"

He chuckled. "Yeah. They were following me *everywhere*."

Tizzy lifted her hand out of the water and watched the droplets roll off her fingers and back into the tub. She could barely see her submerged body. "The water might get cold. I can get out now if you want."

"No, it's fine. A little cold water isn't going to bother me."

She rolled her eyes. "That is unacceptable."

"I don't care."

"Have you seen this thing? It's huge! Do not make me sit in here all by myself! I'm not some *princess*, but if I was, that'd make you a prince. So get your fancy ass in here."

"Absolutely not."

"Fine. I'll just get out now, and none of us can enjoy hot water."

There was a long sigh from the other side of the tapestry. "Why are you like this?"

A smug little grin of triumph worked its way onto her face. "I can't exactly stand in the corner like you told me to at Secret Teller, but how about this—I'll *turn away*."

"Thanks." It was a sarcastic response, but it meant that she had won, so she took it with glee.

She faced away from the tapestry and rested her head on her arms. The minerals in the water soothed her skin. "How did you first find this place? Those girls said it's warded."

"That's a long story," he said, pumping new water into the buckets. He had wrapped up in nearly every towel he could get his hands on. "Let's just say it's similar to how you came to find this place."

She tried to imagine such a scenario. "Who is big enough to carry *you* on their back?"

He laughed. "Maybe it was a little different. One of the many times I found trouble in the Bogwood, I got hurt. Bad. It was greenkind that time. Kenway found me and brought me here, even gave me a job for a little while. But then I blew it."

"Is Kenway the owner?" She tried to ignore a pang of guilt from his story.

"Yeah." He sniffed the soapweed pulp. "Jasmine? Ugh. He'll probably come by to yell at me. Don't jump in and do what you do. Just let him yell at me."

"You know I'm not going to listen to anything anyone tells me, least of all you."

"Hey, you owe me! Your ass is heavy." Then he laughed again. Tizzy could hear it echo from the bucket. "My hair is awful. Was there this much dirt in yours? There had to be!"

"Yeah, it wasn't pretty."

Something was eating away at her as they continued their banter. This wasn't right, she thought. It wasn't normal. They were doing it again, trying to pick up where they'd left off. She knew they couldn't just ignore the past, but that's exactly what they were doing. Part of her wanted to shut him out again and keep arguing, but part of her had simply had enough of that. She had made things unbearable up until now. Maybe it was time to forgive and forget—she remembered her talk with Talora.

The water moved and suddenly tore her from her thoughts, and instinctively, she turned around. Then she gasped.

"You told me you weren't going to do that!" Aleth yelled, jabbing a finger at her.

She covered her mouth and found herself blinking back tears. "What the hell happened to you?" His body was riddled with scars—no wonder he'd been hiding from her. "This is my fault. Oh gods, all of it! This is my fault!"

"No," he spat. "You do not get to take credit for what I've been through!"

"You even told me it was my fault! You said you left because of me. That if I had never turned my back on you the way I had, you would have stayed!"

He bit his lip. "That's not exactly—"

"Yes it is, and you know it is!" she sobbed. "All those things that happened to you after you left, every awful thing you had to go through—" Her voice got small as she hid her face. "They were my fault!"

Her confession was not as satisfying as he had imagined it. He moved through the water to confront her, trying to rub the frustration from his brow as she stared through her fingers with guilt and horror.

"Alright, calm down. See this one here?" He pointed to a jagged line down one of his forearms. "I slipped on a boulder and fell halfway down a cliff, just slid right past this knife of a rock. It had nothing to do with you! In fact, if I had never left, I would probably still have something like it from Rhett *throwing* me down a cliff. Some of these we can pin on you, sure. I can think of a few." He said it sourly. "But I'm stupid enough to earn my own scars, I promise."

She looked up at him, big tears rolling from puffy eyes and down her flushed cheeks. "You'd have been in a warm bed every night instead of sleeping in dirt, or whatever that was at Secret Teller. You wouldn't have—"

"Tizzy, stop. Please."

"I'm so, so sorry. I should have been better to you."

He heaved a tense sigh and sat down in one of the tub's corners. "For ten years," he said, resting his elbows on the edge behind him, "that was all I ever wanted to hear."

She returned to her corner and hugged her knees. "All that time I was such a mess. Every day, I was crushed that you weren't there, and at the same time I was furious with you. I didn't realize I should have been the one apologizing."

Aleth shook his head. "I messed up too. I left. It didn't matter that I had a reason, I still just left you there. I didn't even say goodbye."

Tizzy wiped away her tears with the water. "Will things get better? Are we going to be okay?"

It was a delicate question. He slicked back his wet hair, cold water from the earlier rinse running down his face. He chewed on his knuckle.

"Who knows?" he said finally. "I can't tell you how all of this is going to go. In fact, there's only one thing I can tell you, one thing that I know for certain."

She saw fear in his eyes again and was starting to understand just how much he couldn't say. "What's that?"

"No matter what happens, as long as we stay together, we'll be okay."

She nodded. "Alright." She let it all sink in. "I trust you."

He cocked his head. "You do?"

"Yes. So don't let me down." She sniffled, and suddenly she was stern. "If that's all you can give me, it'll have to be enough. I'm getting out now. I know I just woke up a little while ago, but I'm exhausted."

He didn't know how he had won her trust exactly, but it was a relief. He had expected a longer battle. "I'll be out soon," he told her, shutting his eyes.

Tizzy stepped out of the bath, water pooling out onto the floor beneath her. Her towel was thoroughly soaked. She looked back at Aleth, who had leaned his head back in a state of relaxation bordering on sleep, then shrugged and ditched the towel for a robe.

There was a lot to consider, now more than ever. She used another towel to dry off and sat on the other side of the tapestry. Aleth opened his eyes and watched her silhouette.

"Are you okay?"

"Yeah," she said, rubbing her knees. "You got a lot of those scars from other people, didn't you?"

"Most of them. If it makes you feel better, I don't scar anymore."

"So theoretically you could have even *more*?"

"On second thought, I guess that wouldn't make you feel better."

"How did you find so many people who wanted to hurt you? Usually when people find a boy in the woods, they try to help him get home. But you—"

"People don't like what I am, Tizzy. What we are. It didn't matter how young I was. Look, I know you have questions. I know there's so much you don't understand. I'm going to tell you everything, I promise, but I'm just not ready yet."

She left it at that. Soon, Mayriel and Velana returned, knocking on the door and giggling.

"Your stuff is done!" Velana shouted through laughter.

Tizzy opened the door with an arched eyebrow. "Thank you, ladies. I appreciate the service."

"Yeah, we're not done yet. Move over." Velana gently shoved Tizzy aside with one of her arms and led Mayriel inside.

"You see, we're here for your used towels now." Mayriel wore the biggest smile on her face.

Velana leaned over and whispered. "Hey check it out, May! I think he's hiding from us!"

"Oh, that's precious!"

"Hey!" Tizzy snapped. "Give me my clothes!"

"Yeah, yeah." Velana sighed and took her basket over to the hearth and started laying garments out onto the rack. "I'll just leave them here for you. We washed his, too. You know, the one outfit he owns. We were careful with it. See?" She held up his worn gray tunic. "He's had to fix the seams on this about a hundred times. And sew shut some of these stab wounds too. What a mess."

Tizzy furrowed her brow. "Between the two arms, he's only got about a sleeve left of this thing."

"Hey, lady," Mayriel called from the other side of the tapestry. "I see you've got all these nice, dry towels sitting next to the bath here. I'm just going to take—"

Tizzy growled. "*Leave 'em*! Will you two please get out?"

With mischievous cackles, the quadramanus pair grabbed the wet towels and dashed out of the room. Tizzy, with plans to file a complaint, raced back to the bath. Aleth had held his breath through the whole encounter, hiding under the water. She knelt down, reached her hand in, and tapped his shoulder.

He came to the surface. "They're gone?" He coughed.

"Yes, you've been saved. You've got quite the fan club, don't you?"

"Fan club?" He wiped the water off his face. "They've been laughing at me since the first time I came here. They're half the reason I always cover up."

"Oh!" Tizzy started to chuckle. "What, you think they're making fun of your scars? Is that it?"

"That's obviously it."

"Boy." She grabbed a comb out of the basket and sat down next to him on the floor, starting to work out the tangles in her hair. "Believe me, they don't even notice them."

"That makes no sense. Why else do they act like that? Stalking me, pointing at me, cackling like that."

She stopped what she was doing and just laughed. "Are you serious?" He stared back, confused. "It's like two wolves staring down a piece of meat."

It took him a moment, with Tizzy howling in amusement behind him, and then his eyes widened, and his face went pink. "That's even worse."

She stifled more laughter and ran her fingers through his hair, catching on a tangle. "Good to see you're still the densest thing in the world. And good lords, you could use a trim."

"No, I couldn't." He pushed her hand away before she could take to it with the comb. "I will cut my own hair when I think my own hair is ready to be cut."

"I could just cut it now."

He glared. "That is the least trustworthy grin I've ever seen."

"Okay, fine." She got to her feet, laughing. "When you want to see something other than your own damn hair in your face all the time, let me know."

She sat by the fire to continue combing through her curls and noticed the girls had brought a small loaf of warm bread. She tore into it.

Before long, Aleth parted ways with the bath and was reunited with his towels. He came out from behind the tapestry, drying off his hair. When he came over to the fire to inspect his clothes, Tizzy looked up at him.

"We've got to do something about those," she said through a mouthful of bread.

He grabbed the loaf out of her hand. "They're fine. Besides, we don't really have the kind of time or money to just waltz over to a tailor. I'm six-foot-five, Tizzy. It's harder to find clothes than you think."

"Time," she corrected him. "Time is the only thing we're lacking. If you think I came without any money, you're *dumber* than an idiot."

He scoffed and tore off a piece of bread before tossing it back to her, then took his clothes. A hefty wave of embarrassment stopped him, however, and he returned his tunic to the rack—he couldn't bear to walk around in it. He wandered off to partially dress, and Tizzy stayed by the fire, dutifully working out every tangle until her hair lay neatly in damp black waves down her shoulders and chest. Then she grabbed something comfortable to wear and dressed.

"I feel a hundred times better," she said, stretching. "I'm sorry I was such a pain in the ass, but thanks for bringing us here."

"I feel a hundred times better too. It worked out for both of us." He fought the chill by standing by the hearth, peering over at her pile of belongings. Attached to her belt was a familiar hilt poking out of a scabbard. He couldn't believe he hadn't recognized it earlier. "Is that Wish?"

"What, this old thing?" She picked it up and grinned as she revealed the black blade. "Of course it is! Do you still have Mercy?"

Aleth retrieved his own weapon from next to the bed and revealed its black blade. "I'd never get rid of this. When did we get these? It's been so long, I don't really remember."

"Wish and Mercy, let's see. I think Lazarus got them for us one year at Winter Solstice. Was I eleven? I think I was eleven. Yeah, because *you* had just turned eleven about a month before Winter S—oh my gods, it's almost your birthday!"

"Don't you get excited about that. I mean it!" He playfully pointed the sword at her.

"Don't tell me what to do! And are you still any good with that?" She pointed back.

"Good?" He smirked, sheathing it. "Please. I'm the best."

"Such a humble young swordsman you are. You know, Adeska's husband says *he's* the best." She watched the lambent light glint off the metal.

"Nope. I'm the best, I promise you that." He sat down and stared into the flames.

"No doubt about it at all, hm? We should find out for sure someday." She returned Wish to its sheath and rested it next to her bag. "Do they serve anything besides bread here?"

"Yeah, but you're paying for it, moneybags."

Tizzy rummaged through her bag for her coin purse, excited at the prospect of a meal. Going downstairs to place an order would be awkward, she thought, given how she had made her entrance, but food would be worth it.

She never got that far. Before her hands had found any gold, her headache returned. Aleth noticed her wince and grabbed her shoulder.

"Did it come back?"

"Yes!" She clenched her teeth and shut her eyes tight. The pain was like hot knives all over again, sinking slowly into her head from every angle. Slicing, searing, maddening pain that squeezed her and was needles in her eyes. Every time she told herself it couldn't get worse, it did. "I can't keep doing this!"

"Yes, you can. I know you can, you can beat them. I don't know how long they'll keep being like this, Tizzy, but I know you. I couldn't beat mine, but *you can*."

"No!" Tears welled up. "I can't take it anymore!" She looked him in the eyes, and this time it wasn't fear she saw. It was desperation.

"You're sure?" he asked, his voice breaking.

"Why are you saying that? Can you make it stop?"

He wore the heartbreak on his face. He always did. She held in a sob when he wouldn't meet her gaze.

"I can, but—" He swallowed hard. "If I do, Tizzy, it will change everything. And there'll be no going back."

"I don't care!" she screamed. There was red in her eyes again.

He knew she didn't understand—she couldn't possibly foresee the consequences of succumbing to the impulse, but he couldn't force her to endure its pain any longer.

"Okay. But nothing will be the same. I need you to stay calm. Don't be afraid."

The agony kept her from saying that she was afraid, and she knew her life had changed forever when he came back into it. She was frozen with pain, looking into the face of a man she had just let down. He fixed his stare onto his wrist. For a long time, he couldn't find the strength to act, and then Tizzy watched his incisors grow sharp, into fangs. He bit deep into his flesh, and her pain was replaced by hunger as the blood dripped down onto the floor.

Instinct took over. She asked no questions when he offered her the wound, thought of nothing as she drank of it gluttonously. Aleth watched her, numb to the feeling, and defeated.

This wasn't supposed to happen. This was not why he had come for her. He had *promised* himself it wouldn't happen this way. And now he was either stupid for believing it ever could've gone the way he wanted or a coward for not trying harder.

"You have to believe me that I didn't want this for you." She didn't even look up at him. "Maybe it was inevitable, but I refuse to believe that. Gods, why the hell did I give into you? I was supposed to protect you from this! I should have helped you fight. I—I know I could have convinced you to keep fighting the impulses somehow. I'm sorry my faith in you wasn't enough," he said. "Tizzy, I'm sorry that it had to come to this."

The sound of his voice saying her name broke her trance, and she backed away from him, trembling, blood trickling down her chin. "I— I knew it!" She covered her mouth, still tasting copper. "You're bloodkin! I knew it! I *saw* it!"

"So are you!" he yelled. "Look in the mirror, Tizzy! Your eyes are red, just like mine!" The rust-brown of his irises became crimson. He had so much more to say; the time had finally come. But when he opened his mouth, a sense in the air made him shudder, and he went quiet. Tizzy wiped the red off her lips and watched him approach the door.

"Get behind the tapestry, *now!*"

She obeyed, her body buzzing with his blood. Aleth stood next to the doorway, just out of the door's path, and waited. His hands clenched and unclenched as he tried to steady his breathing. Tizzy thought the next moment would never come, but then he swung the door open.

Immediately, a woman's arm grasping a knife came jabbing at him. He grabbed it and threw her into the room, and she rolled harmlessly to her feet. She was tall and lean, pale with a sharp face and a sharper bob of white-blonde hair.

"Why are you following me?" Aleth yelled.

She ignored him and gestured to his bloody wrist. "What is this? Are you fucking feeding her?"

"Answer me, Lilu! Why are you here?"

"I don't answer to you!" The woman's eyes were yellow and ferocious. Tizzy thought she saw them lock right onto her. "So where is she, huh? Let's see what all the fuss is about."

"Get out!" His fists were shaking. "We'll be at the Convent in a few days! We just had some trouble."

"Aleth, *where is she?*" The woman took a brazen step forward, only inches away from his face. "If she's anything like her pathetic little brother, I've got something for her."

He threw his fist into her face and shoved her back before she had recovered enough to strike at him with the knife. Lilu laughed, wiping away a line of blood, dark like wine, from her bottom lip.

"You little shit."

She lunged forward with the knife, slicing a shallow cut in his chest as he tried to back out of its arc. She went to bring her arm back in, but he swung at her face with his right and twisted her wrist back with his left. The weapon dropped to the floor with a *clang*.

Tizzy watched with wide eyes. Lilu kneed him in the gut and punched him so square in the nose, it sent him reeling back. She smirked as the blood raced down his lips.

"Had enough yet?"

He went to shove her, but she locked hands with him. They struggled with each other, trying to throw each other back, but were stuck at a stalemate.

"You know I'm stronger!" Lilu taunted. "It's only a matter of time before I've pinned you to the ground again! And this time, I brought enough knives to keep you there." Taking in some of his momentum, she bent her arm and threw her elbow into his face.

Without faltering, he swung his body back around from the blow. His hands had grown claws, and he ripped effortlessly into her jaw. Lilu turned her head back from the impact to meet his bright red eyes, blood flowing from the tears in her flesh.

"Not bad," she hissed. The skin sizzled and spat until the wound closed.

Tizzy was now watching the fight outside the shroud of the tapestry. She was transfixed by the blood—both Aleth's and Lilu's—that was spilling onto the floor. A vicious, angry hunger boiled within her, and she felt her own fangs grow and pierce her bottom lip. The impulse overtook her, and she bolted at Lilu, leaping onto the woman's back and sinking her fangs deep into her neck. Lilu cried out, as did Aleth.

"Tizzy, no!"

She tried to drink, but what filled her mouth was black, tasted like ash, and burned her tongue. Lilu twisted and threw her across the room, laughing as she sputtered on the ground.

"I knew she'd be stupid, but this is ridiculous." She took another step toward her. Aleth shoved her back.

"Lilu, don't! Leave her alone!"

With a sweeping kick to his legs, Lilu grounded him and wrestled him to his back. "Oh, shut up." She took two knives from sheaths on her thighs and pierced them through his biceps, pushing them deep into the wood floor. When his cry of pain had sufficiently pleased her, she stood and continued walking to Tizzy.

"Aleth, oh gods!"

"He's *fine*," Lilu sighed, rolling her eyes. "You, on the other hand."

The woman's nails dug into Tizzy's skin as she wrapped her fingers around her neck and lifted her into the air. Tizzy pried and scratched at the woman's hold. Lilu slammed her against the wall.

"You thought you were so special. Well let me be the first to break it to you, *Tizzy*. I've made my observation, and I've decided that you're shit." Lilu took Tizzy's arm with her free hand.

"Lilu, please!" Aleth yelled, struggling with the knives. "Don't!"

The woman changed right before Tizzy's eyes. Silvery scales blanketed her body, and she opened her mouth to reveal long, snake-like fangs that were dripping wet. Tizzy screamed as they sank into her arm. She felt the hot venom enter her blood immediately.

Aleth roared, fighting the pain of the knives cutting into him until he had gathered the strength to dislodge them from the floor. He freed himself and threw the knives to the ground.

"She's never given in to an impulse before!"

Lilu removed her fangs and changed back. She dropped Tizzy and watched her slump over.

"So," she pointed to the slowly closing bite wound on his wrist. "That's the first time she's fed?"

"Yes!" He wiped some of the blood from his nose and rushed to Tizzy's side, turning her on her back. She started to gasp for air.

"Shitty draw." Lilu crossed her arms. "I was only hoping to shake things up a little. Better hope she doesn't die because it's going to be your word against mine. And you know how that goes. See you soon!" She picked up her knives and walked out as casually as though she had never been there at all.

Panicking, Aleth inspected the bite. "No, no, please. Tizzy, breathe. Look at me! Come on, you're okay!"

Her vision was in the wrong colors, she thought, wheezing. With every breath, her body felt jittery and stiff, her skin tight and prickly. She sucked in a breath. "Aleth."

He touched her face, wiping away sweat. "This is bad, do you get that?"

"I'm sorry."

"Aleth!"

A man waited in the doorway. Aleth looked up at him, choking back tears.

"What? I'm sorry, okay? There was nothing else I could do! I had to come here!"

Tizzy didn't recognize him, not that she was lucid enough to anyhow. He wore a long black coat and looked down at them with an expressive face full of black stubble. His skin was dark brown, and his wide eyes black like onyx. A thick, jagged scar across the back of his head, from ear to ear, announced him louder than anything else.

"I saw Lilu come out of here. What's all this? Who is that?"

"She's my sister." He said it through the tiniest escaping sob. "Lilu bit her. Kenway, I don't know what to do!"

The man couldn't stop staring at her. He tilted his head and crossed his arms. "Your sister? Aleth, I swear I've seen her before. Why is she so familiar?"

"Are you listening at all?"

He scratched his chin and then sharply motioned to her. "Aleth, is this Tizena fucking Hallenar on my floor?"

"Yes! *Help me!*"

Kenway knelt down beside them and shrugged. "What's the matter? She'll be fine in a day or so. If she's here at all, it means she's like you, right?"

"Not enough!"

"So then—" He inspected the wound and the glistening venom still on her skin. Tizzy couldn't feel him at all. "Damn. Lilu bit her good. Girls! Get in here!"

At once, Mayriel and Velana filtered into the room and stood behind Kenway.

"Go to the kitchen and find Troll Daughter. See if she has anything for lilitu venom!"

"Yes, sir!" They left as quickly as they had entered.

Kenway clapped Aleth on the shoulder, then noticed the blood dripping down his stab wounds. "Stay calm. We'll figure this out."

"I can't lose her again. You don't understand!" he said, shaking his head. "Tizzy, you're an idiot!"

She coughed. "M-my bag." Her hand twitched as she tried to point to it by the fire. "Ribbon."

In the blink of an eye, he was ransacking through her things until he saw a pink ribbon at the bottom of the bag. He brought it back to her.

"This?"

"Mmh."

"What does she expect us to do with a ribbon?"

"I've got an idea," Aleth said. He stood up and held it with shaking hands.

"Why didn't you ever tell me you were royalty?"

"Because I'm not."

Kenway could only manage a frown as he stood and tossed him a rag from one of the baskets. "Clean up. She broke your nose. Again."

He covered his nose with the rag. "That's the one thing I'm not worried about." Wincing, he set it into place with a vile-sounding *crack*. "It's seen more abuse than this. This thing is in it for the long haul." He threw the rag aside and stared down at Tizzy. Hoping that he understood her intentions, he wrapped the ribbon around his hand. "I'll be back by dawn. Stay with her, *please*."

CHAPTER 7

A VERDANT VEIL

The rain had eased into a gentle drizzle over Suradia. People started to wander out onto the streets to fix damage to their homes and businesses once the the threat of flooding had passed. Lora held up her black sari just enough to pass through a puddle unharmed. She padded through town, shadowing Rori, holding a black shawl over her face.

Farther down the road, the blonde hugged herself for warmth, but the effort was futile. She hadn't seen a cold season since the last time she'd visited, which had been about two years ago, for Mariette's birth.

It would always be home, but she'd have to leave Suradia again eventually. She was a knight now, for the prudish High Elves on the faraway mainland of Sila'Karia. It was a beautiful place with lush forests and a mild climate. She missed it, but she had to admit that there was no place quite like Mirivin Mainland.

Lora followed her to the southern side of town. It was a long way to go for some errands, she thought. But then, she saw the building Rori entered—Emrin's Home for Youth. After the door closed behind her, Lora waited a few moments before entering the establishment herself, conjuring an air of false wonder.

Emrin was the Goddess of Family, Fertility, and Children. Across every mainland on Rosamar, there were Homes and Orphanages in her name that were dedicated to caring for children without a place to live. Lora turned away and feigned interest in various depictions of the goddess while Rori, completely oblivious to her presence, flagged down a priestess. The statues were chipped. The tapestries that hung on damp, stained walls were worn and fraying. Scrolls with well-known verses were barely readable. The Home had only one story, now flooded, and the children carried around their soggy bedrolls looking for a dry corner. Lora watched the priestesses hand out bowls of cold, thin porridge.

"Excuse me, Priestess, I'm looking for a boy I came in with yesterday morning. His name is Alor," Rori said.

The woman, wearing tattered robes in Emrin's colors of peach and light green, turned and pointed to the back of the building. "He's been alone in the corner since you brought him by. Hasn't said a word to anyone. I must say, he acts *quite* a bit different than the other children his age."

Rori blushed. The priestess was not the first person to make such a comment. "He wasn't raised by humans," she explained. "High Elves, actually. They don't treat children the way we do."

The priestess folded her arms. "Believe me, it shows."

Rori broke away and darted off into the room at once. Curiously, Lora neared.

Another priestess cleared her throat and Lora jumped. "My lady, can I help you?"

"No!" Lora said. "No, I'm sorry. My husband is a merchant. We are passing through town." She laid on a thick Besqi accent. "We are thinking of making a donation. May I take a look around?"

"Of course. Please ask if you have questions."

Lora nodded and continued to wander around the Home as though she might be admiring artwork. She stayed within earshot of Rori but was careful to keep her back to her.

"Alor! I'm back, little guy!" Rori said, trying to hide the apprehension in her voice behind a smile. She bent down to a child who looked between three and four. "Sorry it took me so long."

"Ro, it's all wet here. Can we go back home now?"

"No, we can't." She sighed, tucking a wisp of his wild brown hair behind his ear. "Something happened at the queen's house. We have to stay."

"Do I have to stay *here*?" The boy pouted. It broke her heart.

"I'm sorry."

"How come my real mom won't come for me, Ro?"

"Oh!" She wrapped her arms around him. "Alor, come here. Your mother, she wants you, she does. But she just—she made bad choices and chose to deal with them very irresponsibly. Unfortunately, that means you and I have to deal with it. But she loves you, Alor, and I love you." The boy was practically radiating sadness; Rori could feel it as she held him close. But he didn't cry or whimper. The situation was so bleak, she almost wished he would.

Then she stopped and leaned back, squeezing his tiny shoulders.

"You know what? No." She stared into his big, brown eyes. "No, I've had enough of this. You've had enough of this. Let's go."

"But you said you have to stay at the queen's house."

"I did. And I do. And you're coming with me! But it's a secret, okay? Nobody can know you're there."

He got excited and nodded. "Okay, it's a secret! Is it dry? Will they have blankets?"

"It's dry, there are so many blankets, our room will have a hearth, there's food and toys. Alor, they even have a dog! Come on, let's get your bag, and we'll go. I just have to talk to one of the priestesses, okay?"

"Yes!"

Lora had heard enough. She found the priestess who she had spoken to and tapped her on the shoulder. "I am ready to make my donation now."

"That's very kind! I will return in a moment with the documentation—"

Lora held her finger in front of her shawl where her lips were hidden and placed two white coins into the woman's hand, staying perfectly silent.

"Platinum godpennies?" she gasped. "Who will I thank?"

"Just pretend it is from the queen," Lora whispered with a wink. She left without another word.

***

"Are you ready to try again, Isa?"

Gavin thumbed through a tome much too advanced for his student, dividing his attention between Akashic knowledge he already knew and a view of the dusk-shrouded town from a second-story window in the Hall of Anatanth.

Isa's sigh came out more of a grumble. "No."

"You'll get it," he told her. "Don't be so discouraged. Gather up the ingredients again."

She was sitting at a long table with her head in her hands. *Amethyst Spells Vol. I* had been tossed several feet away, joined by a handful of spell components, in a failed attempt to cast Arcane Illuminations. Had the spell been a success, she would have been able to absorb whatever knowledge she wanted from the next book she touched.

"Why don't I just try Arcane Blast? Clearly I'm already halfway there."

"Let's wait until we're outside before you try that one," Gavin laughed.

So many lessons. She was exhausted. Now that she'd mastered petty magic and general spells, Isa had no idea what magic she wanted to learn or which deity she wanted to follow. So, in an effort to pique her interest in something, Gavin taught her everything. She felt like she knew the life and backstory and city registration information and second cousin's birthday of every Ancient that had ever walked Rosamar. She knew about the gemstone magics—Amethyst, Quartz, Topaz, Ruby, Emerald. She knew about the gods that gifted them and the tale of their truce and how Anatanth, the God of Akasha, had gifted them with stones to share his gratitude.

She knew of the other magics too—the ones like Fire and Storm and Time and the branches of Druidism, all of which required special tutoring and licensing by the Academy. There was so much to keep track of, Isa thought she'd be better suited to getting a job and filling out Academy paperwork than pursuing magic.

She didn't know if she'd ever find her focus, but in the meantime, Gavin was happy to teach her his own.

"Come on, Isa. Amethyst Magic is some of the most useful there is. You'd do well to learn it from me."

"Gavin, I can't do this. You keep telling me I just need to focus more, to study more, to practice more. But I know I can't do it. My magic just doesn't work like this."

He closed the tome and chewed the inside of his lip. "I know." He set the book down on the table beside her. "I've seen your magic, Isa, and it's very destructive. If you're going to get any control over it, you need structure."

"We should go outside. It just doesn't *work right* in here."

Gavin opened his mouth, but his thoughts were interrupted by a distant sound. He narrowed his eyes. "Is that a dog?"

"Aw!" Isa stood up and ran to the window. "I bet he ran out of someone's home to play in the puddles! I hope his owners find him and bring him back."

With a quick scan, Isa found that the incessant noise was coming from a medium-sized dog at the front doors of the Hall. An attendant was trying to shoo the mostly black border collie away.

"Gavin, look! What a rough little pooch."

He crossed his arms. "He doesn't look like he's going anywhere, either." The attendant was getting more belligerent, as was the dog.

"Come on!" Isa said, skipping away. "Let's go see what's going on! Maybe we can get him to settle down till the owner shows up." She raced downstairs, Gavin barely able to keep up. When they reached the front doors, the attendant was more than ready to hand the situation over to someone else.

"Wonderful! You two can do something about this filthy, beat-up old thing. He won't stop!"

"Hello there, Puppy!" Isa rushed up to the animal. Gavin rolled his eyes. "Look at you! Gavin, maybe he doesn't have a home after all. He looks like he's fought off every single animal in the Bogwood. He doesn't look very old, either."

"Isa, *please* be careful. He's caked in mud." The dog sniffed Isa's hands, and his barking subsided.

She watched his tail and giggled. "Yeah, boy? Are you friendly?"

With a little jump, he barked in response. Isa broke into laughter, but when her eyes found one of his muddy paws, she stopped.

"What's this you have here?" A scrap of fabric was tied to him. Gingerly, she took his paw and pulled it loose. "Gavin. Gavin, look at this!"

He hadn't been paying attention. "What is it? A bandage? Don't touch it, Isa. You could catch something."

"Gavin, it's not—it's not a bandage." She could barely speak. After wiping the dirt away and wringing it out, she handed it to him. "Just *look*."

The first thing he noticed were the pink lace edges. "This is your ribbon!"

"I gave it to Tizzy when we went back to House Hallenar yesterday morning! I was just trying to be nice; she was in such a bad mood, and I wanted her to know she could talk to me. Maybe I thought it would cheer her up. Gods, I told her pink was her color; what was I thinking?" She grabbed the dog's face. "How do you have it? Is she okay?"

He barked frantically and turned around to lead them. Gavin and Isa exchanged glances.

"I'll get the horse. Grab your cloak, Isa."

"Are we gonna follow the dog?"

"We're gonna follow the dog."

***

Tizzy's eyes fluttered open. Sunlight poured in from cracks in the room, blinding her. Talora's face hovered over her.

"Fantastic job, Tizzy. Absolutely brilliant."

She was dreaming. Again. The seasonal differences peeking through gaps in the wood betrayed the illusion of reality. The sun was up high in a cloudless sky, beaming warmth. Foreign summer birds chirped and tweeted and sang.

Tizzy rubbed her eyes. "That sounds like sarcasm," she grunted. A wave of nausea hit her as she tried to sit up. Surrendering, she laid back down.

"Of course it is!" she snapped. Tizzy could hear a shaking teacup and saucer in her hand. "In the few short hours I've known you, you've already managed to nearly get yourself killed! So yes, congratulations."

"Where am I?" She tried to crane her neck and get a good look around. A tree grew right through the middle of the single-room space.

"My home," Talora said plainly. She took a tiny sip of the tea. "I live in a treehouse. I call it that, but it's really only a few feet off the ground."

"I thought this was my head and that you could only go to places that I knew. I don't know this place."

"Well, I had to put it here, *in your head*!" Talora put the cup and saucer down and shrugged. "You left me no choice. I have to be able to help you right now, so I moved on in. Just for now. *What did you do?*"

"You think this is my fault?" Tizzy regretted yelling immediately. Nausea immobilized her.

"Wasn't it?"

Tizzy grumbled. "It was. Probably."

The scent of the woods coming in through the walls was revitalizing. She breathed in deep and could feel the malaise being worked away.

"Well, spit it out. What did you do?"

"I tried to attack Lilu."

"*Lilu?*" Her hand drifted over her mouth. "Oh my."

"You know her? Aleth sure did."

Talora leaned back against the countertop. It was covered in dry herbs and little jars, and a small candle flame kept her iron teakettle warm. "Lilu is why I moved to this place. Out of the Convent. Her and I don't get along. She's always wandering around, trying to prove that she can kill you if she really wanted to. Her kind are insufferable."

"Aleth mentioned the Convent when they were yelling at each other. Before they started to fight, and before I—"

"Tizzy, listen to me." The woman glared at her. Her lips were drawn into a tight frown. "You're going to die."

"Thanks for the confidence!"

"I'm serious." Talora crossed her arms and looked away. Her eyes were glassy. "If she bit you, it's all too late. All of this, it's just—it's too late."

"That's not fair!" Tizzy fought the nausea and sat up, willing it away with heavy breaths. "I was finally starting to get some answers! I gave into this stupid impulse, found out that Aleth is a *vampire*—"

"No, he's a *nightwalker*," she corrected. "Wait, you did? You gave into it? You fed? But—" She rubbed her forehead. "Before he left, he said he didn't want that—"

"He grew fangs. I saw them in the dream I had, but I kept trying to convince myself it was just my imagination. How could it not be? I was wrong. He bit into his arm, and then I just lost control. I *drank* his blood."

"Well, yes, you're a nightwalker. That's what we do."

"I saw his marks!" Tizzy shouted, touching her neck. "I don't have any! Anywhere! So how?"

"He has to be the one to tell you that, Tizzy. I've heard the story, but he's the one who *knows*."

"Shouldn't I be the one who knows?"

"You do," Talora told her. "It's somewhere in your head. You just don't want to face it."

Tizzy fell back into the bed. It was itchy and uncomfortable. "Why did Lilu come after him? Why does she hate him?"

"She's a Greater Daemon called a *lilitu*. She hates everyone. It's all she really knows, and even then, she hardly understands *that*. And you know what? Now that I think about it, you might be able to survive this." She started to pace around the tree trunk. "Lilitu venom is fatal to humans. Up until your first impulse, you were as good as human. Each time we feed, a nightwalker becomes less and less human, and gains more of their bloodkin traits. It's what separates us from vampires. They can't survive without blood, but *we* can if we can withstand our impulses. Giving into your first one may have tipped Hanarn's scales in your favor."

Tizzy swallowed a lump in her throat. "I'm not human."

"No, you're not. You haven't been for a long time. But you've done a great job masquerading as one." She picked up her teacup. "Are you ready to fight? We can't afford to lose you, Tizzy. You're more important than you know."

Talora's words filled her with purpose, and she managed to sit up and swing her legs off the bed. Sitting there on the edge, she thought of Lilu's face and how the woman's form had changed. Then she thought of her own body, probably still on the floor at Sheerspine, dying and full of venom while her mind was a thousand miles away. Her hands shook with rage.

"Yeah, I'm ready."

***

Rori remembered enough about House Hallenar to know she could get in undetected. There was an outside entrance into the kitchen pantry, but the kitchen had always been a hotspot. She couldn't take the risk that she'd walk in on one of her siblings preparing a meal. The orchard entrance was the safest route, and it was close to her old room on the first floor.

"We really are making this a secret!"

The voice came from underneath her cloak. Alor was riding on her back with the garment draped over him.

"Yes, we certainly are, so stay quiet until I say the coast is clear, okay?"

"Okay."

Allanis had the orchard full of trees that would be producing fruit all year round. Many were dormant, waiting for their preferred season, but Rori could already see some trees bearing ripe apples, Shimara pears, plums, and figs. Soon, pomegranates, persimmons, and walnuts would be ready. She took careful strides underneath the sweet-smelling shade, avoiding stepping on fallen fruit. She plucked a plum free of a branch and passed it to the boy, then made a beeline for the back door.

She passed Tizzy's woodshed and sighed. She had hoped to catch a glimpse of her older sister about town but had no such luck. Giving it no more thought, she took a bundle of firewood and went inside.

A chill set in throughout House Hallenar. It was evident that Tizzy had never come out of her room to light the fires. A few sconces had been lit, likely by a hurried and overslept Athen, but everything else went untouched. When she made it to her room, she dropped Alor onto her bed and set down his bag and the firewood with a grunt of relief.

"Ro, this is nice!"

She shut the door, and his eyes wandered all around: to the plant sketches she had done before leaving the mainland, to the little clay statuettes of faeries she used to collect, and to the floral tapestries she had sewn that all featured white doves. She sat next to him on the bed and covered his shoulders with a downy green blanket.

"It's not quite as nice as the Avendilar High Keep, of course, but it's nicer than the ship we came in on and the Emrin's Home we just left. Will you be okay staying here for a while?"

"Yeah!" He took a bite of the plum. "Wow, what's this?" Still chewing, he jumped off the bed and to a quaint bookshelf. Rori panicked for a second that he would choke running around so carelessly, but he got to a book without any trouble and inspected it with his plum-free hand. The book was one she hadn't thought about in years. Its pages were big, and the paper was thick and bumpy. Alor sat on the floor and flipped through it.

"I used to press flowers and leaves in that book when I was younger," she told him. "I loved learning about plants. I was going to become an apothecary. At least, that was the plan before the ambassador from Sila'Karia and his retinue came to Mirivin. For some reason, they just *had* to see Suradia."

Alor laughed. "That's how you met Raph!"

The thought made Rori smile and blush. "Yeah. I was sixteen when I fell head over heels in love with him."

"Ew!" The boy laughed and chewed on the plum again.

"Hey! One of these days, the very same thing could happen to you!"

"No. Grown-ups are gross."

They laughed together, and Rori decided that he wasn't entirely wrong. She had started making a fire, telling Alor more stories about her youth, when the door opened. Lora casually let herself in, still wearing the black sari.

Rori gasped. "Lora! What are you doing here? You could have knocked!"

"If you don't have to let anyone know you're hiding a child here," she said, clearing her throat. "I don't have to knock."

"I can't believe you were following me!"

Lora was unfazed by Rori's cry. "And it wasn't for naught, it seems. Who is this?" she asked, gesturing to Alor. "Why are you hiding him? We would have been more than happy to have him, you know that."

"I have to hide him, Lora. You don't understand!" She held her head in her hands. "It's a messy situation, okay? But I wasn't going to make him suffer at the Emrin's Home because of it. It isn't his fault!"

"Whose son is he?" Lora raised an eyebrow. "I'm going to find out, eventually. And I won't make a secret out of it because I will keep no secrets from Allanis. My duty is to her, not to this dysfunctional family and the messes it makes."

"I'll tell you, and I'll tell everyone else, when the time is right! Good lords, Lora, you don't get it! This is going to be a, just a—" she threw her hands up, "—a shit show! Nobody is ready for it yet. I just need a little bit of time, Lora. Please don't tell anyone he's here! I'm begging you!"

She crossed her arms. "I will inform Allanis that you have news, and I will leave it at that. But only because you're begging. You have until she decides to inquire about it to get ready for this *shit show*."

That was the last thing she said before leaving and slamming the door. Rori groaned and hid her face.

"That lady is mean," Alor said.

"She is. But she's the best thing that's ever happened to my little sister." She looked up, weary and filled to the brim with anxiety.

***

A cold breeze rustled the leaves as it howled through the Bogwood. Isa tightened her hold around Gavin's stomach as they raced through the forest on horseback, following the mysterious dog with Gavin's magenta flame lighting the way amidst the darkness. The dog's paws padded through the mud, cut deep by every jagged stone and rough branch underfoot. Wherever they were going, Gavin thought they were making good time. The rain was little more than dampness in the air.

"Do you know where we are?" Isa asked, her voice broken by the horse's gallop.

"No. I hope this was the right thing to do."

It felt right, Isa thought. She didn't know where they were, either, but she felt safe among the trees despite the Bogwood's reputation for danger. She couldn't be sure, but it seemed as though the trees swayed out of their path as they went by.

The dog led them to a cliffside covered in wisteria. Gavin didn't understand. "Is this it? Is this where we're supposed to go? There's nothing here."

"Gavin, there's something out there!" Isa dismounted. Her eyes perused the forest. "Gavin—"

"I feel it too."

The dog started whimpering and scratched at the cliff. Gavin stared at him and shook his head.

"This doesn't make sense. It doesn't feel like it was supposed to be a trap." He stayed on the horse and materialized his staff. "Stay back, Isa."

A knife came singing through the air, missing him only narrowly. Lilu cackled, hidden by the trees.

"The next one won't miss!"

The dog barked and scratched relentlessly, Isa at his side. Gavin reached into a pouch on his belt, keeping his eyes on the woods ahead. Then Lilu came out and lunged at him. The horse reared and Gavin tossed a shimmering powder into the air. His staff glowed, and a blast of purple energy shot up from the earth before she could reach him. It knocked her back and sent her rolling into the mud.

"Get in here! Now!"

Isa snapped her head around. A door had appeared from behind the wisteria. A three-eyed woman beckoned.

"I said *now*!" Naia yelled at them. The dog scrambled inside, and Gavin and Isa followed. Naia slammed the door, and her third eye glowed white. "*Vo ar'dansha garuwan lilitu gan asha dor*!"

"You know the Arcane Bindings!" Gavin said breathlessly. "That's incred—"

"Upstairs!" Naia jabbed her finger at the dog, who was already heading up without them.

Mayriel and Velana emerged from down a hall, having amassed a collection of books in their arms.

"Is that gonna keep her out of here?" Mayriel asked.

"Not forever!" Naia snapped. She wiped sweat from her brow. "Akasha is great and all, especially the Arcane stuff, but a daemon is a daemon. Especially *that one*."

"We can't find Troll Daughter," Velana said. "But we found some of her books. I hope this helps."

"What do you mean you can't find her? She never leaves the kitchen!"

"She left this time," Mayriel replied.

"Great." Naia threw her hands up. "Just great. I'm going to stay here by the door and make sure this thing holds. Get the books to Kenway and the others, and then you two need to get back to doing your job! We are trying to run a business, after all. Get to it!"

"Yes, ma'am!"

Upstairs, Kenway sat beside an unconscious Tizzy. He had cleaned the venom out of the wound to the best of his abilities and was flipping through the pages of *Creature Codex 'Daemons'* while he monitored her breathing. The dog ran into the room, tracking mud everywhere as he went behind the tapestry.

"You're back!" Kenway cheered.

Isa gasped. "Gavin, it's Tizzy!"

The two that Kenway had not met came in next. Isa, her eyes wide and glassy, stood over Tizzy.

"What happened to her?" Gavin asked. He dropped to his knees across from Kenway and took his glove off to feel her forehead. "This is bad."

"She thought you could help!" Aleth suddenly peered his head out from the tapestry, trying to wipe enough mud off himself to dress. "Please tell us you can help!"

Isa gasped. "*Were you the dog?*" Aleth didn't answer, instead looking down at his bloody, dirty hands that were trying to heal.

"Here's the situation." Kenway sighed, putting the book down and folding his arms. "She was bit by a lilitu daemon. It's likely the venom will kill her unless we do something. I don't have any ideas."

"I don't think we can help." Gavin frowned. "Isa and I, we're not very skilled healers. She's studied a little bit of Topaz Magic at the Hesperan Hospices, but that's not going to help here." He rubbed the back of his neck. "But, you see, Isa and I think she might actually be bloodkin. Which might mean she'll pull through, right?"

"She's only fed *once*," Aleth said bitterly. "I don't know if it's enough."

Velana and Mayriel barreled in next. Velana squinted her eyes. "Ah, Kenway, we've got bad news." The two of them set down a pile of books and Isa sat and started rifling through them.

"Wonderful. I could always use more bad news."

Mayriel bit her lip. "No Troll Daughter. But, um, here's some of her stuff out of the kitchen! Maybe it'll help!"

Velana grabbed Mayriel's hand. "Alright, back to work! Good luck, everyone!" They ran off and left Kenway grumbling and scratching his head.

"Books. I don't need more books!"

"Hang on a minute." Isa laid one of them out in front of her. "They're not all just books. There are a lot of notes in here too. Look at this stuff!" Her hands traced over words written in barely legible handwriting. "It's like a mix of Rosamarian Druidism and herbalism. *Dark* herbalism. These ingredients aren't going to be easy to come by."

"Let's say that they were easy to come by." Kenway stood and looked over them. "Is there anything useful in there?"

"Maybe not this one," Isa said, turning through more pages. "This is mostly love potions, but I'll keep looking. What did the Troll Daughter do here?"

Gavin and Kenway both started going through books, looking for ones littered with poor penmanship. "She's our cook but also kind of a doctor. We have a lot of patrons that come here with different needs. She always knows how to prepare the right thing. Originally, this was just supposed to be a bathhouse, but since we cater strictly to beings who don't easily exist within normal populations, they started coming here more long-term, or they'd come when they were hurt or in trouble. Whatever the situation and whatever the physiology, Troll Daughter always has a fix. She just whips something up in the kitchen, and it works. Lilu has been a pain in the ass here enough times, always out to stir shit up with Aleth, so I just figured she would have a solution this time."

He looked back at Tizzy. Aleth had finally come out and was sitting by her, still and quiet. Isa stopped digging through books and crawled over to him.

"You're him. You're Aleth, aren't you?"

Wearily, he met her eyes. "Do I know you?" He had torn up towels to wrap his hands.

"No. I'm Isa. The queen told me and Gavin about you."

"I'm sure she had a lot of wonderful things to say," he scoffed.

Isa couldn't think of anything comforting to tell him and returned to her work.

***

Outside in the woods, Tizzy stood tall. Talora's treehouse was in front of her, barely blocking the intense sun. She crossed her arms.

"Now what?"

Talora came out of her home and down a small flight of wooden steps. She tossed Wish to her. "Now you fight!"

Tizzy caught it with surprising ease. "Fight what?"

Talora stepped into the dry dirt and breathed in deep. That was when Tizzy watched her face and body contort until it was no longer Talora in front of her.

"Fight *me*." Lilu ripped away the black and green veil with a fanged grin.

Tizzy swung immediately but was far too slow. Lilu reacted with a punch, and she juked back just in time to avoid the hit.

***

"Venomous daemons!" Isa exclaimed with joy. "I think I found something!"

Gavin and Kenway dropped their books to run over and see. Aleth didn't move from Tizzy's side as she twitched on the ground.

"Is it an antidote?" Kenway asked.

"I'm not sure." She squinted at the writing. "Alright, it says... *Several species are known to be venomous. My chart on each venom's effect on different beings is far from complete.* For someone you guys call Troll Daughter, she is very well-spoken. *Until then, to ease the effects of the venom to facilitate a more painless death, use the instructions below.* Oh. Nevermind. Not an antidote."

"Let's try it anyway. The kitchen might have most of the ingredients. What's it say next?" Kenway asked.

"It says *For venom via spine or barb, use A. For venom via skin, use B. For venom via bite, use C.* Simple enough."

"Bite. Perfect. Let's head downstairs."

Isa stood with the book, her eyes still glued to the notes. "I think I can make some changes to this. If this is supposed to be a vague catch-all, I *should* make changes, right? And if she's bloodkin—"

"She's a *nightwalker.*" Aleth stared into the floor, clenching his jaw. "They're completely different."

"Well, I should add blood, right? That makes sense, doesn't it?"

Gavin put his hand on her shoulder. "Maybe we shouldn't change such an unfamiliar recipe, Isa. We don't know anything about nightwalkers."

"We're wasting time. Let's figure it out in the kitchen." Kenway led them out. Aleth stayed.

He was afraid to look at her. Every bone in his body ached, and his hands weren't healing fast enough. He crossed his arms over his knees.

"Maybe I should have just taken you with me ten years ago."

"Hey! Are you coming?" Kenway called from downstairs.

Aleth ignored him. "What could I have done to keep her away from you?"

"Aleth! Get yourselves down here!"

He knew Kenway was right. He picked her up and carried her down to the others. The kitchen was a wide-open space, messy with fires in pits and jars and tools strewn about without a home. Isa set the book down on a countertop and started trying to match jar labels to the ingredients listed.

"She has so many blank jars and weird names for things! I can't tell what anything is! Ew, are these eyeballs?"

The commotion went in one ear and out the other as Aleth walked out the kitchen's back door. It led to a small clearing in the woods where Troll Daughter would chop firewood. He laid Tizzy down on a pile of fallen pine needles and sat with her. Gavin looked outside.

"What is he doing?"

"Brooding," Kenway said. "He knows he's no help here."

Isa was getting more frustrated with each jar. She couldn't make heads or tails of anything and huffed, throwing the book down and storming outside with Aleth. "I can't do this. I'm trying it my way."

"Your way?" Gavin tilted his head. "Isa, wait!"

She came out into the clearing, wind stirring with her arrival. It carried a sound with it that was distantly musical. Aleth stood up and confronted her.

"What are you doing? I thought you guys had some kind of plan!"

"Give me space, everyone!" she shouted. "I have no idea what I'm doing!" The wind picked up and circled around her. Aleth backed away from her as she had warned and shielded his eyes from the leaves and pine needles whirring through the air.

"Isa, are you ready for this?"

She smiled at Gavin and a little green orb in her necklace started to glow—her casting tool. "I don't think I've got a choice."

He had never seen her use her magic on purpose. Maybe the rigid structure of Academy magic was working after all, he thought. Isa tilted her head back and took in the sensation of the wind, listening to the musical sounds that were just barely there, like a faint tune from long ago finally catching up to her. The trees and their rustling sang, and when she moved a little, she could orchestrate a new tempo. The plants and the rocks and the trees in the area hummed, then gave up tiny glowing orbs that floated in the air like dust. They caught in the wind and Isa absorbed them through her fingertips.

The wind died. The debris fell to the ground in a circle. She approached Tizzy with glowing hands and touched her forehead.

***

Tizzy's fight with her mind's version of Lilu hadn't progressed. She could hear Talora's voice in the air.

"You can't just run from her forever! Do you want to wake up or not?"

"What does it matter?" Tizzy yelled back. "I'm just going to have to fight her in real life when I wake up! Why spend the effort?"

Lilu materialized in front of her and slid a knife through her stomach. Tizzy cried out in pain, and the daemon laughed as the blood poured out onto her hands.

"This was your last chance!" she cackled. "Looks like you fail."

Tizzy fumbled with the hilt of the knife, slick and red. Her fingers found their grip, and she pulled it out and sank it into Lilu's neck. Merlot-colored blood sprayed out like a fountain. Tizzy knew she had bought herself only a few seconds and ran, pressing down on her wound, gritting her teeth through the sharp pain. It felt so real, *looked* so real, as the warm blood seeped out from between her fingers.

"Gods dammit!"

Lilu reappeared before her with breakneck speed, her neck healed like nothing had happened. She jabbed with the knife, and with a grunt, Tizzy swung her sword, knocking it away with a *clang* that reverberated through her bones. She could taste blood in her mouth from biting her lip.

"I'm going to kill you!" Tizzy spat. "I refuse to die before I get the chance!" They were tough words, she realized, for how close she was to passing out. And what would happen to her then? "Go on!" She threw Wish to the ground—it was too heavy. "Let's get this over with!"

Lilu smirked and dropped her knife, then punched Tizzy in the jaw. She returned the motion, landing her fist in the daemon's eye. Tizzy had learned how to fight from Lora years ago when the girl first moved to House Hallenar. She knew she was sub-par at best with a sword, but she could hold her own unarmed. With each punch, the pain ebbed away, and she could feel herself growing stronger. She finally kicked Lilu in the gut, sending her back a few steps.

When Tizzy looked down at her wound, it was covered in little specks of glowing dust.

Lilu stared at it too, her face twisted in anger. "What kind of trick is this?"

"What kind of trick is *biting me*?"

They were both startled when Aleth walked up.

"Tal, what is he doing here?"

"You tell me. It's your head."

"She can't attack me," he said. "The venom is fighting *you*. Hey, Lilu. Try it."

Lilu glared at him, gritting her teeth, then threw a punch at Tizzy. It landed on the corner of her mouth. Aleth only shrugged and stood behind the daemon, pinning her arms at her sides.

"Go ahead, Tizzy. Make a Wish."

She picked up her sword and drove it through Lilu's chest.

***

Aleth rushed back to Tizzy's side as Isa's magic faded away. The girl's shoulders fell in exhaustion, and the woods returned to normal. Nature's voices had left her, leaving behind only the sounds of chirping crickets in the night.

Tizzy opened her eyes, her lids heavy with fatigue. Aleth grabbed her hand, and she knew it was real—there was no chance her mind would have known how to paint a more wide-eyed look of shock and relief on his face.

"You're not dead! Isa, you did it! She's awake!"

She couldn't speak—she'd won the fight, it seemed, but recovery was next on the agenda. She worked her hardest to pull the corners of her mouth into a smile for him, then succumbed to a deep sleep.

Isa looked over to Aleth and caught a yawn now that the excitement was over. "I told her that if she ever needed anything, we were here for her. I know she didn't really like me that much, but I still meant it."

"If it makes you feel better, she's never really liked anyone."

Gavin helped Isa to her feet and hugged her. "Your magic. It was incredible, Isa!"

The praise was the best feeling of all, and Isa beamed. "I think it works better when I'm outside." She rubbed the weariness from her face. "I just listened to the trees. They didn't say anything, but I could still sense what they wanted me to do."

They walked back into the kitchen, discussing more of Isa's ability. Kenway stood at Aleth's side and offered him a hand. He was hesitant, then relented and took it.

"The last thing I wanted to do was cause you more trouble," he told Kenway.

He crossed his arms and shrugged. "Follows you like a plague. There doesn't seem to be anything I can do about it, either. Lifetime ban sure didn't work."

"I was desperate. I'm sorry."

Kenway's look wasn't exactly a glare, but there was a definite hardness in his eyes. "I never would have done that if I had known you were a Hallenar. I know you have a story, but—"

"There's a reason I don't use that name. Being a Hallenar never did me any good back then, so there's no point in being one now. Anyway, as soon as she's feeling better, I'm gone for good."

Kenway clapped him on the shoulder after a long silence. "I was hard on you, I admit." A grin snuck onto his face. "But you don't have to be a stranger. Look, I know you heard that Troll Daughter vanished. She's probably lost as hell out there. On your way out, if you see her out there, maybe send her this way for me? If she gets here safe and sound, I'll see to it that you and your sister always have a place to stay with us if you need it."

Aleth pursed his lips. "You're making it sound like you actually liked having me around."

"I did! And you were good at your job. Every once in a while, an old patron comes in and asks about you. It was good to have you around, but you would just get in your little moods, and Naia and I would have to drag you away from a fight—"

"I remember, Kenway, you don't have to tell me. I was there. This is literally about me."

"Hey," the man gestured down at Tizzy. "Let's get the princess out of the dirt, shall we?"

"Don't call her that," Aleth told him, bending down to pick her up. "She gets so upset. I do it just to piss her off."

CHAPTER 8

ORIGIN

RUSTAUMN 30, 1144

Dawn was breaking over Suradia. The rain had stopped, and clouds lightly dappled the sky. House Hallenar was cold and dark save for the Queen's room. Allanis stood in front of her mirror, staring right through it with stark determination as Lora fitted a delicate piece of armor over her shoulder.

"You're lucky," the woman said, fastening a silver clasp. "The armorsmith was already making these for his daughter. There's probably a month's work in this filigree alone."

The armor was hardly functional on a battlefield, but as an ornamental showstopper, it worked perfectly. Each silver pauldron was curved like a puff sleeve and decorated with filigree in the shape of wings and feathers. As soon as Allanis had made the decision to go to Saunterton, she knew she wanted to wear decorative armor.

"It's very symbolic of my new militant approach, don't you think?" she asked, fluffing her curls.

"If you want to look militant, stop playing with your hair. I love you, but it makes you look like a little girl."

Allanis sighed, trying not to look deflated. Lora was always brutally honest.

"And I don't think you should be going alone." She fastened a sparkling chain between the two pauldrons that draped across Allanis's chest, catching light from the hearth fire. "I should be going with you at least."

"I need you to stay with Athen. If anything happens to me—gods forbid—he'll be king, and he'll need you. Lazarus is a great help of course, but he doesn't know how things work here. You do this every day with us. Athen would *need* you."

"Then take Lazarus!"

"I'll be fine, Lora, I promise. Lazarus said my magic was good when I was practicing yesterday. Rusty, but I can conjure up what I need to if it comes down to that." She adjusted the crown on her head. "Besides, I know you'll hardly believe it, but I've got a strategy behind going alone. I thought this through."

Lora whistled. "Really? I'm impressed, my queen." Her smile was beaming as she looked Allanis over, and the faintest blush grew on her cheeks.

A slip of paper rested on Allanis's vanity—a response from Queen Anavelia Lovell that had arrived late in the night. Saunterton's ruler was excited to see her friend and would be welcoming her warmly. Once Lora had the armor in place, Allanis did a turn in the mirror and smiled.

"Perfect!"

Lora kissed her on the cheek. "You look ready for anything, Little Bird."

"Oh, I almost forgot!" Allanis held the woman's hand. "Last night, you were trying to tell me something, but I fell asleep. I'm sorry. It was important, wasn't it?"

"It was," Lora said, jutting out her jaw. "It was about *Rori*."

"Is everything okay?"

"She has something she wants to tell you. I told her I would relay that much to you."

"Sounds bad. Can it wait until I get back?"

"You are the queen," Lora said. "Of course it can." She stood behind Allanis and gazed into the mirror at their image as a couple. "Don't let it worry you while you are away. Everything here will be fine. Have fun visiting Anavelia."

***

Tizzy's restful slumber was coming to an end; she could feel it. She wasn't ready to leave. The nest of plush, downy blankets and pillows had been so welcoming. Maybe if she persisted, she could fall back into the quiet black depths of sleep, but something pulled her out even farther. *Thumping*. She started to wake as she focused on it.

She opened her eyes and groaned. The door to the room was open and dim sunlight was pouring in from somewhere down the hallway. And the tail of an excited border collie thumped wildly on the blankets at the foot of the bed.

"Why is there a dog in the bed?"

No one answered, which was expected. She got up, and the dog barked and jumped off with her. She raised an eyebrow but said nothing. By now, she'd learned it was a waste of time to ask questions.

Even though she had dressed in clean clothes before the incident, they now felt grimy with the sweat of her fever. There was no time to clean them again. It would just have to wait till later. Sighing, she went to the empty hearth and took new clothes off the rack. The dog made a tiny bark of acknowledgement and padded out of the room.

"I guess I was just blessed with the company of a random, lonely dog. What else will I consider normal now?" Sarcasm laced her musings.

She finished dressing, laced up her boots, and looked at herself in the mirror. Good, but not great. She combed her fingers through her hair and tied it up into a ponytail. By then, a woman was standing in the doorway. Naia picked at the dirt perpetually stuck under her nails. Tizzy tried not to stare at her third eye.

"Can I help you?" she asked.

Naia smirked. "That's supposed to be my line. I'm Naia. I co-own this place. Kenway said he recognized you. Are you really Tizena Hallenar? I mean I already know, *third eye* and all, but I have to ask."

"He recognized me? We're a little far from Suradia. How can he know my family that well? And it's Tizzy. Please just call me Tizzy."

"Really? Your full name is so pretty," Naia said. "That was a genuine compliment. I don't give them out often; be grateful." She took a few steps into the room to observe the evidence of Aleth and Lilu's fight stained into the floor. "Kenway's a regular in Suradia. A lot of the engineering of this place relies on spell stone enchantments. There's a woman who set up shop in Suradia's Hall of Anatanth, and she makes impressive ones. She creates them for all the different functions we need, and they last a couple of months. Kenway visits when he can to buy from her."

"I must have bumped into him before, in that case." Tizzy couldn't stop staring at her. "Are you—I'm sorry, this is really inappropriate of me, but are you Tainted?"

Naia sighed. "Triclops Minora. Not Tainted. There's a whole world out there, Tizzy, that you don't know about. A lot of us go into hiding because humans and other more perfect folk call us monsters. Minoras and Majoras of my kind, quadramani, the half-breeds and the demis, the shifters, so on and so forth. We prefer a gentler name, though. We're not monsters; we're the Uncommon."

"No wonder you all hide. Society must always assume you're Tainted."

"Shit, even being Tainted isn't *bad*. We see plenty of them here. They're just people mutated by the energy from Akashic tears, and most of the time, that isn't even their fault. Sure, when it's something pretty like an exotic eye color, they're welcomed with open arms. But gods forbid you're unlucky enough to grow a horn or a tail. Then you're out. When it comes down to it, though, they're still human. That doesn't change."

Tizzy felt heavy from the revelation. The Uncommon were a whole race living right under her nose. She began to wonder how many the Hunters in Vandroya were out to kill or how many had been caught in Adeska and Centa's raids.

"Thanks for letting us stay here, and sorry we made such a mess," she said finally. "Do you know where my brother is?"

Naia shrugged. "He's around here somewhere. So are your friends. Try outside."

With a parting wave, she left the room. Tizzy took her things and followed her out, noticing for the first time that light was coming in from gaps in the stone, filled by massive quartz crystals that formed all the way through to the outside. Sheerspine Spire was a combined effort of man, magic, and mountain.

Now that there was so much more of the place to see, Tizzy was a little disheartened to leave. The Spire had at least three main parts—a public bathhouse, lodging with private amenities, and a lovely tavern. As she left, she saw that some folk were gathered at the tables in the tavern with their own meals, mostly bundles of travel rations. Others were being served hot food from the kitchen. A charismatic man with faintly blue skin and pointed ears was serving dark, hearty beer to patrons who preferred a liquid breakfast.

To her surprise, Tizzy was not hungry. Naia opened the front door to let her out, and just as expected, there was a small crowd waiting for her. The dog was running circles around Isa while Gavin laughed and Kenway stared off into the distance. Isa skipped over and hugged her.

"Lady Tizzy! I'm so glad you're awake!"

She couldn't contain a smile. "Was that your magic that saved me?"

"No way!" Isa put her hands on her hips. "My magic helped, but you're the one who pulled through. I couldn't have done anything without your determination."

Tizzy remembered how it had felt when she drove her sword through Lilu in her fever dream. Then the dog came over and sat at her feet.

"Whose dog is this? He keeps following me around."

Isa laughed. "He's yours."

"I have a dog," Tizzy said. "This is not him."

Gavin folded his arms. "Well, this one is yours now."

"Hey boy, do you fetch?" She picked up a branch and threw it, but the dog stayed put, unamused. Tizzy shrugged. "Whatever. Where's Aleth?"

Suddenly Naia was standing by the door, howling with laughter. The dog growled. "He's stuck! *He's stuck*! Kenway—" She stopped to breathe, wiping away a tear. "Oh, this is good."

Kenway approached Tizzy and handed her the black cloak and a belt with Mercy in its scabbard. "You'll have to carry these for a while."

She took them and stared at the dog. The myriad of scars that broke up otherwise smooth fur was the only clue she needed, and she narrowed her eyes.

"He's the dog, isn't he?"

Naia couldn't stop laughing, and Kenway waved his hand to shoo her off.

"I'm sorry for your troubles here, Lady Tizena. That isn't the kind of establishment I'm trying to run. I hope you understand."

"Kenway, sir, I don't know what kind of person you think I am or what you assume the Hallenars are like, but please don't treat me any different than you'd treat—" She looked down at Aleth and rolled her eyes. "Nevermind. But I don't need special treatment. You can speak to me plainly."

"Then if I'm allowed to be honest, your first impression was a little lousy."

She scratched her head. "That is a fair assessment."

"But your brother is a good person, and I'm sure you're redeemable, yourself. I'll tell you the same thing I told him. If you run into a friend of ours out there, Troll Daughter, just send her this way for us. If you can do that, I'll consider us even and lift his lifetime ban. I've never been to the place he's taking you, the Convent, so I don't know what you can expect. But if it isn't good—" He shrugged. "Well, that's the deal."

"Who's Troll Daughter?"

"She works here. He'll tell you everything you need to know when he's able to." Kenway grinned.

There were schemes brewing away in Tizzy's head, and she tapped her chin. "Alright. We'll be in touch, Kenway."

"Stay safe out there, you two." He walked back inside. The door closed and the wisteria branches crawled over to hide it again.

Tizzy was alone now with the dog, Isa, and Gavin. A gentle breeze swayed through the trees and their red-leaved branches. Gavin closed the distance.

"It's a relief to see that you're well, *la dama*. What has you all the way out here, anyway?"

"Gods, where do I start? Remember Allanis's dumb party? The estranged brother showed up after all." Tizzy cracked a smile. "Just to make a scene, of course. But when he left, I just—" She shrugged. "I don't know. I had to follow him. I couldn't take the chance that I'd never see him again. One thing led to another, and here we are."

"Will you be going back?"

She sighed. "No. Believe me, part of me thinks I should, but I have to see this through. I need answers."

"Then I hope you get them. Thank you for taking Isa's words seriously the other day."

Tizzy blushed. "Sorry I was so *rude*. Gavin, could you do me one last favor?"

"Of course, *la dama*."

"I'm going to be asking a lot," she warned, fidgeting with the strap of her bag. "I was hoping you'd be able to go back to Allanis and tell her that we're okay. And then—look, I know that you're busy and that you already have responsibilities, so please decline if you have to, but Allanis has a tough job right now and lacks people she can trust. Her advisors are dead. She needs a new Council. Would you consider offering that service to her? She would benefit with you at her side."

"You really think she would be so quick to trust me with that? To be on a royal Council?"

Tizzy nodded with vigor. "My sister has precious little common sense and is a terrible judge of character. She'll trust anyone. But *I* trust you, and I can give you something to take to her that will let her know it."

She set the bag down. It felt heavier today and as she started digging through it; she found it stuffed with her clothes and Aleth's. She gave the dog a very serious look.

"Oh *no*."

The dog whimpered, and Tizzy kept rummaging through things until she found a leather-wrapped pencil and a scrap of paper from her diary. In seconds, she handed a note back to Gavin.

Allanis, the dress was beautiful. I'm sorry I ruined it. Gavin and Isa saved my life. If you need to, please trust them with yours. -T

"She'll know what I'm talking about. She'll know it's really me," she assured him. "Let her know that I'll write again."

"We will deliver the message, Lady Tizzy. Be safe."

Gavin and Isa departed for Suradia. Isa was confident she could use the guidance of the trees to navigate a safe way back. Meanwhile, Tizzy stared down at the dog and gestured ahead.

"Well, it looks like I'm following you. This is ridiculous."

The dog barked and leapt forward to lead the way with a wagging tail.

"Aleth, *why* are you a dog?" She grumbled out a long, dramatic noise. "You know what? You probably aren't. You, dog, are probably just a literal dog, and my brother is going to catch up to me eventually and ask me what the hell I'm doing."

The dog whined.

"Oh, give me a break! You're a cute dog, but I don't know where we're going, so pardon me if I'm a little skeptical, just blindly following you." Then she laughed. "Listen to me! 'A little skeptical,' I say. My brother is a dog. I'm *highly* skeptical."

The terrain they traversed was less perilous than before. Fewer roots and branches blocked the way, and the trees were more spread out. There were dips in the ground as they lost altitude a little at a time, but overall Tizzy found the journey much smoother.

"I want to be angry," she admitted. "I'm used to it, so maybe it's just a desire out of habit. Or maybe the uncertainty of all this is annoying me. Whatever the case, you're only off the hook because I feel amazing!" She took a deep breath of the post-rain forest air and sighed. "For the first time, I woke up without a single trace of pain. The headaches are gone. They're finally gone!"

They walked for a while longer, the sounds of a river growing close. Then the dog raced away from her and disappeared behind a tree.

"What's going on?" When she tried to get close, the dog barked and growled. She stepped away. "What is your problem?"

"Throw me the bag!"

His voice was frantic. Tizzy smirked. "Or what?"

"Tizzy! I'm serious!"

"Yeah? You sure you're serious? Sounds like you could be joking."

"Give me the damn bag!"

"This one here with your clothes in it?" She threw it down by the tree. "Alright, calm down. There it is."

He did not share her same light spirit. In fact, the animosity in his stance when he finally dressed and came out startled her. She backed away as he stormed over and jabbed his finger at her.

"What the hell were you thinking?"

She swallowed hard. He had wasted no time bringing Lilu up. "I-I wasn't, okay?" she yelled back. "I wasn't! I admit it! I know it was stupid, but I couldn't help it!"

All he could do was make a noise of outrage and turn away. "I swear to gods, Tizzy, it's like you're *trying* to get yourself killed! Was once not fucking enough for you?"

"Hey!"

She pouted, picked up the bag, and chased after him as he paced deeper into the woods.

"Aleth! Will you please stop and look at me?"

He was quiet at first, but then she heard him scoff.

"Or what?"

She smiled in relief as he slowed to a halt. But he couldn't bring himself to turn around.

"I can't go through losing you again. I *can't*. But I know I'm bringing you into all these dangerous situations, and it kills me, knowing what could happen. So, when I tell you to do something like *hide*, what I really mean is 'hide because if you don't, you're going to die.' I'm not asking you to; I'm not negotiating terms with you. I am telling you to do it because you will die. You don't listen to anybody. That's your thing, I get it. But please, Tizzy, listen to *me*."

"Okay."

With the faintest sniffle, he turned around. She was too ashamed to look him in the eyes, but he hugged her anyway.

She swallowed the lump in her throat. "I know I require a lot of patience—"

"Yes."

She grunted. "But I'm learning. I'm learning about what I am and what it means and what I have to do about it. You'll need to have even more patience than usual if you're going to keep being cryptic and secretive about things."

"Don't worry. You'll learn, and so will I." He squeezed her shoulder and continued the hike. "Let's go. We're making a bit of a detour. I have to go somewhere." He rubbed his face. "And think. I have to get all of this out of my head."

She remembered the important question. "How can you turn into a dog?"

He welcomed the subject change and kicked a pinecone. "Oh, that? When you feed on blood, you become more nightwalker and less human. And when that happens, sometimes you can turn into a dog. I don't know. Or maybe a cat or a possum or a worm. Whatever. I turned into a dog."

"So if I decide to *be more nightwalker*, I'll be able to turn into a dog? Or something?"

Aleth shrugged. "Maybe. Not everyone can shift. As far as I know, I'm the only shifter in the Convent."

Tizzy kept a frown. When he spoke, she could still hear the depression lingering in his words. Guilt pulled her down with him as they wandered through the trees, and after a while, the forest floor started to show signs of a trail. Once, long ago, it had probably been well worn and easy to follow, but now it was almost completely grown over. She looked up at the treetops. They seemed distantly familiar.

"Aleth, I think we circled back somehow. It looks like we're getting closer to Suradia."

He said nothing and kept walking. Eventually, the trail opened up into a clearing, and Tizzy finally knew where they were. Aleth went to sit on a stump underneath an autumn-touched oak tree. In front of him was not an open, grassy field as Talora had shown her but a stone sarcophagus. Every fiber of her being tried to convince her to stay back, but she was driven by an emptiness in her mind that she had to fill. She knew this was the way. Slowly, she approached.

Aleth didn't look at her and wouldn't speak. He stared blankly ahead, slouched over with his elbows on his knees. The sarcophagus was small, made for a child. There was a small headrest at one end for the body during the Rite of Crossing. Once, a touching poem had been engraved around the edges of the lid, but now it was worn away. The only thing that remained clearly was a name. *Tizena Hallenar.*

"*This* is where you come to think?"

"Just give me ten minutes. Then we'll leave."

Think wasn't even the word for it, she realized. He came here when he needed to feel numb. He was a thousand miles away as she circled the tomb, running her hands along the rough stone. Something about it pulled her in until she decided to sit, to lay atop it. She stared up into the blue sky above them, wondering how her place of interment could still be standing all these years later. She had always thought Lazarus would have it destroyed.

With a deep breath, she rested her eyes and her consciousness was ripped away. There was a darkness deeper than the bleakest night swallowing her and everything around her. Then, one by one, stars glistened above, and she was watching a scene from somewhere else behind the trees. It was pitch black save for the starscape. There she was, twelve years old and lifeless on the tomb lid, dressed in her white funerary gown. Sunburst blossoms littered the ground, still bright with color. No one was around.

Not until a creature entered the clearing. Why was she seeing this? The creature resembled a lynx, but its pelt was black and glossy, and it stared at her body with bright red eyes. Tizzy was frightened it would eat her in this vision, but it merely perused the body with feline curiosity. Satisfied, it leapt on top of the tomb with her and sniffed her face, then sat with its paws at her collarbones. Tizzy couldn't believe the creature hadn't crushed her child-sized body. Thick black fog formed around the creature as though it had been conjured up out of nowhere. A growling voice hummed in her mind.

"Daughter between Realms, know that I am the Father, I am the Ancestral, I am the First. You hover here, following the silver thread to Botathora's underworld to find your fate, but that is no longer to be. Be of my Blood, be my child. See that we thrive. I will return your soul, and with my touch, you will be my Second."

The fog formed tendrils that wove through the air until they pierced the veil to another Realm. Tizzy wasn't well versed in them, but when they reached into the hazy tear and pulled out a ghostly figure, she knew it was the Ethereal Realm. She couldn't make out any details of the figure—it just looked humanoid and small. The tendrils wrapped around it and forced it into the body on the tomb with loud, thunderous crackling. The fog dissipated, and the creature leapt down, paws landing softly in the dirt.

There was movement among the trees and bushes, and the feline's ears perked up.

With a sniffle, Aleth, just a boy in her vision, came into the clearing, wiping away tears. He stopped in his tracks when he saw the creature. For a long moment, they locked eyes, and then it ran off, vanishing into the forest. Aleth sighed, shaking with exhaustion, and wiped his face.

"I'm sorry," he said, the wet tears slipping down his cheeks as fast as he could dry them. "I know I'm not supposed to be out here right now, but I had to come back. I'm sorry."

Her heart broke as she watched him stand next to the tomb, looking up into the sky. He was lost without her.

"I couldn't sleep. I was worried about you. There were so many things we were supposed to do. Could you just—could you just please wake up? Please come back." He sobbed. "The physician says you aren't dead, but Lazarus says he's just too afraid to give us bad news because Alli's the queen." He got on his knees and rested his head on the tomb, on top of folded arms. "I miss you so much. I don't want to do all of this without you."

The girl's bright red eyes opened.

"Tizzy!"

She sat up in a fluid motion, effortless, like she'd used an unearthly force and not her muscles. Her eyes were unblinking as Aleth threw his arms around her.

"I knew it! I knew you were alive!"

Tizzy had no memory of this. The girl tilted her head and opened her mouth, revealing two sharp fangs. Aleth's emotions were too tangled to produce fear. All he could do was stare up in awe and cry out as she bit into his neck. Blood spilled over them both as she drank.

"Tizzy. You're alive."

He put his trembling hand on her shoulder, and she jumped back, his touch forcing her lucid again.

"Aleth!"

She screamed, her hands shaking violently as she saw all the blood. Her fangs had slipped back into her gums, and her eyes had gone rust-brown.

"Aleth, please wake up!"

He fell to the ground, blood flowing from the bite wound. She pressed down on it with one hand and fumbled around in the dirt with the other, feeling for something jagged.

"I'm sorry! I'm so sorry!" she cried. "I-I didn't mean it! I'm sorry! Oh gods, what do I do?" She rolled him onto his back, weeping uncontrollably. With the sharp side of a stone, she scratched at her wrist until she tore open the skin. "Here, take it back! Take it back, please! I'm sorry!" She let the blood fall into his wound and then brought it over his mouth. "Please, please work! Something work!"

Tizzy wished she could have told her younger self that it wouldn't work, that blood loss simply didn't work that way. But she couldn't move or speak. Two more people emerged into the clearing—Lazarus and Adeska, teens in this vision. Adeska gasped.

"Aleth—*Tizzy*! Oh my gods! What happened? How?"

Lazarus ran to Aleth, his face a mix of stern terror. He stared at Tizzy. "What happened to him?"

Tizzy was hysterical as Adeska tried to embrace her. "I don't know! I-I can't remember. I woke up, there was blood everywhere! Lazarus, is he going to be okay?"

He looked him over while Adeska tried to console her.

"I can't believe he snuck out!" Adeska said.

"Yes you can." He pressed his wrist to Aleth's forehead. "He's warm. We need to get him back."

"Are you hurt at all?" Adeska asked Tizzy, wiping away some of her tears.

"I have this cut, right here—" She showed Adeska where she'd torn into her wrist with the rock, but it was just a shallow scratch. She pulled it away slowly and stared at it. "I thought it was deeper."

"Adeska, we need to go *now*." Lazarus carried Aleth away and she followed. The last thing Tizzy saw was herself passing out behind her sister and Adeska shrieking in alarm.

She opened her eyes, and the world came back. Blue sky hung overhead. When she sat up, she was dizzy with recovered knowledge. Nausea roared through her, and she covered her mouth with shaking hands, trying to catch her breath.

"I—no." She swallowed hard. Her chest hurt. "No, that's not—that can't be what happened."

Aleth didn't look up at her. "You remembered, didn't you?"

She grabbed his shoulders and shook him, fighting back a sob. Her fingers found the collar of his tunic, and she pulled it down to see the scar. "Why do you keep telling me that nothing is my fault? Aleth, *everything* is my fault!"

He closed his eyes. "No, it's not." He finally looked at her and she brushed the hair out of his eyes.

"What happened?" she asked. "And why do you keep protecting me from this?"

"Because I don't blame you!" He blinked back tears. "You did not decide to become this! The Father chose you—you had no say in it because you were dead!"

"I was dead because I decided to jump out of a tree! That was me! I was the idiot who did that!"

He hid his face in his hands. "You did. You did do that."

"I turned you into this. I gave you this life." A chill ran through her. He sat up straight and took her hands.

"Stop saying that. I am not like this—*we* are not like this—because you chose it. Alright?" His eyes were welling up. He looked down. "I'm going to tell you what happened. Everything. And then this is done. I'm never going to shed another tear over this ever again, and neither will you. It is what it is. We can't go back."

She couldn't let go of his hands. "Tell me."

He took a deep breath but still felt like he was drowning. He wasn't ready to say any of this, but he never would be.

"All nightwalkers can be traced back to either the Mother or the Father. However it happened, whether they were Ancients or something else, they were the first of our kind to ever be. The night of the Rite of Crossing, you were turned by the Father of Nightwalkers. He chose to turn you himself. He can only turn someone when they're between realms, so the Rite of Crossing was the perfect scenario. Then I showed up. You woke with your initial impulse that took over, and—"

She had gone twelve years with the memory blocked out, but when she looked into his face, she could see he relived it almost every day.

"I know," she stopped him. "I know what I did."

"You had no idea what you were doing. You couldn't have. You were just trying to help. But that's how we turn others. You feed them back their own blood after it's been laced with the nightwalker's. You fed from me. When you tried to give it back, you—" He looked up, away from her, the next words not willing to leave his mouth. It was an answer to a question he could have kept dodging forever. Saying it finally made it real. "You turned me."

She looked up at him and he continued. "Things got complicated after that. I wanted to ask about it, but when I woke up from my fever, everyone acted like nothing happened, so I started to wonder if it was all just a dream. The impulses we started having were never so bad that we recognized them or gave in, but everyone could sense that we weren't *right* anymore. They didn't *know*. They didn't realize there was anything to know, but it's why they felt the way they did. It's just how humans are. They were rejecting us.

"I didn't find out what I was, what we were, until I left. I was in the Bogwood, lost, and I found this woman surrounded by greenkind. I can't really describe what it was, what I felt, but it took over, and I jumped in with this hungry, reckless abandon. It was the first impulse I gave in to. It took over, and that's when I knew what it was. *Bloodlust*. And it was the reason we escaped with our lives.

"The woman was a faerie, the same one you probably saw in your dream. Ilisha. For helping save her life, she granted me a wish. Tizzy, after seeing what I became in that fight, I knew that if you ever gave into an impulse of your own, you'd *slaughter* House Hallenar or die trying. So I wished for you to never know what you were. For you to keep having a normal life. And all those years, it seemed to work.

"But Ilisha came back to me before the night of Allanis's party. She was using too much of her power to keep my wish fulfilled, and she needed it back. She came to collect, and I had to undo my wish."

"That's why you came to get me."

"I couldn't let you go through this alone and suffer the same things I did. I got lucky and eventually found the Convent. They knew about you. Sort of. They knew that for the first time in about fifty years, the Father had turned someone new. He doesn't have any more living protégés left. It's just you. And that means you will be the strongest, purest-blooded nightwalker, second only to the Father himself. But recently, the Convent found out that person was *you*."

"Why do they care?"

"Because they need you. The Hunters are cutting us down more and more, and they need you to help fight them off. They think you'll be the one to do it. And if I don't bring you back, they'll kill us both."

"They threatened to *kill you?*"

"Because I told them I wouldn't do it!" he shouted. "I'm not going to let them use you! If you want to help them, that's your choice. We'll go, you'll meet them, you make your decision. And if you want out, I'll get you out."

"They don't seem like nice people."

"Most of them aren't. But they need you, and they'll treat you like a queen up until they decide you're not worth it." He recognized the scheming look on her face, the smug calculations behind her eyes, and stood up. "You don't have to go down this path. You can't exactly go back to the way things were before, but you don't have to live like bloodkin if you don't want to. I'm with you, no matter your choice. And I know you. I know you're only happy when you get your way."

She stood up beside him. "Don't say it like that; that makes me sound like a child. It's not that I have to have my way, it's, um—" She tilted her head to the side. "I just want control. Over my own life. And *occasionally* others."

"Whatever you want to call it, if you want it, I'm going to help you get it."

"Why? After everything I've done to you, why are you like this?"

He rubbed the back of his neck and kicked at the dirt. "Because." He could feel her staring, waiting for an answer. "You're the only one who doesn't feel like a stranger."

The heaviness and the pain fell from her, and she was weightless.

"What I said back there, back in Allanis's room at the party—" He bit his lip. "It was true. The city of Vandroya is a real threat. Real for us, and real for her and the rest of them, when the Hunters find out you're the Protégé."

"Do you think they'll find out?"

"They always do. It's just a matter of time."

"Do they know about you?"

He felt cold. "I don't matter."

"That's stupid. If I'm so important because I'm second only to this Father, that makes you third! You're *my* protégé. That should count for something!"

Then he started laughing. He couldn't stop. She put her hands on her hips.

"What's so funny? You said none of those other people in the Convent can even turn into a dog! That seems like basic stuff, not that I know what I'm talking about."

When he finally caught a breath and stilled himself, he looked back at the tomb and sighed.

"Come on." He put his arm over her shoulder. "Let's get out of here. I'm never coming back to this place again."

CHAPTER 9

MALEVOLENCE

S tormy followed Athen, showing the young man more attention and excitement than he ever had before, circling around while he carried firewood up and down the halls of House Hallenar. At first, Athen was amused and even grateful for the attention, but as the morning grew on, it was tiresome.

"I thought Tizzy was the only one you really liked," he said, standing by the flames he'd made in the grand hall fireplace. "But you know what? I'm starting to think you just like anyone who makes you a fire."

The thought of his sister saddened him. He hadn't seen her since the night of the party when she had returned from her encounter with Aleth. After the way she'd blown up at everyone and stomped off, he knew he was probably not on good terms with her. None of them would be. He wished he could convince her to come out of her room or at least say something so he knew she didn't hate him.

"What do you think, Stormy? Should we go see what Tizzy's up to?"

The dog wagged his tail, but his enthusiasm died fast. Athen scratched him between the ears.

"C'mon boy, what's the matter? She's probably not even here right now. But shouldn't we find out for sure? She's never going to get over this if we don't give her a little push."

She would be perfectly content locking herself in a room, never to speak another word to them for the rest of eternity. Athen knew that if there was going to be any resolution, someone would have to make it happen. He started for her room upstairs, and Stormy followed with a whimper. Outside of her bedroom door was the rug the mutt dragged out every morning.

"How long has this been here? Tizzy, are you in there?"

No response. Had anyone checked her room? Of course they hadn't. She would be furious if anyone walked in without her invitation, and that's the last thing anyone wanted. Had she locked her door? Athen took a deep breath.

"Tizzy, I'm coming in!"

She didn't tell him not to. Carefully, he opened the door and stepped in, flinching in case she was standing with a blunt object at the ready. She wasn't. He started to inspect.

"Looks like she ain't here, huh?"

Athen leapt around. "Rhett! I didn't know you were—"

"I know you didn't."

Hands in his pockets, Rhett entered. Athen noted his soft steps and cautious stride. His rust-brown eyes followed his brother around the room, and then something in his chest grew tight. Tizzy's room was her haven, her safe space. Rhett was the person least qualified to cross the threshold.

"It looks like she's gone," Athen said. "Like she *left*. Her sword is gone, and her dress is still on the ground."

Rhett stood still, chewing his lip, staring into the mirror at the desk while Athen scrambled around for more clues, huffing.

"What's the matter with you? Are you just going to stand there?"

A short, bitter laugh left Rhett's nose. "That damn mirror. I can't believe it went to *her*. It was Mother's, you know."

Athen rolled his eyes. "I know that."

"I just figured since you never knew her—"

"Yes, Rhett, I'm aware of that too. Thank you." He looked through Tizzy's wardrobe, noted the missing clothes, then shut the doors. "What's so special about the mirror, anyway? Why do you care?"

Rhett couldn't tear his eyes away from it. "None of you really knew Mother." He had their father's blue eyes and hated it.

"Why would you say that?" Athen finally came to his side. "Adeska and Lazarus grieved over her for years! I still don't think they're over it!"

"They're not the only ones."

Rhett remembered the first time he'd seen her use the mirror to speak to daemons. The words still burned in his ears, still made his blood rush. The second time he saw her use it, he'd thought to ask why. That was when she had sat him down on her lap, wrapped her arms around him, and used her sweet, loving voice to say words that were ice cold.

"Not every soul on this world deserves compassion. Don't give it away without purpose."

A month prior, a man had stolen their family's crop in the middle of the night. The very next day after Mother Hallenar's chilling sentiment, the man and his wife and children were all found dead. Every single bone in their bodies broken. *Shattered.*

Mother was grinning for weeks. During her favorite chore of skinning rabbits for dinner, she had even hummed and danced a little.

Suddenly, Athen brushed past him and went to the desk. "Wait, is this a note?" He let out an exasperated grunt. "I can't believe it! She did; she left. Tizzy left!"

The haunting memories were swept away like nothing but dirt on the floor, and Rhett just chuckled. "Look at that. Another one bites the dust." He rolled his shoulders and walked away, whistling their mother's favorite tune.

"Hey!" Athen's growl fell on deaf ears. Rhett paid him no mind, lost to House Hallenar to cause whatever trouble was on his agenda for the day. "What do we do now, Stormy? Allanis already left for

Saunterton. Should we send a carrier?" The dog barked. "You're right. We should tell the others first."

He sought out Lazarus or Adeska and hoped Tizzy's leave wouldn't be a permanent one.

***

The sun graced the land for only a short time, its morning light filtering through the branches, touching the earth with long, gauzy white rays. But light clouds returned before it was even noon. Tizzy and Aleth hadn't conversed much during their journey, both lost to their own thoughts. The woods were quiet except for their footsteps crunching through the forest floor.

Tizzy was relieved that, after all this time, she was letting herself stand on amicable ground with him. All it took was realizing how awful she was, she thought. Everything was out in the open, and they shared the same goal.

Then Aleth cleared his throat. "Can I ask you a question?"

"Fire away."

"This is weird, but—" She watched him muss up his hair in thought. "When did Adeska have a kid?"

Tizzy laughed. "Mariette? She just turned two in Madefloure. Adeska waited till *Valanned* to have a dumb little party for her out by the Undina Loch. Two whole months!" She sighed. "Gods, summer this year was hot. I thought I was going to melt that day. You're lucky you don't have to deal with her, you know. Mari's creepy. And the way she talks? She doesn't talk like a child."

"Adeska used to go on about wanting a big family of her own, at least back when we were kids. It seems like she got her fill with just one."

"Either that or she got her fill by having to raise all of us. Or maybe she can't bear the thought of raising another one with that asshole husband of hers. Would it kill him to stop calling me Tizena?"

She heard Aleth scoff from several paces in front of her. "*Centa.*"

"How do you know that?"

"The two of them and their raiding party, as they call it? I bet they never told any of you what they did. What they *really* did. They killed a lot of people I knew. They'd come to clear out encampments I hid out at, places where I thought I was safe. Me and dozens of others. Some of the encampments housed daemons, sure. But some of them didn't."

"Uncommon?" Tizzy recalled her conversation with Naia.

"Yeah. Thank gods they never found the Spire."

"So you were at some of the raids? And Adeska didn't notice you?"

"Tizzy, please." He looked back at her with a grin. "Of course she didn't notice me. If I don't want to be noticed, I won't be. I'm good at slipping out undetected; it's half the reason I've survived this long."

Imagining Adeska and Aleth in the same place on opposing sides during the raids chilled her to the bone. But it wasn't just that. She also noticed the unnatural silence around them and stopped.

"Something isn't right," she said.

"I know. We should keep moving."

He slowed his pace so she wouldn't fall behind and kept looking back. She was right. Something was off. He stopped her and strained his ears. Voices. He put a finger to his lips, and she nodded. Silent as a wraith, he moved between the trees until he counted six people gathered in an area with a fallen evergreen. One of the six, a young man with a flintlock pistol, wore a decorated, oversized tunic with Vandroya's colors—navy, light blue, and silver.

The other five appeared to be a ragtag bunch of hired mercenaries: A woman with a sleek black braid and two hand axes on her belt. A wood elf in black wrappings with a myriad of throwing knives along their body. A bald man with a leather vest and gloves studded along the knuckles. An old woman in a cowl with a whip and a short sword. A pale man with a tattoo and two snake-hilted daggers.

They were gathered around a hulking figure that was slumped over on the ground. Its skin was green and badly bruised. Aleth could see two pierced pointed ears jutting out from a ponytail of scruffy brown hair. He returned to Tizzy.

"Six of them. Three or four with ranged weapons. They have Troll Daughter!" he whispered.

"What do we do?"

She was astonished to see a smile on his face. "Watch and learn!" He unsheathed Mercy and traipsed into harm's way with an unshakeable confidence.

"No wonder you have so many scars. You're a damn idiot." She followed just enough paces behind him to remain hidden and watched as he made his entrance.

"Hey everyone!"

She groaned. He walked in with wide arms and a friendly smile.

"Guys, thank you so much. You've found my friend! News sure travels fast around here."

Troll Daughter looked up at him, grunting in desperation, and Tizzy realized she did not simply have a nickname—she was a literal troll. Her face was long and square with beady black eyes, a flat nose, and a wide mouth full of sharp teeth.

"Stay back and drop your sword!" The man who seemed to be leading the excursion pointed the flintlock pistol at him.

Aleth rolled his eyes. "Are you sure you want me to do that?"

The elf kicked Troll Daughter, and she made more terrified grunts. "Who is this guy? Do you know him, General?"

The man with the pistol narrowed his eyes. "No. Drop your sword, or I'll shoot!"

The old woman didn't wait and lashed her whip around Aleth's arm. He grabbed at it with his ensnared hand and pulled hard until she fell into the dirt. Then there was a loud crack. The general had fired his pistol, and the bullet lodged itself into Aleth's shoulder.

He clenched his jaw through the pain. "Shit! What is the matter with you?" He jammed his fingers into the wound, trying to dig the bullet out. The man with the studded gloves and the man with the snake daggers came running at him.

They slashed and swung at him, but he didn't fight back. He was focused only on getting the bullet out and side-stepped out of the way of every oncoming attack with ease. The general was preparing his pistol for another shot, fumbling with gunpowder. Laboriously, the old woman got to her feet with help from the elf. The woman with the axes chose to stay out of the fight, more interested in picking something out of her teeth.

"We need to get rid of him," the old woman hissed. The elf nodded and threw a whistling knife through the air.

Tizzy couldn't believe Aleth's reflexes. He should have been struck dead in the chest, but he pushed the man with the daggers into the path with little effort. The elf gawked, and Aleth finally freed the bullet, flicking it at them with blood running down his fingers.

"Good aim. I'll give you that. But you're just too slow."

The man looked down at the knife in his chest and at the blood gushing down into his hands. He sputtered in shock. Aleth dropped his sword and took the snake daggers from him before he fell to the ground.

"These have some nice weight to them. I bet they're worth a lot."

The fighter rushed at him, joined by the elf. Aleth stuck both knives into the fighter's gut, caught an incoming kick from the elf and threw them aside, and then reached for Mercy. Suddenly he heard a click, and the pistol was two feet away, pointed at his face.

"General, no!" the old woman cried out. He looked over to where she was pointing.

"Ah, ah, ah!"

Tizzy grinned, holding firmly onto the other woman's braid with her right hand and steadying Wish's blade against her throat with her left.

"The thing about *long hair*—" She tightened her grip, and the woman whimpered. "Is that it makes for such a nice thing to be caught by. Not very practical for a mercenary, now is it?" Nobody said a word. "Great! Now whose lady is this, hm? She's somebody's big deal."

The old woman dropped her whip. "Please let my daughter go!"

"Just as soon as this guy stops pointing his pistol at my brother's head."

"Not a chance!" the general spat. "I don't know who you think you are, but you're interfering in official Vandroya operations. When I find out where you're from, I can declare this an act of war and *reign hell*—"

"No, you can't," Tizzy said. "You're not a general. The crest is on the wrong shoulder, and that tunic doesn't even fit you. You stole it."

The old woman looked up at him with her jaw agape. "General, is this true?"

"Of course it isn't—"

Aleth grabbed Mercy and sliced into the man's underarm, and the gun fell to the ground. In one fluid motion, he picked up one of the elf's fallen daggers and slid it into the gut of the woman Tizzy was restraining.

"We have to move, now! Doddie, you too!" He sheathed Mercy and helped the greenkind to her feet. The elf and the old woman rushed to their fallen while Tizzy followed Troll Daughter and Aleth away.

"Wait, what's wrong? I hate to suggest this, I can't believe we— no, *you*—you just killed those people. I didn't, did I? That was all you—forget it—shouldn't we get rid of the rest of them so they don't tell anyone about us?"

"They're all going to die anyway, and so will we if we don't leave!"

She tried to follow while scanning the forest for the threat, but she couldn't see anything but the trees. It was quiet. No animals, no breeze, not even the sounds of the others they had left. It was never quiet. Then she found herself completely alone. It was only natural that she would fall behind and get lost.

"Aleth?"

Even her own voice was soundless. Her eyes went wide, and she tried again. Nothing. Her heart pounded as panic raced through her. What was happening? She darted from tree to tree, hoping to catch a glimpse of Aleth or Troll Daughter, but they were gone. She stumbled back to the others without knowing the way. Four of them were slain—only the old woman and the elf remained after what Aleth had done. The elf tried to get the woman to leave, but she was immobilized by grief over her daughter and the fear of the silence.

Tizzy watched the scene in horror. The area grew dark like night, and a thick black fog swooped in, filling out the form of a hulking beast. The elf tried to fight it, throwing knives that passed through the fog like it was nothing. It reached out with a claw-like appendage and tore right through the elf. They exploded into thousands of black wisps, leaving behind a dripping black skeleton. The old woman tried to scream, but she suffered the same fate.

Tizzy had to run. She had to run and never stop. She turned away and sprinted as fast as she could. The branches scratched and nicked the skin on her face and hands as she fled. She took only a second to look behind her—the night was closing in, and tendrils of fog were creeping up by her feet. She pushed her legs to carry her faster.

She shrieked in the soundlessness as she was whisked behind a tree. Aleth grabbed her out of the creature's path and held her tight, his hand clamped over her mouth. When she looked up at him, sweat was at his brow and blood dripped down a gash near his left temple.

He was fixated on the path next to them, waiting and watching for the creature to pass them by.

And they waited. She didn't know how long it was. They didn't move, didn't make a sound; she wasn't even sure they breathed. Then it happened. The fog came by, carrying the beast's form with it. Aleth kept them still. The night surrounding the creature loomed overhead.

Tizzy heard a voice from far in the distance. A woman's voice, light and airy. She squirmed in Aleth's grasp—they had to warn her. But he didn't let go.

There was an otherworldly screech. It shook the trees and blasted away the shroud of night, and a sharp ringing hung in the air. Tizzy caught glimpses of it from between the trees, of the creature being torn asunder, daylight ripping it apart bit by bit until it was just a breath of dark air disappearing into the forest, giving up the last of its form.

Aleth released her at last and she hobbled away. The creature was gone. The forest returned to normal, the sounds of life gradually restoring themselves to the land. She looked back at him with horror in her face.

"*What was that?*"

"Malevolence," he replied, catching his breath. "It comes from the Abyss Realm. The veil around here is thin, and they come through sometimes. When it gets quiet like that? That's what that means. Nothing else can steal sound like that. But hey, nobody ever called the Bogwood safe, right?"

"Aleth!"

The voice was loud and present, attached to a woman who came flying by. Tizzy did a double-take. She was ghostly, floating a foot off the ground and passing through the trees as though they weren't even there. She was pale with narrow red eyes. Tizzy thought she could have been from the Shimara Tail Mainland, but her long, straight hair was white instead of black. Her eyebrows and eyelashes were so white, they looked nonexistent.

"Eidi, that was good timing!" Aleth congratulated her. She gazed at him with adoration, and Tizzy could see it in her posture, in the way that her shoulders went up and her hands flexed a little, that she was itching to give him a hug. But instead, she hugged her arms close to her and tucked her hands under her chin.

She started to laugh. "You corporeal beings sure weren't going to do it any harm. Who is this? Is this her?"

"Tizzy!" Aleth came to her and put his hand around her shoulder. "This is Eidi. She lives at the Convent. She's a banshee."

"That explains the scream, I guess."

"Eidi, this is my sister, Tizzy. Is it just you out here?"

"Oh goodness, no. The others are catching up. They have to actually go around the trees."

Tizzy started looking around. "Where's Troll Daughter?"

"She's okay," Aleth said, stretching his arms and checking the bullet wound. It wasn't healing as fast as he'd hoped. "I sent her in the opposite direction while I went to get you out of that thing's way. She'll be on her way back to Sheerspine. There's something about greenkind that the Malevolence doesn't like. They'll completely avoid each other."

"Just how many of these things have you come across?" Tizzy asked.

"This was my fourth." He grinned.

"We're here!"

A familiar voice announced itself. Two others entered the area, waving.

Tizzy's jaw dropped. "Talora?"

"Tizzy!"

Aleth narrowed his eyes. "What?"

Talora was sweating bullets underneath her dark green veil. She couldn't come up with something to say fast enough. Tizzy's quick mouth cut her off.

"Oh, right! I guess she wouldn't have told you that she hijacked my head a couple of times already since I've left home. She's very invasive."

"Tal!" Aleth jabbed his finger at her. "I thought we agreed—"

Talora locked her eyes on Tizzy, clenched her fists, and huffed. "That's not fair! You left out the part where I helped save your life! Did you forget? Lilu's venom would have killed you had I not stepped in!"

"It *might* have!" Tizzy crossed her arms. "We don't know that for sure."

Aleth threw his hands up. "No point in introducing you two, then. Tizzy, this other one over here is Dacen. Dacen, this is my sister."

Dacen gave her a small, shy smile. She approved of him already. She couldn't tell much by looking at him, and he certainly didn't say anything, but he appeared to be around Aleth's age. He was short and showed off three bony spines on each of his forearms. She spied a short bow and quiver on his back.

"Not that I'm upset about it, but why are you three out here?" Aleth asked them.

"Lilu came back to the Convent," Eidi explained. "She had a lot to say about you, and boy was it ugly. A lot to say about your sister, too, but she said that in private to Louvita. Since Louvita's chambers are still warded, I wasn't able to eavesdrop."

"It seemed like a good idea to come find you after that," Talora said.

"How far away are we?" Tizzy turned to him. "You said we'd be halfway there once we reached the Sheerspine River. I haven't seen any rivers."

"We've been parallel with it for the last few miles. It's maybe a quarter mile from us now," he said. "We're close to a bridge, so we can cross soon and reach the Convent at a little past noon tomorrow."

"*Or*—" Talora cleared her throat. "We could avoid the public bridge and cross at the Helamine Stone! Eidi is here, after all."

Tizzy watched Aleth's face twist with a grimace. He looked away and scratched the back of his head.

"I'd like to stay away from the Helamine Stone this time."

Tizzy hated knowing so little. "What's that?"

Eidi's hand shot up in the air like she had been picked to answer a question. "It's a marker for the Helamine ley lines. It's a path that connects all the different Realms. If you can find it, it's a quick and safe way to traverse, and you can even use it to take shortcuts. Helamine is an old and obscure goddess of crossroads and travel. She set these up when Ancients still walked the land."

"Don't lie to her!" Aleth snapped. "It's not safe!"

Talora rolled her eyes. "He went with us *once*," she told Tizzy. "And there was a little bit of trouble and he was stuck in the Ethereal Realm for about an hour before Eidi could get him out. It was no big deal."

Dacen didn't have anything to say, but he was stifling giggles.

"You two are terrible navigators!" Aleth shouted. Tizzy felt bad for him. He was upset, and his so-called friends weren't taking it seriously. It made her wonder if they ever did.

"We were perhaps a little negligent." Talora sighed. "But it won't happen again. It'll be a first for Dacen and Tizzy! Come on, Aleth, it'll be fine!"

He gritted his teeth and finally threw up one of his hands. "Fine. But if you get me stuck again, I'm going to be pissed."

"Wonderful!" Eidi spun around, her tattered gown passing through the trunk of a tree. "The Helamine Stone is two miles east along the river, past the bridge. We'll get there and camp out until I can open the ley line. The veil will be thin enough to get through about an hour before dawn."

Tizzy was uncomfortable with how friendly the three of them were. She had liked it better when she and Aleth traveled alone. Even Lilu made her less nervous than meeting Talora, Eidi, and Dacen— there was never any doubt about what was going through Lilu's mind.

But she relented. They put Aleth at ease, and if he thought they were trustworthy, then perhaps traveling in numbers was for the best. She took a cue from Dacen and stayed quiet, walking behind Aleth as he conversed casually with Talora and Eidi. There was a lot she had to learn about these people if she was going to fall asleep in the middle of the woods with them.

She still couldn't put trust in Talora, even though they'd already met. The woman was a nightwalker who could invade the unconscious mind; how could she? It was true that Talora had maybe saved Tizzy's life, but Aleth had already told her that ulterior motives were at play in the Convent.

Eidi was stuck in a non-corporeal state, so Tizzy wasn't sure what harm she could cause them even if she wanted to. Then there was Dacen. On the outside, he seemed a little monstrous, sporting literal spikes on his arms, but he wasn't argumentative, didn't have wit or pride to show off with stupid remarks, and wore a calm smile almost permanently.

"Do you talk?" she asked him. He nodded and shrugged at the same time. "Do you just not like to?" This time, he nodded with confidence. "No harm in that, I guess."

"He's a tough shell to crack," Eidi said. "But he's brilliant. We've watched him a few times on the roof with his tools, calculating stuff about the stars."

"*Planets.*" He twisted his face up and cleared his throat as though he had to force himself to speak. His voice was faint and hoarse.

"How can you even tell the difference?" Eidi asked. "They're all just dots."

"Planets are closer," Tizzy said, shrugging. "It's easier to see them move in the sky over time. Stars don't move. The only reason constellations shift in the sky is because Rosamar moves. Haven't you guys studied anything the dragonkind have discovered?"

Aleth smirked. "Told you she was smart."

"Then we'll just consider the stunt with Lilu a lapse in judgment," Talora said.

"Alright, I'm getting sick of this." Tizzy stopped moving and folded her arms. "Yeah, I challenged her when I shouldn't have, and I got bit, and I almost died. But she was going to do it anyway! She was going to find me in that room. You weren't there; you don't get it! Biting me was probably her plan from the start. Can you quit acting like fighting for my life was such a stupid thing to do?"

Talora hugged herself as a breeze picked up. "Sorry, Tizzy. I suppose I'm just being hard on you because—"

"I don't care! It doesn't matter why! I don't need someone to be hard on me!"

Talora looked to Aleth, but he put his hands up. "Don't come to me to fix this. She's got every right to speak for herself. This is who she is."

"You all know way more about me than I know about you." Tizzy met the eyes of each of them, even Dacen. "And I don't like it! But I'm not asking for anyone to level the field. I just want to make sure that the information you've been told is *accurate*. I am not here for any of you. I don't care what significance I have. I am only here for *him*."

Aleth could feel his face get hot. He knew they had made amends, but he hadn't thought he'd ever see her fierce loyalty again.

Eidi approached her, floating only inches away. "I respect your walls, Tizzy, but give us a chance to win your confidence. You have ours."

"How? We've just met!" she snapped. "Shit, give me a chance to let you down!"

Aleth stifled a laugh and squeezed her shoulder. "Alright. We should keep moving."

Tizzy relented to him, her mind racing to figure out her new acquaintances. She trusted Talora the least, if only because of the woman's ability to get inside her head without permission. But it was Eidi and her cheerful, desperate optimism that Tizzy liked the *least*.

Tizzy walked side by side with Aleth, leading the way. Their pace was more relaxed with the new plan to utilize the ley lines. At dusk, they reached the Sheerspine River.

She hadn't seen a more dangerous body of water in all her life. The river was at least a hundred feet across in the area they were stopping. The current was choppy, white, and swift, and she watched it carry giant fallen branches that were bigger than cattle. At the halfway point, a conical stone jutted up from the water's surface. A purple marking wrapped around it like a spiral.

Aleth pursed his lips. "Are you guys sure about this? We can still go back and use the bridge like normal people."

Talora smiled. "But we're not normal people. Besides, there's a warden posted there now. He has Vandroya's colors."

Aleth rolled his eyes. "So what? I'm hungry anyway."

Tizzy stared at him with feigned horror. "Boy, did that mean what I think? That was sinister."

"That was nothing," he said. "Is everyone okay with this spot?"

They all nodded in some manner. Tizzy set her bag down. "Do we want a fire? I can make a mean fire."

"Are you sure?" Talora sounded both doubtful and impressed. "Everything out here is soggy. Did you not see the storm?"

"Tal, I'm unstoppable."

"I have learned this about you."

Tizzy had never stayed outside before without a tent and bedroll. She dreaded the idea of laying on damp brush on the forest floor, but Aleth and Dacen were setting up a boastful camp as she dug the firepit with a rock. They amassed dozens of long branches and started building two tripod-shaped frames off to each side of the firepit, out of harm's way but close enough that they would be warmed by its flames. Talora draped each frame with leaves and brush until they had two covered shelters. Aleth threw down fir boughs to keep them off the ground, and the campsite was nearly done.

Tizzy finished the pit off with a ring of rocks, then left to hunt for dry tinder and kindling. She'd spent enough time outdoors hunting firewood for House Hallenar to know a few tricks. With little effort, she located a fallen tree. All the dry components she needed were safely underneath, protected from the rain. She gathered a handful of leaves and fungus and headed back. With the hatchet and flint she had packed in her bag, she got to work stripping nearby branches of wet bark, and the fire was ready as Aleth, Dacen, and Talora finished up.

"We could live in those." Tizzy put her hands on her hips, unable to contain a grin. "Nice job."

Talora gawked at Tizzy's results. "I can't believe you pulled that off without magic."

"I watched her!" Eidi said.

"You guys need to calm down." Aleth knelt by the flames. "You're going to scare her off."

"You really are." Tizzy joined him and threw a twig into the pit. "So, you made one of those for me, right? I'm a princess, after all."

"If you're a princess, that makes me a prince."

"Guess the rest of these peasants are sleeping in the dirt!"

Talora sang from inside one of the shelters, "Nice try, but we've claimed the big one!"

"What? I made that one for me!" Aleth threw a tiny rock, and Eidi and Talora started giggling. Dacen shrugged and joined them. "Eidi does not count as a third body! She's see-through!" None of his grumbling got them to come out.

Tizzy reclined on her bag and made herself comfortable by the fire. "At least I don't take up much room."

"I've noticed."

Grumpiness had consumed him entirely. She knew she had an uphill battle. "What's on your mind?"

He sighed and threw a leaf into the fire. "Nothing."

"You're an awful liar. Still."

"That's what everybody tells me."

She started clearing away larger debris on the ground until there was just a fine layer of dirt. He paid her no mind as she dragged her finger through it. Then she lowered her voice.

"You know, there's a banshee over there who is absolutely infatuated with you."

He winced. "Yeah."

She drew a heart in the dirt. "Have you had any steamy Ethereal relations? Hm?"

"Tizzy!"

"That's a no, then. Interesting. Why not?"

"What's the matter with you? Why are you so *nosy*?"

She drew a crack in the heart. "So you just don't feel that way about her. I see."

He hid his face. "Can we talk about something else?"

"Sure! What's on your mind?" she asked, wiping the doodle away and giving herself a blank slate.

Aleth slouched forward and groaned. "It's nothing. I have to keep *some* things to myself."

"Guy stuff."

"Tizzy. Shut *up*."

She giggled, tracing a new shape in the dirt. He sighed and got up to make a comfortable spot, setting his cloak down and lying on his stomach. Tizzy rolled her eyes at the laughter from the others.

"I don't know what those losers have against my fire."

"It's a good fire," he said, folding his arms and resting his head on them. "Hey, there's something I've been wanting to ask you."

"Well don't stop now. You've been asking me things since this all started."

"Why'd you stop drawing after the accident?"

The question made her cold and she swallowed hard. "When I woke up from, well from being *dead*, somehow I woke up left handed.

I don't know how or why, and it sounds stupid, but I just couldn't get my right hand to work the way it used to. It just *wouldn't*. I had to re-learn how to do everything with my left, and with all the stress from the way everyone was treating us, I never really felt like going back to re-teach myself how to draw. Something about it felt trivial."

"You were good."

She bit her lip as a smile forced its way onto her face. "I was okay." She drew a squiggly line, and he peered over to see what was in the dirt. She started to chuckle.

"Hold on, is that supposed to be me?"

She was laughing so hard, she gasped for air. "Look at your *hair*!"

The others heard the commotion. Talora peeked her head out of the shelter. "Eidi, look. Look at this jerk smiling."

"I never noticed how unhappy he was before. I mean, I knew he was, but—" She stopped and stared. "They're really close." She watched with Talora as the siblings started shoving each other to make amendments to Tizzy's drawing.

Aleth grabbed her hand and wrestled it away from the dirt. "What are you doing now?"

She cackled and wriggled around until her pinky could touch the ground. "Rabbit ears!"

"*Don't you dare!*" He dropped his shoulder to the ground, obscuring the drawing and wiping it away for good. Then he laughed with her when he saw how he'd fallen. "I think I threw my back out."

"Goodness, the fragile back of a twenty-three-year-old." She wiped away a tear, her face still red from giggling. "You really have to be careful when you get to that age."

They stayed by the fire until the flames could barely reach up from the coals anymore. Then they watched the final ember die from the shelter. Tizzy expected to be cold, but the space was cozy. She looked at Aleth as he stared off in thought.

"You ever going to tell me what's on your mind?"

"I didn't think it would be like this."

"You mean how all of us are right now?"

"I mean you and me."

She was quiet and stared out with him. "How did you think it would be?"

"Difficult. I thought being around you would be harder, that all we would do was fight and bicker, and it'd never end. I thought for sure that things could never be the way they were."

"That's what I thought too. How the hell did we manage to make it this far?"

"I don't know. I hope it stays this way."

***

"What do you think of this, Lora?"

Lazarus offered the woman a taste of the stew he'd been making over the hearth. She blew on it a few times and took a try.

"The potatoes are bland. Add mustard seed and pepper. And go easy on the rosemary next time."

He chuckled. "*Mustard seed*? I can always count on you, Lora."

For several hours, he'd been in the kitchen preparing dinner. Lora, however, was away from Allanis's side and therefore rife with anxiety. She had spent the latter half of her day with Lazarus creating an elaborate pie to busy her mind. She had picked the apples fresh, ground away at the spices with a mortar and pestle, and had even cut little leaf shapes out of the dough. Now that it was finally finished, though, she felt worse than before. She couldn't even show it off to Allanis.

Adeska came into the kitchen, singing as though she didn't have a care in the world. She sat at the counter and breathed in deep.

"It smells wonderful in here! Lazarus, you haven't cooked dinner in ages. I can't wait!"

"It's been awhile," he admitted. "But I'll always have a few tricks up my sleeve."

Lora rolled her eyes. "Your potatoes would be lifeless without my guidance."

"See?" Lazarus gestured to her. "I can do anything as long as she's around. Will your family be joining us, Adeska?"

"No, I'm afraid not. I let Centa head back to Kamdoria with Mari. I told him I'd probably head back once Allanis returned, so long as things started to calm down."

"Even if they don't, you're only a day away at the most! We can send for you if it's important."

"Stop trying to get rid of me!" she laughed. "Let me enjoy this for a little while longer."

Rhett and Athen came into the kitchen some time later, smelling food. Athen sat at the counter with Adeska, his face stiff and somber. Rhett pestered Lazarus for a taste of the stew.

"Cheer up, Athen. Lazarus is cooking, just like way back when!" Adeska put her hand on his. "Isn't that exciting?"

No one noticed Rori slip into the kitchen except for Lora. The blonde avoided the stern woman's glare.

"It's not like way back when," Athen said.

"Well." Adeska drummed her fingers on the countertop. "It's not, you're right. Allanis is away, and let's see—" She felt her face grow hot the more she thought about it. "And *Aleth* isn't here. And Tizzy's cooped up in her room—"

"No she's not." Athen's sigh shook. "Guys, she's gone."

"Wait, Tizzy left?" Everyone looked to Rori after her sudden outburst. "Are you sure?"

Rhett smirked. "She packed her shit and even left a note. I guess when the going gets tough, the best solution is to run away with your tail between your legs."

"We knew she was gone," Lazarus said, ignoring Rhett. The frown he wore was his weariest one yet. "Adeska and I didn't know how to tell you." He poured the stew into bowls.

"So you just lied to us?" Athen narrowed his eyes. "I don't care how estranged she might be to you; she's still my sister!"

Adeska reached for his hand again. "Athen—"

He snatched it away. "Here I was, thinking she was still upset or having another headache or something. I thought all I'd have to do was give her some time and things would go back to normal. But no, it turns out I should have been worried sick because I have no idea where she is or if she's even okay!"

"I really misread the situation." Rhett sat down at the counter with his bowl. "I didn't know anyone really cared. Is it that big of a deal? No one liked her."

"How can you say that?" Athen got to his feet. "So maybe I don't understand her, and she can be a little rude, but so can you! The difference between you two is that she's looked out for me and Allanis and has had our backs all this time! What's the last thing you've done that wasn't for yourself?"

Rori grabbed a bowl and hurried out of the kitchen. "I don't want to be a part of this."

Rhett shrugged away Athen's rage. "Everything I do is for myself. Why not? I can be that way because nobody needs me, especially not in this family. Someone will always offer to help before the burden actually lands on me, so why bother? And anyway, when's the last time any of you cared to know how I was doing? I can spin this on you just as fast."

Athen left the room, spewing explosive profanity.

Lora took a long, contemplative bite of stew and then sighed. "Gods, this family. Listen, if anyone cuts into that pie, I will have every single Hallenar scalp under this roof. Good night." She left for a more peaceful place to dine.

Rhett ate proudly and quietly as Lazarus and Adeska sat.

She stared blankly at nothing. "What happened? How did everything get this difficult? Time makes things so complicated."

"There's eight of us," Rhett said, his mouth full. "You should've expected some dissidence. We're still people, and some people hate each other." He pointed his spoon at Lazarus. "This is pretty good."

"Thanks."

***

Rori escaped the suffocating atmosphere of House Hallenar as night set in. It was cold and misty outside, a still-bloated waning moon in the sky. She'd given Alor her stew after the family had caused her to lose her appetite and had a good laugh watching Stormy lick the bowl clean. Then she found one of her favorite old story books to read aloud before tucking the boy into bed.

The events on the horizon would continue to shake the family. She knew that well. With a cold sigh, she explored the outer courtyard until she came to a little shed along the fence. After years of neglect, she knew it'd be home to spiders now, cute and little and terrifying as she'd always found them. She opened the door anyway.

It still smelled of eucalyptus. Since the very first time she'd brought a branch back from the marketplace to cut up, the scent had permeated her workstation, sometimes making it impossible to finish herbal concoctions that she could only work on by scent. At least it kept the spiders out of the drawers. She fumbled around with a flint until at last she had lit a candle. The orange glow caught the shadows of a few empty webs clinging to the corners.

She traced her hand along the wooden desktop, cut deeply with work and stained green by plants. She missed what she used to do. She missed her dreams on her home, on Mirivin Mainland. Some of her tools still remained in their drawers, including a white-handled boline that had been a gift from Adeska. Rori cracked a smile when she saw the notebook that she'd made completely by hand, including every wrinkled page and the drop-spindled thread that bound them together.

"You sure snuck off fast."

Rori gasped. Rhett stood in the doorway.

"Lords! Could you announce yourself next time?"

"If I remember to."

She grumbled, sighing away the scare, and pushed past him. It was cold, or maybe the chill was from circumstance. Either way, she hugged herself and looked up into the sky.

"What's wrong with you?" he asked.

She rolled her eyes. "Always a way with words, haven't you? Nothing is wrong with me. Would it kill you to say something nice?"

He shrugged. "What if it would?"

"So there's no one in the world right now who you'd bother to be kind to?"

"There's no one in the world right now who needs me to tell them something kind."

Rori stared at her boots, wet from the dewy grass. "I do."

"Why? You have no shortage of people to go to when you need to hear nice things, Rori." Rhett picked at the dirt under his nails. "I don't have to be the one to do it. It's not necessary, that's all."

"Rhett, it's not that I have a general need to hear something nice or to be lifted up right now. I just need to hear those things from *you*. I need to know that *you* feel that way for me. The only way I could possibly know is if you do that."

"You changed."

She turned and glared at him. "People do that! Time and experiences change us! Of course I changed, and I'm glad I did!"

"I liked it much better when you came to me for guidance. Not pampering." He rolled his eyes, and then they locked onto her.

"I'm not asking to be pampered!" She balled up her fists but then stopped and vented her stress with a deep breath, combing her fingers through her hair. "Why did you even come out here?"

"To reminisce!" She thought his grin looked sinister beneath the moon. "We made a great team back then. But I'm sure New Rori doesn't remember any of that."

"Hold on." She wanted to laugh in disbelief. "Are you calling what we did *good teamwork*? Rhett, I almost killed my brother and sister!"

"But you didn't! And it was funny, just like I said it would be. You sure laughed at it back then. You did a lot of things back then."

"Why did you want to hurt them so badly?"

"Don't try to call me out like I'm a villain!" he snapped. "You wanted to, Adeska wanted to, Lazarus wanted to. Hell, I'm willing to bet that if Allanis and Athen had been any older, they would've wanted to! If we all felt that, why didn't we listen to it? What if it was trying to tell us something?"

"Do you think Mother would have wanted to, also? Is that what you think she would have wanted? For you to viciously attack your siblings?"

"Don't talk about her like you ever knew her! She *died* before you were ever old enough to understand her!"

Rori's fists shook. "I don't care what you think you know. Our parents were not people who would have condoned our actions."

"Ha!" Rhett flung his arms out. "There wouldn't have been any question about it! If she had been here, Mother would have seen to it that the two of them were driven away or worse. She didn't waste her time caring about people she knew weren't worth—"

"She was our *mother*. She loved all of us! She *never* would have done what we did. How could you say things like that? The way you talk about her, you make her sound horrible! Do you really think Father would have loved someone like that?"

"Father was a spineless piece of shit!" His body trembled with fury.

It grew quiet. All Rori could hear was her own heartbeat until her voice came out, low and gravelly, weighed down by contempt.

"You shouldn't talk about him like that. For all the visions of us and our future that he had, you should be grateful he could always look you in the eyes and still love you."

Rhett scoffed. "Look at that. You've still got some bite, after all."

"Look, Rhett, the point is that we stopped." She clenched her teeth hard, her contempt washing away to something more fragile. "That feeling we had, we didn't listen to it." She sniffled. "And guess what? Life went on. We're all alive. We're all okay. Maybe all that hatred and violence was for nothing."

"If you're hoping I'm going to feel guilty about it, don't waste your time." He stepped in close to her, and she shivered. "Not only do I not feel guilty, Rori, but what I did was *good*. If Aleth was bad, then what I did got him away from us. And if he wasn't bad, then you know what? Oh well. It built character."

"You call breaking his bones and beating him bloody *building character*? Rhett, where is your moral compass?"

"I've decided I do have something nice to say, Rori." He tucked a curl behind her ear. His eyes were dark. "You were a damn good apothecary. It's a shame you left it behind."

His grin under the night was the last she saw of him before he turned and left for the manor. Rori went back into the shed and sat at the desk, in the light of a single candle, and cried.

CHAPTER 10

CROSSROADS

VAYVEN 1, 1144

T izzy didn't know where she was, but it was cold and wet outside. The sky was dark yet glowed dimly with the promise of sunrise in a couple of hours. Red leaves crunched underfoot as she walked through quiet woods. It wasn't the Bogwood—these trees were pruned, and the ground was worn with regular foot traffic. She continued to wander and stopped at a wrought iron fence.

"Wait, this is House Hallenar!" Her heart beat a little faster. She was home.

Beyond the fence, in the courtyard, she saw someone. A man in a hooded cloak. He was coming closer. Rhett. For a split second she panicked, but he didn't seem to notice her. He kept walking until he vanished inside a small shed.

"I can't believe that old thing is still standing," she mumbled, inching closer along the fence to get a better view. She had forgotten all about her younger sister's old stomping grounds.

She heard the sounds of drawers squealing open and slamming shut. Something felt terribly wrong. He shouldn't be in there, she thought. She heard him laugh. Paper ripped. He walked back out, balling something up in his hand.

"Tizzy! Come on, Tizzy, wake up!"

Startled awake, she was overcome with a wave of dizziness and nausea—something she was becoming well-acquainted with as of late—and her dream was torn away.

"If you don't wake up, I'm going to smother you." Aleth picked up her bag and held it over her face.

She opened her eyes. "What?"

"Good, that worked." He smiled, but she wasn't amused.

When she sat up, she groaned and held her head. She was still inside the shelter, still at the campsite. Not at home.

"Everything okay?"

"Yeah." She wiped the sleep out of her eyes. "Just had a really weird dream."

"I've been thinking about those and how you said you only started having them after I had the wish taken away." It was too early to think, but she let him talk anyway. "Maybe they're clairvoyant. They could be one of your nightwalker abilities or maybe even something inherited from Father." He dusted his cloak off and put it on.

"That's stupid. I'd rather turn into a dog. Is it time to go?"

"Yeah. The others are dismantling camp right now. Are you ready?"

"Guess so."

Tizzy learned that dismantling camp was more fun than it sounded. Throwing rocks and branches in all directions was a great way to wake up underneath the twilight and work off the chill of the misty air. By the time the task was done, her hair was frizzy, and her nose and ears pink.

"What's next?" she asked. Everyone had gathered at the river's edge. Tizzy could cut the sudden tension with a knife.

"It's time to take the ley line," Eidi announced. The banshee's eyes drifted to Aleth for a moment in uneasiness, then stared at the river.

"We should go over a few things first," Talora said. "We neglected to tell Aleth when he went with us, so that experience went not so well."

"Thank you for finally taking responsibility for that," he grumbled. "It was your fault."

Dacen was still quiet, fidgeting with his hands. Talora gripped his shoulder and smiled.

"It'll be okay. But when we get to the ley line, we're not really supposed to be there. You'll have to be completely silent. Don't make a sound."

"We should have used the bridge." Aleth crossed his arms. "This is a bad idea."

"We'll be fine!" Eidi said. Her smile convinced no one. "I do this all the time. There's a lot more of you coming with me than usual, but I'm confident it'll be fine."

Aleth and Tizzy exchanged glances.

"You'll all get in trouble if this kills me, right?" she asked.

Talora frowned. "Actually, Aleth is probably the one who'll get in trouble. But nobody is going to be killed! Let's go! We're wasting time."

They relented, and Eidi floated over the river current and to the Helamine Stone. Talora lined them up and gave the banshee a signal, and Eidi traced a glowing pattern over the stone's markings. Tizzy heard a hum in the atmosphere, and her surroundings started to shift as though she were being swallowed. Everything around her looked like she was seeing it through violet-tinted glass, including herself when she looked down at her hands. They were still in the woods but in a different area. The Sheerspine River that was once in front of them was just a ghostly visage.

Eidi led them in a straight line. Tizzy stared at the ground, careful of rocks and roots, but then found she could pass right through them, just like the banshee. She didn't like it, and she didn't like the noises, either. Traveling the ley line sounded like being submerged under water. But then it changed. Muffled voices were coming from nowhere in particular.

Tizzy was in front of Dacen, who was at the rear. He tapped her on the shoulder, and she craned her neck back to him. His eyes were wide, and his head shook as he pointed to the rapidly changing landscape behind him. Trees and vegetation wilted and decayed, and the ground turned to mud.

She shoved Aleth. He turned around, furious, but she started gesturing. Talora and Eidi soon noticed the others were stopping. When the banshee saw why, she gasped.

They stared at her. She slapped her hands over her mouth.

"Oops!"

A dozen pairs of yellow eyes started to glow around them.

"We have to get out of here!" Talora whispered.

The ground became thick mud beneath them, and suddenly Tizzy couldn't move. She looked at the others struggling beside her. The eyes came closer and brought their insect-winged silhouettes with them, and the air grew heavy with the stench of rot.

"Eidi, scream!" Talora begged.

"They're in their native Realm. It wouldn't do any good! I'm powerless here!"

"Then take us back!" Tizzy snapped.

"I don't know where this spot will take us!"

"Forget that! We'll figure it out!" Aleth yelled.

"Fine!"

Tizzy knew for a fact that she was standing, yet it felt like she was falling as the environment raced up past her and left her in a void. She was alone except for millions of glistening purple specks. It felt familiar, warm and inviting almost. Then she knew. *Between the Realms.* She blinked into existence again beside the others and vomited in the brush.

Aleth confronted Eidi at once. "What the fuck was that? You said everything would be fine!"

"I don't know. I've never seen that before!" she cried. "It was supposed to be a quiet walk to the other marker!"

"Surprise! It wasn't!"

"Aleth, quit yelling at her!" Talora stood between them.

Dacen rubbed Tizzy's back as she heaved a few more times. When she finished, she stood straight and wiped her mouth. "Thanks." He nodded, still staring in concern as she wiped the sweat off her brow. "Where are we? That's the important question, right?"

"Looks like we're by Tal's place, so we're close." Aleth sighed. "I can get us the rest of the way there. No more tricks! You two are going to get us killed!"

Tizzy was a mix of emotions as Aleth led them away. Eidi—overly positive and eager to please—was her least favorite of the three she'd newly met, but the defeated droop of her shoulders and pout on her face pulled at Tizzy's heart. She had only been trying to help.

But on the other hand, Tizzy didn't really know her. She shrugged the sympathy away and continued on.

***

At midday, a carriage pulled up to tall stone city walls. It was small, but the guards dressed in plum and silver recognized it immediately. They opened the gates for Queen Allanis Byland-Hallenar. She was happy to be back in Saunterton and spent the next half hour primping herself as the carriage took her to Lovell Keep.

Saunterton was impressive, ripe with culture, wealth, and cleanliness. Sometimes when she was in a lesser mood, the sight of the city would make her feel pathetic, but she always came back to her excuse: she hadn't been raised noble. The small town that she ruled had fallen into her hands by chance, not by strategy or birthright. There was no point in competition. Allanis worked with what she had, and right then she had Queen Anavelia Lovell.

The everyday fashion in Saunterton was inspiring. Allanis wished she had brought Lora to see but remembered her plan. There were sculptures of great cats, colorful buildings reached into the sky, and wide streets with beautiful designs laid into the cobblestone. It would be hard to go back home, she thought with a smile.

As the carriage neared Lovell Keep, a knight and the queen's chamberlain, both on horseback, ushered her into the keep's outer courtyard. Allanis didn't recognize the knight but knew the chamberlain from past visits. Sir Troyer was a tall, lean man with long hair that was graying prematurely. A scar went down his mouth and through his lips, but his smile was known throughout the city.

The courtyard was extravagant, full of finely dressed people. Peacocks ran between the fig trees and gathered by the edge of a small pond, screeching at Allanis's arrival. Three statues were erected in random locations, each one landscaped with exotic plants and stones to be areas of contemplation. The statue of Rosamar, the Goddess of the Earth, greeted her first. The back of the statue's head was carved hollow to display a plant with bright red leaves, mimicking depictions of her wild hair. Then Allanis saw Libevven, the God of the Animals and the Wilds. A lone stag with a peaceful gaze sat beside his stone form, watching her pass. Finally she saw the statue of a minor goddess whose story she couldn't recount. Simia, the Goddess of the Hunt. She was depicted as a young woman with a bow slung around her shoulder and a falcon perched on her arm.

Seeing the falcon made Allanis's heart hurt. She hoped Tizzy was well.

The carriage stopped. Sir Troyer opened the door and ushered her out onto the steps of Lovell Keep.

"Queen Allanis Hallenar! Her Grace has been expecting you. Shall I escort you and—" He paused and looked inside the carriage as Allanis took out a jeweled satin bag.

"I came alone, Sir Troyer. It's just me you'll be escorting." She smiled as he stammered for a second.

"Yes. Follow me." He had to pull his eyes away from her armor as it gently shone in the overcast sky.

Allanis walked beside him but not before taking careful note of the way the knight inspected her from a distance.

Lovell Keep, just like the courtyard, was full of people. It usually was whenever Allanis came to visit, but today it was packed beyond what she'd ever seen. There were people of all ages, sizes, races, and origins dressed in their best and stretching their social capabilities to the limits, sometimes with accents she couldn't place. There were attractive suitors, too, for all tastes. Servants scurried back and forth with their tasks, avoiding the guests as best as they could.

She was led into the grand hall, clutching at the satin bag she came with.

"Allanis, my darling!"

At that moment, she was happy to have left Lora behind. Allanis's better half had trouble holding her tongue at all the pet names the other queen threw around.

Anavelia rushed over with open arms and embraced Allanis, pulling her hard into her small, bony frame. The strange woman and her personal stories of accomplishment had inspired her since the day they'd first met—Anavelia's coronation day, about eleven years ago. Anavelia was nobility from Kasatta Mainland, affectionately called the Land of Silk by the rest of the world, and she had been raised with the goal of marrying an emperor. But her father made a gamble that had disastrous effects on the family, and Anavelia was forced to flee to Mirivin with her baby brother. She stuck to what she knew, played her cards right, and married a king. Allanis didn't know the story of why the king was no longer in the picture—Anavelia didn't like to talk about it. Before the last advisor had passed from pneumonia, Master Elengin told Allanis it was an assassination.

On this day, Anavelia was her typical self. Allanis didn't know a single person alive or dead as garish as her friend, but she enjoyed every second of it. The queen of Saunterton had touches of red makeup on her small, dark eyes. Her petite face was twisted into its standard wiley, mischievous expression. Her black hair was braided intricately at the sides of her head and adorned with a silver garnet-encrusted hair comb that glittered in the light. The clothes she wore were always uniquely her own, today a collection of wispy silks layered together until they made a decent garment. Her favorite colors were in every outfit—plum and fuchsia—and her favorite parts to flaunt were her small shoulders and flat chest.

Allanis loved the woman more and more every visit. Much of the jewelry she owned had been gifts from Anavelia. Saunterton's queen was displaying many new pieces today, including slippers with little citrine gems.

"Darling, you are welcome here any time! It's been too long since your last visit!" She kissed Allanis on the cheek. "And I love what you're wearing. A bold new look! What do you think of mine?" She did a little twirl, holding onto the black fur stole around her shoulders. "It's getting cold, so we made something to look like our beloved Jade!"

"Where is Jade today?" Allanis asked. "And it's lovely, by the way!"

The Lovell crest featured a black panther, and for generations, one had always been kept as a family companion. Jade, a melanistic jaguar, was the most recent addition. Every black pelt in Lovell Keep, from blankets and rugs to accessories, was an imitation of a black panther pelt, crafted by the Queen's own team of furriers employed at the Keep. Allanis looked at the stole closer and could see the faint jaguar markings woven in. Had she not known Anavelia's passion for imitation, she would have suspected it for the real thing.

"She doesn't like all the people today," Anavelia huffed. "And neither do I. But this area is public space, so it can't be helped until sundown. Now that you're here, though, let's go to my study! Where is Lora? Would she like to join us?"

"Actually," Allanis drew in a deep breath. "I came alone this time."

Anavelia pursed her lips. "Dear, if she was sick, we could have postponed!"

"She's not sick. I just came alone."

The queen tapped on her lips in thought. Allanis recognized the mannerism at once and knew she was troubled. "Very well. Follow me."

The Keep was more and more beautiful every time Allanis visited. Scenes from the Lovells' history were painted on the walls, and a façade of fine gold filigree layered over them like a frame. Curtains of luxurious fabrics were draped over open windows, and they billowed in the walkways. Candles burned within glass sconces, and smoke from frankincense resin poured out from hanging brass censers.

Anavelia's study was tucked away in a corner of the castle. Allanis had been many times before and felt relief walking into it. The warm glow of the candles on the white columns, the plush chairs upholstered in magenta brocade, and the polished cherry wood desk were the focal points of memories of girlish conversations and fits of laughter. Anavelia took two glasses from a shelf and set them on the desk.

"Now, Allanis, why did you come here alone? Is this related to your new fashion choices?"

She went back to the shelf to find a wine she liked when a woman came to the doorway with a bottle in her hands.

"Your Grace, shall I serve you?"

"No. Leave," Anavelia sighed, waving her away. The cup-bearer left at once.

Allanis handed Anavelia the satin bag. "Before we get into that, I brought you something!"

The other queen smiled and blushed. "Oh sweetheart, you know you didn't have to! Let's see what this is."

She tugged at the drawstring and pulled out a large, heavy bottle of pale wine. Anavelia's face lit up.

"Oh, how sweet of you! Did you and your brother finally get—oh. Allanis, dear, I think something went wrong." She held up the bottle and looked at the bottom. "I think it has bubbles."

Allanis had a proud smile on her face. "You should try it. Trust me; it isn't a mistake!"

Dubious, Anavelia worked at the cork.

"Oh, but be careful because—"

It popped out with a hollow *thunk* and shot across the room.

"Allanis, are you trying to kill me?"

"No! Of course not! I didn't think it would come out with so much gusto. I'm sorry. But you should try it!"

Anavelia sniffed it and then shrugged. "You should consider it a great honor that I don't have that woman come back here and try this for me. If you were anyone else, I'd think you were trying to poison me." She poured two glasses and watched the foam dissipate with wonder.

"Athen and I, we're not good at making wine," Allanis said, taking one of the glasses. "Everyone keeps telling us that it isn't hard, but for whatever reason, we keep messing it up. Then this happened!" She took a sip and swayed her shoulders. "A rather pleasant accident, don't you think?"

Anavelia took a sip and was taken aback. "Allanis, oh my gods! It's like—" She took another sip. "It's sparkling on my tongue! I feel like I'm drinking stars! Are you making more?"

"We are. I'm glad you like it! I'll be sure to send you a few cases when it's ready."

"What do you call this?" Anavelia poured a little more into her glass.

"I haven't thought about that, actually."

"Stellina!" She took another sip. "Call it Stellina! Imagine it: a trader comes to Suradia and he says, 'I'm looking for a bottle of the queen's Stellina!' It's an old word they used to use on the Western Peninsula. It means *little star*, I think."

"You have such amazing ideas, Ana!"

"I have too many people kissing my ass today. I do not need you to be one of them." She laughed.

They shared a moment of giggles together and made themselves comfortable on Anavelia's expensive chairs. Then two others entered the room. A young boy with shoulder length black hair and a doublet boasting the Lovell crest walked in with folded arms. He was followed by a tall woman in simple leather armor.

"Sister! Jade fell asleep in the library again!" the boy announced. "She's sleeping up against the doors, and I can't get inside!"

Anavelia stifled laughter. "That's your cue to quit reading for the day. Ashbel, Titha, say hello! Allanis arrived just a while ago."

Ashbel, the boy, bowed slightly and said a greeting under his breath. Titha bowed deeply until her long brown hair swept the floor.

"I'm sorry Lora isn't with me this time. I know she enjoys talking with the two of you."

"Unfortunately, there could be no talking today. I am *very* busy," Ashbel replied solemnly. Anavelia rolled her eyes and he continued. "And I cannot continue with my work until Jade lets me into the library!"

"Titha, take him to the archery range or something," Anavelia grumbled.

He plopped into a chair and stuck his nose in the air. "No! I'm not going anywhere until the library is accessible!"

Titha shrugged. Anavelia sighed.

"Boy, you're a surly kid, aren't you? That's fine. What could we talk about that'd get you to leave? Ah, I've got it! Allanis, let's talk about sex."

"That might make *me* leave!" she said, her face turning red.

The other queen chuckled. "What? You mean you and Lora still haven't—"

"It's not going to work, you know!" Ashbel shouted. "I'm only going to ignore you!"

"I don't know Ana." Allanis followed her friend's lead and ignored the boy, playing with a pet curl. "I just—I don't know. I've never really wanted to do that. With anyone. Maybe she and I will someday, but I don't know how to get to that point."

Anavelia took another sip of the Stellina. "Darling, everyone is different. I'm almost thirty. I have no children and no desire to be a mother, but I know responsibility is calling. Well, actually—" She looked over at Ashbel. "Even if I never produced a child, the throne would be fine. Ash is more than capable. We are lucky to live on a mainland that favors the leadership of Royal Magic over the leadership of blood. If it didn't, the throne could have gone to Venta's brother after he was killed since Venta and I never had any children. But Ash and I are both very skilled with Royal Magic. So we stay."

She readjusted in the chair and crossed her legs. "Now, what happens to Suradia when your time comes? It's not a pleasant thought, but it happens to us all. And you're a queen, so you *have* to consider these things."

"Lora and I can't have children, Ana. Obviously."

"There are ways." Anavelia smiled and swirled her glass. "The priestesses of Emrin don't just run orphanages. If you can find the Order of the Midwives, they have a ritual to help couples conceive who otherwise could not. Granted, the information is often illegally acquired and misused—you don't want to know the grotesque beings that have come out of the practice—so it's locked away tight. But if you, the queen, were to marry and want a child with your wife, I doubt the Order would refuse. Don't let me stop your train of thought, though, dear. What are the other options?"

"Well, I guess the crown would go to Athen. At least that's what I'd like. I hope he could use Royal Magic if it came down to that! I love my family, but he's the only one I would consider to rule. No one else is really, um—"

Around, she thought. But did she really want to say it? Anavelia watched her get lost in her words. She put her hand on Allanis's knee.

"Sweetheart, how have you been?"

"*Now* you ask," Ashbel mumbled.

"Shut up!"

Allanis tried to smile. She thought she was smiling at least, but the corners of her mouth just wouldn't turn up. "I've been—" She swallowed hard. "I've been—"

"Your party didn't go the way you wanted, did it?"

The tears welled up in her eyes and spilled out with a sob. "*No!*"

"Oh, honey."

"It was going so well, and then so much went wrong! Everything is wrong!"

"What happened?"

"Everybody—" She hiccupped. "Everybody was there. Ana, it was amazing! They were all there, for maybe five whole minutes!"

Anavelia tilted her head and set the glass down on the desk. "All of them?" That couldn't be right. "You've told me before about the one that—"

"He was there!" She sobbed again as she recalled bits and pieces of the night.

"I remember him, just barely, from the coronation day. Ashbel was just a baby! Let's see if I can get this right. Out of your brood, your estranged brother was one of those two cute ones with the reddish hair, right?"

"Well, now they're both gone! Not only because their hair isn't red anymore, but—"

She was cut off by Anavelia's gasp. "Tizzy left?"

All Allanis could do through her tears was nod, and Anavelia leaned over and hugged her.

"Allanis, I'm so sorry. She left after he showed up? That couldn't have gone well. You've told me an awful lot about your family."

"Ana, I hate to say it, but it's why I'm here."

She rubbed Allanis's shoulder and then sat back in her chair, folding her arms. "Okay, spill it. What went down?"

Allanis took a deep breath and then a long sip of Stellina. "Aleth came to the door that night, and we didn't know it was him. It was just *someone*, and he wanted to talk to me. But everyone, ugh, they're so protective! He came in once I said it was okay, but they attacked him. He was a little threatening; I suppose I can see why. You had to be there. But that's when we finally realized it was him. I took him to talk in private, and he told me why he'd shown up. He was warning me."

"Warning you about what?" Ashbel was suddenly over himself and was leaning forward, following the conversation.

"He said Vandroya was planning to attack Suradia. He left after that, and Tizzy chased after him. I don't know what happened between them, but she came back, yelled at us, and went to bed. I thought that was that. But when I went to wake her up in the morning, she was gone."

Anavelia crossed her legs again in thought. "Vandroya. So that's why you've got armor. You're willing to go to war, and you want people to know it. You want them to see that you're strong."

"You can't be serious, though!" Ashbel jumped up. "You are not ready for war!"

"That's why I'm here." Allanis wiped away a stray tear. "I knew you'd know more about it than me. I was hoping you could give me some advice since my advisors are dead."

"That's right, your Council. It was just Lora, Athen, and Tizzy, right?" Anavelia asked.

"My oldest brother Lazarus is staying for a bit to sit on the Council now, but I don't know how much help he can be. They're all I've got."

"Our Council is enormous, and our court—" Ashbel threw his arms out. "It's made up of almost a hundred people. That's half the reason why this place is so crazy today. More people want a seat! Allanis, at the very least, you should start making changes to your own Council. You need to expand it to have eyes and ears and control."

"And you're going to need an army." Anavelia nodded.

"Those things require money! And I don't have much of that to spend on an army, nor do I have people enough for one!"

"It's alright, Allanis. Ash and I know a lot about this. We can help."

Ashbel cleared his throat and started pacing. "Suradia is the smallest independent land on Mirivin. If somebody wanted to conquer you, they could. But they don't, either because they have nothing to gain by doing so or they know we'd show up to defend you and we have the biggest army and the biggest economy.

"There are now only five independent lands left since Ebinno pledged fealty to the King of Vandroya. Saunterton, Suradia, Vandroya, Yzen Vale, and Caequin. There is pressure on you now because as an independent land that doesn't really have any way to *stay* independent, if it came down to it, everyone is looking to see who you'll pledge fealty to in order to stay safe. King Mabus probably expects it to be us. Maybe he wants to conquer Suradia before that happens."

Allanis wanted to tell them she thought it was more than just land politics, but she kept that to herself. "I owe Saunterton for all it's done for me, but I intend to stay independent."

"That's my girl!" Anavelia cheered. "You have plenty of room to expand Suradia, even within the walls you have now."

"How exactly do I get people to come here, to expand, when I have nothing to offer?"

"You have to spend wisely," Ashbel told her. "People will leave a place if it's bad enough, but they will go to one of the other independent lands before they go to yours. Unless you have better opportunities."

Allanis's mind was racing. She had nothing. Farmland was average, the arts were average, education and even the Academy teachings were average. There was nothing exciting to be a part of—

"Wait." She was breathless. "I think the Undina Loch falls into Suradian territory."

"Does it?" Ashbel seemed surprised. "Let's go to the map room."

They followed him to a chamber with a hearth. In the center was a large, low table painted with a map of the Mirivin Mainland, the Besq Mainland, the Kasatta Mainland, and the Shimara Tail. There were figurines set down in different areas to represent people, armies, and other factors that were kept secret. One wall was a bookshelf, and another had notes from carriers pinned in chronological order.

"What is this place?" Allanis asked in awe. Anavelia rubbed her shoulders.

"First order of business, my dear. Construct a map room in House Hallenar! We use ours to keep track of current events. It's absolutely critical."

Ashbel went to a bookcase and grabbed the biggest, heaviest book there was, off the top shelf no less. Titha rushed over to help him take it down. He sat by the hearth with it in his lap and flipped through its pages.

"This contains all the documentation regarding land ownership among the independent lands. It's a bit old, so it includes information for kingdoms now pledged, too, like Ebinno. You'll have a book like this in your library somewhere," he said. He found the page he was looking for. It unfolded to be four times its size with a drawn map of Mirivin and defined territory lines.

"Gods, it really does include the Undina Loch. Sister, Suradia is massive! I had no idea King Byland owned so much."

"I don't think anyone did." Anavelia looked over his shoulder. "Imagine how many people you have living on your land who aren't paying taxes."

"Look at that!" Allanis pointed at the Undina Loch. "It completely bisects Mirivin! The Roe River funnels in from Death Pass Sea at that harbor, then it comes down and into the Undina Loch, then winds back down and down into a river that empties into the south shore!

The Undina Loch provides access to the Death Pass Sea *and* the Equenhol Ocean. And it's mine!"

"You could get to Vandroya in half the time they'd expect." Ashbel closed the book in excitement. "Or you could charge other armies for access to do the same thing!"

"Ash, I need you to do something for me." Anavelia looked at him sternly. "I want you and Titha to go to Suradia. I want you to join Allanis's Council."

For a second, the boy was red with a tight-lipped frown. But then he calmed. Her words processed, and at last he nodded. "I see." He stared at the floor. "You're finally going to let me do something I'm good at."

"Are you two sure about this? Isn't it dangerous to have him with me, especially after I told you I have a target on my back?"

"I'm positive," Anavelia said. "Ash, could you please give Allanis and me a moment alone?"

"I'm going to check on the library again, anyway," he said. He left, and Titha followed him out.

Anavelia stared down at the map table for a long time before deciding to speak. When she did, she started with a sigh.

"Vandroya has always been a pain in my ass. Mabus thinks he runs the whole mainland just because of his technology and connections. He does have the allegiance of a lot of smaller towns and cities and those damn Hunters too. You know, Allanis, you're really going to be worth something now. *You* always were, of course, but I mean Suradia. You're going to turn it into something that Frankel never could. And we'll be able to help each other."

"I'm sorry that I've never been of any help to you before."

"That's not your fault. Rarely do I need, and when I do, there's not much that anyone can do for it. But what I'm going to do for you is critical. I need you to understand that. In two days, I'm going to send you Ashbel and his handler Titha, and I'm also going to send you my Master Knight to help you get some semblance of an army trained.

Personally, I don't require anything in return, but history does. It might not seem important now, but in the future, when we are gone and our kingdoms are growing beyond what we made them, this deal will stand out, and it will define them.

"That's why I need you to think. What can you offer me? It doesn't have to be anything right now. You have time. You can tell me when you figure it out, but it needs to be something that I can't get from anyone else."

"I understand."

"Some people will think I should demand fealty, but I won't because I respect you, and I know that we're both better off if we keep each other independent. Go home, try to relax, and *think*."

Allanis smiled. "I will think with a new head on my shoulders."

***

Rori brought a plate of bread and fruit to Alor. She put on her best face though she had barely slept. Stormy was fast asleep in front of the hearth, and Alor sat next to him, lost in thought as he stared into the fire.

"I'm a little late with food this morning; sorry about that, buddy." She sat beside him. "Here you go."

He didn't break his gaze. "I'll eat it later."

"Alright. Are you feeling okay?"

"I couldn't sleep last night."

"That makes two of us." She bit into an apple slice, then pressed the inside of her wrist to his forehead and cheeks. "You don't have a fever, so you're not sick. That's good." She set the plate in Alor's lap. "Here. Try to eat a little bit. I'll be back with just the thing to make you feel better!"

He watched her stand up and head for the door. "Where are you going?"

"Outside!" she answered, fastening her white cloak. "Where I do my best work!"

It had been ages since she'd been foraging. Rori was excited to be back at her old game again. The flora on Sila'Karia was vastly different from that on Mirivin and she'd never had the time to learn it, so her old talents withered away. But she could feel the old knowledge unearthing itself as she raced along the edges of the courtyard, looking at the plants. Nothing nearby was in bloom in the fall, which was too bad, she thought. Tea from fresh kanna flowers would have perked Alor right up.

There were dozens of ways to do the same thing, though. She went into her shed and pulled out one of her old notebooks.

"I know I wrote a few good recipes in here! I can use kanna root like the flower, but it's more potent, so I need to make sure I only use a little." She kept mumbling, thumbing through the pages. "And it'll be bitter, too, so I'll have to mix it with cider or honey if he's going to drink any of it."

The notes were scattered without rhyme or reason to their layout. Some pages featured notes added in someone else's handwriting— Mother Tryphaena, the Master Apothecary she had learned under. She smiled, remembering the woman, but an ugly feeling filled her gut as she kept turning the pages.

The notes started to become sinister in nature. Rori's old recipes were no longer about curing stomach-aches or healing bruises. Her fingers trembled as she turned the next page. She choked on a breath.

"Where—"

A page was torn out. Her face turned white. It could have been *any* page but that one. She slammed the book shut and sprinted back to House Hallenar as fast as she could. She'd never run through the halls faster in all her life. She came to the library and found Lazarus and Adeska pouring over books about Vandroya.

"Where's Rhett?"

"Rori!" Adeska rushed to her. "Goodness, catch your breath! What's the matter?"

"Rhett! Where is Rhett?"

Lazarus set his book down. "He said he was getting stir-crazy and left to go wander around town a little while ago. What's the matter? What did he do this time?"

"Oh no."

Her gut lurched, and she felt sick. She turned in circles, torn between going after him and acknowledging it was too late. "No, no, no."

"Rori, you're shaking like a leaf." Adeska put her hands on her hips. "What's going on?"

Rori shut the door and then slid down it till she hit the floor and hugged her knees. When she spoke, her voice was small.

"I need to tell you guys something."

Adeska helped her into a chair. "What is it? We're here for you."

"It's not me I'm worried about!" she cried, holding her head in her hands. "Look, I should have told you two about this ages ago, but I couldn't! I know what's wrong with Tizzy and Aleth. I know what they are."

"What they *are*? What are you talking about?" Adeska asked.

Rori waved her finger with a short, vicious laugh. "Don't act stupid! Stop trying to play me for a fool! I've been playing you one for years, and now—" she wet her lips, "—now I'm sorry. I don't know what else to say. I know what they are, and they are in so much danger."

Lazarus nodded. "Alright. Start from the beginning, Rori."

She tried to steady herself, but deep breaths didn't work. "We all know that I followed Rhett around like a plague when I was little." He haunted her now: his face, the malice in his eyes, and the way he grabbed her arm and dug his nails in. "He'd give me things and tell me how good I was whenever I would do his chores or do something like—"

"Like push Tizzy down the stairs," Lazarus finished for her, glowering.

"Right. You guys know. When I was studying with Mother Tryphaena, Rhett got this idea. He told me I should poison them, that it'd be funny to get them sick." All those years ago, when he'd said it, she could still remember how close he'd gotten. She could still feel his whisper in her ear.

"I knew exactly what to do. One night, Adeska, I was helping you with dinner. You left to make sure everyone was ready, and I snuck a few drops of green drangea oil into their bowls."

"Yes, Rori, I remember when they got sick!" Adeska snapped.

"No, that wasn't when it happened! The green drangea had no effect on them. None! Two drops of it on the tongue is supposed to make a person violently ill for a whole day!"

"I know what it does!"

"It didn't work on them. Rhett was angry with me and said that I hadn't used enough. So I kept trying with larger doses, but it never worked. Rhett was furious." No one had noticed the marks he left. He'd made sure no one would see. "He said that if I couldn't do it, he'd never talk to me again. I didn't know what else to do, so I told Mother Tryphaena about it.

"She was only a little shocked. She said if that much green drangea didn't do anything, then they simply weren't human. I believed her, but I was a kid! I didn't think anything of it! I think my actual response to her was, 'Of course, that makes sense,' and I went on with my lesson like it was nothing. I kept thinking about what Rhett said, though, and I was scared that he'd hate me, so I eventually asked her if there were ways to poison non-humans."

"Oh lords, Lazarus, where did we find this woman?"

Sharing her exasperation, he pinched the bridge of his nose. "Let's let her finish, Adeska."

"She had lots of poisons. *Lots* of them. I crafted them and tested them, one by one, until one day, something worked. I had finally poisoned Tizzy and Aleth and won back Rhett's favor."

She shuddered. They didn't see it.

"Rori, do you have any idea how sick you made them that night?"

"Oh please, Adeska! Don't!" Rori glared at her. "Don't try to judge me like you cared back then because you didn't! Where were you that night? You weren't at their bedsides, that's for sure. As I recall, you were screaming at them from the hallway that if they didn't cut their bullshit and help clean the kitchen, they'd go hungry for the rest of the month!"

"*Rori.*" Lazarus cleared his throat. "What was the poison?"

"I'll never forget. The main ingredient was gray holland. It was used in Mother Tryphaena's nightwalker poison."

Adeska lost her breath. "*Nightwalker?*"

The library grew quiet except for Lazarus's heavy breathing as he rubbed his face in thought. Adeska wanted to shout something but couldn't find words. Rori rubbed her eyes.

"You remember that night, Adeska." Lazarus glanced at her. "The night she woke up. It makes sense."

"How? I don't understand how it could have happened! To two little kids!"

"We weren't there. We can't possibly understand how, but at least we finally know *what*."

Rori swallowed hard. "I'm not done. Rhett found me at my shed last night, and we had an argument, something stupid about the things we had done back then. I woke up this morning and went back out. I was looking for a tea recipe, but there was a page torn out of my notebook." She took another deep breath. The pain in her chest persisted. "The page with the poison. I know Rhett took it. I know it was him."

"Rori, we know how he is," Adeska said. "But he would never—"

"Yes he would!" Lazarus cut her off. "I know you only want to think the best about him, Adeska, that it's somehow easier that way, but it's time we wake up about this, about *him*! I know him better than all of you. I had to leave all of you just so I could take him someplace away from Tizzy! To protect her from him! We all know what kind of person he is, and we all know he is not above taking that poison formula. We should be worried about what he's going to do with it."

"What should we do?" Rori asked.

Lazarus leaned back into his chair, thinking, and Adeska started to pace. She rubbed her arms.

"Lora. Maybe Lora can find him!"

"Rhett's dangerous, Adeska."

"So is Lora! Maybe she can find him and see what he's doing, and maybe she can even stop him!"

He grumbled. "It should be one of us. It's our problem. We shouldn't go dragging her into it, but I don't have a better idea. Maybe she's the best one for the job."

Rori didn't want to say anything since the Besqi woman had caught her bringing Alor into the manor, but she had high hopes for the plan. "Will we tell Allanis about all of this?"

"Yes. We'll fill her in when she gets back," Adeska answered. "I guess we might as well tell Athen too. No reason why we should leave him in the dark. We saw how upset he got."

"Might as well," Lazarus echoed.

A question hung in the air, the one Rori was afraid to ask. The important one.

"What are they? What are nightwalkers? They're bloodkin like vampires, right?"

No one answered, though Lazarus looked like he was searching for words. Adeska bit her lip, and they could see pain twist into her face, and her eyes finally well up.

"I've killed nightwalkers. I know nothing about them except that they're bloodkin. They're Forbidden. And I killed them during the raids. I made no distinction between them and the daemons and the other foul things I fought." Her throat burned as she held the tears in.

"Any one of them could have been—could have been *Aleth*—and in the heat of the moment, I wouldn't have even known. It's a wonder he survived us."

"You and your friends were not some infallible force for good, Adeska." Lazarus stared a hole right through her. "You've done great things at terrible costs. And sometimes, you've just done terrible things."

Rori huffed. "We all have, including you, Lazarus. So let's go to the next step and quit pointing fingers. If we're all going to make it through this, things have to change. We have to change."

"Alright." Adeska gathered herself and stood straight. "Let's get Lora and make a plan."

CHAPTER 11

THE CONVENT

Late in the afternoon, a light drizzle had fallen over the forest. Tizzy, Aleth, and the others had spent much of the journey from the river in quiet contemplation. Tizzy didn't mind it at all. It was too much work trying to converse with new people, and she was in no mood after their debacle with the ley line. But after hours of walking, Aleth finally broke the silence.

"There it is. The Convent."

Tizzy surveyed the land. Except for a sharp plateau in front of them, there was nothing to see.

"It's a mountain. I don't understand."

Talora stood next to her and stared up proudly. "You're looking at the highest vantage point in the region. The Convent is at the top, safe and sound!"

"So now we have to climb a mountain."

"You can if you want," Aleth told her. "I'm not. Come on, I'll show you the easy way."

She followed him and the others around the plateau, seeing a line of smaller plateaus pepper the land in the distance. A creek ran, branching off from another river somewhere, and terminated at one face of the plateau, covering the side with moss and algae. Aleth led her to a cavernous opening.

The creek fed into an underground river. Tizzy looked up and saw a whole world built into the side of a cavern. A rough stairway fashioned out of dirt, stone, and wood spiraled along the walls, stopping off at wooden doors along the way, ending at one massive iron-studded door at the top.

"This is incredible." She stood by the river in awe.

Aleth grinned. "Stick your hand in."

She was skeptical, but no one challenged him, so she did as she was instructed. "It's not even cold!"

"It doesn't make it any more enjoyable to be pushed into," Talora said bitterly, glaring at him.

He led them up the steps. "The worst part was that after you climbed out, you tried so hard to push me in!"

"I'll make us even someday."

They progressed up the cavern, and darkness took over. Eidi conjured a bright white orb in her hands to light the way, and Tizzy watched the cavern walls glitter with crystal formations. Maybe she would love it here. They climbed on, passing the other doors. She wanted to ask about them, but Aleth, Eidi, and Talora were already deep in conversation.

The final door waited for them at the top. Tizzy looked down and suddenly realized what a deadly drop it would be. Aleth saw her and grabbed her hand.

"We've got you. I've fallen before. Twice."

"Are you at least a little more careful now?"

"Yeah, *now*."

Talora pushed open the heavy door, showing them into an antechamber. Hazy sunlight crawled in from cracks between the next door ahead of them, and Tizzy rushed over to push it open herself. The others followed her out into tall, dewy grass.

"What do you think?" Eidi asked.

"I love it." She'd never felt so close to the sky before. "Half of this place is the cave, and the rest is up here?"

"Yes!" The banshee floated past her. "Though the additions you saw in the cave weren't there when we started." There was a short walkway just a few paces from the antechamber that led to the actual Convent. Tizzy stared ahead at a run-down brick abbey with a statue of the Death Goddess, Botathora, that was in shambles. The top of her scythe was broken off, and the features of the skeletal face beneath the goddess's shroud were eroded. Beyond the walkway, the plateau was covered in lush vegetation and tall evergreens.

"This place was plenty big enough back when the Convent first started," Eidi told her. "But over time, Louvita and Ziaul needed more room, so they dug out extra space below. They decided to leave the abbey run-down like this to keep anyone from suspecting we were here, not that they'll ever see it this high up."

Tizzy made a noise of vague interest while following the walkway to the entrance. She helped Talora push open the doors and was welcomed by must and soft candlelight. Tattered rugs in different colors and patterns covered the stone floor. Dim light came in through slits in the walls. Beyond the entrance was a staircase and more hallways.

Talora turned to her and Aleth with a nervous smile. "We're all going to wander off while you take care of this. Good luck, Aleth."

"Great." He chewed his lip and looked away.

"Wait, what does she mean 'good luck'? What the hell is that for?"

Talora waved, and the others followed her away.

"Don't worry about it."

"Well now I'm especially worried about it."

"Just—" He sighed and put his hands up. "Don't worry about me. Whatever happens, they're going to want to talk to you about all of this, and I need you to *not* worry about me. In fact, while you're with them, just forget I exist entirely. Do you hear me?"

"I hear you."

"Are you going to listen?"

"We'll see."

"Tizzy, please! This is important!"

She put her finger in his face and glowered. "Look, I don't know how things are here! And I don't know *why* they work the way they do, and it makes me nervous, okay? The only thing I have to give me peace of mind going into this is knowing that these people want me here. Badly. So if they want me to stay, things are going to go my way. Because you were right about me."

He rolled his eyes. "Which part, specifically, was I right about?"

"I need control. And I'm going to get it."

"Just keep what I said in mind, okay? You don't exactly have these people in the palm of your hand yet."

"Aleth, you're back!"

A woman interrupted them, swaying her hips as she stepped down the stairs. Tizzy could tell by the shape of her ears that she was an elf, but beyond that, she could guess nothing. She was frail and willowy, like she could snap at any second under the weight of her long, bushy white hair. Her skin was the color of a purple bruise, blue veins visible wherever thin skin was exposed. Her cheekbones jutted from her small, gaunt face, and her black eyes were shaped like a cat's. They were locked onto the siblings with an ominous glimmer.

"Yes, Louvita. We're back." Aleth didn't look at her.

"Wonderful. Tizena, is it?"

"Tizzy." She fought the urge to narrow her eyes.

"Tizzy!" The elf tried it on for size. "I'm Louvita. We are so glad to have you." She smiled warmly with thin, blue lips, but then her tone turned harsh. "Aleth, leave."

"Yep."

"No, he stays with me!"

He drew in a sharp breath and turned away.

"Tizzy." Louvita folded her hands across her stomach. "There are private matters we need to discuss."

"That's fine, but he stays with me."

By now, Aleth was starting to walk off. "Forget it, Tizzy. It's fine."

Louvita was pleased. "Now then, let's go somewhere to talk."

Tizzy watched him grow farther and farther away. "I don't understand what just happened." Fury was growing in her chest, and her face was hot. She knew the woman was picking up on it. "Why can't he be a part of this?"

"How can I put this delicately? There's a hierarchy here, my lady. We don't make the rules; they make themselves. That's just how it is."

"Don't call me *my lady*. That is not who I am. It never has been."

Louvita clenched her jaw for only a second. "Very well. Tizzy, follow me. Normally, Ziaul would be a part of this process as well, but he's away to tend to some other matters. That means it's just you and me!"

She rolled her eyes as she walked behind the woman. They went up a set of stairs and down a long hallway and then up another set of stairs that creaked louder than anything she'd ever heard. Dust covered everything.

"This place is massive." All of the walking she had done in the past few days was catching up to her. Her body ached.

"There used to be a lot more people staying here," Louvita said. "Both as the Botathoran Abbey it was originally and as the Convent. The last few years were rough on our numbers, though, sadly."

There was one final staircase, narrower and darker than the others. There was a hallway with a standing clock and a door that led to the most beautiful room she'd ever seen. It was a bedroom fit for a queen with a four-poster bed and linens in yellow and mint. An enormous cherry wood wardrobe was against a wall, joined by a mannequin, a vanity, and a chaise. One whole wall had curtained archways leading directly onto a balcony.

Louvita beckoned for her to sit with her at a desk. "I don't know what Aleth has already told you," she said. "But I'm here to fill in the gaps. I'm sure you have questions."

"My questions are less about what I'm doing here and more about your motives." She sat with folded arms. "No point in denying it. What are you, anyway?"

"I'm a Mire Elf. I come all the way from the Alevan Wastes."

"The north fucking pole?"

"It took me a hundred years to wind up here in the southern hemisphere. But I'm still young. There's a lot ahead of me, and I need you to help me make sure I get to see it. We all do."

Tizzy crossed her legs. "Well, Aleth is the one who can turn into a dog, not me."

Louvita chuckled. "You'll be able to do much more than that, Tizzy. Your potential is staggering. We only need you to realize it."

She stood back up. "No. Something is not adding up here. I met Lilu. She's plenty strong enough for whatever issues you guys are going through. You can't possibly need me."

"You're right. Lilu is strong. She's one of the fiercest, most capable people here. When the time comes, a lot will fall on her shoulders. Yours too. You are the direct descendent of the Nightwalker Father."

"That's what I've heard, and I have no idea what it means for me."

Louvita rose to her feet, taking her time. There was a sly grin on her face. "It means you could be invincible if you chose to cultivate that potential," she said into Tizzy's ear. "No one else alive holds so many possibilities the way you do now."

"Is the most powerful nightwalker even still comparable to a Greater Daemon? That seems unlikely."

"They are *certainly*." Louvita wandered around the room. "This Realm, the Mortal Realm, is still your home, after all. It doesn't matter how much power a Greater Daemon has. They still do not belong here, and their true name is their biggest weakness. And vampires—goodness, don't get me started. The old ones may be powerful, and their growth is sharper than a nightwalker's, but their abilities aren't as varied, and they are *so very* susceptible to their weaknesses.

"What makes a nightwalker so interesting is their mystery. Your abilities could be anything! We won't know until you acquire them. They could be worthless, they could be earth-shattering, they could mutate you. And the best part of all is that no one really knows how to kill you."

"Just wait about fifty years."

"Tizzy, I don't think you understand what you are. You're practically immortal. Well, you will be. You have to be able to heal faster than a wound can kill you, so avoid fatal encounters until you've grown into yourself a bit if you can help it. But dying old is a thing of the past. There is so little known about what hurts your kind. So far, we know decapitation works, but that'll kill just about anything. Honestly, any weaknesses that are known beyond that are Aleth's fault."

"Excuse me?"

Louvita came to the yellow curtains and parted them to look at the landscape below. "That's not fair of me, I suppose. He was a boy under the care of someone else at the time. A man named Torah, another nightwalker. Quite an accomplished one, at that. They were in the forest and were cornered by Hunters. Torah ditched your brother so he could escape."

"*What?*"

"I assume the Hunters had quite a few theories they wanted to test, judging by the shape Aleth was in when Talora and Ilisha went after him. He was still alive though, clearly."

"Is that why you treat him the way you do?" Tizzy's voice was shaking. "Because that's got to change."

"That has nothing to do with it." Louvita folded her arms. "And you should worry about yourself. You have things to focus on, and so does he."

Tizzy wasn't satisfied with Louvita's answer at all. The hair on the back of her neck stood, but she ignored it and pressed on.

"I should have asked him or even Tal about it, but I'm here now, and I guess you're as good as anyone else. If I can be immortal, as you say, how will I age? In all the old stories, you hear about bloodkin staying the same age they were when they were turned. But I was a *child*. Look at me now!"

"Those old stories are about vampires," Louvita said dryly. "You should get used to that from now on. *Your* people stick to the shadows and are barely known of. You'll all age until you reach a peak, and it's different for everyone. We used to have a nightwalker here who was eighty years old but hadn't aged past sixteen. Talora seems to have stopped at about forty. You'll just have to wait and see for yourself."

In the days leading up to this, she'd had a seemingly infinite amount of questions, but her head was a fog now that she finally had access to the answers. She stared down at her hands, struggling between wonder and anger.

"How did you know it was me?" she asked. "That I was the one turned by the Father?"

She could see Louvita's smile even from where she stood. It was not a friendly one. "Talora. She can get into your head real good, can't she? It was a lot harder for her to get into Aleth's, but we knew he had the answers. She got them, eventually."

"He tried to protect me from you." She felt sick.

"A futile effort, as here you are."

Tizzy clenched her fists. She wasn't sure how much longer she could keep herself from doing something stupid. "And what am *I* supposed to be protecting all of *you* from?"

Louvita turned to face her, a frown on her lips but a smile in her eyes. "Our common enemy. The Hunters in Vandroya are after each and every one of us."

"And you really can't defend yourselves? They're just *people*. Their weapons and magic are completely ineffective against most of you!"

"You don't know the first thing about the Hunters, do you?"

Louvita's words struck her. Up until then, she expected them to be like Adeska and her raiding party, and it had taken twelve of them to take down a single Greater Daemon.

"No. I don't."

"Did your brother tell you that they're coming for your family?"

The question invigorated her. It was the opening she had been waiting for. "What? No!"

Her anger shifted, evolved into something more. The smugness inside of her felt ugly but good. It wasn't even difficult to keep a convincing expression as she began her game.

"I'm not surprised," Louvita said airily. "He's probably keeping a lot of things from you. We were able to intercept a message from Vandroya to Duke Orin of Davrkton about it. It didn't say very much—there only seems to be a faint suspicion—but it is the *Hunters*, specifically, that have interest. Granted, they almost run Vandroya, but as far as we can tell, the king is not invested. We don't know if they're just after Aleth, or if they know about you, too, but mobilizing the Hunters for Aleth would be—" She searched for the word, running her tongue along the inside of her cheek "A waste of resources? An overreaction? Pointless?"

The Convent didn't seem to know about the other Forbidden things lurking in her family with Lazarus and Rhett. That was a relief, Tizzy thought. "Davrkton is in on this?"

"Well the duke has been sworn to Vandroya for almost a decade, now."

"No, the duke has been sworn to *Saunterton* for almost a decade."

Both women looked shocked. Louvita laced her fingers together. "Oh dear. I'm afraid he's been serving King Mabus behind Queen Anavelia's back this whole time. Perhaps I should care more for current events."

"Interesting. Alright, Lou—can I call you Lou?"

"I prefer Louvita, but whatever makes you happy."

"Lou! Great! Tell me something. How am I supposed to protect you from the Hunters? I have no abilities. I don't think you understand how unprepared I am for this."

"I'm glad you finally asked! I need you to keep this a secret from your brother, but Ziaul is on his way back with a bloodslave for you.

He had to travel all the way to the Western Peninsula to find the nomads with the condition, but he was successful."

Tizzy sat back down. "Bloodslave. There's a lot in a name. Is that what I think it is?"

She smirked. "There are people from this tribe of nomads I mentioned who are cursed. It's like they build up too much blood in their bodies. The only way to relieve the pain and maladies is by bloodletting. I'm sure you can make the connection from there. They form a symbiotic relationship of mutual benefit with bloodkin, and you're going to have your very own because you will only grow if you feed on blood."

"You have a lot of faith in me."

"For now," Louvita said, inspecting her nails. "And by the way? You should stay away from him." She tilted her head, gesturing to the Convent outside the door.

Tizzy narrowed her eyes. "Stay away from Aleth? My brother? This had better be good."

"It's a shame, you know. You were made by the Father, and he was made by a *nobody*."

Tizzy tucked a black curl behind her ear and cleared her throat. "He was?"

"He didn't tell you? Ironic, isn't it? You both become nightwalkers, but you are a legend, and him—" She stopped and sighed, a pretty noise. "Well, he runs away from home and gets turned by some lowlife who finds him in the woods. His maker isn't even alive anymore."

Tizzy frowned quickly to hide the grin that threatened her face. "I had no idea. That's sad, really. I feel bad for him."

"We mind the hierarchy here. It's important. It's kept us in order since the beginning," Louvita explained. "It would be best if you adopted the practice now. Your brother is nothing but the dirt beneath us, I'm sorry to say it. That's just the way it is."

"I get the feeling Lilu's pretty high up on the hierarchy. Does she understand where I sit, or does she just not care? The way she introduced herself to me could have used some work."

"You'll have to excuse Lilu," Louvita said. "She has a habit of throwing her weight around, so to speak. She'll antagonize anyone. Even if it wasn't in her nature, if she was just a regular *mortal*, she'd probably still be this way. She likes to make sure no one forgets what she's capable of, and for some reason, she's got this obsession with your brother. I'm sure he's done something to deserve it."

"Lilu almost fucking killed me."

Louvita's little smile would have been darling on anyone else. "It was quite the learning experience, I'll bet." She made her way to the door. "We'll be talking again soon, Tizzy. In the meantime, feel free to get acquainted with the Convent. Ziaul is still a few days out. And before I forget, this room is yours."

"Wait! Lou, I-I have another question. One more."

The woman locked eyes with her, and for a split second, Tizzy thought she saw something genuine about her.

"Yes? What is it?"

"Why me? And not the Father himself? If he's the one who gave me all of this, wouldn't he be your best hope?"

All she could do was shrug. "If he were easy to find, Tizzy, he'd be here."

She left after that, and Tizzy was numb. She looked around and swallowed the sickness crawling up her body.

"This is going to go horribly, horribly wrong."

She didn't think she could process everything she had just been told; the words bounced around her head for a long, long time. So long, she lost track of how long she'd been in the room lost in thought until the uncomfortable sensation that had crept in during her meeting with Louvita finally left. She breathed a sigh of relief and walked out.

There was a lot to see in the abbey as she descended, but none of it caught her immediate interest. She was in the clear for the moment, leaving her with only one thing on her mind. One goal. It was time. Through the windows and archways, she could see dark clouds on the horizon like the world was trying to tell her something. She tore through the building with abandon. The abbey was a maze of new faces, but before long, she saw one that she knew. Talora was in a hallway leading to a courtyard. She took one look at Tizzy's face and shied away.

"Look at me!" Tizzy yelled. "You know why I'm here!"

"I can't read your mind when you're awake! That's not how it works!" Talora's laughter was weak in her attempt to lighten the mood. Tizzy shoved her, and she whimpered.

"Who knows?"

"Who knows *what*?"

Tizzy grabbed her shoulders and pulled the woman close with a heated glare. "I just had a chat with my new friend Lou. Guess what? She thinks that Aleth—"

"Oh! That!"

"Yeah." She let Talora go free. "I don't know what you guys are doing because nobody ever wants to say anything until it's already a disaster! If that's how you guys want to do things, *fine*. But tell me who else knows the truth."

"It's just me and Eidi. And Aleth, of course. He didn't want Louvita to know, so I played along. I thought it was the least I could do after ripping through his mind to get to the information in the first place."

"Why does Eidi know?"

Talora's eyes were wide with confusion. "Why wouldn't she? Eidi knows everything."

"Why? Did you tell her?"

"Yes, of course I did. She's my friend. I trust her. Besides—" She smiled nervously. "She'd do anything for Aleth."

Tizzy crossed her arms. "There's a distinct line between *anything for* and *anything to have*. Make sure she stays on the correct side of it."

"Tizzy, please! Eidi isn't like that!"

"Where's Aleth?"

She hesitated.

"*Now* what's the problem?"

"It's just—" Talora fidgeted with the hem on her veil. "Tizzy, he should be left alone right now. He really should."

"Well I'm not going to do that. Where is he?"

She grunted. "I really wish you'd listen to someone for once. He's in his room. It's in the cavern."

Without a word, Tizzy left and wandered the abbey until she found the antechamber leading back into the cavern. The hair on the back of her neck stood again as she pried open the door. This was the second time she'd felt this prickle. It was beginning to paint a picture.

She shut the door behind her and pretended not to notice.

When she was back in the cavern, she realized that Eidi was no longer lighting the way. It was pitch black, save for the faintest touch of muted daylight at the mouth down below. Tizzy traversed slowly, one hand brushing the crystal-laden wall and the other hand out into the nothingness beside her. Her boots found one step at a time. She strained her eyes staring at the ground, but soon they adjusted to the low light.

They adjusted *too well*, Tizzy thought. It wasn't as clear as a sunny afternoon, but the walk no longer felt dangerous. She quickened her pace until she came to the first door. It didn't fit right in its frame, but with a little shove, she got it open and shut it behind her.

It was time.

The room inside had been carved out of the ore-streaked earth and left unfinished. It was warm, outfitted with four tiny beds and a hearth that was lit—at least Louvita and Ziaul had seen it fit to dig out ventilation. Aleth sat on one of the beds closest to the fire, staring into the flames with an open bottle in his hand.

He took a long drink when she came into the room and didn't look back at her.

"Get out."

"No."

She felt a little cold and came over to the hearth. She could feel his glare on her back.

"Is this your shit?" She turned and drummed her fingers on the trunk. "Come on, let's get it upstairs. You're moving in with me! I'll even give you half my stuff."

"Get out!" he yelled.

She hurt, listening to the bitterness he aimed at her. It hurt to even look at him, but she did. She glared and found her footing.

"What is your problem? I'm sorry that you feel like brooding, but I'm in a new place surrounded by new people who I don't like, and the last thing I'm okay with is being alone! So snap out of it!"

His jaw tensed up as he debated yelling back, but all he did was glower at her and take another drink. That was when she saw something in his eyes.

"Hey, wait a minute." She studied them, recalling a time when he'd done the same thing to her. She remembered the frigid rain pouring down in the Bogwood, the mud on her face, and him staring into the red in her eyes. "How long has it been since you've fed?"

Slowly, calmly, he answered her.

"A very long time."

"Have you been fighting your impulses? *Why*? And is it a good idea to be drinking right now?"

"Why do you think I told you to get out?"

"You have a million reasons for telling me to get out. But there's one reason in particular that I'm here for, so you'd better get your head straight."

The stubborn part of her, which was also the stupid part, was not leaving without what she came for. But there was also the sensation at the back of her neck she was worried about, and it was more intense now than ever. As terrible as her plan was, she hoped it would fix both problems.

"That's what this is about?" Aleth asked. "You're here to nag me about my feelings?"

"Yeah! Quit being an asshole and get on with it! You know exactly what I'm asking about!"

He chewed his lip. "Did you ever wonder if maybe the reason I was so upset was because sooner or later you were going to sit down with Louvita? And listen to her try and convince you of how worthless I am? That maybe I was afraid of you buying it and turning into just another person here who treats me like shit?"

"How dare you!"

"Tizzy—" He sighed and rubbed his brow, knowing full well he wasn't going to get a word in.

"You think that little of me, that I'd just turn on you? Just because of what some purple bitch has to say? I kept your stupid secret for you, by the way! She still thinks you're worthless!"

"Between Allanis's party and getting you here, I didn't think we had anything good left! I thought everything we used to have died! I was wrong. I never thought I would ever have this with you again, so when I *did*, I got scared of putting it in Louvita's hands for her to destroy."

"You're stupid!" Suddenly she wanted to cry. This was not going as planned. It hurt more than it was supposed to. "You're stupid for not feeding, you're stupid for holding something back from me, and you're stupid for thinking that I would ever be *anything* less than loyal and possessive over you!"

He almost smiled but stopped, letting her have her frustration for however long she needed it. She shoved the inside of her wrist in his face.

"Do it."

"Get it away from me."

Her heart was beating too fast. "What, is mine not good enough for you?"

"Obviously it is. It fucking made me, but I am not feeding from you!"

"Yes, you are."

It was working. The anger was bringing out the red in his eyes.

"No, Tizzy, not everything gets to happen the way you want it to! I am not taking your blood!"

She traced a finger down the vein. "Look how well it stands out. It's nice, isn't it? Sooner or later, those headaches are going to be too much for you."

"I don't get the headaches."

She looked down at him and felt cold again. "No?"

"No. I just get mean."

Leaving sounded like a good idea for a split second before the stubborn part of her took the lead.

"Oh, you do? Somehow I doubt you're better at it than me."

"Tizzy, I don't want your blood. Get the fuck out."

"That was rude, but I still think I'm going to win this round."

She shoved him. But then he stood, and she felt dwarfed. A small part of her was willing to accept that she had made a poor decision, but at least something was going according to plan.

"How mean are you going to get now?" she taunted. "Because so far, I'm not impressed." Yet she was backing away from him as he neared.

"You should have left." He was disappointed.

"No! We have to talk! This is not going to wait anymore! And if I've got to fix this first, then so be it!"

"There is nothing to fix!" He said it through clenched teeth as he picked her up and slammed her against the dirt wall. "Fighting down my impulses is my choice!"

"It's stupid! I'm right here!" She grabbed at his arm and tried to pry him off, but he was much stronger. "Gods, what is the problem? Quit doing this to yourself!"

He slammed her again, and her head and back lit up with pain. He dropped her.

"Shit, what am I doing? Tizzy, *please*. You have to go."

Now there was no stubbornness or fear or logic left. Now she was just angry. Before rational thought could stop her, she punched him in the jaw and saw the impulse take him over fully.

Then, finally, the strange presence that had been making her hair stand on end went away.

She cursed and slid into a fighting stance. "None of this would have happened if you would have just fed!"

But there was bloodlust in him now, and he was too quick and too strong for her to fight off. He was on her in a second, twisting her head around to expose her neck. He paused, and she could feel his breath.

"It's okay. Just do it." She winced as he tightened his grasp in her hair.

"Stop saying that."

"Why? It's fair!"

He looked up to keep himself from staring at the vein in her neck. "No. Not like this."

"What? Do you want to have a fucking picnic, then?"

A response caught in his throat, and he went quiet. She started to writhe around in his hold, but he didn't let go. Then he stifled a laugh.

"Seriously?" She turned around and raised an eyebrow.

He released her, trying to bury the last of the impulse in a deep breath. "Fuck you." The words had never felt more freeing. He put his arms around her, and she relaxed into his embrace.

The room was quiet. Soft. They stayed still, staring at the hearth ahead, hearing only the cracking flames and their own breathing. Finally, Tizzy spoke.

"I thought you hated my jokes."

"I have never hated your jokes." He was afraid to let go. "I don't hate anything about you, even if you're annoying. I want you to know that."

She smiled. "That's good because if you've been acting like you hate me lately, I've been completely oblivious."

He made his way back to the hearth and sat against the trunk, picking the bottle back up and trying to calm his nerves again. She joined him. It felt strange to witness a bad habit he'd picked up in the years without her, and for a moment, he seemed foreign.

"Sorry I picked a fight with you," she said. "But we're in the clear now. Eidi isn't watching us anymore."

"Eidi was watching us? Wait, you did all of that on *purpose*?"

She rolled her eyes and took the bottle from him. When she took a sip, she gagged. "What is this? It's awful!"

He took it back with a grin. "It's in my budget. I thought it might be strong enough to get a starved nightwalker drunk."

"Is it working?"

He shook his head while gulping it down like water. "Not even a little. How could you tell Eidi was here?"

"Ever since the incident with the Helamine Stone, I can feel her. I know it's her, and I'm pretty sure she's only watching to report back to Louvita. She's got too much of an upper hand not to be playing sides. Why else would she sneak around, right?"

"And you wanted her to see us fighting?"

"Yeah. If Louvita doesn't want us to get along, I'm going to make her believe we aren't getting along."

"You're weaving a dangerous web."

"Don't worry! If there's anything I am only barely skilled at, it's weaving a dangerous web."

Unconvinced, he kept drinking. A silence started to grow between them, and she knew she had to keep pushing.

"Aleth, it's time."

"Time for what?"

She knew he was holding something back. He had been since the beginning. "You know what I'm asking you to say."

"Gods, will you just get off that already?"

"No! You need to tell me what's been bothering you! *Say it!*"

He stared into the fire and rubbed his brow. "Tizzy, I can't."

"You can tell me anything!"

"*No*, I can't." He looked at her with a brittle smile and shook his head. "I can't. I just can't, and I can't make you understand." There weren't enough words to tell her how much it even hurt to say that much.

"That's bullshit, and you know it." She took the bottle and started to chug.

"What are you doing?"

"You can't get drunk. But I bet I still can!"

"Why do you do things like this? Why do you go so far out of your way to be completely intolerable?"

"I'm much less difficult when I get what I want!"

"I am not letting you manipulate me!" he yelled. "So have fun sitting here, drunk and alone, speculating about shit that doesn't matter!"

He stood up, and she panicked and reached for him.

"Aleth, wait!"

He stared down at her, and she could see the knife she was pushing through his chest. It was now or never.

"Please," she said. "I-I'm not asking because I need an answer. Aleth, I know the answer. All I want is to hear you say it."

He shook his head and swallowed hard. "If you really knew, you wouldn't make me say it. You wouldn't put me through this! You would let me be and let me keep ignoring it because it's the way it has to be."

"I can't believe you think I would be that thoughtful! That doesn't sound like me at all." When she stood up, the room spun, and her stomach turned. He steadied her and threw the bottle down.

"You're a fucking mess."

She scoffed. "*You're* a fucking mess!"

She pointed at his face, and he moved her hand away and pressed his lips into hers. It was short. She tried to draw it out, but he pulled back. He couldn't even look at her, but there she was, looking up at him, her hands gently at his waist. His voice broke.

"How long have you known?"

"Aleth, I've always known, as far back as I can remember. I've always known."

"Why did you want this? Why aren't you horrified? This is wrong."

"This is hardly the most wrong thing about us anymore."

"Yes! It is!" He turned away and pulled at his hair. "This isn't happening. What the hell have I done?"

She walked around to him and grabbed his shoulders. "We're wrong no matter what!" She shook him. "We're nightwalkers! Our entire existence is wrong! This doesn't matter!" She stood as tall as she could on the tips of her toes and kissed him again, something delicate but hungry. "It doesn't *matter*. This is how it was always supposed to be; we've both known that."

His hands trembled as he caressed her cheek. He wanted so badly to believe her. "I can't do this."

"You just need a little momentum."

When she met his lips again, he didn't push her away, but he was afraid to touch her. She leaned into him, pressing her body into his until he started to kiss her back. His movements were hesitant but curious. She never imagined his lips on hers would be so warm and soft. He drew each kiss out longer and longer, passion starting to dissolve the fear, until she pulled away and grazed her teeth down his neck. He pried her off.

"What are you doing?"

She looked up, her eyes full of mischief. "Will you feed from me *now*?" She wrapped her arms around him.

"None of this should be happening."

"But it is happening." She shrugged. "And I hope it never goes back to the way it was."

They sat down by the hearth, and he went against every sane thought in his head. He locked onto her lips long and slow, his heart beating so fast he was faint. And then he broke away and bit into her neck.

She cried out. It hurt so much more than it did when she played it out in her mind. He pulled back and wiped his mouth.

"You drank a *lot*."

She started to laugh, feeling the blood trickle down her neck. "You said you wanted to get drunk."

It hit him—she'd planned the whole thing. Something in him hurt as he returned to the wound, but then she was running her fingers through his hair, and he didn't care anymore. He drank, and when she couldn't take any more blood loss, she guided him back to her lips. She could taste her own blood.

"The room is spinning," she said.

"It is."

They leaned back against the trunk. As soon as her head found his shoulder, she fell into sleep.

CHAPTER 12

GENESIS

It was late. Deep blue had enveloped the sky, and stars were glimmering over Suradia. Tizzy was in the orchard by House Hallenar. Dead leaves littered the ground, but when she moved forward, she couldn't feel them. In true dream fashion, she wasn't really there.

"This had *better* be a dream," she grumbled. "If it's Tal again, she and I are going to have words." An almost ripe pomegranate fell to the ground, and she sighed. "Alright, why am I here?"

She tried to remember what had happened leading up to her slumber, but her mind was a fog. She headed for the outer edge of the orchard.

"If there was something I was supposed to see inside, I assume I'd have shown up inside. Is that how this works?"

There was a tree nearby, a large and old tree that didn't look like others in Mirivin. Its trunk was enormous, with smooth, gray bark. Some nights when she had snuck out to see it, the shadows from the moonlight made the trunk look like giant pythons from the rainforests in her books, all slithering up into the canopy. Some people tried to say it was just an Ancient Oak and nothing more, but Tizzy knew better. Late King Frankel and previous generations of Bylands had called the tree Genesis.

It waited at the orchard's edge, along a short wall of piled stone and a small pond that Frankel had commissioned early in his rule. And tonight, there was light from a lantern. Tizzy kept her distance, hiding behind a dormant peach tree.

Lambent light played on Adeska's face as she sat at the pond's edge, gazing over the waning moon's reflection. She clutched her thick shawl as a breeze picked up. Even from afar, Tizzy could see the forlorn look on her face and the droop in her shoulders. She moved in closer behind another tree.

Adeska sniffled and wiped her nose. A leaf fell onto the pond's surface, sending ripples through the reflection.

"Viaeuro, Mother in the Moon, Guardian in the Stars, Daughter of Time and Death—" She paused for a deep breath. "Please send me guidance." A small hiccup marked the end of her words. Tizzy wondered how long she had been crying. "I know in the past I've ignored you. I've gone my own way despite the answers you've given me, and I have paid the price of each mistake. But now I'm lost, and it's different." Silence stretched for minutes and minutes. No animals made a sound for her, and the breeze died in the autumn leaves.

"All this time, I thought I could fix things. I thought my solutions and my solutions alone were the ones that would fix the world! Conceited of me, isn't it?" Her voice trembled. "To think that I'm the one that always knows the way. And when I don't, I ask the gods, and I don't even listen to them. I deserve every problem that's found me—" She wet her lips. "But now they've become other people's problems. I need to do something about what I've done. Where do I start?"

It was still quiet. Was her goddess finally abandoning her? Fresh anguish started to well up in her eyes, and then she heard a voice from afar. Tizzy heard it too.

"Adeska? Are you out here?"

She could see another lantern light between the fruit trees.

"Athen?"

"What are you doing out here? It's freezing!"

The baby brother closed the distance at last, sporting a thick wool blanket. He set the lantern down beside Genesis, and Adeska hugged him.

"I just needed a little bit of time alone to think," she said.

"I can understand that." Athen picked up a pebble and tossed it into the pond. The ripples obscured the moon's reflection. "These past few days, there's been more people in House Hallenar than there usually is all year. I forgot how suffocating it feels."

Adeska found the strength to laugh and sat between Genesis's roots. "That's a good word for it. What brought you out here?"

He sat at the edge of the pond, looked up into the treetop, and sighed. "I'm just confused. I thought I'd be able to sort it all out if I came here."

"This mess that's going on?"

"Not so much that stuff. *Yes*, it's confusing too, but that doesn't surprise me. It's supposed to be confusing."

"What exactly are you hung up on, Athen?"

It took him a moment to find his words. "It's just—you know, the day before the party I was so mad at her. Even the morning of the party, I was frustrated with her. And that's not new! I'm always frustrated with her, one way or another!"

"Who? Tizzy?"

Tizzy rolled her eyes.

"Yeah. But then I tore into Rhett when he said those things, and I tore into all of you for not telling me she was gone. I genuinely got worried. I still am, and it's got me thinking how I never really got to know her despite seeing her every single day of my life."

"You keep thinking that there's more to her, that if you just crack that shell, you'll get to see the Real Tizzy. Athen, who you knew *was* the real Tizzy."

"Was she always like that?" he asked. "I don't remember how she was before the accident."

Adeska threw her head back with a smile and a sigh. "Oh boy, before the accident." She laughed. "That girl was a hurricane. Lazarus and I aren't surprised to see that she grew up hard and jaded. No matter how much she was forced to see the world a certain way, she saw it differently, sometimes purely out of spite. She knew what was real before anyone else did.

"She was born early, you know. Almost too early. Mother said Tizzy waited for no one! Not only that, but as a little girl, she was unstoppable. She was always getting into trouble. *Always*. Everything had to be tested. Poor Aleth didn't have a mischievous bone in his body, but he followed her everywhere, getting sucked up into her whirlwind of chaos. When they were together, she was fairly cooperative after causing her mayhem. But alone? She was the brattiest, most defiant child you could imagine!"

"Oh please! That's not accurate at all!" Tizzy shouted. "Why are dreams so damn self-reflective?"

Athen and Adeska froze. Tizzy froze too.

"Who's there?" Adeska asked. They looked in her direction.

"You guys can hear me?"

"Tizzy, is that you?" Adeska scrambled to her feet.

Tizzy emerged from behind a tree and approached them. Adeska gasped.

"Oh my gods! It *is* you! You're home!"

Athen scratched his head. "Adeska, she looks transparent."

Tizzy inspected herself. From her end, she seemed perfectly solid. "This is new. Really new."

"I think you're Ethereal!" Adeska sputtered and started walking back to House Hallenar. "I can get you back to this Realm, hold on, I just need—"

"No!" Tizzy waved her arms. "No, don't do that! It's fine. You're hallucinating. This isn't real. And I'm fine! We're fine! Nobody panic!"

***

VAYVEN 2, 1144

She woke with a start. She was still slouched against Aleth, who was deep asleep, slumped over with his head resting on the trunk. She started to recall the previous events and shivered. With stiff joints, she crawled away and got to her feet. Her head was pounding.

"Ugh, what was this stuff?" She picked up the empty bottle.

"Anise and rye whiskey." Aleth started to stir. "It's everywhere in Yzen Vale. Costs a handful of silver." He tried to stand, then groaned and sat back down.

"That bad, huh?"

"Guess your idea worked."

The thought of it caused a flair of pain in her neck. It was bruised. "Gods, you've got an iron jaw."

"Tizzy, I'm sorry. About everything. I don't know what the hell I was thinking."

"Come on," she said, grabbing his arm. "Let's get some fresh air."

"Why are you still talking to me?"

"I guess I feel bad for punching you in the face."

Her sarcasm was a slight relief. He followed her down to the bottom of the cavern, fighting nausea and a dull headache. The morning light was pale and gray, accompanied by a gentle rain. Aleth tilted his head back and sighed.

"That's right," Tizzy said. "We're gonna talk."

"I don't want to talk."

"No." She waved her finger. "You're not running from this. It happened. Now we have to talk about it."

"I'm sorry it happened!" He moved the hair out of his face. "I never should have let it happen!"

"Are you trying to take responsibility for what I did too?" Tizzy put her hands on her hips. "Stop it!"

"Somebody has to feel guilty about the shit you do!"

She narrowed her eyes. "What was that?"

He grumbled and rubbed his eyes. "That's wasn't—that's not exactly what I meant to say. Sorry."

"Are you sure?"

He didn't say a word. He didn't even look at her. She crossed her arms and took a step closer.

"If you say *sorry* to me one more time, I'm gonna knock you out."

He scoffed. "You've got a nice swing, but you're not there yet."

"Are you challenging me?" Her smile said she knew but didn't care.

"No. My face still hurts from last night."

This was getting tiresome, she thought. She took a deep breath and grabbed his hand. "Can we please talk about this? Like adults, for once?"

"I don't know what to say except for that thing you told me I can't say anymore."

"Then just say yes or no. We'll start simple."

"No."

She stifled a laugh. "I'm trying to be serious, you ass."

With a weary smile, he relented to her. "Alright."

They sat where the river met the plateau. Tizzy let her hair down to catch the rain, combing her fingers through a mass of black tangles. The pain in her head started to ease, but the pain in her chest grew as she looked for how to begin. She hugged her knees.

"There's not really a good place to start, so I'll just jump in. Aleth, I want this to happen. But you don't. Yes or no?"

The first question already had him reeling. He shrugged and threw his hands up. "I don't know. I can't answer that!"

"Well you'd better."

"I—no."

"No, you won't answer the question? Or no, you don't want this to happen?"

He swallowed hard. "The second one."

Her heart sank, but she continued. "But you've thought about it happening. Obviously."

He hid his face. "Yes."

"And in those thoughts, you *wanted* it to happen." She wanted to study his face, but he still wouldn't look at her.

"Yes."

"So, you do want this to happen, but now that it's a possibility, you're scared because—let's see if I can guess this—it's disgusting and immoral?"

"Look at that, you can see inside my head."

"Next question." She clapped her hands together. "You've killed before, taking their blood. Right?"

"*Tizzy.*"

"That's why you barely feed, right? You don't want to get caught, lest you wind up with a bounty on your head. That means if it's going to happen, they've got to die. Right?"

He exhaled sharply. "Yeah."

"That's what I thought. So, to be clear, we're already in the category of *disgusting and immoral.*"

"That is not a good reason for diving headfirst into everything else that's fucked up!"

"I'm not talking about everything else! I'm talking about this! About *us!*" She could see that he was thinking, struggling. She bit her lip. "You told me that as long as we were together, we would be okay."

"I did."

"Are you trying to tell me that when you said that, there wasn't a tiny part of you that meant it like this?"

He rested his head in the palm of his hand, looking into the river, remembering how many times he had told himself this would never happen. That it would never come to this. That it never *could* come to this. His eyes were glassy and stung in the cold air.

"Put your shame aside for a minute and just say it. All of it. Get it off your chest. You might as well because there's no point in arguing with me."

"Forget it, Tizzy. You're the last person in this world I can bear to be judged by."

She came closer and took his hands. "I'm not asking so I can judge you. I couldn't." She shrugged with the faintest smile on her lips. "I think everything of you. You're perfect."

He wanted to smile back, but all he could do was shake his head. "You're usually a good liar."

"And usually you're not! But you had me convinced early on in this mess that you hated me. Especially when we first started through the Bogwood."

His fingers brushed her cheek, and his shoulders fell. "I had to do something to hide that you had me wrapped around your finger."

"It didn't work for very long," she laughed.

"It didn't." The way she beamed broke him.

"What's the matter?" She laced her fingers with his. "Why do you always look like that? If we both want this, why can't we have it?"

"Tizzy, I'm *scared*." He finally said it. "I don't know what's going to happen, and that doesn't make this exciting; it makes it terrifying because it's *us*, and there's a darkness in our family. You know there is. It's in Rhett, and it's in you. It's in all of us.

"I've fought to keep my humanity with everything I have, and I'm perfectly happy staying at your side, fighting that fight for the both of us. I am; it's what I was prepared to do. But I'm afraid if I let *this* happen, I'll fall right into the darkness with you, and I know I'd be happy there. Because I would do anything for you."

Her gaze drifted to the ground. He'd struck a nerve. Her brow furrowed. "You say that, but you think I'm like Rhett?"

"Tizzy, I didn't mean it like that. I—" He stopped himself. Apologizing would just make her angry. "Rhett has no conscience. His monster reigns free, but you and your obsession with control keeps yours in check. But it's still there, and this life is only going to make it harder for you to control it. This life will rip your humanity away from you like it was never even there. I have to fight for us to keep what we've got left."

"Unless you follow me down the path with my monsters. Right?"

"I think you're upset with me, but I can't tell."

"No." She sat up straight and scratched her head. "I'm not. You're right about all of it. I could be angry and yell at you, but why? You're right."

She thought about the things she had heard Adeska say to Athen.

"I just never thought, not in a million years, that you'd compare me to Rhett. Of all the people."

"That was wrong of me. I'm so—"

"Don't. I will still knock you out if you say it."

He huffed.

"This is starting to make sense now, though," she said. "Somewhat. Louvita didn't want me to tell you about the bloodslave. She *wants* me to lose my humanity. She probably thinks it'll make me strong or useful or something, and she knows you feel differently."

"It's one more reason why she doesn't like me."

"What are we going to do about the bloodslave?" Tizzy asked.

He shrugged. "I don't know. It's going to make things weird."

"Things are already weird."

He bit his lip, trying not to smile, and she giggled. He knew right then that if the sound had been his only reason for living, he could live to see the world end.

"Is this what it's like?" she asked.

"What do you mean?"

When she tried to suppress more laughter, she could feel her face grow hot. "I don't know. It sounds stupid. Forget it." She looked up at him again, and he couldn't remember the last time he had seen shyness in her eyes. "I've been in love with you for so long. Finally admitting it—is this how it feels?"

His lips brushed hers, and every shameful thought they'd ever had was laid bare. He drew her in deeper, and she could feel the rain on her face as it rolled off his lashes.

"If we're going to have this—" he whispered, "—promise me you won't fall away."

"I won't fall out of your reach."

With a faint smirk, he ran his thumb across her chin. "Is that the best I'm going to get?"

"It might take a little bit of darkness to save us."

She got to her feet and gazed down at him with the roguish look he knew her for.

"That wasn't very comforting," he said, standing up with her.

"When have I ever been known for saying something comforting?" she teased.

The rain faded, turning into a mist that clung to the air, cold and grounding. She grabbed his hand.

"Let's leave this place. It's terrible. We could go back to Sheerspine!"

"You just want hot water."

"Who doesn't?"

He looked up the plateau. "Okay. We'll go, but let's see how this bloodslave plays out first. If they get here and we're gone, I'm worried what'll happen to them."

"You don't think the others will protect them?"

"No. Most bloodkin would do anything to get their hands on one. And *we* need to be careful." He shot her a wry glance. "We're going to have to keep our distance from each other as long as Eidi's going to keep poking around."

"She's Ethereal, right?"

"Yes. Why? Tizzy, I can see you scheming. Stop it."

"I've finally got a trick of my own. It's not as neat as turning into a dog, though."

"An ability?"

"I went Ethereal in my sleep last night. This morning. Whenever it was."

"Where did you go?" he asked. "How did you figure it out?" He was ten times more excited about it than she was.

She walked into the cavern, and he followed. "I thought it was another clairvoyant dream, like you said, or maybe Tal screwing around in my head again. I was back home in the orchard, so I headed for Genesis. Adeska was there. She was mumbling something to the moon; you know how she is. Then Athen came out, and they started talking about me, and I thought it was *ridiculous*, so I started yelling. It was a dream. Who cares what I say? Except they heard me. And they could see me."

Suddenly he was serious. "What did you tell them?"

"Will you relax? Adeska was the one who pointed out I was Ethereal. She said she could fix it, and I told her not to, and I said we were both fine and everything was okay. Then I woke up. Hungover."

He grabbed her shoulders. "Tizzy, *do not mess with the banshee*."

"I won't as long as she minds her own damn business."

"If you take her on in the Ethereal Realm, her voice will rip you apart. Do you understand?"

"I'm not going to let that discourage me."

He threw his hands up. "What am I supposed to say to that? I'm glad you're confident, but second guessing yourself from time to time might help you live longer." He started to lead her up the steps.

"Sure thing. Where are we going?"

"Before you get yourself killed, there's someone I want you to meet."

***

The Hallenar carriage had at last returned to Suradia. It pulled up to the front steps of House Hallenar, and Allanis climbed out to pet the horses and give the driver some gold coins for his time.

She watched him leave and then sighed in contentment.

"That went better than I imagined!"

The journey home had been smooth and her meeting with Anavelia unexpectedly fruitful. She slammed the iron knocker on the doors and waited patiently for someone to let her in.

Moments passed. Nobody came. She cleared her throat and called out.

"Hello? I'm back, everyone!"

She knocked again and waited, and it dawned on her just how right the Lovells had been—not simply about hiring for her Council but hiring around the manor in general. A queen should not be waiting to be let into her own home. She could hear Stormy barking inside, and finally Athen unbarred the doors and beckoned her inside.

"Hey."

Allanis looked up at him and cringed. "You do *not* look good."

"I didn't get any sleep last night." He barred the doors behind her. "Some things have transpired."

"To say the least."

He chuckled without smiling. "To say the least."

"Alright, where is everyone?"

"The kitchen. How was Saunterton?"

"It was great! I kind of wish I could go back," she grumbled.

She sensed the tense air filling the manor as they walked down the halls. They were joined by Stormy as they stood outside the kitchen.

"We're stopping." Allanis's expression remained dry as she lifted an eyebrow. "What exactly transpired?" She put her hands on her hips. Something shattered on the other side of the door, and Lora started yelling.

Athen shrugged. "I don't know how to prepare you for this. I'm sorry. But Lora's upset because of Rhett. Well, because we've asked her to find him."

The door was ripped open, Lora on the other side staring him down, red with fury.

"You ask me to find him this morning when he's already had an entire day ahead of me! You could have mentioned that instead of making me look like the bad guy!" Her face softened a little as she turned to Allanis. "Little Bird, I'm so glad you're back. Your family is on my last nerve!"

"I missed you too!" Allanis hugged her, unsure of what else to say, and followed her into the kitchen. Her stomach writhed with anxiety. "Alright, I'm back. What'd I miss?"

It was quiet as everyone tried to find a way to start. Rori found her footing first.

"We know what Tizzy and Aleth are."

Every fiber of her being told her not to do it, but Allanis threw her arms in the air anyway and landed them on her thighs with a *smack*. "So do I! Tizzy is our sister, and Aleth is our brother. Please tell me you've gotten farther than that, that you've been working harder than this while I've been away, because so far it only looks like you've made a giant mess of everything."

"They're nightwalkers," Lazarus said.

They waited for his words to sink in, for a telling expression on Allanis's face, but the idea wasn't registering. She stared right through them.

"Allanis? Honey?" Adeska came closer and put her hand on her sister's shoulder. "Is everything okay?"

"Yes. Of course." Allanis shrugged her off. "Why wouldn't it be?"

"Did you hear what Lazarus said?" Athen asked. "Why aren't you acting shocked? It's shocking."

Lazarus cleared his throat. "Alli, they're bloodkin. Nightwalkers are bloodkin."

"Oh my gods, like vampires?"

"Like vampires," he repeated. "Sort of."

"I don't understand!"

"None of us really do, either," he said. "But there's no doubt, not anymore. That's what they are."

"But she was dead." Allanis buried her head in her hands. Everything was fuzzy. She couldn't link her thoughts together. "Vampires don't turn dead people."

"Maybe nightwalkers do." Lazarus shrugged.

"No, that's what *you* do!" She didn't know why she was so angry. "That couldn't have happened to Tizzy! It doesn't make any sense!" She felt lightheaded. "She's been living here all this time. You really think we would have been living with a monster like that?"

Rori chewed her lip. "When I poisoned them, the only poison that worked was Mother Tryphaena's nightwalker poison. That's how we know."

"Well that's not, not a very good—"

They looked on as Allanis stopped, as the pieces fell from her hands. She sighed with watery eyes. They thought she might collapse, *she* thought she might collapse, under the weight of everything that just wouldn't fit together. Even if they started to form a picture, there was still one piece that stuck out and cut into her.

"But *Aleth*."

"I don't know, Alli. I can't explain any of it. But when Adeska and I came to get him in the woods that night, they were both covered in blood. She was alive and well but didn't remember anything. And he—he had been bitten. By *something*."

Allanis found a seat at the counter and rubbed her head. "But I've never seen a bite on Tizzy. All these years, all these stupid dresses I made her wear and the days at the lake, I would have seen one. I would have noticed something like that."

Lora stood by her side. "Now kindly tell her about part two."

The words spilled out of Rori the second she had the opening. "Rhett stole the poison formula from my notes." She curled her bottom lip in and bit down hard to stop the quivering. It had been *hers*. She was the one who had such a terrible thing for him to take at all. "Now he's gone."

"*What?*"

"Yes." Lora crossed her arms. "When did you know he was missing?" It wasn't a question at all—it was an accusation.

"Yesterday morning." Rori bowed her head.

"Your family corners me this morning asking me to find him, after he's already had a twenty-four-hour head start!" Allanis swallowed hard but didn't say anything. Lora continued. "This is insanity. You all know it! I can't believe you come to me looking for a way out of this!"

That was when the queen stood and left the kitchen. Lora watched her go, choking on air, her heart shattering. She started after her, but Adeska rested a hand on her shoulder.

"It's alright," she said. "Let her have a minute."

"What did I say?" Lora was breathless.

"She's just overwhelmed. We didn't even ask her how her trip went before we threw all of this at her." Adeska looked across the room at her family and sighed. "Lora, I'm sorry. *We're* sorry."

She averted Adeska's eyes. "Finally you give me that. I can't fix the problems you make! Especially not when you set me up to fail!"

Far away, Allanis was racing down the halls, fists clenched in a flurry of emotion. Stormy followed at her side with a whimper. She didn't know where she was going; she just wanted to go, and before long, her escape brought her to the orchard. The cold, gray air of the afternoon slowed her down until, with a heavy heart, she was slogging her satin-trimmed shoes through the dead leaves.

"When did this all get so bad?"

Stormy howled half-heartedly.

"Yeah, you said it."

She ambled farther into the orchard, trying to ignore the nagging feeling that she had acted foolishly. She came to its edge, where Genesis grew tall and proud, and a sigh shook her to her core. Then she heard a voice.

"Look, there she is, Gavin!"

"Isa, wait—"

Beyond the little piled stone wall bordering the orchard, Allanis saw the figures of Gavin and Isa coming closer. In the current atmosphere, she found their presence a relief.

"Your Grace!" Isa called. "Good afternoon!"

She pulled herself together enough to smile at them as they approached her from the other side of the wall. "Hello, you two! How have you been?"

Gavin's face reddened with a grin. "I can't for the life of me come up with an answer for that. However, we do come bearing news and a message."

She was taken aback. "A message? From who?"

He handed her the note. "Lady Tizzy."

She gasped. The note started to tremble in her hands. She couldn't look down at it. "You've met with her?"

"Her and Aleth both!" Isa said. "They're well. Aleth is nice. He wishes he wasn't, but he is. He turned into a dog!"

Allanis blinked through more disconnected thoughts, and Gavin retold their adventure for her. When she finally read the note, a relieved tear slipped down her cheek.

"She wants me to put you on my Council."

Gavin cleared his throat, trying to respectfully avoid her eyes. "Well, she told me a little bit about—"

"You're hired."

"Your Grace?"

Allanis shrugged. "If you want it, of course. You and Isa can both stay here; there's plenty of room. Or I could have one of the old advisor's villas cleaned out for you, if you'd like."

Isa knew it was rude, but she couldn't help it. She leaned on Gavin and started to laugh. "She did say it would go a bit like this, didn't she?"

Allanis put her hands on her hips. "That doesn't sound like a no. Come on, jump this stupid fence and follow me back to House Hallenar. Maybe you can help me wrangle in my family. We've got problems, some of which I haven't even told them about yet."

"My queen, how shall we conduct ourselves around the royal family?" Gavin asked, taking a large step over the wall.

Allanis rolled her eyes. "Hah! They don't want to act royal, so no need to treat them royal."

He helped Isa over the wall next, and before long, the three plus Stormy were back in the kitchen. The family did not expect her to return with newcomers, and they especially did not expect her to return with renewed confidence. Lazarus started to speak, but the queen put her hand in the air to silence him.

"We're taking all further discussion to my study."

No one challenged her. They followed her out and into a large, dusty, mostly empty room with a desk and some scattered seating. Lazarus and Gavin used their magic to light the sconces, giving the space some light for the business Allanis was preparing to conduct. She stood behind the desk and ran her tongue over her teeth while the others situated themselves.

"I'd like to officially name my Council."

She waited, giving one of her siblings the chance to snap at her, to tell her that this wasn't the time for such a matter, but they said nothing. The look on her face was a stilling one that she had learned from an overbearing sister whom she missed dearly.

"I name Athen Hallenar the Queen's Right Hand. He is to be my proxy in any situation where I cannot be present." She paused, and Athen gave her an awkward nod. "I name Lazarus Hallenar the Master Advisor. All future Councilmembers must receive his approval for their seat." Then she extended a hand to Gavin and Isa. "This is Gavin

Castillo of the Mage's Academy and his student, Isa Vega. They will both be staying here, as I name Gavin Castillo the Master Battle Mage and the first official staff of the Suradian Army."

Gavin looked incredibly satisfied, she thought, and it made sense. Amethyst Magic was known for its practicality—it was an even split of knowledge acquisition spells and battle spells. She could have simply asked for Gavin's focus, but her gut served her well on a guess. The others glanced up at him for moment, and then all eyes were back on Allanis.

"Is that all?" Adeska asked.

"For now." Allanis rolled her shoulders. "I'll be drawing up a list of vacancies and comparing them with the ledgers to see what we can afford to pay. Then, hopefully, I'll be fit to start filling them in. I need to get control of this place. Of Suradia. If war is coming, I have to have my claws in deep. I need to be more than some person wearing a crown. My visit with Queen Anavelia went well, though.

"The problem is that I need to figure out how to repay her for what she's giving us. Today, she will have sent two of her most trusted to help me. Her Master Knight, Jurdeir Jashi, and her brother, Prince Ashbel. They will be coming to join the Council. They should arrive by the fourth. How about we get our shit together by then?"

"Where do we start?" Rori asked.

"Gavin, Isa, this is my family," Allanis said, introducing Lazarus, Rori, and Adeska. "There is one other who you haven't met. Our brother Rhett has gone rogue. He never really cared for Tizzy and Aleth. I guess with the revelation that they're nightwalkers—" She faltered at the look of surprise on her siblings' faces. "Nobody panic. Gavin and Isa have already had this revelation since running into them. It's fine. But now that Rhett's got the formula for your poison, Rori, it looks like he's connected the dots too. Now he's taken the formula and run off with it."

"But do you really think he'd take it to Vandroya?" Athen asked.

"No." Allanis folded her arms. "It's too far, and I doubt he knows where the closest Vandroyan representative is. Even I don't know."

"Then where could he be going?" Rori asked. "Vandroya was my guess too."

"Come on," Allanis said. "Think about it. He'll be looking for Mother Tryphaena, I bet. He'll get her to make the poison, and then he'll sell it to the highest bidder." Some of her siblings seemed mortified. "Don't do that. We all know he's greedy."

"Your Grace—" Isa paused. "I'm sorry to say this, it's completely out of turn, but your brother Rhett sounds awful."

"He's—" Rori tried to find an excuse for him, but she was finally too weary of it. "He's selfish, and yes, he's greedy, and he has no interest in redeeming himself. He thinks those are good things too! Like they're going to take him far someday! I thought maybe if I turned away, if he saw that he was losing me, he'd wake up. But the joke is on me. I was never important to him."

But it was Lazarus who felt like something had truly withered up, dried, and turned to dust in his soul. He looked at Rori and wanted to smile to make the words bearable, but he couldn't.

"It hurts, the way he is." He stared through Rori. "You'll be having a good moment, you think. You're laughing, you're having fun, sharing something like kin. And then it happens. Something comes out of his mouth that's so dark, so disturbing and out of touch. It shakes you right out of the illusion that you were ever close. Where does it come from? How did he become this person? None of us showed him that. He's our brother, we loved him, but he feels nothing for us. He will take any of us down the second it gets him where he wants to be. I think he was just born that way."

Lora scoffed at them. "And you want me to track down this cruel man… who is trained in Forbidden Arts, I should add! I would die for my queen, but I will not die for her family's senseless drama. I can cover up my tracks, I can disguise myself a thousand ways, and I know this town inside and out, but you all mistake me for this highly trained *spy*. I'm not! I cannot go on some *mission* with these scraps you throw at me!"

"A spy?" Isa's little voice got everyone's attention. "I might know someone who can help. Your Grace, shall I arrange a meeting?"

"What? Yes, please do! In the meantime, Lazarus and Rori, see if you can track down Mother Tryphaena. I don't think she lives in Suradia anymore, but see what you can find. Hopefully we can get to her before Rhett does."

***

Anavelia shut the door to her study. She was alone with a tall man in bronze armor and a short elf with a braid of silver hair down her back. They watched their queen sit down at her desk.

"I need some input," she started, shuffling through papers. "But as you know, I sent Master Otes to the physician for his cough. If I wind up catching pneumonia or the red cold, I will be quite cross."

"Of course, my queen," the man said with a handsome grin. He was a dashing knight in his early forties, with sunny brown skin, a mop of black hair, and a jawline that was rumored to have landed him the job in the first place.

"Master Jurdeir, are you prepared for your journey?" Anavelia asked. "And I don't just mean to ask whether or not you're packed. I mean mentally. Because my brother will be joining you, as you know."

"I am ecstatic!" Jurdeir proclaimed it with a straight back, sweeping his arm out in an over-the-top gesture. At times, Anavelia thought he would be better off on the stage than a battlefield. "Prince Ashbel is one of my favorite people!"

Anavelia's smile twitched with a chuckle. "Good. Titha will be accompanying you, so she will have him mostly under control. But while you're there, Jurdeir, I need you to keep your eyes and ears peeled for me." She shuffled through the papers until she came to a list. She had spent the last two days compiling information on the Hallenar family.

"Does this pertain to the job you've assigned *me*, Your Grace?" The elf stepped forward, her stature strong and confident, her piercing violet eyes avoiding her queen's face out of respect. Her voice was silky and low, the soft tone that one wouldn't hear unless they were listening for it. She was striking, yet her very presence was unremarkable like it was barely there at all. Sinisia Alvax was a Whisper Mage sitting on Anavelia's Council as the Master of Dusk. The position was suited for reconnaissance and espionage.

"Yes," Anavelia answered. "Please keep this a secret. From everyone. Even Ash." She looked away from them, her hands finding an ornamental letter opener. "Queen Allanis is my friend. She has great potential with Suradia, but she's under threat from Vandroya. When she came here and told me about everything, it was clear that there is one person who has the answers that she needs. But I know her. She'll never do what needs to be done to get those answers." Idly, she twirled the tip of the letter opener into her fingers. "Master Sinisia, find Aleth Hallenar and bring him to me."

"Alive, Your Grace?"

"Holy shit, yes. *Alive.* Good lords, do not kill Queen Allanis's brother. Start by just telling him I want to see him, alright?" She leaned back in her seat and huffed. "If he's anything like Allanis and Athen, he'll probably be perfectly agreeable about it."

Jurdeir chuckled. "And if he's like Tizena?"

Anavelia jabbed her finger at him. "Don't do that."

The door to the study opened. Anavelia's face fell when Ashbel came in fuming.

"Master Jurdeir, Master Sinisia, leave," he told them. They obeyed.

"What do you want?" Anavelia asked, folding her arms. "I'm very busy drawing up material for you to take to Allanis."

"I've already got that handled." He glowered. "You know that."

"Then what is it?"

"What you're doing is wrong, sister. You're making a bad decision. You should stay out of Allanis's family affairs."

Anavelia rolled her eyes. "Oh for gods' sake, Ash, don't act like you've suddenly forgotten how the game works! You heard it with your own ears: Tizzy left! She walked out on House Hallenar. That's not like her! The only reason I can imagine she'd do such a thing is to find answers, and if I want those answers too, I have to look in the same place she did."

Ashbel threw his hands up. "What do *you* need those answers for?"

"Don't worry about it. It's between Duke Orin and me. You just focus on helping Allanis. She doesn't need to know about any of this! Aleth will be left unharmed, so long as he cooperates."

He narrowed his eyes. "Of course. Duke Orin. You act like you've got him in your pocket, but you know what? I think it's the other way around."

"Hey!" Anavelia rose with clenched fists. Ashbel stuck his nose in the air.

"Anyway, I just came to say goodbye. Titha and I are ready to leave. I don't know when I'll see you next, but I'll write."

He turned on his heel and left, slamming the door. Anavelia sighed and rubbed her forehead before deciding to see him off.

***

Tizzy learned the plateau the Convent sat upon was vast. Aleth had led her through a small wooded area surrounding the abbey where the oaks and the evergreens competed for space, reaching up high into the gray sky. It was colder and quieter than the Bogwood, which was solace Tizzy needed. Soon, they reached the edge. She stared down the cliffside at her feet and then to the expanse of woods far down below. She could even see the gates to Davrkton in the distance. When she looked back up, a third person had joined them.

She fought to suppress a gasp. A woman stood beside Aleth. A faerie. The same one she had seen in her first dream. The glow from her green eyes perfectly highlighted her brown cheekbones, and a trace of her wings could be caught beneath her feather-trimmed cloak. Twisted bronze and copper held an impressive opal at her throat.

"Ilisha!" Aleth couldn't contain a grin. The faerie wrapped her arms around him and pulled him into a gentle hug.

"Welcome back." But then her smile disappeared, and she drew back. "You smell."

"Uh." He blushed and sniffed his clothes. "Sorry, I guess they're a little—"

"You reek of the *Glades*."

"Oh, that." He rubbed the back of his neck. "Eidi and Tal took us through the Helamine ley lines."

"What? Those are not for you to take!" Ilisha hissed. "Those ley lines are for the Fae!"

"You mean those were faeries we saw?" Tizzy gasped. "What the hell? No wonder you went off on Eidi like that!"

Ilisha crossed her arms. "Boy, explain."

He looked up into the overcast and tried to keep the irritation off his face. "There were too many of us there to start with. We must have drawn attention that way. Everything around us started to rot, and then Eidi made a noise. The next thing we know, we're surrounded."

"Blight Fae." Ilisha said it with such distaste, Tizzy felt her blood go cold. "They're moving too fast. They'll destroy my grove before long." She sighed deeply, trying not to sound as defeated as she felt. "This must be her, then. Tizzy?" She extended her hand.

As she accepted Ilisha's gesture, Tizzy couldn't decide how she felt. She wanted to be hot with rage for what she'd seen her do to Aleth in the dream, but all the stories she'd heard so far made it seem like it was also Ilisha who cared for him and kept him safe when he was young.

"Yes." She glanced up at Aleth with a faint smile. "You must have told her how much I dislike my full name."

"I did." He grinned.

"For ten years, you're damn near the only thing he's talked about. I am Ilisha of the Willow Clan."

Tizzy's cheeks tingled as they went pink. "He talked about me *that* much? The awful things you must know about me." She coughed. "Hold on. What did you say about something being destroyed?"

Ilisha looked out over the cliffside. "I could turn you both into little frogs right now. Tiny creatures that I could keep close and safe. Then maybe this whole thing could be over."

"Ilisha, what's going on?" Aleth asked. "What are you talking about? This sounds different from what you've told me."

"It isn't. There's just more to it. The Blight Fae are plunging the Glades into a season of decay that it will never recover from, and they're moving closer to the home of the Willow Clan. As their queen, I have to protect them, but I don't have the power to stop the Blight Fae. I've spent too much time in this Realm, spreading my power too thin. That wouldn't matter so much if I had *help*, but many clans have already been decimated, and I haven't been able to track down survivors.

"So I remain here, trying to tie up loose ends. But the longer it takes, the more frayed and tangled it all becomes. I am ribs-deep in the politics of this place. It's more convoluted than I ever could have imagined." She glanced across her shoulder and looked them over. "Both of you promise me you'll lie low and stay out of this mess."

Aleth answered immediately. "Of course."

However, Tizzy crossed her arms. "I had every intention of diving into this mess headfirst and tangling it up a little myself."

"It's bad enough as it is. Your touch is not needed," Ilisha replied. "If you are bent on those intentions, I will spare enough of my power to make you a frog. For the sake of convenience."

"Forever?"

"If you persist."

Tizzy pursed her lips. "Fine. Lie low."

"*Thank you.* I would now like to speak to your brother in private."

"I'll be in my room. Come find me when you're done, Aleth." She shrugged a goodbye and vanished into the trees.

Ilisha rolled her eyes. "Charming."

"I wish I could say it gets better."

The faerie cleared her throat, and her demeanor softened. "How is everything?"

He considered the question, looking back at Tizzy. She was already gone.

"I guess it's been—"

"Boy, don't even think about lying to me. Without the wish, it's more or less how I told you it would be, isn't it?"

"Yeah." He looked down at the grass. "I was afraid it wouldn't be. It doesn't help that she's such a handful."

"You feel different." She surveyed him. "Like you've had a weight taken off your shoulders."

He knew he was red in the face. "Maybe."

She squeezed his shoulder. "I told you it was for the best. Go find her, stay together. Keep each other safe. I'm sorry, but things are going to get much worse before they get any better. For all of us."

He nodded. "Be careful, Ilisha."

CHAPTER 13

THE BOOK OF STARS

"How many chairs will you need?"

Adeska dragged another piece of seating to the table and watched the unblinking expression on Allanis's face. The Queen's Council room was lacking in grandeur in its early stages, boasting little more than a scuffed communal table, mismatched chairs, and a collection of half-burnt pillar candles.

"Allanis? Honey?"

"Sorry." She shook her head. "I'm just having trouble picturing it all." Out of the corner of her eye, she could see Rori wearing a sympathetic smile and dusting off chairs. "It feels like there's no possible way this could happen. I can't picture people in this room, coming together, working with me. Working *for* me. I know that's what will happen, but I can't envision it."

Adeska stood beside her to take in the future grandness of the room. "It's funny," she said, staring down at her hands. "Your brother used to have the same problem when he was little."

Allanis grinned and rolled her eyes so far back it hurt. "Which of the four?"

"Aleth." A touch of reminiscence brought her a laugh. "For so long, we avoided talking about him, but now I'm remembering all of these things I made myself forget. I never told you anything; it must feel like you don't even know him."

"I remember a lot." Allanis put her hands on her hips. "I was ten. It's not like I was a baby when he left."

Adeska couldn't stop smiling. "He hated to read. Absolutely hated it. Thankfully, Tizzy loved it—it was the only thing that would keep her out of trouble. She could just disappear into a story for hours. But for him, when he read, the words were just words. He couldn't picture any of it. At least, not the way the rest of us could."

Allanis frowned. "That's why I hate reading too. The words sound nice together, but they never mean anything to me."

"By the time we understood that about *him*, that he didn't learn so well from written material, we knew to get a tutor for you who could teach you without relying on it so much."

"Is that what you did for him?"

"Back then, we still lived on the farm. We couldn't afford a tutor for any of you until you were crowned. But Tizzy has a big mouth and loves hearing herself talk, so she'd read aloud to Aleth when Lazarus and I couldn't be there. It seemed to work just fine. Both of you are sharp as a tack."

Allanis smirked. "She does have a big mouth."

Adeska sighed, suddenly tense with more recent memories. Allanis waited patiently for her to speak.

She swallowed a lump in her throat. "We saw her, Athen and I, just last night."

"You saw Tizzy?"

"Yeah."

Rori dusted her way over to her sisters.

"We were going to tell you when you first got back," Adeska said. "But things got a little, eh, you know. You were there."

"So she's here? She's still in Suradia? She just ran away?" Allanis asked.

Adeska shrugged. "I don't know where she is. When we saw her, she was Ethereal."

"Like a ghost?" Rori asked. "What does that mean?"

"It could mean a lot of things," Adeska told them. "But she didn't know that she was Ethereal. I think she thought it was all a dream, which means she could be using the Ethereal Realm to travel in her sleep. Whatever the case, I hope she woke up alright."

"What did she say?" Rori asked again.

She wished she had said so much more. "That she's fine. They're both fine. She doesn't want us to worry about anything. Then she vanished."

Allanis cracked into a wide grin. "I believe her. Gavin and Isa have seen them too. Under much worse circumstances, of course, but it sounds like they're back on their feet and things are going their way. Good!"

"Much worse circumstances?" Rori echoed. "Gods, what happened?"

"They tried to tell me about it, but I'm embarrassed to say I didn't follow their story at all. I don't know if I was just stressed or if Gavin and Isa are terrible storytellers. Aleth turned into a dog? I don't know."

"I think you may have missed a few details," Rori said.

Allanis's face brightened. "I forgot! Rori, Lora mentioned you had something to tell me earlier."

Rori's hand crept over her mouth. She had forgotten too. Dread filled her insides like hot tar all over again.

"I guess I do."

"Should I leave?" Adeska asked.

Then the hot tar burned, dried up and flaked away, leaving Rori with growing indignation. She had no reason to be scared.

"Actually, this is something both of you should see." She locked eyes with Adeska and saw the color drain from her older sister's face.

"Rori, you *didn't.*"

"It's time, Adeska." Her hands quivered at her sides. "It was time long ago."

"You brought him with you?"

"What was I supposed to do?"

"Leave him with Raphael!"

"Raph is not his father, and I am not his mother! It's time he knows the truth. It's time everyone does!"

"Hey!" Allanis's voice was cold. "What is going on?"

Adeska's deep blue eyes burned as they glassed over. "Rori, please."

She reared back. "*Rori, please*? Are you serious? I'm the one who should be begging you! This was your responsibility from the beginning. I'm tired of hiding your mistakes for you!"

"Oh gods." Allanis sighed a tired, irritated moan into her hands. "You have got to be joking. We don't have room for this. Do you two understand? No room! We have reached a limit with family drama. What else are you trying to add to the plate?"

Adeska looked up and finally the tears spilled over. "You're right." She clapped a hand over her trembling lips. Her throat was tight with a sob she wouldn't let out. "It's time."

There was more Rori wanted to say, more built up from the unfairness of the last three-and-a-half years, but she wasn't about to waste a rare moment of compliance.

"Follow me."

She led her sisters to her room, and the silence gave Allanis a moment for insight. She realized the way she was beginning to feel in these moments must have been what Tizzy felt day to day. Annoyance. Like she was dealing with a bunch of children. Her family was stunningly unable to conduct themselves like well-adjusted adults, and it was only now that Allanis understood. The hole in her heart grew a little wider.

Before long, they were standing in front of Rori's door. They looked back at Adeska, who was about to fall apart at the seams, but Rori was free of remorse and had no more pity to give her. She opened the door and showed them in.

"Ro!"

Alor looked up from his place on the rug by a lit hearth. He had been thumbing through a storybook with pictures. Adeska was breathless.

"Hey, buddy!" Rori smoothed down a few locks of his wispy hair. "I thought you'd like to meet someone. We have to talk about everything now."

"Is that the queen?"

Allanis's smile was wrinkled with guilt. "He looks like a tiny Centa. But happier." She knelt down and extended her hand.

"My name is Alor." He wiggled her hand like an almost-four-year-old interpreting a handshake. "Ro said I could stay here. Did I break any rules?"

"Not a single one of them!" Allanis told him. "Have you met Stormy?"

"I love your dog!"

Adeska's tears were steady. She hiccupped, and Alor looked up at her.

"Are you okay?"

Her body shook with a sob, but she did her best to show him a smile. "Yes. I'm okay." She sat down to look at him and he stared back.

"You're my mother."

She brushed aside a wisp of his brown hair. "Did Rori tell you?"

"No. She wouldn't tell me about my mother and father."

"Then how—"

Her confusion morphed to dread when she noticed the fire. She had studied hard to learn how to communicate in the elements, learned from Rosamarian Druids and their tomes. But her daughter could do it instinctively.

"Oh *no*." She ran to it. "Alor, have you been talking to anyone?"

"Just my sister."

And so could her son.

Allanis stood up and crossed her arms. "Adeska, what's going on?"

"Mari, this is your mother!" Adeska yelled into the flames. "Come out! I need to talk to you!"

Allanis ran her tongue over her teeth and grumbled to Rori. "This, all of this, is why Tizzy was always in such a bad mood. I get it now."

"I didn't do anything!" Rori whispered back. "This is all Adeska's mess! These are her bad decisions!"

"And you should have grown a spine and made her deal with them from the beginning!"

"I know that!"

They looked on. A shape appeared in the fire, one suspiciously like Mariette. Adeska knew she shouldn't be so nervous talking to her own daughter, but she couldn't stop shivering.

"Hi, Mari. How are you and your father doing?"

"Good."

"That's wonderful. How long have you been talking to this boy behind me?"

"My brother? A long time."

The flames couldn't warm the chill in her bones. "You knew all along?" Mariette didn't answer. "Could you get your father for me?"

"Oh my gods." Rori put her hand on Allanis's arm. "She's really gonna do it. She's going to tell him!"

The shape in the hearth changed. Centa.

"I don't feel good about this anymore, Allanis." Rori hugged herself. "You don't know Centa. Not that I know him much better, but— but maybe I shouldn't have pushed her to do this."

"No, don't you dare do that! This has to happen, for the boy's sake at the very least. Adeska has to face the situation she's made if his life is going to get better, so don't make excuses for her!"

"Adeska?"

It was Centa's voice. The girls quieted for a sickly sigh from Adeska.

"Hello, sweetheart."

"Is everything alright?"

The words were stuck in her throat. As the silence drew on, the flames grew.

"Adeska? Are *you* alright?"

"Um, can you and Mari come back to House Hallenar? Everything is—" she swallowed hard, "—it's not alright, Centa. We—" she tried to drown out her nerves with a deep breath, "—we need to talk."

"What happened?"

The alarm in his voice made her quake. "Nothing happened. It's okay. It *isn't* okay, but no one is hurt, if that's what you're asking."

"I don't know what I'm asking." His silhouette didn't say anything for a moment. He scratched his neck. "Adeska, what did you do?"

"You'll find out." She barely suppressed a sob.

"We'll leave in an hour. I love you."

The fire dissipated until it was nothing more than tiny blue wisps crackling at the bottom of a log. Adeska turned to look at her sisters and her son.

"This will be very, *very* ugly," she said. "I apologize."

"Don't apologize," Allanis said, narrowing her eyes. "Just start explaining. Consider it practice."

Alor sat down with the storybook in his hands, his eyes big and scared and sad. He knew this was the moment where his mother would tell him why she never wanted him.

"Mariette isn't really Centa's daughter," Adeska started.

Allanis shrugged. "The only person who doesn't know that is Centa."

"Will you please tone it down a little?" Rori snapped.

"Sorry." She wasn't sorry. "The longer you all stay here, the more things seem to go wrong, and I'm getting tired of it."

"Look," Adeska wet her lips. "Do you remember when I moved out?"

"What about it?"

"Do you remember what *happened*?"

Sorrow escaped Allanis through a sigh. "Of course. Centa left to see his family for an emergency, and while he was gone, Cato's sister went missing. Instead of writing him and telling him about it, though, you decided to handle it yourself and help Cato investigate. I swear I didn't hear from you for almost a year."

"Eight months," Adeska said, sitting down with Alor. "We'd finally banished the Greater Daemon that destroyed the city of Burshen back to the Hell Planes, right before he could put together enough forces to do it again. The party disbanded and went on with their lives. We thought we were finally free. Centa and I settled down outside Caequin, in Kamdoria. It was nice.

"But then he got a letter from his brother. He never told me what it said, but he left to go back to the Cerulendas Islands immediately. It had to have been something dire because he hates his family. He'd never go back to them. That's why I didn't want to bother him when Cato came around. He was hoping Centa would help him find Marika, and at that point, she'd been missing for three days, so I offered to help in Centa's place. I didn't think it would be hard. It shouldn't have been; it should have been easy! My second focus is in Rosamarian Druidism, so there's no reason why I can't find a person lost in the woods!

"But Marika wasn't just missing in the woods. She went missing in territory that had been affected by a tear in the Glades. You'd think something like that, something touched by the land of the fae, would be beautiful and overgrown with flowers or something. But everything was diseased and rotting, like plague had just poured out of it. Cato and I tried to be careful; the Glades had twisted the trees into these creatures like dryads, but they were *vile*. We were stuck there for weeks, trying to avoid them. I wanted to let you know that I was okay, though, so I tried to send you a carrier."

More hot tears slipped down her red cheeks. "That's how they found us. I was stupid. I don't know what to call her—a dark fae? Her name was Myentra. She had an entire operation in that territory, and it was growing so fast. She took Cato and me and threw us in her prison, but we didn't think we would be there for very long. How could no one notice what was happening? Someone would come, I thought. But a month went by. That's when I realized I was pregnant. With *you*." Gingerly, she took Alor's hand.

"Myentra knew. I think she had known from the beginning. When we didn't obey her commands, she threatened me, saying she'd kill all the life growing inside of me. So we were compliant. As the months went on, I swelled until you were finally born. Cato was desperate to find us a way out. A baby doesn't belong in a dungeon." She sobbed, and her second-long smile shattered. "You were about a month and a half old, Alor, when he finally figured out how to escape.

"But she found us. She found us and put us back in our cage, and she took you away. And I thought—" she swallowed a sob, "—we thought it was over. We were devastated. I cried, and he comforted me." She wept more, shaking and gasping as the memories ripped through her. "Y-you have to understand, we thought we were going to die, that it was the end for us, that we'd never see anyone again. We just wanted to feel one last moment of peace. Of love. The day after she took you, Alor, Myentra came to us. She said we had to choose.

"She'd had Marika all along. Just like she'd had us."

She wiped away tears. "I couldn't say anything. I just froze. She had Marika, and she had you, and I couldn't say a word. So Cato made the choice, and Myentra killed Marika right in front of us. You all know the rest. Rori, you and Centa and the others had found us at last—"

"And that's when you hid Alor with me!"

"I did. Centa knew that Cato had loved me for years. I was afraid if he saw a baby, he'd jump to conclusions. He'd think it was Cato's, and I'd never be able to do or say anything to salvage our relationship. He'd be angry and jealous and mean, and he'd push both of us away."

"But you *did* have Cato's child! And that's the one you let him believe was his own instead of the one that actually is!" Rori shouted.

"I know it's stupid!" Adeska yelled back. "Trust me, I know! But it's not like I could take it back. I can't say, 'Oh no, nevermind! This one is yours too.' I just panicked!"

"That would be infinitely better than what you actually did!"

Allanis rubbed her temples. "So what are you going to tell him?"

Adeska sighed. "The truth." She considered her options, watching Alor's big brown eyes search her face. "All of it. It would be easier to leave out the part about Mariette, but I've been dishonest enough. I should just come clean and get it over with."

Rori put her finger in the air. "I'm not against leaving out that part. I've seen Centa when he's angry."

The look Adeska gave her was chilling. "Trust me. You haven't. You haven't seen either of us angry."

Alor's little voice cut through the air. "Marika died so I wouldn't?"

Adeska hugged him tight. "Yes. I'm sorry you had to know that, but we *did* want you. Do you understand?"

"But you didn't want Marika?"

"Honey, we wanted her too. We wanted her very, very much. But we could only have one of you. Cato chose Marika to die so that you could live."

"Does he not like me?"

"Cato?" She kissed his forehead. "He was there when you were born. He can't not like you. He's not around much anymore, though. He's still sad about Marika."

Allanis and Rori looked on as Adeska and her son shared a tearful embrace. Allanis fidgeted with her hands. The day she knew something was wrong, the day she *really* knew, the feeling when it struck her in the chest and reverberated through her like a broken violin string, it haunted her.

"I never told you." She twisted her pearl wedding ring around her finger, the one from her coronation day. "I never told you how we knew something was wrong. Phio and Tizzy figured it out. I had him over to paint us a new portrait, and he was talking about it and mentioned how long you'd been gone. Tizzy suggested that by that time, you'd be stupid enough to try and send us a letter, dangerous territory be damned. It was just to make small talk, but when she took that jab at you, we thought about it and got worried that she was right. That's what sent the rescue in motion."

"I'll be sure to thank her next time I see her."

***

Isa could tell the days were getting shorter. She could feel it in the skies more and more. The sun still danced above the horizon as evening came closer, but she knew there could only be another hour of daylight left before hazy purple dusk stretched out overhead. She watched people spend it gathered around entertainers on street corners, awed by captivating songs or daring talents and tearing into peddled street food. Suradia could be a magical place when it wanted to be.

A honey roll *did* sound good, Isa thought. She'd been waiting for her friend for the greater part of the day now and hoped they'd be making an appearance soon. Isa sighed inwardly and went to find the man with the honey rolls. He was across the street from a woman juggling knives.

"Gio, good evening!" Isa called to him. He was perhaps Gavin's age but tall and with a generous stomach and black beard. He smiled for her.

"Little Isa! Come for a roll?"

"I have." She dug through a pouch on her belt, through all the new wealth gained by working at House Hallenar, and gave him a silver star—double the ten brass pennies that he typically charged. He looked around his cart for the biggest pastry he had.

"It's getting close to dinner time. Won't this spoil your appetite?" he asked, handing her a glossy, golden roll dusted in spice.

"It will," she admitted. "But things are so busy, I'm not sure anyone's going to remember dinner." She tore off a piece and chewed it up in excitement. Then her eyes went wide. "Gio, this is a different recipe!"

He beamed. "Isa, I've met someone." He gazed right through her with a dream in his eyes. "A brilliant woman from Wakhet, the *capitol* of Besq! Brilliant and talented and so kind. She made some adjustments to the recipe."

Isa tasted a bouquet of warming spices that she wasn't familiar with. "It's good. Is that ginger I taste?" She didn't have the faintest idea, but it sounded smart.

"We're going to marry!"

For some reason, the notion shocked her. Worried her, even, as she realized she didn't know many married couples.

"I'm so happy for you, Gio." She tried to say it with confidence. "When will it happen?"

"Truthfully, little Isa, I'm not sure." Now he was the one who sounded worried. A group of townspeople carried on behind him, looking for another promising entertainer.

"I am hoping to consult the queen," he said. "But I know she doesn't meet people very often. I have very little to offer my love, Safiya. Nothing but this silly cart of sweets. But maybe if the queen took an interest in what I do, she would consider lowering the cost of an empty building near the Square so that I might start an empire of my own."

The dreamy look that came back to him made her smile, but she was confused about his words.

"You would call the lots in the Square expensive? Or just too much for *you*?"

"No, little Isa, they are very expensive. They have always been that way since before our queen."

Isa squared up and put her hands on her hips. "I'm sure Her Grace has no desire for those lots to remain so—" she searched for a big word, "—unattainable." Good enough. She chewed on another bite of the roll. "Her Council is small, so I'm sure it just fell unnoticed next to all the other pressing matters. You know what, Gio? You should meet with the queen. You and any other artisans hoping for a lot. I'm going to arrange the affair myself! For all of you!"

Gio started to laugh the way old men do when a child amuses them. Isa folded her arms.

"I appreciate that you believe in my dreams, little Isa. Truly."

"I'm serious, Gio. Gavin works for the queen now. He's spoken with the dean at the Academy about it and everything. It's official!"

"What?"

"That's right! I can come and find you when I draw up the details. How about that?"

The people who were stirring behind Gio finally shuffled farther down the street. That was when she saw them—two scruffy boys about her age who had stopped moving at the group's pace. One plucked the sack of coins from Gio's cart so deftly that she had barely noticed it.

"Hey, give that back!" she yelled. The boys shot off with speed like a wild animal. Isa huffed and tried to remember her lessons— some of them unwisely ahead of curriculum—and reached into her pouch for ingredients. She pulled out a thick pinch of shimmery purple Akashic powder and an amethyst chip, and her casting necklace started to glow. Keeping her eyes on the boy with Gio's money, she aimed and flicked the ingredients into the air.

The Arcane Blast spell erupted from the ground in a thunderous crackle. It was uneven, terrifyingly powerful, and missed its target entirely. Isa's heart sank as a minstrel went flying alongside a stall of embroidered sashes.

"Oh no!" She tried to rush forward, dropping her roll, but Gio rested his hand on her shoulder and pulled her back. A Topaz Mage from

268 · AJ GALA

the Hesperan Hospice had already emerged to tend to the minstrel's wounds. The woman selling the sashes ran with her mother to pick them all up before sticky fingers saw to it first.

"Gio, let go! I have to fix this!"

"No Isa, look." He pointed to a couple of men in heavy blue and gold cloaks. The Watch. "Let them sort out the bystanders first. Maybe they will have lost interest when it's time to look for you."

"But your money!" Isa gestured to the boys who were getting away.

But when she looked at them again, she wasn't so sure that was the case. A short figure in black wrappings and mismatched leather armor came around the corner. Isa could see just a glimpse of a yellow scarf around her neck as she padded effortlessly down the streets, dancing between crowds with utmost grace. Isa smiled.

"She's here!"

Her contact had finally arrived.

The boys, while fast, were clumsy, but their pursuer was like a gust of wind, sailing over obstacles with delicate leaps and tumbles. When they took notice of her, they turned down an alley, their worn boots sliding on the cobblestone. She didn't let the turn slow her down at all. Her momentum carried on as she ran halfway up a wall and spun off into the side street with precise acrobatics. The boy with the bounty lost his footing and stumbled to the ground. His friend stayed by his side and pulled out a dagger.

"Stay back!" he warned, shaking it.

The pursuer removed her skull cap and shook out two little pom-poms of black hair. A dashing smile crept onto her dark, freckled face.

"What's all this for?" she asked.

Isa finally caught up, out of breath. Her necklace was aglow, and her hand was full of purple powder.

"Give back the money!" she panted. "I won't miss this time!"

The boy on the ground groaned and tossed it at her feet. "Fine." He looked up at his partner. "I told you we wouldn't be able to get away with it."

His friend helped him up and they started away in shame. The pursuer cleared her throat as Isa picked up the coin sack.

"Why don't you two try an honest day's work for once instead of ruining someone else's?"

"There's not enough work to get by in this stupid town!"

"That'll change!" Isa shouted, putting away the spell components. "It is. And soon!"

The boys left the scene with mumbled profanity. When all was finally quiet, Isa threw her arms around the girl and hollered.

"Djara, that was amazing!"

Her friend giggled. "Ma just says I'm good at running around." Her fingers tangled idly in her yellow scarf. Now that she was close, Isa could see the flower-shaped splotches of color in it.

"You like it?" Djara asked. "Ma and I made them for each other. Just hammered a bunch of flowers into the fabric and it stained like this. Pretty, huh? This one that she made for me looks so much better than the one I made for her."

They laughed, and Djara tucked the scarf under her leather vest until it was only a thin pop of color at her neck.

"Speaking of your mother, would she want to meet with the queen about a job opportunity?"

"Are you serious? That's what this is about?" Djara's jaw dropped. "Yes, but only if I get to come!"

"Of course you're coming!" Isa linked arms with her. "Come on, let's get this back to Gio. He'll be so relieved. Did you know he's getting married?"

Djara laughed. "Isa, I know everything around here."

And it was true, which gave Isa an idea. She looked back over her shoulder at where the boys had been. "Did you know those two?"

"Sure. Rupert the Robber and Sydar the Stabber." Djara rolled her eyes at the cheesy monikers. "Ma says they're bored and lazy, but there's still some truth to what they said."

"What do you mean?"

"There really isn't enough work to get by around here. At least not for them. There's no family business to inherit or work from because they're both orphans. They've got no real skills, and fat chance of finding a mentor with an opening for an apprentice. They're at a disadvantage, it's true. But Ma says you have to work hard for anything, and honestly, she'd know."

"Why don't they just go to Saunterton?"

"Saunterton is a glorious place of opportunity!" Djara poured on some dramatic flair. "But it's demanding. You can't be lazy there because if you're gonna prowl the streets for a living, it's competitive. You're gonna get swindled by people ten times better at it than Rupert and Sydar."

Isa made a contemplative noise. "Do you think they're okay guys, though? Deep down? Do you think they'd do the right thing if enough depended on it?"

"What on Rosamar's Green Earth do you have going on in that head of yours, Isa?"

"You'll see!"

***

Crickets came out to sing and explore as the sun set over the woods. It was cool and the clouds in the distance promised rain by morning. The black blades of Wish and Mercy met with a gentle *clang*.

"You're slow!" Aleth said it with a grin, striking playfully.

Tizzy swung upward with much more effort. "It's heavy!"

"It wouldn't be—" he jabbed, and she parried, "—if you had kept practicing. Now you've got princess arms!"

Her jaw hung open, and he laughed.

"I'll show you *princess arms!*"

She attacked recklessly, but the strikes were fluid. And weak, Aleth thought. He parried with a little too much force, and Tizzy went stumbling back. Swiftly, he grabbed her hand and pulled her steady before she could fall to the ground, but instead she fell into him with a mischievous giggle that said it was anything but an accident.

"Goodness. You two are having some fight now, aren't you?"

Talora's voice startled them both, and they stared at her with blushing faces. They untangled themselves.

"That's right," Tizzy said. "He's awful, and I hate him."

Talora smirked. She leaned against an old fir, her smile friendly but dry.

"That *is* how Eidi's been telling it. Arguing and even getting physically violent." She looked up into the canopy, and they could tell she hadn't believed it. "You two must have settled your differences, though. You're getting along famously."

Aleth looked at Tizzy with all the contempt he could possibly fake. "Getting along? With her?" He jabbed Mercy in her direction. "It's impossible. Look at her! And she smells. Like—"

He stopped, frozen in his thoughts. The rest of the sentence wouldn't come to him. Tizzy sighed and motioned for him to go on, but the only word that came out was a noise of indecision.

"You could have said literally anything." She rolled her eyes. "You picked a good direction, you did, I'll give you that. But you have to run with it! Instead, you stood there and broke your own legs."

Talora grumbled. "I knew you two were faking it. Why?"

Tizzy sheathed Wish. "Because Tal, I don't like everyone knowing my business! But they're going to stick their noses in it anyway, so I'm giving them something to think they know."

Why did she tell her that? She didn't trust the woman enough to reveal her thoughts, so why would she say anything at all? It was too late now, Tizzy thought. Talora just stood there, nodding thoughtfully.

"Smart."

It was the opposite of what Aleth had been telling her. Tizzy stuck her nose in the air. "See? I told you."

"You're going to get yourself in trouble," he said, sheathing Mercy. "You're going to get all of us in trouble."

"He's absolutely right," Talora said. "But until that happens, you're at least buying yourself a bit of freedom."

"It's going to buy me a lot of freedom, Tal." She folded her arms and came closer. "I'm not staying here." She studied Talora's face, watching the notion disturb her. "If everyone is really as afraid as Louvita says they are, maybe you should leave too. And make sure Dacen leaves. I like him."

Talora cleared her throat and pulled at her veil. "We shouldn't talk about all of this out here. Will you two come to my place?"

"The Treehouse?" Tizzy asked. When Talora nodded, she looked back at Aleth. "What do you say? Is my training over?"

"Gods no. You're terrible! But nothing else we do tonight is going to change that, so we might as well call it."

"Yes!" Tizzy smacked Talora on the shoulder and smiled. "Teacher says I can go!"

Talora's little grin was warm. She squeezed Tizzy's hand and led the way.

"What's this part of the woods called anyway?" she asked. "I know we can't still be in the Bogwood. The trees are different." She tried to imagine her exact location—seeing Davrkton from the plateau had helped. Suradia, Saunterton, and Davrkton were sister cities forming a prim triangle on a map, one not more than a two-day ride from another. Suradia was to the west, Saunterton to the southeast, and Davrkton to the northeast. She imagined they'd be just outside of the triangle's boundary at the Suradia-Davrkton line.

"This area is technically the Wistwilds," Talora told her. "There's more evergreens this way, while the Bogwood has more oaks."

The Wistwilds were indeed much greener than the Bogwood. It was the first thing Tizzy had noticed. Autumn had kissed the leaves back home, making it a fiery, copper-colored paradise. As she looked at the firs and cedars and their needles and the crunchy brown forest floor underfoot, she realized the Wistwilds wouldn't get the season's love.

But the *air*. She took in a deep breath. It was divine.

Talora's home wasn't far. She scolded the siblings along the way as they threw pinecones at each other and found things to squabble about. But she couldn't help but smile to herself despite it all. Never in all the years she'd known him had Talora seen Aleth so at ease. She approached her tree and sighed with content.

Tizzy turned to Aleth and grandly gestured out to it. "I have both been here and never been here. How weird is that?"

It was exactly as it had been in her fever dream fighting Lilu but with the added detail of a sitting area by the Treehouse's steps. There were a few worn chairs, a table for tea, and a fire pit that had been dispersed by the last storm.

"I guess weird is one way to describe it," Aleth said. "I'm trying to get over the fact she jumped into your head when she told me she wouldn't."

"Aren't you happy that I did?" Talora scoffed, showing them up to the door.

Aleth looked back at his sister. "I guess I'm happy she's *alive*."

Tizzy smiled even though she stuck her nose in the air. "Oh you guess, huh?"

He loved her dry remarks the most. He responded with a smile that made her cheeks pink.

The wooden steps creaked under their weight. The sky was dusty blue with its first showing of stars as Talora unlocked the door and let them inside. Tizzy couldn't believe how real everything was when she had already found it so real in her head. They stood in the dark waiting for Talora to light candles, and Tizzy reached out to touch the tree trunk growing through the middle of the room.

It only took her a single encounter with Lilu to understand why Talora had left the Convent, but Tizzy could've left it for the Treehouse alone. Lilu be damned. The cold smell of pine, the fragrant wooden walls, and the countless jars and pots of tea made the cramped space cozy enough to settle into forever. Or until the tree in the center outgrew the structure.

Talora finally had a fire started in a tiny clay oven. Its orange glow cast their shadows long on the walls, waking up the sleepy details around them.

"Tea?" Talora asked, pouring water from a jug into the small iron kettle.

"Sounds nice." Tizzy helped her pick out a cup for each of them as Talora lit the candle beneath the kettle.

Aleth sat on Talora's bed and its scratchy blankets. "I miss coming here. Sorry it's been so long since I've visited."

"You know I'm not upset," the woman said with a smile. "We've both had our fair share of problems to deal with. It wouldn't have been good timing."

For a split second, Aleth was rife with anxiety, staring wide-eyed at the floor. It bubbled up from nowhere and filled him until he realized no one wanted to discuss said problems. It passed as quickly as it had come.

Tizzy stood at Talora's countertop, going through all the tea. "What's this one? Can we have this one?"

The woman leaned over and sniffed. "That's one of my favorites! It's got tea from Kasatta that's rolled into little pearls, and I added blackberries and blackberry leaf. We can have this one; I was hoping to bring it out for company anyway!"

She sprinkled the dried mixture into three cups and waited for the kettle to heat.

"Hey, Tal?"

She glanced over her shoulder at Aleth. "Yes?"

"Do you have any *food*?"

Tizzy suddenly felt the emptiness in her own stomach. "I'm starving too. I don't think I've ever gone three days without something to eat. I didn't even notice I was hungry!"

"Three days?" Talora laughed. "That's how I know you two are still babies. It's been well over a month since I've had real food, and that was only because I really like the apple tarts in Davrkton. Had nothing to do with hunger." She rummaged through a crate sitting on the floor beside the counter, eventually pulling out a cloth bundle. "That's what happens when you lean into your bloodkin side more, Tizzy. You just lose the need for food. Lucky for you both that I was expecting a visitor a couple days ago." Then she sighed. "They never showed up."

She handed the bundle to Aleth, and he and Tizzy immediately started fighting over the travel rations inside. It couldn't have been more than a few pieces of cured meat and hard tack.

"Why do you get that many pieces?" Tizzy asked, watching him divvy it up.

"Because I'm two of you!"

"This—" she waved around the single piece of meat he'd given her, "—is not going to sustain these massive thighs of mine!"

He went red in the face and looked away from Talora. "Let's not talk about your massive thighs in front of other people."

She pouted. "You really think they're massive?"

"What? No!"

"*Tizzy.*" Talora was laughing. "Leave the poor boy alone."

"Fine." Her devilish smile returned, and she sat down next to him, making sure he was dividing up the rations evenly. "Let's go to Davrkton tomorrow! What do you think?"

"Really?" He broke the tack in half.

"Yeah, there should be one last good run in the marketplace before it's all just onions and potatoes and blankets."

His mouth twitched as if it were fighting a grin. "Gods forbid we go all that way just for onions and potatoes and blankets."

"We can get you fitted for some new clothes too."

"I don't want to get fitted," he grumbled.

"Aleth." Talora was pouring hot water over the tea. "Please go with her. And while you're there, you can replace my sewing kit you took."

"You weren't even using it. I had things to fix!"

"Go see a tailor." She handed them each their cups. "Now, what's this about you two leaving the Convent?"

Silence. They watched Tizzy's face twist with thought as she came up with a way to explain herself. She crunched on a piece of hard tack.

"Well." Her mouth was full. "I hate it."

"That's it?"

"That's typically all it takes, isn't it?"

"But—" Talora shook her head, exasperated. "Louvita told you everything, didn't she? About how we need you, and, and—"

"It's bullshit." Tizzy sipped the tea. "I find it hard to believe that somehow I'm going to be the one to save everyone from the Hunters. You'll either make it or you won't. I'm not going to make the slightest difference. No." She stared into the cup at the little pearls unfolding. "There's something else going on. There has to be."

Talora's cup started to shake in her hand. She frowned. "Something else? Like what?"

"I don't know. And for once, I'm not interested in sticking around to find out. This feels bad, Tal."

Aleth tilted his head. "Do you honestly believe what Louvita and Ziaul have been telling us?"

"Didn't *you*?" she asked. "You finally agreed to fetch her. I thought that meant you believed them!"

"No." He scratched his head and stole a glance at Tizzy. "I just wanted to see her again. They were threatening me. Then there was Ilisha doing what she does. It just seemed like the right time." Tizzy hid her smile in her cup.

"Okay, fine. You're leaving. But where are you going to go? What's your plan? Have either of you thought this out? Because you know they're going to come looking for you."

"Haven't really thought about it," Tizzy admitted. "I just want out. But we've got somewhere to go for a little while, and then after that, who knows? Maybe we—"

"We are *not* going back to Suradia," Aleth declared. "Don't even think about it."

The look she gave him challenged his very soul to drop dead. "I'll do what I want. And if I want us to go back to Suradia, I will drag you there myself."

"Tizzy, we can't go back! If you care about any of them, let them be!"

She folded her arms. "The problem is that they aren't going to let *us* be. I would rather go back to them with this mess than have them accidentally walk into it, trying to track us down to see if we're okay. They're going to be in this whether we're there or not. At least in one scenario, we can protect them."

"You can protect them." He looked away.

"Alright, your obvious and understandable hatred can be discussed another day." Tizzy sighed.

There was more silence. Talora gulped down her tea.

"It sounds like you two have a lot to work out."

Tizzy sat close beside Aleth. He still wouldn't make eye contact.

"I guess I miss them," she said. "I didn't expect to. I'm sorry."

"It was bad enough showing up at the party. All of them there, just fucking *looking* at me. I don't think I could do it again."

"It would be a little different if we went back." She held his hand. "You'd be with me, and if anyone looked at you wrong, if Rori so much as opened her fat, stupid mouth again, I'd take a candlestick to her face."

One small laugh came through his nose, and he chewed on his lip. "You would. I know you would."

Talora softened with the mood. "I understand if you leave the Convent, but I do wish you'd stay. I'd miss the both of you."

Tizzy's eyes started to wander to Talora's belongings. She collected cups and jars mostly, but when she saw a little bookshelf opposite the bed, her interest piqued.

"Maybe you should go with us," she suggested. "As long as you aren't a pain in the ass. There's only room for one, and I'm it."

Aleth rolled his eyes. "So self-aware."

"You're inviting me along?" Talora watched Tizzy sit down in front of her books. "I guess I'll consider it."

Tizzy mentally kicked herself. Why did she invite her? That was not what she wanted, but she forgot all about it as she perused the titles on Talora's shelf.

"You have a lot of really good plays, Tal."

"I don't know many people who read them. You can imagine the others at the Convent have better things to do. Which is your favorite?"

"Knight of the Red Castle," Aleth answered for her, crossing his arms smugly. "That's still the one, right?"

Tizzy laughed. "I've probably read it a thousand times at least. I'm surprised you don't have it here!"

"Sadly, no." Talora stared at the soggy tea leaves at the bottom of her cup, trying to decide if the shape was a snake or some kind of tall bird. "No copy of my own, but Aleth has tried plenty of times to tell me about it. His rendition has a lot of plot holes."

"I've never read it myself," Aleth explained. "Tried to, but Tizzy read it to me a few times when we were young. I guess I missed some things." He coughed. "I'm not a very strong reader."

"They had a troupe performing it once at a theater in Saunterton," Tizzy said, starry-eyed. "Just a few years ago. Allanis took me to see it, and we sat with Queen Anavelia in her seats. The actress playing Lady Olivine was perfect! But when I heard Sir Lyzan say his first lines, I walked out. The actor *ruined* him! And I think I might have offended Anavelia. She still jokes about it to this day, but she's never invited me back to see another play."

Talora's body heaved with genuine, squeaky laughter. "A play so old and rare that you'll probably never see it on another stage again! Your favorite, no less! And you walk out because of a single actor's delivery?"

Aleth slid off the bed to sit beside Tizzy and scoffed. "It wasn't just any character. It was *Sir Lyzan*."

"He's the best character! All the other characters just *love* Lady Olivine," Tizzy said. "They all think she's so charming, so beautiful, they all obey her every command because she's just so nice. But then there's Lyzan who doesn't give half-a-shit about Lady Olivine. He's the only one who has the sense to stop her from running the Red Castle into ruins."

"Are you upset because the actor portrayed him with more charisma than a pile of dirt?" He suppressed a giggle as she swatted at him.

"I would love to read it sometime," Talora said, catching their humor as she poured more hot water into her cup. "If you find it while you're in Davrkton, will you pick it up and let me borrow it?"

"Of course she's going to pick it up; it's probably been an entire ten days since the last time she's read it—ow!"

She observed the two wrestling and swatting and shoving, noting how Aleth let himself lose and the way he grinned when Tizzy roared in triumph—triumph that she had sense enough to know was probably fake. Talora sipped, and soon they gathered themselves and went back to searching the shelf.

Just as Tizzy had caught her breath, she gasped. "You have *Shaken Spear*! I heard a playwright in Suradia was going to adapt this for the stage."

"He's got his work cut out for him, then," Talora said. "That saga is over two dozen books long. You'll be at the theater forever!"

"Wouldn't that be something? They could completely change the theater experience. You'd have this enormous inn attached to it and the biggest stage you've ever seen. And the size of the troupe and the orchestra and—*that* would be an attraction! Hey, what's this?" Tizzy paused to take out a slender little book. "*The Tale of Clydewick Boyle?*"

"That's *his*." Talora rolled her head in Aleth's direction. "It's here because he doesn't want anyone finding it in his room."

Tizzy narrowed her eyes with suspicion. "You don't read." She cracked it open to a random page and cleared her throat. "What? *Poetry*? Wait, did this guy just get eaten by a gargoyle?"

"Shut up! Clydewick comes back as a ghost on the next page," Aleth told her.

"So you won't read *Knight of the Red Castle*, but you'll read this garbage?"

He shrugged. "It's funny. He dies on every page."

"Funny? This is so dumb." She turned the page to read on, just for good measure, and Aleth waited with bated breath. After a moment, Tizzy snorted. "Alright, the next part was better. I don't think that's how you kill a ghost, though." She shook her head and returned it to the shelf.

There was something comforting about the way the night was unfolding in the Treehouse, Tizzy thought. It was comforting to feel like she could let her guard down, to feel close without the nagging resentment. Perhaps Talora wasn't as bad as she'd first thought.

She gave the shelf one last look before finding a way to change the conversation, and that's when she saw it. She felt her whole body light up.

"*The Book of Stars*." Breathless, she stared at the book's worn blue leather spine. "We had this when we were little. I haven't seen this since—it couldn't have been very long after our mother died."

"Oh Tizzy, be careful with that please. It's old—"

It was as though she hadn't spoken at all. The book was in Tizzy's hands, having the dust worked away with cautious fingers.

"Mother used to read it to us all the time. I remember sitting in her lap sometimes. Usually I'd have to sit next to her to leave room for someone else who was on the way. She was pregnant a lot." She chuckled, the pages gently gliding past her thumb. The memory of huddling around her mother, sitting carefully beside a belly swollen with a healthy, growing Athen was vivid. She knew there had been other siblings around somewhere too. But in her reconstructed memory, it was just her, her mother, and the book.

"Then, when Mother was too sick to read to us, Adeska would do it. We'd all get in close, and someone would pick a story, and we'd all watch her, listen to her try to tell it exactly the way Mother used to. Adeska loved this book."

She didn't notice Talora's nervous, wide eyes. All she could see when the last page fell was the inside cover. It was old and yellowed, just as their old copy had been, with a similar stain in the top left corner. Then she saw something scrawled along the bottom edge. She swallowed hard.

To Adeska, my wise little girl with her heart in the moon. Love, Mother

She was cold. Her hands trembled.

"Who are you?" She stared at the writing. "Tal, *how do you have this?*"

Aleth looked over her, down at the book. Adeska's name in his mother's handwriting stood out like a sore thumb. "Tal?"

"I can explain!" Talora said it, but she wasn't sure it was true. Her cup was shaking, and she set it on the counter to rub her temples. "I can explain."

"Then do it!" Tizzy yelled. "This is my sister's! How the hell do you have it?"

Talora leaned with her back against the counter. "Adeska and I know each other." She took a deep breath. "We're friends, even."

"She's friends with *you*?" Tizzy shuddered. Betrayal was cold. It was colder not knowing who was at fault. "That's great. A random nightwalker, yes, let's be friends! That's sure not a courtesy she was willing to extend to the ones in her own family!"

Talora swallowed the lump in her throat. "I'm sure the kindness she showed me was her heart's way of trying to undo what she'd done to you two. At least at first. It was a long time before I told her what I was, you know. I think from the beginning she could tell something was off, and she was trying to be different."

"A long time?" Tizzy repeated.

"How long have you known her?" Aleth asked.

"I blew my cover eight, almost nine, years ago." Talora sighed. She didn't look at them as they both scowled at her. She especially couldn't meet Aleth's eyes, not after how long she had owed him the truth.

"What do you mean you blew your cover?" Tizzy asked through clenched teeth.

The woman fidgeted with the lace on her gloves for a long time before she had the courage to speak. "After you ran from House Hallenar, Aleth, your oldest brother took a ship to Besq. He was gone for quite some time. Do you know where he went?"

"Do *you*?"

"Sonaghaatee. A wealthy city about a hundred miles from Wakhet. I know he was there because I saw him. I saw him come to the Palace of Nabirye every day. On Besq, that's the name the goddess Emrin takes. But the Palace of Nabirye is much more than an orphanage. Your brother would speak to the priestesses; he would speak to the children." She paused and took a deep breath. "There was one in particular he had taken a liking to. She was stone-cold and capable, sharp of tongue, wit, and mind. The priestesses were all dedicants to Nabi-rye as well as the Whisper Goddess, Kadesh, and they were training this child and seven others to be spies and assassins. I watched this girl too. Every day. Because she is my granddaughter."

Tizzy gasped. "*Lora!*"

"She's an amazing girl. I had hoped to see her stay at the palace with the priestesses, but the reality is that anyone could come adopt her at any time, and I could lose her. I was so scared when your brother came to take her. I didn't know him. I didn't know what he'd do to her. The priestesses deemed him worthy, but they've made mistakes before. I know because I've had to fix some of them.

"Lora never saw him as a father, and why should she? She's never needed one. And he knew that, but he wasn't looking for a daughter. I stowed away on the ship back to Mirivin. I followed them onto the riverboat that sailed down the Undina Loch. And finally, I shadowed them back to House Hallenar, where Lora was introduced to the rest of your family and invited to serve the queen. It was everything I could have dreamed of for her.

"I tried not to make a habit of spying on her—she doesn't even know I exist, after all. I tried, I did. But Adeska found me anyway. I like to think it was because she's good at sniffing people out and not that I was maybe too conspicuous. I told her half-truths, and she believed me and pitied me. In time, I came to depend on her for updates on how Lora was faring. Then she went on the raids. I tried to keep her away from places where our friends were, but sometimes there was nothing I could do. Thankfully, I steered her away from the Convent."

"And Adeska knows you're a nightwalker?" Tizzy asked. "And she didn't try to kill you?"

"Goodness, no. When I told her, I tried to educate her a little bit, since you both know the reactions we usually get by now."

"Vampire?" Aleth folded his arms.

"Yes." Talora stared down at her boots. "I got her to understand that, just like anyone else, we're dangerous if we want to be. Most of us hold onto the Order that we followed in our mortal lives quite well. *I* certainly don't think I'm very dangerous."

"Why do you have the book?" Tizzy persisted. "This is a family heirloom!"

"She left it here by accident. I've had it for a year now, maybe. She doesn't find me to be a threat in the least, clearly. She'd come visit with Mariette, and we'd read it to her." She saw pain behind Aleth's eyes that she couldn't place. "Are you alright?"

He wasn't, and she knew it. He stared at the floor again, his mouth open as though he had something to say, but nothing would come out.

He furrowed his brow. "Tal, I lost ten years with them." He stopped, still trying to put his disjointed thoughts into words. He chose to lose those years. Right? "Ten years. Because I left. Because no one wanted me there." And he was fine with that. He would tell himself every single day that he was fine with it. He hated them. "I had *tried* to stay. I tried to make things better, to fix them in case they were my fault. I knew they weren't, but—" There was a tightness in his throat, and suddenly he felt vulnerable. "I was desperate to be loved by them all the same."

Talora's hand drifted over her lips in shame.

"But it wasn't going to happen. I left. And you walk in and, and you just—I don't even know my niece! And you're *reading* to her?"

"I'm sorry, Aleth. I should have told you from the start."

"No! You shouldn't have! You shouldn't have said anything, you should have lied, or maybe you shouldn't have been caught in the first place! How could you think this was okay?"

He went to stand, but Tizzy pulled him back down and wrapped her arms around him. "Those assholes don't deserve you."

"I got her to talk about you," Talora said. "At first she'd say that she didn't like to talk about it, about anything that happened. But then she'd let little things slip. Sometimes she'd get so angry with me for no reason, but she'd always apologize and talk about her anger problems and how she would blow up at the two of you the same way. She would sometimes wonder how to make things better. I almost told her about you. I thought it would help, but I know how you feel. So I didn't."

"But she doesn't miss me." He felt Tizzy pull him in closer. "She wanted to make things better. But did she say she missed me? If not, it sounds a lot more like she just wants to clear her own conscience."

Talora sat on her bed. "I miss you for her. How's that?"

"It's not good enough to bring me back to them." He broke away from Tizzy and hung his head between his knees. "Fuck them."

They were far from perfect, Tizzy thought, but she imagined he might like Allanis and Athen if he ever gave them a chance.

"Can you forgive me?" Talora asked.

He grimaced, rubbed his face, and finally sighed. "I'm sorry, Tal. None of this is your fault, I just get so screwed up whenever we have to talk about my family. I'll get over it someday. Besides, I'd rather they were your problem."

They decided to leave Talora's home soon after. It was dark, and they didn't feel like trying to find space in the cramped Treehouse to sleep. Talora bid them goodnight and closed her door. Creaking wooden steps turned into soft earth beneath their boots. A full chorus of insects and owls serenaded them as they started back to the Convent.

"Are you okay?" Tizzy asked, squeezing his hand.

"I will be," he told her. "All of that happened a little fast. I don't know how I should take it."

"You should be confused." She nodded. "Angry, sad, confused, probably a hundred other things. That would be a perfectly acceptable way to take it."

"What a relief." He smiled.

"I don't want to go back to the Convent. Do we have to go back right now?"

He shrugged. "We don't have to. I just thought you'd be tired. I'm tired."

"So let's sleep somewhere else!"

"You mean out here?"

"Yeah!" She skipped ahead and found something to kick. She didn't know what it was, but it flew beautifully. "That camp you set up was great."

He grumbled. "That was too much work. I don't want to do that right now." He stopped and looked at their surroundings. "But I'm pretty sure there's a cave around here. The ridge is over that way. Let's hope there's not a bear in it."

"Let's hope!"

They ran through the Wistwilds, excited and impish like children. The cave was at the ridge as he'd said, and it was quiet and empty of territorial wildlife. Aleth started collecting boughs, and Tizzy made a small fire to give them an hour's worth of warmth. When the ground was plush with pine they settled in, looking out past the jagged mouth of the cave and into the sky, catching glimpses of starlight between clouds.

"I could get used to this," Tizzy said, lying on her stomach. "Let's just move in here. Forever. Tal has a tree. We can have a cave."

"It's a good cave." He lay on his back and closed his eyes, breathing deeply. When he opened them again, Tizzy was crawling on top of him. "You don't waste any time, do you?"

"Why should I?"

"Because it's fun."

The glimmer of darkness in his voice made her hot. She crept closer until her curls brushed his cheek.

"Then how do you suggest we waste time?"

"My first suggestion—" he put his finger on her nose and gently pushed her away, "—is that we don't waste it in the dirt."

"Oh, come on." She maneuvered around his hand and nestled her face into his neck. "I just want to talk." Her lips softly grazed his skin as she spoke.

He bit his lip. "Talk about what?"

"The party. It was the first time you'd seen me up close since you left, right?"

It was an annoyingly sensitive subject to be coy about, but he played along. "It was." He could feel her lips turn up in a grin.

"Well, what did you think? Did you like my dress?"

He could just barely suppress a moan. "That *dress*." His hands were suddenly on her as he thought about it, and in the next moment, she was on her back, looking up at him.

"Yeah?" She didn't know how to wipe the smirk off her face.

"I loved that dress." He bit down on her neck, and she gasped.

"Even after I ruined it?"

"Especially after you ruined it." He kissed her deeply, tasting her, keeping one hand on her wrist and the other firmly on her hip. He squeezed, and she turned away to whimper.

"Maybe—" she moaned as he kissed down to her chest, letting go of her wrist to pull down her collar, "—I should ruin another one."

"Shh." He dragged his fingers across her lips, and she went quiet.

She loved the way he did everything, the way he kissed her and touched her, and how it was soft yet deliberate. His fingers raked down her thigh. Then they stopped.

"You've never done any of this before, have you?" There was a hint of panic in his voice.

"Should I answer or stop talking?"

He sighed and crept back up, kissing her forehead. "Speak. I don't know how I feel about this anymore."

She pursed her lips in thought. "How would you feel if I said I do this all the time?"

"First I'd say bullshit." He nibbled on her ear. "And then I'd say *prove it*."

She wanted to prove it so badly. "And how would you feel if the only things I knew were from the steamy books in the back of the library?"

He groaned, and it turned into a laugh. "That's what I thought." She pouted, and he took her face in his hands and kissed her once more, long and sweet. "I love you."

"I love you too. Are you making fun of me?"

"A little." He pressed his forehead to hers. "Tizzy, how far were you thinking this—us, together—was going to go?"

"I don't know. What's the farthest that such a thing *can* go?"

"We can't entertain this. We have to stop."

"How do you figure?" She traced her fingers around his jaw. "We could live forever. I'm not holding out forever."

He chewed his lip. "I don't know any delicate way to put this Tizzy, but your first experience cannot be with—" he choked on the word and was instantly red, "—your *brother*."

"It's okay if my second one is, though, right?"

He rolled off her and covered his face with his arms. She sat up, threw her head back, and laughed.

"You just had a handful of my ass, so it's a little late to back out now!"

He groaned. "How are you okay with this? I was just—oh gods, I was just lusting after you. I've *been* lusting after you. I'm gonna be sick. What the hell is wrong with us?"

She lowered herself back onto him, gleaming with the usual sin in her rust-brown eyes and the no-good smile that made his heart race.

"Look, even I know I was a fucking knockout in that dress."

"You were. It killed me to be so mean, looking down at you in the rain—" His lips found her again, and he turned her on her back. "Soaking wet, that black silk clinging to you, your makeup running."

He was back where she wanted him. She knew better than to let him talk himself out of what he wanted, and they both knew what he wanted. When she kissed him so clumsily and so hurried, she couldn't help it. Every touch was like fire on her skin, and his lips were the only place in the world she wanted to be. She wanted more, she was going to get more, but then he had her wrists pinned.

"Slow down."

"That's stupid."

"It's not." He kissed the corner of her mouth. "I don't want to rush this. That's not what I want with you." He laced his fingers with hers. "Can you contain yourself?"

"I'll just open up with the dress bit next time."

"You should."

They parted, and she lay on his chest, listening to him breathe. Her heart still raced for him. It took every fiber of her being to calm herself and settle for drinking up his presence.

"Sounds like you've been around," she said.

He laughed. "Ugh, you'd be ashamed of me."

She loved the sound and the way his chest moved. She loved imagining him and what he'd done to others and what he would do to her. He weaved his fingers through her hair as she watched the fire. It would die soon.

It didn't take her long to fall asleep, and it didn't take long for her Ethereal body to wander. All she wanted was some restful slumber, but curiosity sank in deep, and she crept around, taking in her surroundings.

The Wistwilds.

She was close. She looked up at the tallest trees next to her and realized they had passed the area earlier on the way to the Treehouse. Then there were voices. Tizzy hid, phasing through a bush.

People. At least four, two with torches. But the commotion told her there had to be more. They dressed in normal clothes that betrayed no royal allegiance, but one woman stood out. One woman she thought she had seen before. The ears of an elf and a long silver braid were giving her away.

"I'll be glad when this whole thing is over," Sinisia grumbled.

One of the men holding torches laughed. "Why's that? Don't like being a traitorous bitch?"

Sinisia crossed her arms. "That's got nothing to do with it. And I'm not a traitor. She left it up to me to decide how to carry out my task." She rubbed her shoulders. "It's just this guy and his *mother*. He's an asshole, and there's definitely something not right about her."

Then, two others came running past Tizzy's hiding spot.

"We found them!"

Tizzy's stomach turned. They were looking for other people. They had to be.

Sinisia thrust her arm into the air. "Alright, rally everyone! You know what happens next!" The others gathered around her and then set off back the way they had come, racing past Tizzy once more. She had the idea to follow them, and did for a moment, but then her world started to fade.

"Tizzy, wake up!"

She could hear Aleth's voice, but she was stuck, floating between Realms. What was wrong? Everything was black. The pine boughs were sharp and scratchy beneath her. She felt Aleth's hands on her shoulders, shaking her.

"Tizzy, *please!*"

She wished she could tell him that she couldn't, that she was stuck. Then he gasped. There was yelling and fighting.

"Get away!"

Someone hit someone—she could hear the impact of something blunt on flesh and the sound of a body hitting the ground. When there was no more fighting, she knew it was Aleth who'd fallen. She had to get up. She had to wake up! But even as her body was being dragged out of the cave, she remained in rigid slumber.

CHAPTER 14

TWO DRAMS

D oused by a bucket of frigid water, Tizzy roused, and the world appeared before her eyes. She coughed and gasped, and the water's chill took her breath away.

"Where am I?"

It was a single-room stone hovel. Four torches flickered wildly, lighting the room, and the only door was wide open and revealed a dark, early morning in the Wistwilds. Tizzy tried to move, only to find herself tied to a chair that had been bolted to the ground with iron spikes. Aleth was beside her in the same predicament, out cold with a bruised cheek and a bloody lip.

"It doesn't matter where you are."

The answer came from a man she'd never seen before, and she would have known a hideous face like his. His chin was bulbous, his face a jagged triangle, and his long brown curls were heavy with grime. But his voice was like velvet. If she had heard him speak without ever seeing him, she would have trusted him with her life.

"What did you do to him?" Tizzy growled.

The man shrugged. "Nothing yet."

The rope binding her wrists was tight and strong. Whoever they were, they didn't take their chances. She would've asked more questions, but panic drowned her, and she couldn't stop herself from fighting with the restraints.

"Aleth, wake up!"

If anyone could save them, it was him. She kicked but couldn't reach him.

"Please, do your best!" the man laughed. "He's the one we're waiting on."

Sinisia came into the room, tucking a wisp of silver hair behind a pointed ear, keeping her head high. The elf tried to avoid Tizzy's stare and folded her arms. "We should leave now."

"Are you crazy? This is exciting!" the man said.

"I've seen you." Tizzy searched Sinisia's face. "I know it. Where have I seen you?"

With a shiver, the elf ignored her. "You do what you want, Peyrs, but I'm not going to hang around here with that asshole and his weird hag. We did what we were supposed to do. I'm done. I'll be waiting for his half of the deal somewhere else."

Aleth started to stir. Sinisia glared at him.

"You got a weak stomach or something?" Peyrs asked her. "I don't think it'll be that bad. Sounds like the Mother is gonna wrap things up all nice and neat. Come on, stick around! I'll take you to town afterward!"

"Drop dead, Peyrs." She left without another word.

The man shook his head, then looked at Aleth and smirked. "Rise and shine, fucker."

Tizzy kicked and screamed, and Aleth hissed at her, "Be quiet!"

"*Be quiet?*"

He tried his binds. They were strong. "Just be quiet. Don't say anything; *don't make this worse!*"

Her gut writhed in horror when she realized what he meant. She couldn't breathe. "You, you can't get out?"

He didn't say anything and looked ahead, licking at the wound on his lip. He didn't know the man or the woman who had left, but they clearly knew enough about him.

"Any guesses why you're here?" Peyrs asked them. "I'll admit, I haven't been told very much about you two. I *have* been told that you're both stupid, but you—" he pointed at Aleth, "—you're smarter than you let on. I see you calculating over there."

"Maybe I'm smart," Aleth said. "Or maybe this is just routine by now."

Peyrs threw his head back with a cackle. "I promise you this won't be routine!"

The only thing that fazed Aleth was Tizzy's presence. Whatever he was going to face, he knew it would have been easier if she didn't have to go through it too.

"Who are you with?" he finally asked. "There's a lot of parties with an interest. Who won this round?"

"The most interested party of all!"

This voice was a new one from outside. It hummed a perky tune, then came inside and revealed itself a woman in black. She carried a small trunk. She didn't look old, but something betrayed the many decades she carried in her. Her fair skin seemed smooth, and her short, bushy hair seemed brown, but she looked at them with the eyes of an old woman. From her neck down, every inch of her was concealed in glossy black goatskin leather that hugged her body, and a heavy black tunic littered with pockets hung loose over her torso. She opened her trunk and pilfered through it, humming again.

"You!" Aleth's voice trembled.

"Tryphaena." Tizzy fought her bindings again, more desperately than before.

The woman scolded her. "*Mother* Tryphaena!" She held up a small glass vial to the light and shook it. "I didn't spend eighty years of my life between mainlands, dedicated to the path, just to be called by my name! How silly."

There was nothing cruel or anxious in her voice. She was merely completing another day's work.

"I am not the interested party," she clarified. "Not to say that I'm not interested, though. This makes for excellent research! And it's so nice to see you children again, all grown up." She had a thick glass syringe in her hand next. "I am sorry it's under these circumstances, but you will make a wonderful entry in my logs."

Tryphaena extracted the liquid from the vial until there was nothing left but residue. With a glittering smile, she stared into it, watching the gray liquid bead up at the top of the needle.

"Your sister was such a good student," she said. "Rori had so much potential. Sadly, it was ruined by that feeble heart of hers." With a wistful sigh, she stood next to Aleth. He could smell it, the noxious herbal aroma dripping from the needle. It brought him back to the night he'd gotten sick with Tizzy. He remembered fighting to breathe, his body burning and shaking, and Adeska screaming at him.

"So they sent you." His words were bitter. "I'm not surprised."

"You look surprised!" Tryphaena told him, working down his collar, exposing his neck. "Why else would you look like that? All that pain behind your eyes. You're making me feel bad."

"They didn't!" Tizzy yelled, kicking. "They wouldn't! They would *never!*" No matter how hard she pulled, the ropes wouldn't budge. She yelled again and then looked up and was dead quiet.

Rhett stood in the doorway.

"They didn't send her." He stared at Aleth. "I did."

Even Peyrs could feel the tension in the room. Aleth tried to glare back, to produce the most vicious look that he could, but his contempt ebbed away to bone-chilling dread as the moments drew on. He tried the ropes again, and Rhett started laughing.

"Don't bother!" He stepped closer, inspecting his brother's face. Aleth swallowed hard. "Who hit him?"

"I had to knock him out, my lord, to get him here." Peyrs proudly puffed out his chest as he said it. Rhett swung his fist into the man's face, and he fell. Tryphaena glanced over from her work with disinterest.

Rhett's face was red with rage. "I did not give anyone permission to hit him!"

Peyrs tried to explain. Rhett kicked him in his ribs, over and over, until he was quiet. Winded, he turned to Tizzy.

"You'll be happy to know that everyone at home is a fucking *coward*."

She pulled and writhed in the ropes till the cold air burned the rawness on her wrists. She kept trying, scratchy fibers cutting into her till she was numb. They wouldn't give.

"You two should have died years ago. And there was a time when we all knew it!" he spat. "But now they're making excuses for what we did. They're defending you, even hoping you're okay! What did you do?" He knelt down to look her in the eye, ignoring Aleth's struggles next to them. "What the fuck did you do to make them forget what monsters you are?"

"Get away from her!"

Tizzy watched Aleth's arms tremble as he put all his strength into the ropes to no avail. Rhett stood straight and narrowed his eyes.

"Phae, do it."

Tizzy screamed. "Wait, no, don't!"

Tryphaena stuck the needle into Aleth's neck without the slightest bit of care. He shut his eyes tight and clenched his teeth, fighting to hide the pain from Rhett. But Tizzy could see something was wrong. The poison entered his blood and worked its way through him. He gave up a gasp of pain.

Tizzy leaned over to him as far as her restraints would let her. "No! Is it going to kill him?"

"That's the idea." Tryphaena was smiling. She put the vial back in her trunk and took out a book and a twine-wrapped pencil.

Rhett folded his arms. "What are you doing?"

"I'm taking notes, you dunce." She flipped through pages until she found what she wanted and then wrote, staring Aleth down. "This is a new recipe. It's not as though I had the resources to test it out."

"This is a test?" Rhett balled up his fists.

"Yes. Look at him struggle. It must feel like absolute fire!"

"This needs to be ready to sell, Phae! The buyer will be here by the middle of the month!"

She wasn't listening. Rhett gave up and tried to join her. "Does he look dizzy to you?" she asked him. "He looks dizzy, right? Dear, open your eyes for me." She touched his face, and Aleth jerked away.

Rhett grabbed his collar. "I can make him dizzy."

"Will you please calm down?" Tryphaena shooed him away, and Aleth fell back against the chair. "I need to see exactly how this works. It's the process! So quit your alpha nonsense and let me work!"

Tizzy started kicking and grunting again, trying to find a new angle.

"This will work though, right?" Rhett asked. "She's getting on my nerves."

"Of course it'll work." She scribbled notes as quickly as she could think them. "Goodness, look at him. He's fighting it. Fascinating!" She took a rag from the trunk and dabbed away the sweat at his brow. "I put enough gray holland in that to kill a horse!" She turned to Rhett and laughed. "A nightwalker horse, I mean."

He wasn't amused. "Phae, it isn't working."

Aleth's eyes opened, bloodshot and crimson with bloodlust.

"Give him more!" Rhett told her, stepping back. He couldn't catch his breath.

"I only brought two drams!"

"What?"

"That's all I made!" Tryphaena closed her book and packed it into the trunk. "One for each of them! I thought it would be enough, I made it so strong—"

"Obviously you didn't!"

Rhett struck her. The woman recovered from the recoil, straightening her back to look at him, wiping away the red dripping down her chin.

"You petulant child." When Rhett raised his hand again, Tryphaena didn't flinch. "You had better not. There's not a single part of my body that won't kill you. My sweat is poison, my tears, my hair, my flesh, my *blood*. I would be very careful if I were you."

He hesitated, and that's when Tryphaena made her leave, taking her trunk and the last dram of poison.

"Stay close, you old bitch!"

"They're going to find you."

Rhett came back to Tizzy. "What's that? You wanna get hit too, little sister?"

She yelled and kicked and fought. "They're going to find out! And they're going to find you, and they're going to kill you!"

He smirked. "They won't kill me."

"You're right," she said. "They'll save the privilege for *him*."

"Him?" Rhett looked at Aleth with feigned pity. "I'm going to enjoy this."

Aleth's breathing was heavy and ragged. The wound on his lip had reopened, and it bled freely down his chin. Rhett gazed down at him, peeling off his gloves and cracking his knuckles.

"It's fine," he said with a sigh. "I don't need a poison to kill you. I think I can take it from here."

The ropes snapped. Aleth stood, his wrists raw, his balance off.

"You will never kill me." He spat out the blood in his mouth.

Something terrible was going to happen. Tizzy could feel it. It couldn't end well. She pulled and writhed and wished for the strength to break her own restraints, but nothing worked.

"I have to get out," she breathed. "Please, I have to!"

No one heard her. Rhett sized him up and took a step back.

"You can barely stand." He put his fists up. "What do I have to worry about?"

Malicious laughter came from outside, and the body of one of his men came soaring through the doorway.

"Light as a feather!"

Tizzy wanted to scream, but fear was the cork that kept it bottled. She knew the voice, the shrewd, incessant, dehumanizing voice. She didn't know whether to be relieved or horrified as Lilu strolled into the room, wiping blood off her hands with the sleeve of a disembodied arm. Tizzy looked down—it belonged to the dying man at her feet.

Aleth saw her, tried words, and then passed out, crumpling to the ground. Tizzy twisted and screamed again.

"What the hell is going on here?" Lilu asked. The longer she stared, the more serious her expression became.

"It's him!" Tizzy shouted. "*Him*! Our brother! *That* brother!"

It was a chance she had to take. She didn't know how long Aleth and Lilu had known each other, but she hoped it had been long enough for Lilu to learn about his past. The woman studied Rhett with curiosity.

Tizzy's stomach lurched—it dawned on her that whether Lilu knew the past or not, the truth of it was that she probably didn't care. A worse thought ran through her like ice. Maybe she was here to help him.

Rhett looked down at the blood and the dying man and finally grew hostile. "Who are you?"

"I was the first one to ask a question," Lilu said plainly. "You're being rude. Aren't you a lord or something? You've sure got the prissy boots of one."

Rhett swung at her, but she parried easily and threw her elbow into the side of his head. She started gesturing furiously to Aleth's motionless body on the ground.

"Did you do that?"

He wiped away the new blood trickling down his ear. "No, but I was responsible for it nonetheless. Is that good enough?" He put distance between them and summoned his casting tool—a slender bronze rod fitted with obsidian and citrine down its length, shaped into a crane's head at its tip. Lilu rolled her eyes.

"Of course you're an Akasha-loving shitfuck."

"It's more exciting than that," he assured her. With all his might, he swung the rod at the ground. Before it made contact, it hit the edge of another Realm, tearing an opening that gushed with fiery, kaleidoscopic energy. A fleshy pink creature crawled out, human-sized, armed with claws and spines like glossy black arrowheads.

Lilu threw her head back and howled with laughter.

"Stop laughing!" Rhett was shaking with rage. "Do you have any idea what I've done? Do you have the faintest idea what that is?" His blue eyes were wide. His anger was losing to a different emotion. "Normal people can't handle the fucking sight of a daemon, and you're just *laughing*! I said stop it!"

She gasped for air and wiped away a tear. Rhett spoke with words that Tizzy could hear in her bones were Forbidden—vile, painful words of a language no human should speak. The creature he had conjured went flying at Lilu with blinding speed.

She avoided the attack, shifting into the white and gray scaled form Tizzy was all too familiar with. Rhett's eyes were wide as she spoke the same tongue, sending the creature back into the tear. With another phrase, the tear closed with a searing hot crackle.

"You idiot!" She still roared with laughter. "You send a lesser daemon at me? And a fucking *carnitoth*, no less?"

Rhett backed away from her. The fear in his eyes had become awe. "You're a Greater Daemon. Wh-what kind?"

"Ugh, daemonologists. You're all pathetic. I should drag you down into those Hell Planes you're all so obsessed with and let you feel the hellfire for yourself."

She hissed, showing fangs wet with venom, and he ran. When she turned back around, Tizzy was sobbing.

"Oh gods." The daemon scoffed and started to untie her, changing back into her human form. "What's the matter with you?"

"Look what they did to him!" The second she was free, she ran to Aleth's body and fell to her knees. "I'm going to kill Rhett! I'm going to kill him!"

"Give him some space," Lilu snapped, hovering over them. "And you? Killing someone? Don't make me laugh. Now, if Aleth weren't dying, he could catch up and break that man's scrawny neck. But you? I doubt you even have the nerve."

Tizzy's breath was hot and ragged while the tears streamed down her face. She hated Lilu. The promise to kill her had been the only thing giving her the will to live when she had to fight the daemon's venom. It wasn't Talora who had saved her life. It wasn't Isa who had saved her life. It was Lilu. And she hated it.

"You don't know me," she growled.

"I don't have to. You couldn't kill someone. You think about doing it, and I bet you have yourself so convinced that you want to do it. But you couldn't."

She had to argue, to scream, to throw a fit and prove her wrong. But she couldn't. Tizzy couldn't even concentrate. All of Lilu's words fell right through her. With quivering hands, she rolled Aleth onto his back.

"Is he going to live?" she asked.

"Are you blind?"

Tizzy whimpered and cried into his chest. With a grumble, Lilu pried her away and started dragging him across the floor.

"Outside."

She obeyed, stepping over Peyrs and the dead man she didn't know. A drizzle of cold rain greeted them under the twilight. A dropped torch flickered on the ground, fighting to remain alive.

"What do I do?" she said to the daemon. "He can't die!"

Lilu raised an eyebrow. "Why not? People die. It's what they do. Especially monsters like us."

"We're not monsters! *You're* a monster!"

"Watch it, you little bitch. I just saved you." She jabbed her finger into Tizzy's chest. "You're lucky I was in the area when I got hungry. I had to hunt."

And the proof was everywhere around them. Those who hadn't escaped were dead on the ground, ripped open and gutted, strewn about the trees. The taste of copper was heavy in the wet air. Before the massacre, their weapons had rested against a tree trunk, but they were scattered, Wish and Mercy amongst them, laying innocently in the red mud.

"He can't die!" Tizzy sobbed again. "People die, I know that. But not him! And not by Rhett!" She kept her scream behind clenched teeth and raked her nails into her scalp.

Lilu crouched down by Aleth and wiped at his bloodied lip with her thumb. Horrified, Tizzy watched her taste it.

"What are you doing?"

She ran over, and Lilu shoved her to the ground. "Stop it. You're making me angry."

"I'm making you *angry*?"

Lilu leaned in and licked up more of his blood. After a sufficient taste, she sat up and wiped her mouth.

"I'm sorry that you're *angry*!" Tizzy shouted. "Do you have any idea what I had to go through? What it was like?"

"No because I don't have to feel your stupid mortal emotions!" Lilu yelled back. "I'm a daemon! We are not created to feel that which does not serve us! It's a wonder I even know anger."

But she *did* feel something. Tizzy could see it in her face as she spoke. For the first time, there was something other than pure malice.

"He's going to be fine," Lilu said, tasting the blood still lingering in her mouth. "He's scared and ashamed and furious. And he will live."

Tizzy was so relieved, she sobbed again. "You can tell from his blood?"

"It tastes a certain way when they're going to die."

"And what about the other part?"

Lilu gazed down at Aleth bitterly, brushing aside the sweat-slick hair in his face. "I don't have the *capacity*—" she nearly spat the word out, "—to feel beyond hatred and rage, not unless you count being bored and annoyed. I can't feel other things for myself, but I can feel them for others."

"Empathy through blood." Tizzy wiped away fresh tears. "I can't imagine how that serves you."

"No, you can't! You don't even know the first thing about a lilitu!"

Tizzy tried to steady her breathing, but everything in her quaked and trembled and crashed. Lilu was suddenly exploding with emotion from Aleth's blood, and she didn't know what to say.

"Of course I don't. The first time I ever saw you, you came at me—"

"You think you know everything!" Lilu stood and balled up her fists. "You think things are simple! That they are a certain way because you're *mortal* and things are simple for mortal people! Well, they're not!" She shook her head. "You think you know everything. And you think you know *him*! You don't know anything about him or me or what we were or what we did!"

Tizzy stared up at her with glassy eyes. "What you did?"

"I have felt *all* of his pain! Many times over! Stand up, you worthless shit!"

She crawled back as Lilu stormed after her, but she wasn't quick enough. The daemon pulled her to her feet.

"I know who you are! He isn't the weak, lowly bloodkin he plays at the Convent. He's yours, isn't he?"

"I—"

Lilu shoved her away. She stumbled back but kept her footing and stood tall.

"This—" the daemon gestured to Aleth, "—*this*, this idiot! He can't cope with anything! So do you know what he'd do, Tizzy?" She shoved her again. "There was a time when he'd come to *me*." Her nostrils flared with a memory she didn't like. "He'd get high off my venom and lie there, numb to the world. And I'd taste his blood and *feel*. All the people who had hurt him, the ones who had betrayed him, the friends he'd lost, I felt all of it." She looked up into the misty, wet air, and inhaled deeply. "He would come to me, again and again. Addicted to me. That's why Talora hates me. He'd spend more time lost to the fevers than he'd spend lucid, and every time, I would take just enough from him to feel. And every time, amidst the anguish, I could feel *you*."

Tizzy swallowed hard. "Do you love him?"

Lilu roared. "I don't know what that means!" She shoved her again. "But I do know that this is your fault."

She was loud when she was angry. Tizzy could only fight back with more tears. "My fault? What could I have done?"

"He is yours! You made him, he is yours, it is your responsibility to keep him safe!"

The daemon screamed at her, and Tizzy withered inside. Her chest tightened till she could barely breathe.

"He is your responsibility. You're supposed to protect him! I don't care where else your loyalties are. I don't give a shit whether or not you stay and fight for us at the Convent. But you better start taking this seriously. You better make sure this never fucking happens again!"

Every word hurt. Every word shocked Tizzy into silence. She stared up at Lilu, who was drenched. The rain, gently washing away the horrors behind them, was the only sound until Tizzy nodded.

"Okay."

"What are you going to do?"

Her eyes fell on Wish laying in the dirt. "I'm going to get better. I'll train and practice and get stronger."

"What, your sword?" Lilu looked at it over her shoulder. The two blades were snug in their scabbards. "Are you any good?"

"No, but maybe if I feed more—"

"Won't matter. Without skill, it's pointless. Not all of your kind gets stronger or faster with blood."

"Then I'll work harder! I can get good at it, I know it. It'll just take time!"

Lilu scoffed. "Time. Was all of this because you thought you had time? Next time you might not have any. What else can you do? Or are you really as pathetic as I thought you were?"

There were more tears, but Tizzy wouldn't let them fall. She clenched her jaw through them, swallowed them, and put her fists up. "I'm not."

"Your stance isn't terrible."

Tizzy hadn't sparred with Lora in years, but her muscles remembered the way to move. "I'm better at this than I am with a sword."

"Good." Lilu put her own fists up. "For his sake, I'll make you even better."

"What?"

"Do you give a shit about him or not? If you want to protect him, this is the way. No one else at the Convent can match me, so don't waste your time. I'll train you. I'll beat you bloody every day till the day I can't."

She was right, and Tizzy hated it. But knowing she had failed Aleth hurt worse than anything she would endure from Lilu. She was right. He couldn't be the one to always save them, not when it was in her blood to surpass them all.

Her eyes were blurry with tears. "Do your worst."

"Don't worry. I won't."

They fought. Tizzy threw punches that missed. Lilu juked out of harm's way until she finally parried with such force, Tizzy's arm went numb. And then Lilu hit her, repeatedly, finding glee every time the blood hit her own face. Tizzy tried to recover and kick, and Lilu backed away and put distance between them.

"You're awful, but you're not the worst."

Tizzy came at her in a frenzy, striking every way she knew how until she finally landed a punch to the daemon's ribcage. Lilu responded with a backhand that knocked her out cold. Panting, she looked down at Tizzy's body, face down in the dirt.

"I'll make you better. I promise."

The rain became steady. The blood of the slain seeped deep into the earth. Lilu let it wash her clean of the fighting and the emotions and the memories that she had felt. Someday, she thought she might learn to feel them on her own.

"Oh gods, what have you done?"

The daemon's anger returned at the sound of Talora's voice. She was out of breath, leaning against a tree, rain and sweat soaking her veil.

"They're fine," Lilu grunted.

"What did you do?"

"Shut up!"

Lilu slicked her wet hair back and took a heavy breath. Talora approached her, her footsteps small and careful as she looked down at the unconscious siblings.

"I heard screaming, so I started looking around. I saw people running away from something."

"They were the ones who started it." Lilu folded her arms. "These two really would be dead if it weren't for me."

"So then, you didn't?"

Lilu nudged Tizzy with the tip of her boot. "I'm responsible for her. She'll wake up before he does; I didn't hit her that hard. But you've all got a lot to worry about."

Talora crouched down and started to heave Tizzy onto her back. "What do you mean by that?"

"There'll be a nightwalker poison on the market soon. They tested it out on him."

"Then let's head back to the Convent." Talora brushed some dirt off Tizzy's cheek. "We'll discuss it there."

***

Allanis had barely slept. Lora didn't stir at all when she slipped out of bed late at night. No one saw her walk through the halls barefoot. Alone with her thoughts, she stood on the balcony that oversaw the entirety of Suradia, gazing southward across her town. She missed how carefree she'd been before Aleth arrived, and she missed the feeling that she would only ever have to mind her spending habits to keep her people well and stay afloat.

How could she have been so blind? There was an entire world of responsibilities that she'd been ignoring, and a mountain of work that had been casting a shadow over her. Did she know her town at all, truly? She stared into the twilight, watching clouds far in the distance start to take on the colors of a sunrise. None of King Byland's advisors had been ready to help a child. They had left her with nothing but the walls of a dying, neglected empire.

It was fortunate that Anavelia had entered the fray when she had. Early on, Anavelia was vulnerable, foreign, trying to find her place. And Allanis had just wanted a friend. Without Ana's knowledge of the world and its politics, Allanis doubted Suradia would still have its independence. Her arms dangled over the wrought iron rails.

She needed a plan. For everything. And she couldn't get caught her family's nonsense. Adeska and Centa would either handle their situation with grace and poise, or she wouldn't allow them to handle it at all. Anyone within the royal residence would be made to act accordingly. They would not embarrass her.

The plan. What was the plan? She had to be able to defend herself if and when the Hunters came. How would that go?

"The real question is, is it really Suradia that I'm worried about?"

Her words were whispered into the day's first raindrops. As much as she knew House Hallenar and the town should be her priority, her heart wanted to find Tizzy, to protect her and Aleth. She knew they were the real ones in trouble.

"How do I find them? They could be anywhere."

How do you predict the actions of someone you never really knew? Allanis was so exhausted of it all, she wanted to cry. But she couldn't. That wasn't the face she was going to show the world anymore. She watched the town, sound asleep save for the rainbirds and the crows, a mix of silver and black peppering the streets. They made her think of her father. She sifted through memories of a happier time. She could've spent the entire day there, lost in reverie, but as the sky broke into a lavender dawn, she spotted two figures approaching House Hallenar.

She knew no one would be awake to answer their knocking and hurried down to meet them herself. Soon, Stormy joined her. The timing was perfect—by the time she'd made it to the front doors, the guests were coming up the steps.

Djara and her mother shared a look of bewilderment when the doors opened.

"Your Grace?" the woman asked.

"Yes!" Allanis beamed, out of breath. "That is me! Was there an appointment? Did I forget it?"

"No, Your Grace. I apologize if it's early." The woman spoke softly but with purpose. "I was instructed to come by House Hallenar for a meeting. No time was specified." She gave a sideways glance to Djara. "By gods, this had better not be a *prank*—"

Allanis cleared her throat. "Isa?"

"Yeah!" Djara squeaked. "She was telling the truth, right?"

"She was. Follow me."

At first glance, Djara's mother was exactly the kind of person Allanis hoped she'd be. Serious but gentle. Plain but pretty. She could disappear in a crowd or stand in a spotlight and steal the show. She was tall and walked strong. Her skin was brown and freckled like her daughter's, and her almond-shaped, catlike eyes discreetly observed everything. She didn't busy herself with looking fancy and fussy for a date with the queen—Allanis liked that—and stayed true to her trade with functional clothing. But Allanis could see that it still must've been some of her best garb. The leather was sturdy and polished, the boots and the vest and every pouch and strap. The stitching was perfectly fitted to her body and even decorative in some places.

It was only the matching yellow scarves she wore with Djara that betrayed the image her skill set painted.

Allanis led them through the halls and started to feel silly in her bare feet, but it wouldn't do any good to go running for slippers after she'd already made her first impression. Stormy sniffed the newcomers with excited curiosity and bounded back and forth, barking his discovery.

"Cut it out; you're going to wake everyone!"

Stormy gave one last hushed *yap* before obeying his Queen. But he had already achieved what he'd set out to.

"Alli?"

Lazarus appeared from the library as she started leading her guests to the Council room. She showed her disapproval with hands on her hips.

"Do you sleep?" she whispered.

"Very little."

She snickered. "*Night owl*. Of course."

He ignored her. "What are you doing?" His eyes met the guests standing several paces behind Allanis. "I thought you named me your advisor. You said I'd be present for all meetings."

"They were here, and I thought you'd be asleep. I didn't want to turn them away; that'd be rude. And so would waking you! Honestly, I was trying to do you a favor."

He sighed. "Well, I'm not asleep."

"Then let's go."

Once in the Council room, Djara's eyes were wide. She watched Lazarus go from candle to candle, lighting them with petty magic. She'd never seen someone skilled enough to conjure the petty flame with just a finger.

Her mother stood patiently in the center of the room, surveying as inconspicuously as she could. House Hallenar and the queen had thus far not been what she'd expected. The room felt dusty, old, and incomplete.

It was precisely what excited her about this moment. Something was happening, *growing*, and she was about to make her case to be a part of it. The room came to life, and Allanis and Lazarus took their seats at a table at the end of the room. Allanis gestured to a lonely chair.

"Your name is Djara, right? Please, sit."

Djara sat only a short distance from her mother and folded her hands in her lap like a noble.

"You already know me, probably." Allanis quickly smothered her awkward smile with something more curt. "Beside me is my Master Advisor and brother, Lazarus Hallenar. He may interject with some questions of his own."

"Of course, my queen. If I understand this correctly, this is an interrogation?"

Allanis scratched her head. "No, not quite."

"An interview," Lazarus said. "The queen wants you for her Council. The position of Master of Dusk is currently vacant."

"See, Ma? I told you!"

Djara's mother was floored but didn't show it. "I heard it was a job offer, but for the Queen's Council? *Me?*"

Allanis shrugged. "Maybe. Tell me about yourself. Who are you two? Isa didn't tell me very much."

The woman fixed her posture and nodded. "My name is Ravina Songo. That—" she gestured to her daughter, "—is Djara, my little girl. I believe Isa recommended me because I am a member of the Eastern Mirivin Guild of Spies."

"I didn't even know that existed." Allanis tapped her chin.

"That is the goal." Ravina bowed her head. "I am a Whisper Mage with a secondary focus in Ruby Magic, though the days where Ruby Magic served me are long in the past."

Ashenlaa—the Goddess of Love, Beauty, and Romance—was seen in much better light than the manipulative Ruby Magic she gifted her Akasha-inclined followers. Allanis drummed her fingers on the table.

"What made you decide to take it up at all?" she asked. "I'm sure it's a popular choice to pair with Whisper Magic; it makes you a formidable spy. But everyone's choices come with a story."

"It was an assignment, Your Grace." Ravina didn't let the dread onto her face, keeping it cold in her stomach. "I was hired to learn the secrets of an important man visiting Wakhet. Djara's father, actually." She'd told her daughter the story before to lessen the impact of its gruesomeness, but it was never easy to tell. "A member of a different Council had found the means to contact the Guild, and I was chosen for the job. I had to find out how much this man knew about the Council and its skeletons. We knew he'd be making a trip to Wakhet on business—he was a purveyor of historical artifacts—and my plan was to be in Besq at that time and run into him by chance.

"I started studying Ruby Magic extensively in preparation for my assignment. I had convinced myself it was right for me, that *that* was who I was. I was not hired to hurt or kill him, you see. Just to acquire the information, and I knew that this would be the best way to do that. The Ruby Magic could get me harmlessly in his space, and then I could perform the Whisper Magic without him ever knowing. I had my disguise, and I ran into him in Wakhet's marketplace. I wasn't expecting to fall head over heels in love, though. What he and I had was blissful and intense, and it almost made me flee the Guild for good and stay with him.

"And then I found out *he* was a Ruby Mage." She said it as coolly and evenly as she could, though her insides were shaking. "Everything started to fall apart after that. The illusion was shattered, knowing he had manipulated me from the beginning. All I wanted to do was finish the assignment and return to Mirivin. That's what I did, and I did it carelessly, blowing my cover. In the end, things got violent. I had to kill him."

Silence blanketed the room. Ravina waited for a response, keeping her air of indifference.

"Is this why you've ceased the practice?" Lazarus asked.

"Yes. I am capable of doing what I do without relying on love games. It's a cloudy, hazy thing, and I don't care for drama or crimes of passion."

"If you're part of the Guild—" Allanis pursed her lips, "—could you even be on my Council?"

"Yes, of course, Your Grace. There are several others in the Guild who are currently in a position of Master of Dusk."

She thought on it for a moment and frowned. "So the whole Guild knows everything about everyone. You could be a direct line to my enemies, nevermind the fact that it lets the Guild as a whole pull the strings on the entire mainland as it sees fit. There's potential for any-one to know my every move."

"My Ma isn't a talker!"

"*Djara.*" Ravina looked over her shoulder, giving the girl a sec-ond-long glance. "Your Grace, you are correct. The Guild, operating within it, is a complicated game." For the first time, Allanis saw a faint smile on the woman's face. "But see it as a resource. When you want to open a door, sometimes you speak, and sometimes you don't. And if you want to guard your own door, it's the same rule. You have to know which commands to use on whom and to what end. And I have been a part of it for twenty-three years. I know exactly how every member works. I know how to protect what you have and how to get what you want."

"There is no doubt about your capability," Lazarus told her. "It's your loyalty in question. The Master of Dusk is a position that almost leaves us more vulnerable if filled. If we didn't have need of it, it's likely we'd leave it vacant."

Ravina took a deep breath. "Rhett Hallenar and the Poison Mother called Tryphaena were spotted close to Davrkton last night."

Allanis gasped. Isa could have told Djara and Ravina what little she knew about the situation. It was possible that what she'd just heard was a lie. But she knew in her bones that it wasn't.

"We were too late."

"My queen, I am loyal to my family. That's the truth. I can serve you for as long as I can remain that way."

Lazarus leaned over and whispered to Allanis, "Are there any others we know of who could take the position?"

Her heart ached. "No, not yet. What should I do? She told us exactly what we would have asked her to find out."

Ravina cleared her throat. "You have the authority to kill me if I commit treason. That is always within your means, not that I have any intention of being treasonous."

"Ma! You're terrible at this!"

"You are," Allanis said, groaning into her hands. "Lazarus, what do we do? Is there even a point, anymore? He found her! They'll know everything! It's only a matter of time now, before—"

"Alli, stop. We have work to do no matter what stage this is in."

Djara rose from her seat and stood next to Ravina, as tall and proud as she could. "My mother doesn't give herself enough credit."

Both Allanis and Lazarus thought the woman had given herself quite a bit of credit as it was, but they let the girl speak.

"She's a woman with high moral standards." Djara looked up at her, her eyes full of admiration. "And she raised me to be the same way. She might put her family before yours, Your Grace, but it doesn't mean she'll do wrong by you."

Ravina's high moral standards only made Allanis worry more. "Ravina, Djara, what would you think of people—" the queen sighed as she chose her words, "—of people who were good at heart, who wanted good things for others and loved helping those around them, but had deeply questionable interests?"

Ravina raised an eyebrow. "Questionable *how?*"

Allanis made more noises of struggling thought, turning away from Lazarus's expression, which managed to be terrified, pleading, and accusatory all in one.

"For the sake of this example, let's say that they, oh, I don't know—" she shrugged, "—worshipped a Forbidden deity."

"My queen?" Ravina was used to her own answers coming quickly. This one wasn't. "I don't think there are people like how you describe."

"There are," Allanis assured her. "Lazarus, I need you to step out for a moment. And Djara, would it be alright for me to have a word alone with your mother?"

"Ma?"

"Do as your queen asks!" Ravina told the girl.

Lazarus studied Allanis before rising from his seat. "I don't think this is wise," he whispered. "You gave me a job; you should let me do it."

"I will," she said. "But this one is different. This position is different. It's not like hiring for the others."

With nothing more than a nod, Lazarus left, taking Djara with him, and closed the door on the Council room. Allanis stood and started pacing in front of the table.

"Everything's changing."

Ravina didn't speak. She watched her queen and the way she battled her indecision.

"*I'm* changing." Allanis sat on the edge of the table. "You see the state we're in. I know you do."

"Suradia? Or House Hallenar?"

Allanis scoffed. "Take your pick. They'd be one and the same if you really started to compare."

"You have no guards in front of House Hallenar or anywhere in it, as far as I can tell," Ravina started. "For gods' sake, you answered the doors *yourself*, early in the morning when you should have been asleep. I could have had a knife at your throat in half a second."

"I didn't think it had been a test, but now that you mention it—"

"It *was* a test. You failed. More than once. There was no one in this room but you, your brother, myself, and Djara. I don't have measure of your brother's ability, but I'm quite certain that we could've killed you. Even right now, I could kill you."

Allanis shrugged, keeping it to herself that Lazarus was a terrifyingly capable bodyguard. "This is why things are changing. I need all the help I can get. I don't know how King Byland kept the place running; there's no evidence of anything! We're just a bunch of little houses behind a wall that no one is bored enough to knock down yet. But that could all change in an instant."

"It could? Or it *did*?"

"Ravina, do you want the job?"

"I want what's best for my family."

"That's not what I asked."

Ravina stared through her with her hands at her back. She had to think. Even before arriving, she didn't know if she'd want to take a job from the queen, but this was not the job she had expected.

"I want to be a part of something. It's always been a dream to somehow shape this place. I love Suradia; it's my home. I was born here, and I hope to die here. I know everything about this town that there is to know. I'd be *invaluable* to your Council. But my gut tells me I have something to fear."

"Your gut is smart. It's picking up on my family's problems," Allanis said dryly. "That's going to be the hardest part, accepting them and the issues we're facing. The scope of it, of this, of us and everything we're going through, it's too big to ignore. For Suradia's sake."

"Do you want me for this job?"

"I do, but I don't know how to tell if I can trust you. *My* gut tells me I can trust everyone, so I'm trying not to rely on it as much these days. Not since—"

Her words stopped, and the memory of how things used to be hollowed her. She'd always had someone else to determine the motives of others.

Ravina nodded, allowing a little smile onto her face. "Lady Tizena."

Allanis took in the biggest breath she could and then deflated. "What do you know?"

"Haven't seen her around since the end of last month. Last time she was seen, she took the East Gate out."

"Was she with anyone?"

"She was. Unknown male."

Allanis smiled. "Good. Ravina, if you become the Master of Dusk for Suradia, there are some things I'll have to tell you that might make you change your mind. That's what makes this decision hard for me."

"I'm guessing your brother Lazarus is the worshipper of a Forbidden deity."

"I wish it ended there. He is a great man, you know."

"How can a great man worship something Forbidden?"

"I'd love to tell you about it sometime, if I can trust you. Isa and Gavin are residing in House Hallenar, and you and Djara would be free to do so as well if you'll take the seat. Or Byland's advisors all had their own villas just a short distance away if you'd rather have that. I could have one cleaned and ready for you in a few days."

"You're offering us your home?"

"Absolutely." Allanis noticed the dust she'd picked up on the bottoms of her feet. It was the dust that had accumulated during her rule, and now it was time to wash House Hallenar and save Suradia. "There's more than enough room here. Lazarus is going to help me hire to keep this place guarded and in order, so eventually it'll be safe too!"

Ravina folded her hands together neatly. "I accept. I will be your Master of Dusk, Your Grace."

CHAPTER 15

DICHOTOMY

The clouds came in from the north. By midday, a light drizzle turned into a full-on storm. Branches snapped under the weight of the downpour, rain fell in sheets that rippled in the wind, and the ground was mud. Under a cold, gray sky, Centa decided the road to Suradia from Kamdoria was no longer traversable.

"What's next?" Phio asked.

Centa adjusted the hood of his cloak and looked over his shoulder. Behind him, Phio was cloaked and on horseback, holding a warmly bundled Mariette precariously while the horse complained of the weather, snorting and shaking his head and wandering away from Phio's guidance. The mount was a light, agile, temperamental creature but responded to Phio's every movement and command with precision. Just not in a downpour. Centa's own horse was bred in the mountain city of Yzen Vale. A large, broad, and quiet beast, it was stalwart in the face of most anything.

Centa guided his horse back to them with a sigh and took Mariette. "We'll have to turn back. It'll be flooded further down."

"Will you tell her you're not coming?"

After what Adeska had said, Centa couldn't afford not to return to House Hallenar. She sounded like a wreck. Something was wrong, and he didn't feel good about staying behind.

But he didn't feel good about going, either.

"We'll turn back and find another way."

"The fork a couple miles back?"

"Yeah. We can try the east path. The west goes too close to the Undina Loch. It'll probably be flooded like this one."

They headed back the way they came, careful not to press the horses too hard. They still had over half the journey ahead of them.

When the fork was in sight, Mariette started squirming in Centa's arms.

"You're hungry," she said.

"We brought plenty of rations. I can eat when we stop for a break."

"It won't stop till sundown."

Phio looked up, shielding his eyes. "You mean the rain, Mari?"

"Thunder soon," she added.

Centa knew better than to doubt her. "We'd be out of our minds to camp out here. Do you know if there's an inn nearby?"

"Barton Hovel," Phio answered with a grin. "Ugly place and ugly people, but there's food, and they're good to the horses."

"Is it expensive?"

"My treat."

"Phio," Centa grumbled. "You're an *artist* now. You're good, but you're not that good."

Phio led the way down the east path, looking for a grassy side road. "The queen will pay me back. Use your resources, friend."

Using his resources, in this case his sister-in-law, was his least favorite way to solve a problem, but he didn't argue. Mariette was smart, well-spoken, and patient, but she was still two-and-a-half and was going to loudly protest the rain at some point.

The grassy side road was just how Phio remembered it, if not a great deal farther into the east path. The ground hadn't become mud yet and instead was soft, plush, wet grass that held the imprint of hooves as they trotted through it. When the trees grew thinner around them, Centa could see it—a stout stone longhouse with a chimney, belching broken plumes of smoke into the rain.

Centa wouldn't have called it ugly, but it wasn't up to Caequin standards or even Suradia standards. There was not one single decorative feature about it. Even the wooden sign outside was only there as a place marker. But it was big, and the stables were dry and secure, and it wasn't so busy as to be uncomfortable. It would be a perfect resting place, Centa thought.

"The Bartons own this place," Phio said. "Have for generations. I haven't been here since I was a kid, though. Looks bigger than before. Maybe they should call it something other than a hovel."

There were a lot of Bartons, Centa noted. Especially working the stables. A lot of them were scrappy young children covered in mud, playing a strategic game of tag.

Phio led them to the stable master—a tired lady dwarf—and they dismounted. "Good afternoon!"

The dwarf looked them up and down for the drowned rats they were. "Is it?"

"No," Mariette answered.

The dwarf noticed her for the first time and suddenly smiled. "You've got a good girl there, boys. You need your horses cared for while you stay?"

"Yes, please." Phio reached for a pouch on his belt. "How much for these two?"

She looked at them thoughtfully. "Ten silver for each. No, wait." Phio's indignant horse demanded a second inspection. "Make it eleven for this one."

He handed her the silver. "That's only fair. Montague has a slight attitude." He patted him playfully and the horse snorted. "Please don't cause any problems."

"Montague?" The dwarf giggled. "And what's this one over here?"

"Honua," Centa said. "He'll give you no trouble. He'll be sleeping the whole time."

"Alright then. Meeka!" She flagged someone down and a stable girl came racing over. "Get these two settled in. Montague and Honua. It's the small, wiry one that'll make you work. Understand?"

"Yes, Bruna. I'll take good care of them."

Centa took their bags off Honua's saddle and Meeka took both sets of reins and led the horses away. Bruna turned to them again.

"The fare will cover you till tomorrow afternoon. If you're still here by then, I'll need you to check in and pay up. We've no rooms in the Hovel, but it's warm inside and there's space to set up your bedrolls. Cohen and Elle serve meals every two hours. It's mostly roasted birds and potatoes, but I'm told Elle put on a stew for the storm."

"Thanks, Bruna." Phio waved to her and they headed toward the Hovel.

"Is she a Barton?" Centa whispered.

"She married one," Phio told him. "One of the Barton men had a couple of boys with his first wife, but they didn't grow right. Each one was born with a misshapen head and curled up arms and legs. Nicest boys I've ever met, but neither one lived very long. Old Barton was afraid of more short-lived, suffering children, so he decided he just wouldn't have any more.

"His wife became pregnant. She fled the mainland with a healthy baby and another man. A few years later, Old Barton crawled out of his depression and fell in love with Bruna, and since humans and dwarves can't have offspring, it's been a weight off his shoulders."

"Ouch about the first wife."

"If it makes you feel any better, the ship they took was attacked by pirates on its way to the Siopenne Mainland. There were no survivors."

Centa shrugged. "I don't know if that makes me feel better or not. I still can't imagine what I'd do or how I'd react."

Mariette sighed, and neither man knew why. They stepped into the Barton Hovel, assaulted by warmth, smoke, must, and sweat. Centa perused the patrons and decided against letting Mariette down to walk. She could feel his hold on her tighten.

The Hovel, no longer appropriately named, was monstrous on the inside. The west end had a massive hearth that roared tirelessly, warming the space where others had set up their bedrolls. The east side had a smaller hearth and rows of communal tables where patrons ate and gambled. Glimpses of the kitchen could be seen, full of more Bartons who came in and out with food and drink.

A woman approached them after setting two heavy glasses of ale down at a table. She was younger than them and showed her smile on a smooth face framed by dark hair.

"Hello, boys. Shacking up here for the storm?"

Phio felt himself blush. "Exactly! What's the fare?"

"A silver each for the space. The little one can stay for free," she cooed. Phio, hands sweaty, placed two silver stars into the palm of her hand. "First meal is free. Stew's not quite ready yet, but how about a piece of bird and some bread?"

He stuttered. "Oh, uh, yes, please."

She laughed. "I'll have it out to you in a moment. Go set up your space out there." She gestured to the west end and then disappeared into the kitchen.

Centa smacked Phio's arm as she left. "You said they were ugly!"

"They *were*! I don't know what happened!"

Perplexed and embarrassed, Phio led them near the hearth so they could unpack their bedrolls. Centa didn't think he'd be able to sleep but tried to look like a normal traveler following protocol. He watched Mariette fumble around, trying to peel off her wool coat.

"Here." He slipped the cap off her head—it had been knitted by a woman in Kamdoria to look like a rabbit's head—and then he unwrapped her scarf. "Sometimes it's easier if you start with the little things."

"Oh." She found the first clasp of her coat and did the rest herself.

"Most two-year-olds can barely hold a spoon right, much less un-button something."

Her mismatched eyes gave him a dry stare. "I'm two-and-a-half."

He loved her more than he ever could have imagined. She was not what he'd expected, of course. Others had prepared him for a different kind of child, one who was noisy and who cried and who didn't like things. A typical child. Mariette had her moments, but he knew the gods had seen him favorably to give him a girl who was not afraid of the world.

"This place is only going to get more crowded," Phio sighed. He adjusted his bag, fluffing and punching it down until it held a pillow-like shape.

"Some of them will leave when the storm lets up tonight."

"The ones in blue will." Mariette had started gazing into the fire.

"The ones in—" Centa looked around at the others, "—blue?" He didn't see a speck of blue anywhere.

The dark-haired woman returned with two bowls, one boasting an extra serving cut up into little pieces for Mariette. "A hunter sold us some turkeys from his haul this morning. They've been roasting for hours!" Each bowl had a leg and a cut of hot bread that soaked up the fat dripping down the browned skin.

They thanked her, Phio even slipping her an extra silver star in gratitude. Centa tore off a piece of bread and handed it to Mariette. She stared at it as if it had insulted her.

"I want the turkey." She looked up at her father. "All of it."

Phio laughed so hard he snorted. Seeing no other options for nego-tiation, Centa surrendered the bowl.

"Will you at least let me have some of those little pieces?" he asked her.

"Two. No, three. You can have three." The drumstick was un-wieldy in her hands. "Make sure you take the biggest ones."

He did, smiling wryly as the girl tried in vain to tear off meat with her tiny mouth. She got a few bites in and then fell fast asleep, curling up on Centa's bedroll to the murmur of the people and the crackling of the fire. Centa finally took the turkey leg for himself.

"She gets cuter every day," Phio said.

"Smarter too. You wouldn't believe the stuff she says. And Adeska's father was an oracle, so maybe that's why she—"

His words trailed off, and he remembered what Mariette had told him.

"Everything okay? You've got a weird look on your face," Phio said through a mouthful of food.

"She said the people in blue would leave when the storm died. Do you see anyone in blue?" He watched the sea of mismatched black cloaks by the fire and then the sea of mismatched black cloaks in the dining area.

"No." Phio stared at a group of three who were only a few paces away from them, warming themselves at the hearth. His voice went hushed. "Centa, everyone is in black. I don't see blue, gray, brown…"

"So what did she mean?"

Phio scratched his chin. "What's Vandroya's banner?"

"A silver manta ray on *navy blue*. Where?"

As discreetly as he could, Phio gestured to an older man standing by the kitchen door. He spoke to the dark-haired girl who had served them, a money purse in his hand. Centa had to squint to see it, but it was there. A silver manta ray embroidered on the purse.

"What are they doing this far south?"

"What are they doing this far *west*?" Phio added.

Centa folded his arms. "Maybe that guy was telling the truth."

"The estranged brother?"

He grumbled. "Yeah. When Adeska told me what he'd said, I thought he was full of shit. It just didn't make sense to show up and say something like that. But why else would one of their men be here?"

"I thought you said it was the Hunters," Phio whispered. "Would they still be in Vandroya's colors, or do they operate on their own?"

"I don't know, but now we've got to see who else that man is with."

"Are we going to track them down when they leave?"

Centa looked down at Mariette's sleeping little body and frowned. "Phio, I can't. I can't do things like that anymore. Not when I've got her with me."

"I completely understand." Phio nodded. "You leave for Suradia in the morning. I'll follow them on my own if they leave after the storm."

"No! Absolutely not!"

A look of brazen overconfidence spread onto Phio's face. "Come on, Centa! I've got this!"

Centa gave his best friend the same stern look he might have given his daughter. "I am not going to let you do this. It's a terrible idea! The two of us, sure, we could handle something like that—"

"Or even you by yourself, right?" Phio was unimpressed. "But me, by *myself*, you don't think is a good idea."

"Phio!"

"I'll be fine, Centa. You don't give me any credit."

He didn't bother arguing with the man. Centa may have been the notoriously stubborn of the two, but when Phio had something to prove, he couldn't be stopped, and Centa knew he had been guilty of showing Phio up for their entire friendship.

***

The door to Louvita's chambers hummed and crackled. Lilu stared at the sigil etched into the wood as it glittered with energy. She'd never felt this way before. Heavy. Unsure. Sick. Forgetting what had transpired was all she wanted, but she couldn't. Not yet.

It cracked open just a little, and Louvita peered out with a smile. "Lilu, you're back! Wonderful, please come inside. I want to hear everything."

The daemon couldn't come up with a response. She stepped into Louvita's room in silence, completely aware of the suspicion now on her friend's face.

"Are you hurt?" Louvita asked.

Louvita's chambers were truly a reflection of her heritage and race. There were furs from beasts that had never set foot on Mirivin alive before with thick pelts for the Arctic tundra and twisted spines down their backs. Tapestries hung over dark walls, dyed blue and purple and painted with silver. They told nonsensical legends, pieced together a history that started from and went nowhere, decipherable only by the Mire Elves. Candles burned on every surface and in every corner with an indigo flame.

"Am I hurt?" Lilu thought aloud. No, she wasn't. She hadn't been injured in the slightest, at least not past her capability to heal. "I'm in fine health."

Louvita sat down on a nightwood stool with a black fur cushion and crossed her legs. "You seem so shaken up. It's no matter. Really, I just wanted to thank you for recovering my nightwalker. I had started to worry about her."

"I brought the other one back too, you know."

Louvita rolled her eyes. "Who cares?"

"She does," Lilu answered. "For the time being, he's her only motivation."

She raised an eyebrow. "What are you trying to say?"

Lilu was not afraid of upsetting the woman and never had been. But she was afraid of something nonetheless. What that thing was eluded her.

"I'm saying that the next time you push him away, they might not come back."

"That's what I have you for."

Lilu was confused. "Wouldn't it be easier to simply not push him away?"

"Nothing is achieved the easy way, Lilu. But you let me worry about that. What happened when you went after them, exactly?"

She hadn't actually gone looking for them at all, Lilu thought. But she couldn't force the words out. "I picked up a scent."

Then, a different thought entered her mind. *Tell her you weren't looking for them.* The voice sounded like her own, but it didn't feel like it.

She decided to say something else. "I followed it to an abandoned shelter in the Wistwilds. Must've been empty for a hundred years till then." *Tell her. She thinks you were looking. She's wrong.*

"Goodness. What were they doing there?"

The voice in her mind changed. *Let her be wrong.* "They'd been kidnapped."

"What?"

"Must've been the Hunters. I don't know. I killed their captors and freed them."

Louvita ran her tongue over her teeth. "And you came back with Talora."

"The two had been roughed up by the time I found them. They were unconscious. Talora showed up as I was waiting for them to wake. Apparently she heard a commotion. We decided it would be faster to just carry them back."

She laughed. "You. Working together. With *her.*"

Lilu narrowed her eyes. "What about it?"

"Nothing. I just never thought I'd see the day. I thought you hated her."

"I do."

"So then returning my nightwalker must have been very important to you."

No. It wasn't. "You were worried. You wanted her back. When the bitch showed up, I—"

You both knew you had to do something.

"You what, Lilu?"

"I threatened her. I told her she had to help me get them back or else."

Lilu hated the way Louvita grinned at that moment.

"Or else what?"

"Or else I'd kill her," Lilu said plainly. "You occasionally have use for her, but she can't fight. She's worthless, and she knows it, so it wasn't hard to make it look like something I'd be allowed to do."

You'd do it even if you weren't allowed to, if that's what you wanted.

"How resourceful." Louvita's pretty little smile said she was pleased. "I'm worried about their run-in with the Hunters, though. It's shocking that they're in these parts already. You sure that's who they were?"

"No." Lilu folded her arms and looked away. "It was just a guess. I don't know who they were. Didn't see any banners or sigils, but I don't think they were just random people, either. There were a lot of them."

Louvita stood and strolled around her room, keeping one lock of her white hair across her shoulder to twirl and play with. "That's troubling. Ziaul and the others are no doubt being delayed by the weather. Dacen mapped the storm out, and it's covering a lot of ground. It came over from Death Pass Sea so quickly. So this? This issue with Tizena and the Hunters? It's something Ziaul doesn't need added to his plate. Unfortunate."

Lilu didn't have anything to say to the news and turned for the door.

"Oh! Lilu, before I forget, a letter came for you."

The thought was preposterous. "A letter?"

"Yes. It came on this." She sauntered over to her nightwood desk where a sheet covered a large cage. When she pulled it off, a high-pitched howl filled the room.

Lilu yelled in Daemonstongue, and the horrendous noise stopped. The creature in the cage was an aberration of fur, tentacles, and leathery wings. It looked up at her with one monstrous orange eye. With another command, it released a rolled-up note from its tentacles. Lilu slipped her fingers through the cage and picked it up.

"What a cute little thing," Louvita cooed. "What do you call them?"

"Nuntius." Lilu unrolled the message written on desiccated flesh. She did not like the words.

"What's it say?"

"Nothing that I had to be told," she grumbled. She rolled the note back up and gave it to the nuntius, who devoured it with a squeal. "I'm tired. The weather has me foul."

Louvita watched her take the daemon out of the cage. It crawled up her arm and stared back at her, never blinking. "Are you sure nothing else happened? You seem different."

"I must have eaten some bad organs."

She left.

***

The breeze rippled through the yellow curtains in Tizzy's room. She stared down from the balcony, watching the storm flood the grassy area around the abbey. She'd stripped down to a soft slip from the wardrobe. The cold air felt good on her bare skin, soothing the cuts and bruises on her hands and face.

Behind her on the bed, Aleth slept. He hadn't moved a muscle when Lilu and Talora carried him up the steps, or when she'd freed him of most of his clothes to help bring his fever down. Tizzy had never been one to pray, but suddenly she was calling out to any deity who'd listen. He couldn't die.

Despite her distress, she didn't go to him. There was nothing she could do for him, and after Lilu's harsh truths had gutted her, she felt no comfort at his side. Her heart and body ached, but there were no more tears to cry, not that she had the strength for it anyway.

In the past, at House Hallenar, she always thought she had felt alone, but it was a juvenile way to use the word. She had used her bitterness to wall everyone off. Alone, truly alone, was the way she finally felt after everything that had happened.

Aleth started to move. Tizzy glanced at him over her shoulder.

"How do you feel?"

It took him a moment to find his voice, but after a grimace, he answered her. "I've felt worse." He rubbed his face. "That's a lie."

His light mood troubled her. She tried to smile but couldn't.

With a groan, he sat up, fighting a twisted sea of pain and tightness that crashed over him. Every joint and every muscle protested his movement as he tore himself from stasis. But it was his mind that was worse off. It was hazy, and it hurt with an anchor that wouldn't let him think. He was stuck in the present.

"How are you?" He rubbed his chest. "When did I take my shirt off?"

She stayed focused on the rain. "I'm fine."

He didn't think he'd ever heard someone sound less fine in his life. "Tizzy, we're going to be okay. We can talk if you want."

"I don't want to talk!"

"Then will you at least look at me?"

She wasn't sure that she could. She didn't want to see everything that she knew was behind his eyes. He had such an emotionally telling face, and she didn't think she could stand to—

"Tizzy, please say something. I'm sorry you had to go through that!"

"*You're* sorry?" She spun around, damp curls whipping the side of her face. "Is that what you just said to me? That you're *sorry*?"

His jaw opened when he finally saw her. "Your face." A part of the encounter replayed in a searing hot flash that his blood remembered. His stomach turned. "What happened to you? Tizzy, I—"

"Don't say it!" Her voice broke. "Don't you dare say it! You shouldn't be the one saying it!"

He reached for her, and she almost didn't take his hand. Everything hurt in every way that it could, and she was convinced that she deserved no less. She didn't want comfort. But her heart made her lace her fingers with his.

"What happened?" He tried to pull her in. She wouldn't come close. "The last thing I can remember is—" He tried to sort it out in his head. The events swam through him, through the pain and nausea, too quickly to understand. "Lilu? Was that real?"

Tizzy swallowed hard, tasting old blood. "It was."

"She must've gotten us out. Right? Did they hurt you? Did *he*—"

"No!" She burned with rage. All she wanted was to go back to the balcony and feel the rain. "He didn't touch me. This isn't about me."

He tugged at her hand again, and at last she went to him, standing stone cold. She held his head close to her, and he wrapped his arms around her waist. She could feel his warm breath through the fabric of her slip.

She was a hundred miles away. He knew. He could sense it in her movements as she ran her fingers through his hair.

"Are you okay?" she asked.

He came up with something to say but let it die in his chest. "I guess I don't feel much like talking, either." He looked up and brushed his fingers along her cheekbone where the skin had split with Lilu's punches. "Who hurt you? Are they dead?"

"I'm fine."

"That wasn't what I asked."

She took his hands off her and held them firmly. "It wasn't any of them. It was Lilu."

"Lilu did this?"

"Calm down!" she snapped. "It's not what you think. It's fine. I told you it was fine!" She was shaking. "What happened to me doesn't matter."

"Tizzy."

"I want to go home!" Her eyes were wet, but the tears wouldn't fall. She wouldn't let them. "I don't know if I can do this. I *have to*, and I don't know how."

Piece by piece, the picture came together. He finally understood what she had been hiding in her words.

"You don't need to protect me."

"Somebody does," she said darkly. "And it *will* be me. I will be better. No one will ever let you down again."

"No." He buried his face in her again, and she embraced him. "That's not how this should be. Don't do this to yourself."

"It's already started. You can't stop it."

He didn't want to let her go, but she broke away from him and stood at the balcony, the wind tossing her hair and the rain drenching her slip.

***

Anavelia stared down at the polished cherrywood dinner table, the sounds of the storm drowning out the conversations around her. She could see the trees in front of the tall, ornate windows thrashing. Her private dining chambers were a flurry of servants preparing her meal. They asked her questions, but she didn't answer. She barely registered their presence at all.

"We'll have a red," a man answered for her. "Something nice from the Western Riverlands, if we have it."

When Anavelia heard Duke Orin's voice, she eased back into reality. "What?"

"Everything is fine, my queen. They will be back to complete our dinner."

She smiled back at him to make him feel as though he'd comforted her, but he hadn't. Duke Orin Undomien was an attractive man and therefore untrustworthy, but Anavelia had long since admitted to herself that she liked the attention. His brown hair had a touch of silver at his temples, and the little wrinkles at the corners of his blue eyes warmed his smile.

Ashbel had never liked him, but Anavelia noticed he didn't like anyone who flirted with her or gave her nice things. She assumed he was just protective.

"What's the matter, my queen?"

"It's Ash. We had a fight when he left. I wish I could've had some time to resolve things properly, but it is the way it is."

"What did you send him away for, exactly?"

The audacity of the question made her eye twitch. "Why, *exactly*, is it any of your business, Duke?"

"It isn't, my queen. Please forgive me. However, I am on your Council, so perhaps you would see it appropriate to debrief me?"

"It's not something that needs debriefing. I sent him away. End of story."

She watched his handsome face closely. She watched the lump in his throat as he swallowed it.

"Of course, my queen."

Servants returned, bringing a red porcelain bowl for each of them. They filled it with steaming rice, ginger-glazed yams, cranberries, and minced goose. The queen's cup-bearer poured her a generous glass of red.

"How is it?" Anavelia asked.

The cup-bearer, a young girl with a ruddy face, sipped and gave her a wide grin. "It's very good, Your Grace. Light for a red."

"Wonderful. That will be all for now. Thank you."

Anavelia ate with a set of silver chopsticks, picking delicately through the rice and mixing the flavors together. Orin stared down at his food, breathing it in with dread.

"You'd think with so many meals at your table, I would get used to these things." He avoided his own chopsticks and picked up a spoon. "Your cook, that Shen fellow? My dear, you should have him hung! You should be eating boar or bison! Not these paltry *birds*."

Glowering, Anavelia set her chopsticks down. "First, I am not your *dear*. I am your queen. Second, this is exactly the meal I asked for. I don't like boar. I don't like bison. I like *goose*."

"Forgive me, my queen." His words were stiff. "I shouldn't have spoken."

"You shouldn't have! Please take your bowl and leave my table."

"My queen?"

"Did I not say it loud enough?"

He was shaking, either with anger or shame. Anavelia sat back in her chair with her hands folded in her lap and waited. When he finally left, his bowl stayed behind.

She rolled her eyes and grumbled. "I commanded you to both take your bowl and leave. Technically you have disobeyed me, and I could have your head."

"My queen, shall I take the bowl for you?" the cup-bearer asked from the doorway.

"Gods Lishe, you've got the ears of an elf. The bowl can stay, dear, but can you please have someone retrieve Master Otes for me?"

"Yes, my queen!"

She picked at her food in silence, listening to the commotion outside her room as her servants scrambled to find her Master Advisor. She was in the middle of a generous sip of wine when the old man was brought to her.

"Good evening, Master Otes." She wiped her mouth.

"A fine evening it is, Your Grace. And a fine dinner you have here! Am I to join you?"

Otes looked dreadfully old, and he was, yet he was in incredible health. He moved swiftly down the halls and spoke every word clearly and powerfully. As hunched over as he looked under his ivory and plum robes, he danced every night with his personal troupe from Besq, keeping up no matter the tempo. Anavelia always joked that the man would outlive her.

"Yes, please do, and pardon the offense if it's a little cold."

"All the better for digestion, Your Grace!"

She smiled, sipping from her glass. "Tell me your thoughts on Orin again, please. Ash isn't here to remind me."

Otes chuckled. "The young lord and I both agree the man is a damn fool. He eats our food and listens to our plans, desperately courting you while his poor sister governs in his stead."

"Oh, how I would prefer Duchess Oksana."

"To be courted by? Or to represent Davrkton in the court?"

She snorted. "Both! Orin is gorgeous, but he's got all the charm of moldy bread."

They shared laughter through bites of rice and goose. She knew she had to let Orin go, but she saved that conversation for later. She had a more pressing topic for the table.

"I asked for you, Otes, because I need your thoughts. As you know, we have vacancies in our Council. The Master Knight and—" She sighed. "My Right Hand."

Otes nodded solemnly. "How long will they be serving Queen Allanis?"

"I don't know exactly. We never established that. Jurdeir may very well be there permanently. Ash, too, though I hope that isn't the case."

"Your Right Hand must be someone who you intend will rule when you cannot, and you have no other heir without Prince Ashbel."

"Vacant it stays," she said into her glass.

"You have many knights in your guard who would make fine replacements for Master Jurdeir. I believe he was our best only because we never sniffed out other potential."

"Any names at the top of your list?"

"Yes." He sipped the wine. "Milla Deshen. She lacks Jurdeir's humor, but I can't say it will be missed."

"That clueless grin of his was refreshing," Anavelia said with a smile. "But I think he's taken a blow to the head too many."

They sat in silence, a vibrant showing from the storm drowning out all further conversation. It was cold and dark outside, and Anavelia's anxiety beat wickedly within her, praying for her brother's safety.

"Your Grace?"

There was a lull in the storm's thunderous downpour. "Yes, Otes?"

"I beg you, please figure out what to do with the Duke. I don't feel good about him, especially now that Ashbel's incessant barking isn't here to dissuade him."

"You think Ash was keeping him out of trouble?" she laughed.

"Yes, Your Grace. Please, keep your eye on him, yes?"

"Of course, Master Otes." His seriousness pulled her gaze into her glass. She swirled the red around and watched it stick to the sides. "I suppose I should try to mend his stupid heart now."

***

At long last, as darkness set over Mirivin, the clouds parted for a waning moon. The rain ceased, and the wet landscape fell eerily silent. Phio waited outside the Barton Hovel, tucked behind trees. Travelers started to leave. He counted.

Twelve.

The Hovel had to be damn near empty, he thought. He also started to wonder if Centa had been right. Maybe he shouldn't follow twelve mysterious people through the woods at night. But he'd already taken Montague from the stable girl, whose name he was desperately trying to remember. Something cute and meek. *Meeka.* That was it. He didn't want to look silly coming back so soon.

He stayed off the road as he shadowed them. The trek was harrowing, as the storm had left many hazards behind, but Montague handled it with pride. The fallen brush made the mud shallow, and before long, Phio found himself closer to the group than expected.

"Why are we here if they don't know who they're looking for?"

The voices were crystal clear. He almost couldn't hear them over the wild thumping of his heartbeat.

"Because this is where we're gonna find people who have answers."

"Exactly. When we post up in Suradia at the gates, no one's going to come through without us knowing about it. There's another team doing the same thing at Saunterton. Lord-Hunter Cyrus says these queens can't be trusted, but if we're not careful, we'll bring the war to our own doorstep instead."

"Doesn't the Lord-Hunter have someone on the inside in Saunterton?"

"More than one."

"Anyone in Suradia yet?"

"We might have one. Peyrs was working with him, but I don't know how that turned out."

Phio's mental dialogue was firing off thought after thought. He was afraid he wouldn't remember any of the group's conversation.

"It's a shame that the first team didn't work out. We thought they were really onto something. Did you know that General Manar and his mercenaries were all killed? Can't tell what did it, though. Malevolence passed through, but when we saw the bodies, we knew that wasn't what killed *all* of them."

He didn't want to follow them anymore. Phio stopped, letting them disappear into the distance. The crowd of twelve was not one he could afford to be caught by. He stayed quiet and still for almost half an hour before he could finally breathe again.

When he returned to the Hovel, Meeka was waiting for him at the stable in Montague's stall.

"Did you find what you were looking for?"

Phio swallowed hard. "I wasn't looking for anything. Montague doesn't like to be cooped up for a long time is all. He's—"

"You don't have to lie. I know."

"I don't understand."

She stepped aside and pulled away a heavy canvas tarp. Centa lay in the hay, unconscious, with Mariette trapped beneath one of his arms. Phio's breath was tight in his chest.

"Why?"

"Because you shouldn't be sticking your nose in this!" She unsheathed a knife at her hip. Phio felt guilty for what he was about to do.

"Meeka, are you a Hunter? Is that what this is?" His hand went to his belt where he felt the weight of his sidearm now more than ever.

"We're not good enough to be Hunters," she said. "Not yet. Not like the *real* Hunters. They're going to find what they're looking for."

"And what the hell are they looking for? Meeka, I'm not trying to hide anything. I'm not playing stupid with you; I *am* stupid. I have no idea what all of this is about!"

"They want the Protégé."

Phio's hand twitched as it reached the holster. His flintlock felt dry as a bone.

"Don't you dare!" Meeka jabbed her knife at him. "I've got your friend, your horse, and the little girl!"

"It's okay, Phio."

He looked down at Mariette, who stared at the ground with her tiny, unnerving smile.

"Mari?"

"You won't have to shoot her. Too loud, anyway." Her eyes followed a splotched brown spider the size of her fist as it crawled onto Meeka's leg. "I told Old Legs to do it. He said yes."

"Ow!"

Meeka saw it after she felt the sharp pain in her calf. It raced down, back into the hay as she swatted, but it was too late. She whimpered in pain, then her body twitched, went rigid, and careened over.

"It won't kill her," Mariette said. "Old Legs isn't like that."

Phio crawled over and helped her out from under Centa, then shook the man until he stirred. "Centa, get up! We have to leave!"

He groaned. "Where am I?"

"What happened?" Phio threw his hands in the air. "A teenage girl dragged you two out here! How'd she manage that?"

"The woman who gave us our food—" He rubbed his eyes. "She asked if I wanted another meal. I said no, but I was thirsty. She must've put something in my drink."

"Let's get our shit and leave. Are there any other ways into Suradia besides the gates? We're going to have a problem. I'll tell you about it later."

Centa stood and picked up Mariette. Phio did not like the way his friend looked at him. "There's another way. But you're not going to like it."

"Add it to the growing list." Phio crossed his arms and glared down at Meeka. "Because I don't like any of this. You know we have to take her with us."

***

Ashbel stared through the carriage window at the indistinguishable world outside, cloaked in the night. It was cold and wet and scary, the twisted trees staring him down with their branches reaching out like they were up in arms. But he was excited. The last thing he wanted to do was turn around and go back home. He listened to Titha and Jurdeir's voices but couldn't tell what they were saying. Titha drove the carriage, and Jurdeir rode beside them on a monstrous white horse.

Since no one could hear him, Ashbel let out a grumpy sigh and sprawled himself out on the cushioned seat. He didn't want to be in the carriage, but Titha had insisted, and he hated to give the woman trouble.

She turned her attention away from the reins to lean back and knock a few times on the roof of the carriage. Ashbel knocked back, and she smiled.

During the storm, their pace had been slow, but now that it had let up, it felt like they were going even slower. Just as soon as he had thought it, the carriage came to a halt. He heard Titha yelling and grunting in the high-pitched way she always did when she was stressed. He stepped out.

"What happened?"

"Prince Ashbel!" Jurdeir gestured widely to him, always with a smile. "It's nothing. You should get back in the carriage where it's safe!"

"No. What happened?"

"The wheels are stuck in the mud!" Titha sighed. "The horses can't keep pulling on like this. They're tired; they need rest."

"Yes, but we cannot rest out here!" Jurdeir said. "There are green-kind out here. They will see us out here, sitting like ducks, and eat our faces!"

Ashbel glared at them both. "I told you the carriage was a bad idea. I told you to just put everything on horses and be done with it. But did anyone listen to me?"

"On horseback, exposed to the storm? That is no way for a young prince to travel, my lord!" Jurdeir told him.

"No, Master Jurdeir." He crossed his arms. "You are not allowed to disagree with both the plan that could have prevented this problem *and* the current solution. Not unless you offer up a useful idea of your own, so where is it?"

"I say we should keep pressing the horses. We have to."

There was a noise in the distance. Splashing and clopping. Ashbel looked down the road behind them.

"There are others coming! Maybe we can—"

"Prince, get back into the carriage! They cannot see you!"

He did as Titha told him. Sometimes he forgot what being a prince meant. It meant that there were others who wanted to kill him or take him hostage, and he wouldn't exactly say he was being heavily guarded. Titha stood as close to the edge of the road as she could, using the carriage as cover.

It was too dark, and the group was too fast to count their number. They passed the carriage as though they hadn't seen it at all, and that was the only peculiar thing about them. They didn't even have uniforms, and their mounts were all unique.

"Wait a minute." Ashbel came out of the carriage and watched the group move into the distance. "That horse, that black one with the silver mane and tail. That's an elven-bred horse. That's Master Sinisia's!"

Jurdeir cleared his throat. "Are you sure, my prince? I don't think it looked silver. More grayish, if you ask me."

"I'm not asking you."

"What would she be doing going toward Suradia?" Titha asked.

"She's probably working on my sister's stupid assignment. I've half a mind to tell Allanis, you know. But I can't do that. It would crush them both and tear them apart, and we can't have that."

"Shall we quietly sabotage the assignment then, my prince?" Jurdeir's grin could barely be seen in the darkness.

"Of course. And we'll press on tonight, but let's unyoke the horses and give them a rest. I've got something I've been wanting to try out."

Titha started freeing the horses of the equipment. "My lord?"

With a confident smile, Ashbel removed a wand from its sheath. It was carved entirely from a royal blue sapphire, almost a foot and a half in length, polished to a perfect shine.

"Royal Magic!" he said. "Last year, I learned something called Hanarn's Chariot, and I've never had the opportunity to use it." He raised his casting tool, and thick blue fog started to form around it. He uttered a phrase in Kingstongue, and the fog formed two equine shapes at the front of the carriage. With his continued instruction, they became solid.

When the spell finished, they were left with two giant horses. They had thick manes and tails that fluttered from beneath decorated armor in a nonexistent breeze, and each one was magically tethered to the carriage with glittering strings of Akashic energy, ready for their burden. The other horses perked up in their presence.

"There!" Ashbel declared. "Perfect!"

"A wizard of practicality!" Jurdeir clapped. "I do believe this fixes our problem."

***

When Tizzy found access to the rooftop and its midnight view of the Wistwilds, she also found Dacen staring up at the sky. He had tools and instruments laid out in the center of the rooftop, where it was flat. Most of the tools Tizzy didn't know the names of and ones she had never seen before. A tray was on Dacen's lap to give him a flat surface for a long sheet of paper, and before she had said a word, he waved to her.

"Hey. What are you doing up here?" she asked. She looked over the edge where the roof sloped down before coming back and sitting next to him.

He gestured up at the sky, grinning.

"Gods, look at all of them," she mumbled. "The stars always look so nice after a storm. Is this what you came out here for?"

He nodded, opening a book. She spied the word 'astronomy' in the title. "Looks like you've been drawing a map too." She peered over at the paper in his lap, and he pointed to the clouds moving in the distance. "Mapping out the storm. Smart. I always thought it was just the Storm Mages that did that. Didn't even realize there was a way to do it without magic."

Based off the various intricate gauges he had spread out, she assumed his way was not the easier way. Mystery liquids in each gauge reacted to the temperature or the pressure outside or other variables. He took the readings and plugged them into equations scribbled in the margins of his map. A sudden gust of wind whistled by them for only an instant, spinning his weathervane.

"Westerly."

He nodded as she said it and stared into the stars again.

"Dacen, I think I messed up." She didn't know why she had said it.

He turned to her, his frown bunched up in confusion.

"With Aleth. Well, with everything. Does this place ever make you confused about the right thing to do?"

He didn't have anything to say. Instead, he put his hand on her shoulder and patted it. He smiled, but his eyes were cast aside with sadness.

"I don't know if Tal or Lilu started talking about what happened yet, but we had a—"

How could she even begin to describe it? The terror she had felt still lingered in her mind and was trying to convince her it had never happened.

"We had a bad encounter. Let's just say that." She sighed. "I'll get over it, I know I will. My sister used to tell me trauma didn't shake me the way it should. But once I come to terms with this, with what happened, I know I won't be the same." She tried to block out the image of Rhett that was bearing down on her. "Aleth, in the heat of it all, he seemed fine. It was like any other bad situation he'd been in. And then something happened, and it wasn't. It was worse. And then it was *much* worse. We came out of it in one piece, but I'm worried about him."

Dacen rolled his eyes and scoffed. He waved his arm around and gestured down to the empty courtyard below them.

"Oh." The corners of her mouth turned up a little. "Me and everyone else, huh? I guess he does have enough people fussing over him. Tal, and Eidi, and even Lilu in her own way. And then there's Lou. The last thing he needs is me joining the fray, pestering him."

She hugged her knees, and everything was silent save for the wind in the trees. She heard Dacen tinkering with his instruments and flipping through pages.

"I turned away from him," she said. "I know he's not okay. He needed me, and I turned away. And the worst part is that I can't tell what *I* need. Do I need him to be okay? Or do I need him to be broken about it so I don't feel so bad about how much this is messing me up? I don't know what would make me feel better. I want to be supportive, Dacen, but my brand of support isn't usually the one people go looking for."

He laughed out loud, a sound hoarse and cute.

"It's not funny, it's terrible!" But now she was laughing too. "When people need me, I make everything worse."

He shrugged and then gestured to her. She raised an eyebrow. "What?"

He touched his heart and then motioned to hers.

"You're right, I need to figure this out. What do I need?" She rubbed her face. "Shit, Dacen. I don't know." She didn't want to recall the kidnapping anymore, but she had to. She had to picture Rhett's face again. "I need him to get *angry*, but I've just got this feeling that all he's going to do is wallow."

Dacen showed her the map he'd been working on. It showed all of Mirivin to the east of the Undina Loch and about fifty miles to the west of it. He'd watered down ink to draw in where the clouds would start to form, and he had drawn arrows here and there to show the wind and where it would take them. The storm that had left was going to the Western Peninsula, and a bigger one was headed their way.

He looked up at the cloudless sky above them and breathed in deep. She understood.

"The calm before the storm." She stared at the shapes on the map. "When he's ready, he'll be angry."

Dacen nodded, trying not to smile at a little bit of his own brilliance.

"Thanks. Good talk," Tizzy told him. She squeezed his shoulder, stood up, and found her way back inside.

CHAPTER 16

AMELIORATE

VAYVEN 4, 1144

Duke Orin Undomien had been representing Davrkton in Saunterton's court for several years. He remembered the conversation that had led him to approaching Queen Anavelia with a query for the seat, and he remembered it vividly. It had been his sister's idea. Well no, he thought, it had probably been King Mabus's idea. The old king in Vandroya was a nice fellow, if not a little full of himself. Oksana didn't like him at all, Orin knew, and she often passed off his ideas as her own.

At first, Oksana wanted him to govern Davrkton and produce its heir. His sister was a very plain woman, he mused, who would be hard-pressed to ever have suitors. But with his smile, he could choose anyone he wanted. And he wanted the queen.

"Don't be ridiculous," Oksana had said. "You will never gain her hand, and you will never be king. Not unless we somehow undo fealty to *two* kingdoms."

She had said it to sound impossible, but the idea inspired him.

"If you don't think I can marry the queen, dear sister, then I shall undo our fealty one kingdom at a time!"

So she let him go. It was their father who had set up the secret dual fealty originally, a public fealty to Saunterton and a private one to

Vandroya. Ten years later, however, both Orin and Oksana were ready to make changes. But it wouldn't be a clean break.

"They would *destroy* us," Oksana had said. "It would be the first thing Anavelia and Mabus ever agreed on."

And she was right. There had been many secrets passed on to Vandroya and, if Orin was being honest, a few of Vandroya's that had been slipped to Saunterton. Davrkton would become the most hated city on the mainland. There would be no time to rise to their own throne before it was burnt to the ground.

And it was thus that he served Anavelia at Lovell Keep. Not one month after taking a seat on the court, a letter arrived for him. He remembered how it had baffled him at first—it bore Oksana's name and her personal seal, but it wasn't in her handwriting and the letter was nonsense. He thought it could be in code, so he tried for weeks to break it to no avail. At last he turned to Whisper Magic, to a spell that would uncover its secrets.

The letter hadn't been from Oksana at all. It had come from King Mabus. The old man was allowing him several months to figure out how to read it, congratulating him in advance. Then he read the word *alliance*. It wasn't like what they had already. Mabus needed something different, something between the two of them and no one else.

When another letter came for him, Orin was ready. Anavelia found him in the library with a pile of historical plays. The queen approached him hesitantly, dressed in a white gown with a fuchsia bird print and a black faux-fur stole. Once upon a time, he found it hard to stay angry with her, but now he could hold his grudge for ages.

"Good morning, Duke." She put on a sweet smile.

He faked one back.

"Did you sleep well, my queen?"

"No."

She waited to hand him the letter. It made him sweat.

"No, my queen?"

"I was in a terrible mood yesterday, what with Ash being away. I just wanted to apologize for my behavior. I was awful to you, Orin. I'm sorry."

She didn't really mean it; he knew that. She just said it to make him feel better. She always did.

"Think nothing of it, my queen. I was acting like a fool." He grinned. "Now, what is it that you've got there? It looks like my sister's seal."

He didn't know anyone else with pearly white wax and an albino doe stamp. It had to be Oksana's. Which meant it would be Mabus's. Anavelia gave it to him at last.

"Yes, it does seem to be hers. I hope the Duchess is well. You never talk about what she writes to you. She is okay, isn't she?"

"Oh yes, she's, well, she just—" He wet his lips. "Well, you'd never guess it with how prudish she can be, but lately she's been getting swept away with men, tangled up in one terrible suitor after another. Poor thing has to settle for what she can get, and there's nothing but asses throwing themselves at her feet."

"I've got some suitors I'd be happy to send her way. A merchant from Kasatta in particular," Anavelia said. "He's been pushy as ever. Don't worry, Duke; I've no mind to keep him for myself."

He knew that. He knew she was too proud for anyone. And he was getting tired of trying to prove otherwise.

"Well I won't keep you any longer," she finally said. "I've got a Council meeting in an hour that I should review for. It's nothing very important, but you're welcome to sit in if you like."

"Thank you, my queen."

She waved coyly and left the library, heading for her study. Then he found himself alone in the back of the library in a storage room he'd commandeered for himself. He had all the letters from 'Oksana' as well as an assortment of pouches and jars on a desk. At first, the method of unscrambling the secrets was complicated, but he'd since acquired tools and ingredients to simplify it.

He uncorked two jars and opened a pouch, then scooped a little of each into a quartz mixing dish. Akashic powder, powdered snake bones, and powdered dusk stone. They mixed into a faintly iridescent lavender dust. He pulled away 'Oksana's' seal and unrolled the nonsensical letter, then sprinkled the mixture over the words, making sure to coat every drop of ink that touched the paper.

The powder adhered to the words, and he shook away the excess. It fell to the floor, adding to the dust that had collected from previous letters. Then he took a clear quartz lens from his pocket, a lens with snakes engraved on the edges to represent Shilash, the Goddess of Destructive Secrets. When he read the letter through it, the words made perfect sense.

It was indeed from Mabus. The poor old fool was being hounded by Lord-Hunter Cyrus to the point that he barely ran his own kingdom anymore. Orin had grandeur thoughts about striking up a deal—taking down the Lord-Hunter in return for his independence. He was sure Mabus would agree to it, but how could he expect to fulfill his end of it?

He kept reading. Cyrus had over fifty apprentice Hunters spread out between Suradia, Saunterton, Davrkton, and Kamdoria. Cyrus thought he was getting closer to finding the nightwalker Protégé, and Mabus was frantic about it.

It would be any day now that Sinisia would report back with Aleth Hallenar, Orin thought. When she did, they would without a doubt learn the location of the Protégé before Cyrus did. When Anavelia had told him about Queen Allanis's problems back in Suradia, it was the perfect plan. Mabus had done his own research into a place called the Convent. It, too, was seeking out the Protégé, and Mabus had intel on many of the people staying there.

Aleth Hallenar was on the list. Orin had not shared any of this information with Anavelia, but she was easily convinced that Aleth knew important things and that she needed him in her custody, for Allanis's sake and her own sake.

But Sinisia hadn't reported back yet. With anything. He didn't think anyone was too hard for that woman to find. Shrugging inwardly, Orin started to draft a letter back to his king.

***

Tizzy barely slept. It was well past midnight when she slipped into bed, Aleth out cold beside her. It took hours for her mind to finally quiet, and when it did, she woke with the dawn, feeling more tired than ever. Aleth was gone.

She still felt hollow and worn, but meeting with Dacen on the roof the night before had lifted her spirits enough to get her out of her room. Today she'd see Lilu, and she'd fight. She'd put up the hardest fight she ever had, because Lilu would give her no less. And tomorrow, she'd do it again. She would be strong, and she would be feared, no matter the cost.

Before she began the day, however, she wanted to find Aleth. She scolded herself about how distant she'd been when, clearly, he had needed her. The same mistake was what drove him away from her a decade ago. She had to fix this, and she had to stop herself from turning into the cold, alien person she used to be.

But she couldn't find him anywhere. Hours passed, a serene morning wasted tearing apart the abbey looking for him.

She'd messed up worse than she thought. He would come out of the woodwork eventually, right? She took a few rags and her clothes for the day and headed down into the cavern to the river. It would be good to wash up and mentally prepare for brutally losing another fight.

That's where she found him, tucked away behind boulders where the river bent. She guessed that his plan had been similar to hers in the beginning—his tunic and a rag hung on a branch near a small, crackling fire. He sat, hugging his knees, another damp rag over the back of his neck and a bottle in his hand. She planned her words and shuffled up to him with tiny steps.

"There you are!"

He didn't even look up at her. "Shit, Tizzy, just let me be miserable."

Wallowing. At least things were how she expected them to be. She stripped off her top layers of clothing and draped them next to his. "Don't mind me. Continue what you were doing."

"What do you want?"

She stared at him. "Yesterday was rough. I smell, I'm grimy, and we're miles away from Sheerspine. Sorry to invade your space, but I've only got so many options." She inspected his area and spotted a pile of blankets. "How long have you been out here?"

"Does it matter?"

She ground her teeth and kept telling herself that he had earned the right to be annoying. "Look at me."

"No."

"You're acting like me! Is that really something you want under your belt?"

With a deep, begrudging breath, he looked up at her. His face was wet and his eyes bloodshot. "There. Happy now?"

She ran the rag under the river's smooth current and wrung it out. "Of course I'm not happy." She wiped down her face, neck, and arms. "I'm trying to work past things in my own way, but I can't even tell how I feel anymore." She was afraid to say that she felt better. "But I shouldn't have pushed you away."

"You were right to, and you shouldn't have come back."

The bitterness in his voice stunned her. Something else was wrong. She sat next to him, pulling him into her.

"No—"

"Yes, shut up." She wrapped her arms around him, and he relented, resting his head on her shoulder. "Alright, talk. Help me understand. Why should I push you away and never come back?"

He said nothing. His jaw tensed until she started weaving her fingers through his hair. "How can you not be furious with me?"

"Furious?" She could feel the wetness on his cheek as she brushed the hair out of his eyes. "What are you talking about?"

"I should have done something."

"You couldn't!"

"I could have *tried*. You were trying!"

She sighed. "Don't call it trying. It was *panicking*. Whatever was happening, you had been through it already, dozens of times. You thought you knew what to expect. You were trying to stay calm. You were trying to be smart about it. I just thought you had a plan and you were patiently waiting for an opportunity."

"I shouldn't be waiting patiently when you're right there in the shit next to me!"

"Stop doing this to yourself."

"Maybe I could have ended the whole thing before it started."

"You couldn't have, and you *knew* you couldn't have. I'm not mad at you."

"You don't get it."

"Obviously I don't!"

He pulled away from her and rubbed his face. His body still ached. "I was fine. I was nervous, but it was like you said. I was just waiting." He sucked in a breath and let it out. "I was coming up with a plan. Even when things changed, when she came out with the poison, I was fine. I was going to keep it together. I'd find us an opportunity somewhere." He swallowed hard. His hands were shaking. "But then *he* came out.

"I should have been angry. Seeing him, I should have been furious, I should have wanted to kill him. But instead, I was *afraid*." Tizzy watched his eyes glass up again. "I was fucking afraid of him, Tizzy. You should be ashamed of me."

"Yeah, you were afraid of him!" She grabbed his shoulder. "Assess the situation we were in, Aleth! He's abusive and manipulative and a coward! No one else knows that more than you! I'm not ashamed of you. He captured us, and he poisoned you because that was the only way he was going to have the upper hand, so if there's anyone I'm disappointed in, it's him." She looked at him and could see a glimpse of sarcasm in his eyes as he met her stare. "Think about it. If the two of you ever fought on even footing? He'd be fucked."

Aleth didn't say a word as he imagined it. Just picturing Rhett's face made him sick to his stomach. "He would be."

She went back to washing in the river's current. "Exactly. Which means it's time to start planning your revenge."

"Revenge?" He scoffed.

"Yes, absolutely. You'd be ridiculous not to. Revenge is the best is motivator for survival, you know."

"Is that what this is all about? You're afraid for my motivation to survive?"

"No, that's not it." She walked over to her clothes. "Believe it or not, all this effort I'm making is for very selfish reasons."

At last he cracked a smile and her heart leapt. "Oh, really?"

"Yes. I want to see your face—" she leaned down and traced her finger along his jaw, "—when you finally give that asshole what he deserves. I want to see what it looks like when you get that satisfaction, when you've taken all the pain he's caused you and given it back."

"How selfish of you."

"I told you. Does it sound like a good plan?"

Part of him thought it did. He even looked forward to the bloody fistfight that would ensue.

"What's the part you're not telling me?" he asked.

She bit her lip. "We have to go back. I know that somewhere inside of you, you already know that. We have to go back and confront this. There's no other way."

Deflated, he sighed. "How can you not see what a bad idea that is?"

"It's not about it being a good idea or a bad idea," she said. "It's about solving the problem and getting answers. Obviously, it's a terrible idea, but it might get us to the bottom of this situation with the poison, and maybe we'll even find *him* there."

"Is that when I'd exact my revenge?"

"Yes!"

With a lighthearted groan, he shook his head. He watched as she dried off and finished dressing herself and sat back down beside him.

"Are you better?" she asked.

"A little." He looked at the bottle he'd already halfway drained. "I still feel so pissed off."

"Good. Don't let go of it. Just maybe direct it away from yourself." Under normal circumstances, it was probably not sound advice. "Sorry for being a hypocrite."

"You are a huge hypocrite, but I forgive you. You know I always will."

"Yeah." She stared into the river. The current still moved along in a carefree way despite being engorged by the storm. "So why are all these blankets out here?"

He shrugged. "I got moody and thought I'd just stay here. Forever." When she laughed, he rolled his eyes. "I know, I know."

"Is this—" she steadied her giggles with a deep breath, "—is this everything you own?"

"I guess it is."

"Your clothes and a cloak, a knife, Mercy, and some blankets?" Then she saw his chest puff out and his wide eyes avoid her. His telltale suspicious expression. "Oh no, there's something else. What is it? Why don't you want to say it?"

He hid his face. "It's probably tangled up in the blankets. Go ahead; I was going to give it to you anyway."

Now she was especially confused. She tore through them and gasped.

"My book!" Her fingers touched the faded gold embossing of *Knight of the Red Castle*. "You have it! I've been looking for this for years—*you took it*?"

She was about to throw it at him, and he flinched, laughing. "I took it when I left. I'm sorry! It's going to sound stupid, but—" he rested his head in the palm of his hand, "—I wanted to take something with me that would remind me of how different things used to be. How good they were once."

"You took my favorite thing in the world! I can't believe you!" She saw the thin scarlet ribbon keeping his place about a quarter of the way through. "You've had it for ten years and still haven't finished it."

"I'd just read it to imagine you reading it out loud like you used to, but it's not easy to follow a story that way."

She leaned over and kissed his forehead. "Thank you for keeping it safe for me. I think it served you more than it would have served me, anyway."

"You're not mad?"

"I'm definitely a little mad." She set the book down on the pile of blankets and stood with a stretch, glad to have found him. "I've got to go for a while. Will I see you tonight?"

"I'll be here tonight. Be careful, Tizzy."

"You be careful too."

Leaving the cavern changed her. She'd found so much warmth and peace with him, but it seeped out to make room for a dutiful sense of dread the second she walked out. She would leave a shred of her old self behind for him, something for him to cling to when he needed it, but that was it. Things were different now, and she had to construct a new self that was ready to do a job and let nothing get in the way.

Lilu waited for her in a quiet clearing away from the Convent, standing with folded arms and a scowl.

"You brought your stupid sword."

Tizzy looked down at Wish, strapped to her hip. "Old habits."

Lilu shifted into a fighting stance. "Fine. Don't let me be the one to tell you that you're a talentless prima donna. Do whatever you want, whatever you can. We don't fight for skill. We fight to survive because that's how you get strong."

***

The day was bright and cool with passing clouds when Ashbel finally arrived in Suradia through the Southern Gate. The guards had been told to expect him and his companions and escorted them to House Hallenar with awe and excitement. It had been a long time since anyone noteworthy had come into Suradia, or so the guards said. Allanis was typically the one visiting Anavelia; very rarely had it been the other way around.

The prince was tired and wanted a nap desperately but kept his class about him. He wasn't here to nap and whine like a child, he told himself. He was here to work.

"Prince Ashbel, you made it!"

Allanis was overjoyed when she came down the steps of House Hallenar to greet him. She looked just as tired as he did.

"We made it, yes. The storm made things a little tricky, but I can't be easily stopped." He let only the tiniest grin show.

"I'm glad to hear it." Allanis gave him a hug. "I've had a villa cleaned and prepared for all of you if you didn't want to stay at House Hallenar, but we do have the room if you're interested."

"I hate to sound like a spoiled brat, but the villa sounds wonderful. Thank you, Allanis."

He was shown to a villa he'd be sharing with Titha and Jurdeir. It was a short walk from the manor and Athen was already inside, waiting for them with bottles of wine and a plate of fruits and cheeses.

"Settle in," Allanis told them. "Unpack your things, have a little food and drink, rest up. I will be in the Council room when you're ready. Athen will be posted in the main hall and can show you the way when you're ready."

Jurdeir showed the queen a too-deep bow. "Thank you for the hospitality, Your Grace!"

When Allanis and Athen left, Ashbel wasted no time in unwinding. Titha sat beside him at a polished walnut table and picked at a slice of plum.

"I thought you said you were going to jump right in as soon as we got here," she said.

"I changed my mind."

Jurdeir took a tiny fork from the plate and picked at a cube of soft white cheese with honey. "There's not much to this town, is there?"

"It is a little quaint," Ashbel said, stretching out on a burgundy-upholstered chaise. It smelled dusty. "But that just means there's a lot of potential to work with. Let's not forget why we're here. Allanis needs our help to turn Suradia into a force to be reckoned with."

After falling asleep five minutes later, he got the nap he'd wanted. He dreamt about Jade and his room and the red porcelain bowls at dinner. He knew he was getting homesick. He hoped Suradia would be interesting enough to distract him from his slowly breaking heart.

An hour later, he made his way to House Hallenar, Jurdeir and Titha in tow. He'd never seen it before, but he liked it the moment he stepped inside. It was big, but not grand or lavish like Lovell Keep. In fact, aside from the crimson and black eagle banners, there was barely any decoration at all. It was empty. Empty and quiet and welcoming.

As promised, Athen was waiting for him. "Hello, Prince Ashbel. Hello, others I haven't met yet."

"We're going to be working together, Athen. If you'd like, you can just call me Ash. No need to be so *formal*."

"Are you sure? I'm trying really hard to get this right."

"Yes. My sister doesn't rule here. Yours does. If anything, I should be calling you Prince Athen."

"Please don't do that."

"Very well, my lord." Ashbel was grinning, and Athen was clearly uncomfortable. He found it amusing how Athen was so easily disarmed by a twelve-year-old.

They walked, and Ashbel told him about his thoughts and reservations, and Ashbel told him about Titha and Jurdeir, and Ashbel told him about many other things that Athen lost track of. As they walked the winding halls, Ashbel's voice trailed off, and he took in as much as he could, seeing opportunities for House Hallenar with every step he took. He almost hoped Allanis hadn't come up with any ideas of her own.

The Council room had acquired more chairs and a vase with fresh white flowers since it had last been used. Allanis sat at the table with an empty seat to her right, and Lora was in the seat to her left. Three others who Ashbel had not met yet sat at the table, too.

"Allanis, err, *Your Grace*—" Athen coughed nervously. "I would like to—"

"Cut it out, Athen," she grumbled. "Don't be afraid of Ash. You can speak plainly."

"Better do as your queen says!" Jurdeir honked.

Athen cleared his throat and began again. "Fine. Allanis, Council, I would like to announce Prince Ashbel Lovell, Titha Russo, and Master Knight Jurdeir Jashi." He then gestured to the table. "Present at our first official Council meeting is Master Battle Mage Gavin Castillo, Master of Dusk Ravina Songo, Master Advisor Lazarus Hallenar, Left

Hand Lora Sheikh, Right Hand, uh, *me*, and Her Majesty the Queen Allanis Byland-Hallenar."

Ashbel cocked his head to the side as Athen took the empty seat next to Allanis. "Left Hand?"

Looking as prim and pretty as she ever had, Lora gazed over at him with disinterest while inspecting her nails. "What?"

"I've never heard of a seat for a *Left Hand* before."

"I thought it made sense," Allanis said. "There's a Right Hand. What about the other one? Shouldn't both hands be doing something?"

"Very well. It is *your* Council after all." He tucked a long lock of his dark hair behind his ear. "Where on your Council shall I sit, if you'll have me, Your Grace?"

Allanis tapped her chin. "Hm, let me think. It won't be necessary for you to take on the Treasury; I've taken that responsibility myself. And a Chamberlain seems like a waste of your abilities. Well, Ash, what do you think? Where are your strengths?"

"I feel strongly that I could be your Master Cobalt."

She hadn't thought about that position yet. The Master Cobalt—named after the investigative guild of Hanarn-worshippers simply referred to as The Cobalts—dealt with everyday law in town. The Master Cobalt acted as a judge for the people and organized the Watch and the Militia.

"I am exceptionally well-versed in the role. I have studied law and the Codes of Watch. It would give me the ability to see the inner workings of your town up close, to organize the way the Watch works, and to make connections with the people. The position has been empty in Suradia for almost eighteen years, so no doubt there is a lot slipping through the cracks."

"Ash, Master Cobalt is a lot of work," Allanis told him.

"I am well aware. I've sat at hundreds of court sessions in Saunter-ton, and I've seen what gets brought to the table for our Master Cobalt. I've been dying to take over his job for the last two years. The man's an idiot, but of course Ana couldn't have handed the seat over to a ten-year-old." He rolled his eyes. "I'm twelve now, Allanis. I am more than prepared for this."

She shrugged, smiling a little at the typical overconfidence of a child playing grownup. It was adorable. But if there was anyone who could do it, she knew it was Ashbel.

"Alright, but I'm warning you now: The Watch and Militia are a mess, but we're depending on them to provide the foundation for our army. That's actually our first line of business for today. Oh, you know what? I've changed my mind!"

Ashbel tried not to laugh when he saw Lazarus's jaw tense.

"Titha Russo—" Allanis waved to her and all her silver bangles clinked together. "I understand you are to accompany Ashbel at all times."

The woman blushed, not used to the attention. "Unless he tells me otherwise. He's a young man in an adult's world, and I am a trained assassin who makes sure he is safe in it."

"I like her," Lora mumbled.

"Well, we're a little short-staffed around here these days, Titha, Ash." Allanis rubbed her eyes. "Until we have some trustworthy picks for a doorguard, may I offer a shift to Titha when she is not with you, Ash? Titha?"

"I'd hate to part from you, my lord, but I know you're entirely capable of protecting yourself and you only keep me around because I make good tea."

"A partially accurate statement, Titha. I am capable, and you do in fact make great tea, but I keep you around because I like your company. But I will allow it, Allanis!"

"Phenomenal! One problem with a temporary solution. Look at that, everyone! That's what progress looks like."

Ashbel and Jurdeir pulled up chairs, and they continued with business as planned. Allanis had scoped out land to build training barracks, one for the Master Battle Mage to run and one for the Master Knight to run.

"And you have the funds to commission these?" Ashbel asked.

"Yes. Money will be a problem in the future. Presently, it's not. But I'm worried about how everything is going to stay balanced once this gets off the ground and starts growing. We could see a lot of movement from other cities, and with a higher population comes more crime and a heavier burden on our food stores. I don't know how to handle a food shortage, other than to beg for help."

"You couldn't even do that," Lazarus said. "You don't have fealty from any city. *Any.* Anavelia would probably help you because you two are friends, but she certainly is under no obligation."

"How about we make a pledge not to ask her for anything while I'm here?" Ashbel grumbled. "I want her to think I can handle this. Because I can."

Ravina cleared her throat. "Winter's right around the corner. It would be a bad time to see expansion unless you were to rely on the starkfin season in the Undina Loch and Roe River. In an emergency, it could save us."

"Starkfin season?" Allanis asked.

"It's a pain in the ass for traders coming in through the river from Death Pass Sea or the Equenhol Ocean. Starkfin surge to the Undina Loch during the winter for nesting. The last week of fall is the most dangerous time of year for the land by the riverbanks. It'll be crawling with predators readying for hibernation and of course hyper-aggressive greenkind. Starkfin is a mean, dangerous fish, but it's meaty and fatty. It'd be a great food source if we see a shortage in our stores. Plus, thinning out a food source for the predators and green-kind could make the riverbanks safer as long as it doesn't drive them inland toward civilization."

Allanis scribbled down notes. "Holy Hells, Ravina, am I glad to have you. I'm adding to the list. *Build fisher's wharf in the Undina*

Loch. Make small fleet of boats to fish in late fall for starkfin. This is great."

"Our own boats?" Lazarus leaned back in his seat. "We could save funds if we hire captains who already have a boat and a crew. I'm sure we could find a small fleet's worth at the Undina Loch who would work for the crown's coin."

"That's a better idea." Allanis scratched it out and made new notes.

Jurdeir leaned back in his seat too. "Now that we have potential food issues taken care of, where are my young knights hailing from? Is there good stock in Suradia?"

"We'll meet with the public for a few days," Allanis said. "You'll be able to scope it out from there. We'll probably see people from the Militia, from the streets, from farms, who knows? They'll come out of the woodwork, and hopefully you'll have enough to work with when the barracks are complete. Gods, I hope *that* doesn't take too long."

"And weapons. Do we know who is making my weapons?"

"All in due time, Jurdeir, I promise."

Ashbel had never sat in on such an exciting Council meeting.

***

"We're lost."

"We're not lost."

At every break, Tryphaena had been listening to Rhett and Sinisia argue. If it wasn't one thing, it was another. During this argument, Tryphaena learned that Rhett had no faith in anyone but himself and Sinisia wasn't as skilled at navigation as she claimed to be.

"I know exactly where we are," the old woman said sourly. "The fly fern only grows in one area of the Bogwood. See? They're right there." She pointed. "We're about five miles from the edge of the Wistwilds."

They had only made it away from the hovel in the Wistwilds with four of the eleven original Hunters. Lilu had slaughtered the rest. Either that or they had fled. One of them stepped up to Rhett, looking back at his companions as he planned his words.

"We're not from these parts," he said. "I have to ask: Are we headed to Saunterton still?"

"Saunterton? Why would we be going to Saunterton?"

"That's what *she* said." The Hunter motioned to Sinisia.

"That's where we should go!" she snapped. "We're in a vulnerable position right now since everything went to shit! We need protection!"

"And you think your queen is going to give you that when she finds out what happened?" Rhett laughed. "She'll have your head."

"Only because you lied to me!" Sinisia shook as she jabbed her finger at him. "The queen told me to bring her Aleth Hallenar, *alive*, and you said you could do that."

He smirked. "I said I could. Not that I would."

"Settle down, you children," Tryphaena grunted. "What is the plan, exactly?"

"We should head to Davrkton," Rhett said. "It's crawling with Vandroyan spies. We can get word of the poison to the Lord-Hunter in no time at all. Before you know it, someone will be here to buy."

The woman glared at him. "Yes, but it isn't finished yet, and if Davrkton was your goal, we've been going the wrong direction since we left! We're nearly out of provisions. If we're going to turn back now, we'll have to find an inn and hope we don't get spotted."

The Hunter who had spoken returned to his group. They watched the three continue to deliberate, keeping their eyes on Rhett.

"The queen's bitch is the only one who has to worry about being spotted," he said smugly. "I may have my name to worry about, but no one knows my face. And Phae is a nobody."

"That's enough of that. You can all find your own way to Davrk-ton," Tryphaena said. "This nobody has better things to do." She didn't wait for any objections; she mounted her horse and took off down through the trees.

Sinisia called after her, "Wait, Tryphaena! Please wait!"

"We can find Davrkton without her," Rhett said. "Because that *is* where we're going."

There was cold-blooded murder in her eyes when she turned around and stared at him. "You'd better watch yourself, daemon-lover. Those Hunters at your back are going to target you next if you're not careful."

Rhett looked back at his horse, which was grazing without a care in the world. Then he turned back to Sinisia with a terrifying calmness.

"We should talk. How about you follow me somewhere quiet?"

She folded her arms and followed him into the woods. It struck her for a moment as unwise, but then she buried the thought. He was the one who should be afraid of being alone with her, not the other way around.

"What do you want?" she asked, her violet eyes heavy with anger.

His grin was wicked. "I've got information for you to take to your queen. It would change *everything*."

"Is this a trick?"

"Not a trick. But it won't come free of charge."

"Why would the queen want this information? How can I trust it would even be true? You've already lied to me once."

Rhett looked into the distance and scratched his chin. "Back there with my brother, you left before things got interesting. There's so much you didn't get to see with your own eyes." Maybe it was for the best, he thought. If she found out and told Anavelia, the fallout and the witch hunt would be a disaster, and he would no doubt be caught in the middle.

"Like what? You stuck the boy with a needle and tried to kill him."

"Why do you think my brother has all of these answers? Everyone wants him. What do you think makes him so fucking special?"

She couldn't deny that it was a good point. "I don't know. Does it matter?"

"It matters. There's something about Aleth and Tizzy that your queen would die to know. You should have stuck around."

"Fine. What's it going to cost?"

He came closer, and even though every scrap of her soul wanted to step back, she didn't move a muscle. She stood her ground, even when he was inches away. She would not show weakness.

"Depends what you're willing to give me. I've no use for money, you know. And I've got a lot to tell."

She could feel her stomach churning as he ran a finger along her jaw and looked down at her with the infamous Hallenar charm. His blue eyes were incredible. "Please tell me you're fucking joking."

"You'd enjoy yourself."

"Fuck you! I can figure out your secrets on my own." She shoved him away and stormed back onto the road.

"It was worth a try."

It was for the best, he decided. She didn't need to know that his brother and sister were nightwalkers. He could do more if the information stayed in his hands.

Sinisia mounted her horse and took off in the opposite direction. When Rhett came back to the Hunters, he wore a look of satisfaction.

"It's good that they're both gone," he told them. "Things were going to get ugly."

"What about the poison, my lord?"

He chewed the inside of his lip for a moment. "I've got my sister's copy of the original formula; we won't need Phae. The esteemed Poison Mother couldn't even kill my brother with her new one. She must've watered it down. I don't understand how he survived."

"Maybe he's stronger than we thought."

Rhett sized up the Hunter who'd spoken and then materialized his staff.

"My lord, what are you doing?"

"It almost sounded like you were suggesting my brother is too strong for me to handle."

"No. I was suggesting he was too strong for that wretched mother's work!"

Rhett swung his staff at the ground, opening a fissure to the Hell Planes. "You keep using that word. You keep saying he's strong. What is this? Are you fascinated with him or something? Why don't you run off too and take his side? For fuck's sake."

The Hunter apologized over and over again, in any way he could think to, until Rhett closed the tear and let his staff fade into the air.

"Don't ever let me catch you talking about him like that again. He's pathetic, he's nothing, he shouldn't be alive! The same goes for my sister! They're not alive because they're *strong*. They're alive because they had help." He paused to think back on Lilu. "That daemon, *she* was strong."

The Hunters didn't dare speak. They weren't trained to dispose of someone of Rhett's caliber. He looked down the road in the direction of Davrkton, scratching the trimmed blonde beard on his chin.

"Fuck it. Let's go back to Suradia."

"Suradia, my lord?"

"Yes." His grin was more malicious than ever. "The queen's bitch wanted to bring my brother in for answers. You guys are all looking for answers too, right? How much do you wanna bet everyone's asking the same damn question?"

"About the Protégé?"

"Exactly. I don't give half-a-shit about the Protégé, but when it comes down to it, it does seem like we're all looking for the same person, doesn't it? And if we are, no one will have more leads than my family." So far, every thread tied back to Aleth.

"They don't suspect you of anything?"

Rhett laughed. "Oh, I'm sure by now they suspect me of plenty, but they have no proof, and even if they did, they wouldn't let themselves believe it. They've morphed into these pathetic, forgiving, dismissive sheep. The only one who ever held people to who they were was Tizzy."

"To Suradia, then, my lord."

CHAPTER 17

BETWIXT A STORM

VAYVEN 5, 1144

T he sun hadn't yet dawned when Allanis woke. She didn't feel rested in the slightest, but it didn't matter. It was a big day. Lora rose with her, and together they dressed to meet the public. Allanis chose a heavy gown—ivory, silver, and powder blue brocade fabrics—with long, flowing sleeves and a high collar decorated with pearls. Lora's own gown was soft and silver with mandalas embroidered in white and gold tassels at her sapphire-jeweled shoulders. She clutched a matching shawl.

"You look beautiful," Allanis told her. "I've never seen you dress up like this before. It suits you, you know."

Lora smiled sweetly at her and set the crown atop her dark blonde curls. "It is only because I have your confidence, Little Bird."

Allanis drew her in without warning and kissed her. She clutched the woman's hands so tight, she thought she'd never be able to pry them loose. Lora stroked her hair and pulled away.

"Allanis?"

She swallowed hard. "I'm sorry. I'm nervous. About today. And about *this*."

Lora leaned down and met Allanis's lips again, tender and deep. "About this?"

"You've been so patient with me, waiting for me to stop being so scared and closed, and it's only now that I'm annoyed with everything in this world that I'm feeling an ounce of passion."

Lora giggled—a wondrous noise Allanis so rarely heard—and cupped her queen's face. "Don't feel sorry or nervous. I had resigned to the possibility that you just didn't have those feelings. Some people don't, and it's perfectly fine. I was going to love you nonetheless."

Allanis didn't think anything could work away the anxiety eating her alive, but she was sure that tangling herself up in Lora and learning what passion really felt like would help. At least a little.

But she had to be a queen today more than ever. Together, they walked out and down into the main hall where the rest of her Council was assembled in their finest. Athen's black tunic had a brilliant stripe of scarlet down the middle where it fastened with silver, and brand-new steel pauldrons sat at his shoulders, holding his cloak in place. He wouldn't stop brushing away at dog hair on his stomach.

Allanis's grip on Lora's hand tightened as she continued inspecting everyone. Ashbel's confidence was astounding. He stood as tall as his four-and-a-half feet of stature would let him in a black doublet with the outline of the Lovell crest embroidered in ivory thread. Gavin was beside him, choosing to shed the mentor's green of the Academy in favor of colors more representative of his new status—charcoal gray and silver and amethyst for his Akashic focus.

"Your eyes are giant, Little Bird. Feeling better about your Council now?" Lora whispered.

Allanis whispered back, "I can't believe it! Look at them!"

Ravina had even afforded herself some new luxuries, perhaps to make her position less obvious, letting expensive fabrics in purple and yellow pop against her fine leather. Jurdeir's armor had been polished obnoxiously bright and for once, he wore the matching helmet. Lazarus brought up the end. His facial hair was trimmed and his dark clothes were accented with faint silver edges.

Lora eyed him with a raised brow. "You Hallenar boys sure clean up nice when you want to."

Lazarus tried not to smile. "Why thank you, Lora. It's certainly been awhile since I was referred to as a Hallenar *boy*."

"Don't tell me you're starting to feel your age, *Father*."

He rolled his eyes and her demeanor stayed playfully dry as ever. The word brought back memories from the first time he'd met her at the orphanage on Besq. "Feel my age? I'm only thirty-one."

Then Allanis clapped her hands. "Alright everyone, are we ready? This is the first public forum I've held. Ever." As stressed as her people were, they *did* enjoy peace that larger cities rarely had, but her fear told her they were still angry. Somehow, King Byland had kept everything together without breaking a sweat.

"We're ready," Ashbel assured her. "Don't worry, Allanis. It'll be fine. Even if they hate you, we will be able to handle it. You'll be surprised at how well a twelve-year-old can control a crowd."

She smiled when he smiled. "Then we'll stop by the build sites first so you can see what I've been planning. Jurdeir, Gavin, if you both approve, we can have construction begin."

They followed her out and down the steps into Suradia. It was cold and still wet that morning. Allanis saw birds and dogs and rats in the puddles before she started to see people. Suradia was a sleepy town.

They took carriages to the South Gate where both barracks were slated to be built. She reminded them that the new barracks would be used for training, schooling, and lodging for much of the army. Knights and mages would be assigned to towers that would be built at every gate.

"Won't this negate the need for the guards you already have at the gates?" Gavin asked.

"Yes!" Allanis wiggled with excitement. "Hopefully they'd rather be knights! They'll be better trained and better paid, and if they're not interested in that, why would I want them as guards in the first place?"

"Fair point," he replied.

Nobody had complaints about the location or the plans. When Allanis looked over to Lazarus, he was nodding to himself with a little smile.

"You've thought this through, Alli. I'm proud of you."

The rest of her day, to Allanis's dismay, would be spent in Town Square on a hastily built stage, introducing herself finally and truly to her people. She was terrified. Lora held her hand as the carriages took them to the heart of town. Curious people started to gather, and she even saw Isa waiting for them in a pretty pea-green cloak.

Gio stood with Isa in his finest clothes. "I can't believe it." He watched the Council step out from their carriages down the road, spying Gavin among them. "You really are working for the queen!"

Isa thought back to her first meeting with Athen and Tizzy and shrugged. "I was in the wrong place at the right time. That's all."

Allanis marched up to the stage with as much grace and dignity as she could, but somehow it was hard. The crowd parted for her, and she walked up the steps, the creaking beneath her the loudest sound in the whole square. Listening to it felt more awkward as each Council member stepped up behind her and moved to their seat, waiting for her cue to sit.

She waited, standing, staring at her people, her expression a mix of friendliness, authority, and nausea. The people were polite enough— they always had been—but they were confused. She saw it on their faces, the puzzled stances, and the murmuring and the staring. After what felt like an eternity, Isa cleared her throat and stood below the stage.

"Presenting Her Majesty the Queen Allanis Byland-Hallenar and her Council!" She announced it with more enthusiasm and regality than Allanis could have ever hoped for. "Please take part in the queen's first public forum!"

When she stepped away back into the crowd, Allanis took a deep breath and motioned for the Council to sit.

"Good morning, Suradia."

Some of the eyes staring back at her were angry. There was a story in all of them. A life, an experience, turmoil that she had caused by waiting so long to step up.

"If you're wondering *why now*, that's good. That's the question I'm going to answer." She rubbed her forehead. "I'm here to lay out my plans for the future and hear your needs and *your* ideas for the future. You probably all know that I have none of the late King Byland's Council left. I have had no guidance, no one to teach me how to care for a kingdom. At such a point, I know some towns and cities make the decision to swear fealty." She eyed the crowd for signs and saw a sea of nervousness and growing fury. "I am publicly announcing that I have no intentions of losing Suradia's independence.

"But the older I've grown, the more I've noticed movement. A stirring within the mainland. I don't know what it means, but I am here to announce that I have no plans of being conquered, either. This is my town, and you are my people, and it is well past the time I learned what I'm doing and stopped neglecting you.

"If you have enjoyed the lack of a military presence in Suradia, I sincerely apologize. It's going to change. We are building training barracks and guard towers to kick things off. When they are completed, all are welcome to train at the barracks so that cadets may be selected for further training from our Master Knight Jurdeir Jashi—" she gestured, "—and our Master Battle Mage Gavin Castillo." She gestured again.

A man in the crowd yelled, "Are we going to war?"

Allanis shrugged. "I don't know, but I would at least like to have the option to instead of having someone with an army just waltz in and burn us to the ground. People with armies take what they want. We've been lucky because well, to be frank, no one wants us. As lovely of a deterrent that may be, I would still like to change it. I want this place to be better for all of you and safer for all of you. What do you need?"

"A courthouse and a Watch that gave a damn would be a nice start!" someone shouted. Off-duty Watchmen spoke out in protest.

With a grin of renewed confidence, Allanis turned to Ashbel. "Would it? Well then, have I got a treat for you. After eighteen years, a Master Cobalt has finally been appointed. Presenting the Crown Prince of Saunterton, Ashbel Lovell."

If he was nervous, Allanis couldn't tell. He stood, steel against all the dubious faces in the crowd.

"From *Saunterton*? Why not our own?"

"He's a boy! Is this a joke?"

When Ashbel spoke, his voice carried effortlessly over them. "Believe me, the second you find someone more qualified than myself—and I *know* you hear the gossip about me from Saunterton—I will relinquish the seat. But save yourself the trouble. In a week's time, perhaps sooner, you will see there is no one else. I look forward to providing structure to the law in Suradia."

A woman kept yelling. "Why aren't you in Saunterton?"

Ashbel fought to keep his expression from drying out. "Because the Master Cobalt in Saunterton has another twenty to thirty years before *expiring*, and I'm not willing to wait that long."

Isa's snort was heard over all the people. She quickly composed herself.

"Look at it this way," Ashbel said. "I can't do any worse than literally *no one* for eighteen years, so let's start there."

The yelling hushed to a murmur. He heard, "He's not wrong," from one person and then, "I don't know shit about law," from another. He was pleased enough to bow and sit down, though his posture was far less formal than it had been starting out.

Allanis got back to her feet to take over the stage. "See? With structure, we're going to bring in a new era for Suradia. One of stability and growth. But there's more to it than my plans. I'm going to be here all day, so form a line, and I'll give each of you a bit of my time.

Tell me your needs or your ideas or your worries, and if there is anything I can do for them, I will do for them."

The crowd started to move, eager to have the queen's ear.

***

The air in the Bogwood was thicker now, sweet with rot and heavy with flies. Centa knew they were getting close to the bog that the forest was named after, which meant they were close to what he was looking for.

Only an hour ago, Meeka woke to find herself tied up and sharing the man's saddle. She had a mouthful of nasty insults to say, but the only one who paid her any attention was Mariette, who stared right through her from the comfort of Phio's grasp.

"Well," Phio said, trying to keep the mood light, "the bog sure smells a lot *fresher* since the storm, eh?"

"Where are you taking me?" Meeka howled. "How many times do I have to ask?"

"Five thousand times," Centa answered. "If you can ask five thousand times, I'll tell you."

She glared daggers at him, hating that she was stuck to him in particular. If she'd been stuck with the other one, she thought, she might have been able to escape.

Centa guided them through the muck, the reeds growing thicker as they neared the bog. After some wandering, he finally saw a trace of a trail and followed it to an elevated clearing with a cabin. Phio scratched his head.

"Who the hell lives out here? The greenkind would have found this place by now, and—" He stopped as Montague took him closer. "No one's here. Maybe that's just what happened."

Centa had several pieces of news he did not want to break to his friend. He chewed his lip and watched Phio dismount and look around.

"Sure, it looks run down," Centa said. "But it's in no worse condition than the last time I was here. I think someone lives here; we just caught them while they are out." He shoved Meeka off the saddle, and she fell to the ground with a cry.

Phio peered through the broken windows and turned up his nose. "It smells. Bad. Like one of those plants with the berries they're always telling you not to touch. Look at everything in there, Centa! Jars and knives and wax. And look at all the books. What is this place?"

"Must be an apothecary's house," he said. "Guess there's no better place to find unusual specimens than here." He took a deep breath to brace himself. "So, we're going to have to ditch the horses, Phio."

"What?" The look on his face wasn't unlike a scared, disappointed child.

Centa nodded slowly and put a hand on his friend's shoulder. "We can't take them with us where we're going. It just won't work."

"No, I don't believe that for a second. I've had Montague since right after the raids! Centa, I'm not going to find another like him! I can't let him go, especially not out here. There's no way he'll make it somewhere safe!"

"They know the way home, Phio."

"Not from here, they don't!"

Phio was getting frantic. Centa scrambled for the right words. "Alright, maybe not. But on the islands, the Cerulendas elves breed their horses to be able to find their way home from anywhere. They're better navigators than their riders—"

"Honua isn't from the Cerulendas Islands!"

"But *I* am!" His voice boomed, and Phio quieted. "Trust me Phio, Honua can find the way back, I've taught him the best I can with help from the elves in Caequin. If Montague stays with him, they'll find the way back to Kamdoria."

"If they stay together. Fat chance of that, we both know Montague's more of an ass than a horse." Centa tried to keep his face still through his friend's distressed pun. "And what about the greenkind, huh? They don't ride horses, Centa; they eat them! Is Honua also an expert swordsman?"

Centa rolled his eyes. "No. I don't know what to tell you about the greenkind. They'll just have to be careful. That's the best we can hope for."

Phio turned away from him, shaking and bitter. He was glad when Meeka spoke.

"Are you two done yet? This is boring. Go inside the house!" Instead of pressing for answers she wasn't going to get, she decided to be as bothersome as possible. Centa grumbled and pulled her to her feet.

"Then be our chaperone."

She fussed. "But my leg, the bite! It hurts. I don't know if I can walk on it!"

Centa swung his head in Mariette's direction. She was still snug in Phio's arms.

"She's okay."

"That settles it," Centa said. "Come on Meeka, lead the way." He kept his hand on her back to balance her walking. He couldn't tell if she wobbled from her leg or from her arms being tied, but either way he was entertained having the upper hand.

The front door wasn't locked, and neither was the back one.

"You're sure someone lives here?" Phio asked. "This is typically a sign that they're coming back soon, or everyone nearby knows better than to do what we're doing."

Unlit candles and oil lanterns shared space with countless journals and glass containers on every surface. There was a small hearth that was full of ash and a pile of boughs and blankets in a corner in lieu of a bed. Detailed plant sketches hung on the walls with bundles of drying herbs and flowers.

"This is definitely where an apothecary lives," Centa said. "These bundles aren't fully dried yet. They couldn't have been picked more than a few days ago."

"You should touch them!" Meeka cooed. "They're all poisonous!"

Phio looked back at her as he investigated. "How do *you* know that? You're not even from here."

"The bittermile up there?" She cocked her head in its direction. "It grows in Vandroya too. A lot of these do. We're not *that* different of a climate. Just warmer."

Phio shifted Mariette to one arm and pried open a journal. "You seem cold as ice to me." As he flipped through the pages, he grimaced. "It looks like this whole book is one recipe. There's probably a hundred ingredients in it!"

"What's it for?" Centa asked, going through drawers of a desk.

"It's a poison." He skimmed the words all the way to the end. "Whoever lives here was·trying to make a catch-all poison for daemons. They didn't finish it, though. Too bad."

"There's more poison formulas over here too."

Phio set the journal down and clutched Mariette tight with both arms. "Centa, I think a Poison Mother lives here."

"You think so? There's only a few of them this side of the Undina Loch. I wonder which one it'd be."

"Hey, remember when Adeska used to talk about Rori's old mentor? She used to go on and on about how sketchy she was. She suspected she was a Poison Mother, didn't she?"

Centa sighed and rubbed his temples. "Yeah. Let's get out of here. I'll show you how we're getting to Suradia."

They left the house and said their goodbyes to Montague and Honua, taking only one saddlebag from each to make the rest of the journey easier. With a simple command, Centa had Honua off into the woods to find home. Waving and shooing tearfully, Phio at last got Montague to follow. Then Centa led Phio and Meeka down a winding path away from the house and to a well.

Phio stared at it and shook his head. "No. *No.*"

"I'm sorry. I knew you wouldn't be happy about it."

Meeka laughed. "A well? You guys are gonna take a *well* to Suradia? Even if it went anywhere, and I doubt it does, it's going to be full up since this storm!"

"Not this one!" Centa told her. "I don't think it was ever a well. Years ago, I would use it to meet up with Adeska. It's a tunnel all the way to Suradia."

Phio shook his head vehemently. "Not a damn chance."

"I know you're claustrophobic—"

"Do you? Because a dark underground tunnel doesn't seem like an option you'd give to a claustrophobic person!"

"You're claustrophobic?" Meeka tilted her head back and bellowed with laughter.

"You know as well as I do that all the roads are going to be flooded!" Centa said. "And we just sent the horses away, so it's not like we could try and tough it out! There are more clouds headed this way, so everything is only going to get worse. This is the only way!"

Phio groaned into his hand. "I never should have come with you. I *knew* something like this would happen!"

Centa took that as acceptance and started to pull rope and anchors from his bag. Meeka stood beside him, smiling.

"We rappelling down? That means you're gonna untie me, right?"

"Absolutely not."

"What? How come?"

"*We're* rappelling. You're falling."

She started choking on her words. "You're just going to push me down there? I'll break my legs or something!"

He shrugged. "I don't care about your bones. Don't be a spy."

"I'll run! I'll run right now! I'll do it!"

Humming to himself, he hammered the anchors into place outside the well. The dirt was soft, but the stones piled up around it had been still and strong for eons.

"Most people don't announce that they're going to run," he told her. "Most people just do it. You're all bark, Meeka. You should be ashamed."

She let him know how furious she was by stomping and calling him every name she could think of, some of which he hadn't heard before. Once he finished securing the anchors, he looked up at her and sighed.

"Calm down, you're rappelling with me. You'll be tied to my back. But if you kick, bite, or are in any way annoying, I'm dropping you. Understand?"

She pursed her lips. "Fine."

Phio, nerves shot, went down first with Mariette secured to his chest. She looked up and waved at her father as they descended. Centa leaned over the lip of the well and heard Phio's boots hit the ground with a splash.

"How's it look down there?"

"I hate it!"

"Yes, but—" he tried not to chuckle at his friend, "—but how's it look, Phio?"

"There's a couple inches of water. Smells a little stagnant, proba- bly from the first storm that rolled in at the end of Rustaumn, but there's a raised walkway on each side that runs the length of this thing. It's still dry there if we need to rest later."

"Perfect. Get a torch lit, I'm coming down."

Phio rubbed his face. "Can those anchors hold both of you?"

"We're about to find out."

"Just let me go down by myself!" Meeka hissed. "I don't want you dropping me or falling on top of me if those things come loose!"

"If I let you go by yourself, the second you get down there, you're going to try and fight Phio, I already know. Small, scrappy guy; you think you can take him. Well, you can't. Trust me, Meeka, he hits a lot harder than I do, and I am not in the mood to haul your ass all the way down this tunnel when he knocks you out for being an idiot."

And that was the end of it. She huffed and let him secure her to his back and even cooperated as he lowered into the well, praying the stunt wouldn't end with her back broken. The rope protested their weight. The anchors especially protested their weight. For a second, they slipped down several feet in one quick, wobbly motion, and she thought it was over. Centa did too—she heard him let out a breath when the rope steadied. The rest of the way down went as smoothly as it could. Phio handed a torch to Centa and helped get Meeka off his back while Mariette stood on the walkway, picking up little pebbles to throw into the water.

Meeka barely had any breath left in her. "Thanks for not dropping me."

"Thanks for behaving." Centa wiped his brow and removed the last of her binding. Her arms were free. "Don't do anything stupid. You've got nowhere to go but the same place we do." He waved the rappelling rope that he had unknotted and retrieved, and she complied.

Centa let Mariette ride on his shoulders, and they journeyed in silence.

***

"Girls! Get back here! Quit wandering off!"

The old man's voice from atop his horse carried through the evergreens of the Wistwilds. When all he heard in response was giggling, he sighed.

"Come on, you two. Quit this nonsense. You're too old to be acting like children! We must get to Davrkton before the next storm!"

His hair had once been thick and dark, but all that remained that way now were his eyebrows, which were furrowed in annoyance. He scratched his stubble as a forceful wind mussed his stark white hair.

"*Girls!*"

"Sorry Father!"

They came out from behind the trees, leading their horses by the reins. Twins, each fair-skinned with dark, straight hair and high cheekbones. They weren't older than twenty, and they weren't identical. One seemed a little bored as she returned to her father's side, adjusting the axe strapped to her back before mounting her horse. She was taller than her sister, and her shoulders were broader and boasted muscle. Her hair was pulled up high and out of her face in a ponytail that reached down her back with a slight wave.

"Sola!" her father barked at her. "I expect no less from your sister, but you are the one I thought was responsible."

"Oh, come on Father," the other girl said. "The time spent was well worth the look!"

Where Sola's movements were rigid and precise, her sister's were enthusiastic and dramatic. She swept her ponytail over her shoulder and tucked her bangs behind her ear. She gave her father a glittering smile that took up half her face.

"Scara, what do you mean?"

"You want to see?" she asked. "Sola and I can show you! It's disgusting; you *must* see it!"

The man looked at his more sensible daughter, and she shrugged weary shoulders. "Bodies."

"What? Show me!" he snapped. "Is that what young women giggle about nowadays?"

Scara patted the whip at her waist. "I giggled more when I got that boy's ass from across the bar. Do you think that's more appropriate?"

Her father grumbled and dismounted. "I was thinking you could take up a knitting circle or something."

Sola looked up in thought. "I like to knit."

"Yes, and you also like to break bones!" Scara grinned as she helped her sister down.

They went back into the thick trees and bushes. It wasn't long before he could smell in the air that the girls were right. But it wasn't just the odor of dead bodies. It was the wet, heavy stench of what was inside of them.

"See? Look at all of them!"

When they arrived, he was mortified. The longer he looked, the more bodies he could see. Not bodies, he corrected himself. Body *parts*. They were not all where they belonged. Many of the bodies had been torn asunder, their bodies devoured.

"Sola and I thought it might have been an animal at first. But we know better than that."

"It wasn't an animal," Sola said firmly.

"It probably wasn't even greenkind," their father said, crouching down by one of the bodies. "Greenkind use blunt weapons mostly, but if they have a blade, it's a dull one. Orcs and goblins do, at least. Trolls and ogres are more likely to rip bodies apart like this, but—" he inspected the many different wounds, "—claws opened this man's stomach, and a *knife* opened his throat. A sharp one."

"There's a stone hovel over there," Sola told him, pointing several yards in the distance. "We didn't look inside."

"We were going to, but you started nagging us, Father."

"Scara, be quiet!" He put a finger to his lips. "This is serious. It's not some little game of yours. Something in these woods ripped these people apart!"

"Could be a trap," Sola said.

Scara scoffed at them both. "A trap? So what? The three of us can handle it." She murmured some less polite things that her father didn't hear.

He worked a coin purse free from the body's belt. "This one's from Vandroya."

"They all are," Sola said. "Isn't that peculiar." She said it with such disinterest that it didn't sound like it was peculiar at all.

"Alright." He stood back up and shook his head. "Let's have a look at this hovel. Gods, it looks older than these woods."

Their horses stayed outside, grazing peacefully, unfazed by the carnage around them. The man and his daughters stepped carefully into the worn stone building. Sola took a simple rowan wood wand from a sheath on her hip and summoned a petty magic flame to its tip. The shadows of two empty chairs bolted to the ground were sinister, dancing on the walls in the lambent light.

"There's a man. And there's his arm," Scara chirped. "Ooh, and look, a man all in one piece!"

"I think he's still alive!" Her father scrambled to Peyrs, who twitched feebly on the ground. "Son, what happened? Can you speak?"

Scara sat down next to him, and Sola hovered above with her petty flame.

"Father, he's dehydrated." Scara motioned to the canteen hanging from her father's bag. She eyed the room's every detail in the dim light, narrowing her eyes. The smell of blood and rot was strong, but it was laced with a curious herbal scent. Her eyes stopped at a length of frayed, broken rope on the ground by one of the chairs. "Something bad was happening in this room before everyone was torn to pieces."

Sola smiled at her. "Not exactly a casual place to spend your time, is it?"

The water mostly dribbled down Peyrs's chin, but he took a few generous gulps before coughing.

"Anything else wrong with him?" her father asked.

"Oh, definitely." She snapped her fingers in front of Peyrs's face a few times. He could only respond with a grunt before looking away. "His world is surely spinning right now. I bet he hit his head a bit too hard on his way down here. Or maybe it was from that wicked punch! What a bruise you've got on that ugly mug of yours, stranger. And let's see, there's probably some—" She pressed down hard on his torso in different areas until he cried out. "Broken ribs! I hate to say it, stranger, but you're going to have to grin and bear it if we're gonna get you to a doctor."

"Doctor?" Peyrs forced the word out, feeling pain light up all over as he was becoming more and more awake.

"We're headed to Davrkton. I'm Ayvar Garva. These are my daughters, and you're lucky—without their annoying curiosity, we never would have found you."

"Davrkton." Peyrs had barely enough time to consider it before he passed out again.

Scara clapped. "Oh, good! He wouldn't have liked riding on a horse with broken ribs, not at all. So, who is he riding with?"

"I'll take him," Sola said. "If he wakes up, I'll just knock him out again."

"Sister, he has a *concussion*, please don't do that."

Ayvar mounted his horse as his daughters bickered. He led the way back to the road to Davrkton.

***

The gray above deepened as the day was coming to a close. Ilisha breathed in deep, the scent of rain in the wind. She knew he was looking for her; she could feel him in the trees around her. She gazed down the cliffside, waiting for him, watching the current of the swollen river below.

"Ilisha?"

She let herself grin for only a second. "Yes, Aleth. I'm here."

His steps were quiet and nimble—if she hadn't known what his presence felt like, she might not have known he was there at all. He joined her but couldn't focus on the river. He stared blankly out to the horizon instead.

"Talk, boy."

"You were right when you said things were going to get worse before they get better."

"It's barely begun. Don't tell me it's worn you out already."

"Barely begun?" He tilted his head back and closed his eyes, letting his shoulders fall. Ilisha patted his back. "It's not the kind of pain I thought it'd be. It's not the kind where I just grit my teeth and will it away. It *stays*. Nothing I do makes it go away."

"My offer still stands if you don't mind being a frog."

"I don't know how you looked after me for so long. I owe you so much."

"You *did* save my life. I'm only sorry that I couldn't keep looking after you as you got older. There were so many things I should have been there to stop."

When he looked back down, his face was bitter. "Yeah well, the things that hurt the most were the ones no one saw coming."

"And what of this one? What's pulling you down right now? Your anger is making you sick."

"I have to be angry, Ilisha! If I'm not, I *fall apart!*" He yelled it into the horizon. "I've given myself so much time to try and sort it out and get over it, but nothing fixes it!"

Ilisha took his hand and they sat at the cliffside, watching the storm come for them.

"Who, boy?" She put her arm around his shoulder and felt him exhale.

"Home."

"It hurts you to call it that."

"It's not my home, but it should be."

"That's not why you're angry."

"It is."

Ilisha smiled just a little. "I've never had a son before. I suppose I do technically have many children, but it means something different for the fae. I've never had anyone to look after, to protect, to teach, love, and watch grow like this. Not until you. I have learned more than I ever thought I could about this Realm, from you. So if you think for one second that I can't figure you out—"

She stopped and heard him laugh a little through his nose.

"Fine. Why am I really angry?"

"It doesn't matter. Your anger isn't the point. Tell me about your family again, Aleth. One last time, I promise."

"What else is there to say?" he asked. "They hate me. Rhett tried to *kill* me."

She rubbed his back. "At this point, you know why they felt that way. You know it was only because you are a nightwalker. But you didn't always know that. No, in the beginning, you thought it was real as anything else, and that's what you're carrying around still. How can you not? You never got closure for that. Maybe with enough time, you would have been well enough, but something has happened that's stirring everything up again."

Part of him still wasn't convinced it was only because he was a nightwalker. Even before the accident, it felt like Rhett had never wanted to be around him. For the first time, Aleth wondered if what he was even mattered. Maybe Rhett would have hated him anyway. He would have hated all of them. He was the brother who was like a soulless snake in the bushes, waiting for someone to come too close, waiting for someone to take down, no matter who it was.

And then, for just a second, despite it all, he felt like he was on the same side as the rest of them. But *they* had all turned on him too. He shook his head.

"I tried so hard to make them not hate me, Ilisha."

"Tried so hard to make them do what, now?"

He sighed. "To make them *love* me." He hated the way it sounded. "I didn't do anything! They had no reason to hate me. But they did anyway."

"So you hate them back."

"Yeah."

She was quiet, leaving him to his thoughts as another cool, damp breeze met them. He watched his legs dangle over the cliff.

"I remember the night I decided to leave." It had been frigid and bleak. Fitting. The smell of the snow had been cold and dirty when he was spotted in the orchard. "Rhett caught me before I got very far." There had been a storm up north. Distant thunder had rumbled through the clouds. A streak had come close and shattered the black sky, lighting up his brother's face. He remembered being stuck between fear and courage. "When he hit me, I told myself that was going to be the last fucking time." His hand drifted to his neck, touching the cord to his hidden Hallenar pendant.

"He told me no one wanted me around. It wasn't the first time he'd said it, but after Tizzy and I had a bad fight that day, I couldn't keep hearing it anymore. I didn't feel like I had anyone left on my side, so I ran. I ran as fast as I could, and I swore to myself I would never cry over them. They weren't worth it."

"But you were sad. People cry when they're sad."

"They pushed me away. They don't deserve tears, they deserve to be hated!"

"Maybe it's true, but you're not mad at them. You're mad at yourself for still being sad."

"I *know*." He swallowed hard, holding in bitter tears welling up in his throat. "Feeling like this makes me pathetic."

"Such is the way of emotions, Aleth, and you've got more than most. But you have to find other ways to get through them besides drinking, fighting, and fucking. You're a mess."

He groaned and laid back in the grass, having no argument. "She wants to go back."

"Tizzy?"

"Yeah. To see them."

"Do it." Ilisha started to get to her feet. "If it's in your heart, maybe give them one chance to earn you back. If it's not in your heart, go anyway and make them miserable. They're assholes, aren't they? They deserve it."

It seemed easier when she said it. Aleth rolled and stood with her. "Thanks."

"What are mothers for?" she said airily. "I have an idea. You've got your sword with you. Should we spar like old times and work off some of this anguish of yours?"

He folded his arms. "I'm a lot better now. Are you going to be able to keep up with me?"

The tree behind her twisted a branch down into her hand. It toughened and shed itself until it was tempered and sharp to match Mercy.

"Please, you say that like I'm old. I'm only eight hundred and seventy; I'm practically a spring chicken. Perhaps a summer chicken, but I still think I can give you a run for your money."

She had been a good partner when he was younger, he remembered as she lunged forward to test him. It was a slow movement, and he parried it gently.

"Don't play games," Ilisha warned. "You'd better do your best."

She slashed upward almost faster than he could track. He stepped back with just enough time to avoid a cut that would have opened his throat with a thin, vertical line.

"I can't tell if your lack of consistency is a strategy or a weakness!" he said.

"It's definitely not a weakness." Ilisha was laughing. "How audacious of you to think I even have such a thing."

Every time he fought her, it was like fighting different people. She'd taught him to be surprised by nothing and to never get comfortable with his opponent's mannerisms. In battle, people could be unpredictable, and the way she fought proved it. She was graceful and showmanlike and very strong, but he was still faster. He always had been.

It didn't take long for him to realize that this was not for the fun of it. He could feel the sweat cold against his skin as the wind circled and howled around them. Ilisha was grunting and shouting with every swing, giving everything she had, and he had no choice but to do the same. She started to tire, and he would have done the same, but something coursed through him and made him quicker and fiercer.

"Aleth!"

He paused, panting.

"Boy, I *yield*. Calm down!"

"Sorry." He sheathed Mercy and rested his arms over his head, breathing deeply. Perhaps he had more anguish to work off than he thought.

"When you say you're the best, even if it's a little conceited, it's no lie." Her smile held nothing back. "How do you feel?"

He felt sheepish but decided to let the pink in his face speak for him. "Like I can breathe again."

"Then run off. Find your sister. I know that's your next move. The storm will be here soon, so you should be quick about it."

"She'll be with Lilu," Aleth grumbled. "I have no idea where she'll have taken Tizzy."

With the faerie's gentle magic, the tree accepted its limb back and healed beautifully. Ilisha took another deep, full breath of air, stretching her arms and feeling them tingle all the way into the forest around them and down below.

"They're toward the Sheerspine River, by the Arrow."

Not knowing where Tizzy was had been an excuse, one which he no longer had, so he bid Ilisha goodbye and moved down into the cavern and through the Wistwilds.

Tizzy had to deal with things in her own way, he knew that, but he wished they didn't involve Lilu. He knew well enough the way Lilu liked to solve problems, and he also knew how tempting she was about it.

The sky suddenly rumbled with a promise. This storm would not be like the last. The cold bit in deep and he shivered.

The Arrow was a pine tree, hundreds of years old, struck by lightning. The resulting fire had burned everything around it into a small clearing. Only a sliver of the tree remained, blackened and sharp at the tip a hundred feet tall, casting a shadow over the Wistwilds like a giant sundial. That's where he found them.

He heard them before he saw them. Lilu's rage was audible with every hit, and Tizzy grunted as she received more force than she could take. But she wouldn't give up. He'd never seen her so ruthless and determined. She may not have been any good with a sword, but she was doing fine with her fists.

Tizzy got daring, sending a desperate kick with all her weight and momentum. It would have knocked the daemon off her feet for sure. It would have hit squarely in her stomach, but Lilu was a faster fighter than his sister, and she slid out of harm's way, and suddenly Tizzy was wide open. Lilu punished her for the mistake with a punch that knocked the breath from her and sent her to her knees.

"What the hell is this?" Aleth didn't even realize he'd said it. Lilu glared in response, the anger in her face smoothing into her usual condescending smile as she realized who was facing her. Tizzy wheezed on the ground.

"Lessons," the daemon said plainly.

"What could you possibly be teaching her by beating the shit out of her?"

Tizzy looked up, blood in her teeth. "Go away!"

It hurt but not enough to dissuade his anger. "Seriously? This is what you want? What are you going to get from this?"

"It'll make her tough," Lilu said. "It's going to be hard for anyone to train her if she's reeling from every hit. She needs to know pain. And I'd be lying if I said I wasn't enjoying myself."

Tizzy got to her feet, wiping her mouth. "This is what I want. Stop treating me like I can't handle it! Like I can't handle *anything*! I don't need you to baby me!"

"But you need this instead? How is this helping?"

"It was helping plenty before you showed up!"

Lilu loved the sound of them arguing and shouting at one another, in as much of a way as she could understand loving anything.

"Tell you what." The smile on her face was devilish. "Judge how well it's working for yourself. Fight her."

"No."

But his answer wasn't accepted. Tizzy picked up Wish from the ground and came for him, bellowing. He had just enough time to get out of her way.

"Will you stop? This is ridiculous!"

She was dead serious about all of it. If he hadn't drawn Mercy to parry her next attack, she'd have ripped his stomach open. Her new confidence astounded him. It made her faster and stronger. But she was still sloppy, and that made him angry. It didn't look like she had learned anything at all.

"All you've done—" he hissed, swinging, "—is make yourself suffer—" he knew he was putting too much strength into it, driving her back, "—so you can be a bitch!"

When she tried a swing of her own, the force of his parry knocked the sword out of her hands and sent it skidding through the brush. She roared and charged him, her small fist sinking into his gut with power he didn't expect.

He should have stopped right then, but he didn't. He threw his sword down and swung back, and she juked out of the way with a swift, practiced movement. It made him livid. There was no reason he should've missed. She was having trouble hitting him, too, always aiming for his face, which was just out of her reach. It was easy to block her when she aimed high, but then she swept her leg into his knee, and he stumbled. It gave her an opportunity to connect to his jaw, but her fist never landed. He caught it, shoved her back, and punched her in the cheek.

She stopped, and so did he. She held her face and stared at the ground.

"Tizzy, I—"

She ran past him, and Lilu smirked.

"Is this my fault too?" she asked.

He thought of a hundred things to say all at once but bit his tongue and chased after Tizzy. He knew he shouldn't have hit her, regardless of the cheap shots she had taken. She had only been trying to prove herself.

"Stop! Tizzy, please!"

He wasn't far behind her. She slogged through the mud, branches cracking and breaking underfoot. Soon, he was only inches away, but she still wouldn't slow down. He came up behind and wrapped his arms around her, stopping her in her tracks and sweeping her off the ground. She kicked and squirmed.

"Let go! Why won't you just go away?"

He brought her to the ground and kept his embrace as tight as he could. "Because the last time I did that, it ripped us apart."

She quit struggling, but he didn't let go. He listened to her sniffle, then felt her tears on his hand. Finally, she leaned into him and sighed.

"Am I really a bitch?"

He kissed her on the cheek where he'd hit her, and she could feel the tiny grin on his lips.

"You already know the answer to that."

She sobbed. "Gods, the answer is yes, isn't it?"

"A little."

It became hauntingly quiet between them. There was only the singing of the wind and the guttural roar in the clouds warning the world below. He could see bruises on her hands and arms and blood on her knuckles. She felt tired and stiff in his arms.

"I'll go back with you," he said.

She didn't have the energy to understand him. "Back?"

"Yeah." It didn't feel like it was possible to pull her in any closer, but he tried. "We can go back. I need a little time, but I'll do it."

"Back to Suradia?"

When he didn't answer, she knew. He meant *home*. Her heart soared, but guilt cut her down.

"I'm sorry I've pushed and nagged—"

"You're better." He picked up one of her hands as carefully as he could. "You are. Just take it easy, okay?"

She turned and held his face with her mangled hands and kissed him with her bloodied lips. Together, they heard the first crack of thunder.

They didn't make it to the cavern before it started to rain. It was cold, and the raindrops were big, and they scattered wildly in the wind. It was miserable, but Tizzy loved it. There was something enticing and passionate brewing in the air as the sky grew black, and she couldn't wait to get Aleth next to her on her balcony drenched in the rain.

Getting carried away with her thoughts had made her breathless. When they got back to the abbey, it seemed like everyone was excited about something, but she had no interest in what it could be. She dodged everyone as deftly as she could to get to her room, Aleth following like a shadow.

By the time she was there with the door closed beind them, every muscle in her body cried in agony, but it didn't stop her from turning around and peeling off his clothes. He started to free her of her own, moving delicately, sensing she was in pain. He tried to kiss her just as tenderly, but she was voracious, throwing her arms around his neck and changing the pace. He wanted to oblige, but everywhere he went to touch her, there was a bruise or a scrape barring him.

He tried something different, working his fingers down into the muscles of her neck and shoulders. She bit her lip and stopped, completely frozen when his touch reached her back.

He shook his head and smiled. "Come on, let me work on you for a minute." He picked her up and carried her to the bed.

"Maybe I overdid it," she mumbled. He resumed massaging anywhere she'd let him, and she moaned into her blankets. "Why do you always stop me?"

"Stop you from what? Coming at me like a wild animal?"

"Well, *yeah.*"

"I guess I'm still working through some things. Admitting you're about to fuck your sister is a lot to come to terms with, you know."

She leaned back and laughed.

"Cut it out. This is hard to do when you move around so much."

She rolled onto her back and stared up at him, her smile twisted with mischief. He looked down at her bare and bruised skin, concealed by nothing more than damp underclothes, and swallowed uncomfortably.

"Why don't you work on this side a little, hm?"

"You're very persistent."

She took his hand and guided it to the inside of her thigh. "It hurts right here."

"I bet it does."

When he lowered himself onto her, feeling so much of her skin touching his, his worries disappeared. It was wrong, but he couldn't keep denying it was where he belonged. He kissed her slowly and deeply, and she wove her fingers through his hair as he gently parted her legs. His lips moved down her chest, and she shuddered as he inched closer to parts of her body that begged for a touch.

The curtains thrashed in the wind, and a streak of lightning lit up the sky. She pulled him close as the thunder rolled in, and for several moments they didn't move, watching the flashes in the night. It was beautiful, she thought. And then she couldn't bear the thought of any more clothing separating them.

The blankets were soft and cold when they slid beneath them, bare and tangled together like they might never part. She couldn't let go or she would never feel so whole again in her life. She thought she knew what to expect when this moment finally happened, but it felt like nothing she had imagined. He knew exactly what he was doing, every kiss, every caress, everywhere he grazed his teeth so gently, and then his fingers found her, and she was purring and moaning into his chest.

Her face was flush when he guided her hand and she felt him. She loved the sounds he made, the way he kissed her so aggressively, the way he trembled when she touched him. And then he stopped her.

She gazed up at him, brushing his cheek, running her thumb over his lips. "No more holding back. We're ready for this."

He breathed deeply and nodded, lacing his fingers with hers, kissing her. She gasped. The pain was slight but sharp.

The room was frigid, the balcony slick with the storm's downpour, but the cold didn't reach them. He was inside of her, and there was nothing else in the world that mattered. Everything around her melted away, and all she knew was that she had moaned and whimpered into him as everything happened faster, as she was brought to her edge. She could feel his breath hot in her hair, could feel the sweat on him as he shuddered and gasped and cried out with her.

When he stopped, she looked up at him catching his breath, and she could feel his heartbeat. He could feel hers. He laid on her chest, and they watched the storm until sleep took them.

***

Slumber didn't last. Only a few hours later, Tizzy was woken by a familiar sensation. She shook Aleth awake.

"*Eidi!*"

There was nothing they could do but crawl to opposite sides of the bed and look innocently asleep. Eidi slipped through the walls with no warning.

"Hey, you two need to get up!" The banshee tried to hide a curious expression behind her hand as Tizzy rolled to her side and glared her down.

"Could you learn how to knock?"

"I'm so sorry, Tizzy, but this is important! Ziaul and the others have arrived! You should dress and come to the grand hall at once."

She left the same way she had entered, and Tizzy grunted. Aleth's hand found hers under the blankets.

"You should go," he said.

"You should go with me."

"I suppose I have to."

He smiled as he said it. There was a softness to him that she'd never seen before. She slid in beside him again, brushing the hair out of his eyes.

"Are you okay?" she asked.

His face was red. "Very okay. You?"

Her answer was a warm kiss before climbing out of bed to clean up and dress herself. He watched her bare skin light up as a bolt flashed in the sky, then joined her. She stood and leaned on her hip, making no effort to rush, not caring to meet any of these important people.

Tizzy lit the hearth to bring a glow to the room. When she inspected herself in the mirror, her face looked every bit like she'd been beaten by a Greater Daemon. She stepped to the balcony and let the rain cleanse her, letting her drenched, tangled hair hang down her shoulders like two drowned animals. She grumbled, and Aleth stood behind her, his hands at her waist.

"You're beautiful," he said. "And you look like you'll rip someone's throat out if they say otherwise. Can't get much better than that."

"That's exactly the look I'm going for."

She fished through her wardrobe for something dry to wear, noticing their soaked clothes in front of the fire.

"I don't suppose you'd like to borrow a shirt."

He stifled a laugh. "I'll pass."

She layered a black bodice over a warm, heavy tunic. "Who is showing up, exactly?"

Aleth sighed, his gaze fixed outside. "Ziaul. He left with a few others who you'll probably meet, if they survived the trip. Guess it's time to meet this bloodslave." He started his lengthy dressing procedure of trying to make something out of nothing. There was woe in his steps as he picked up the wet clothes.

Tizzy saw movement in the trees down below, and then there were more people in the courtyard. She recognized Louvita but no one else.

"There's more than I thought there'd be," she said.

He rummaged through her drawers until he found a roll of linen bandages.

"Let me see your hands," he said. "We can't have you go down there looking like you punched broken glass all day."

"Lilu's got a bony face. It couldn't be helped!"

His stare was wry. "If you're trying to tell me you landed a hit to her face, you're lying." He made a loop at the end of the bandage and secured it around her thumb, then started wrapping around her wrist. "But you do have a tough parry. Do me a favor though, alright? Do this from now on *before* you fight her. Try to take care of yourself a little."

"This Ziaul guy must be really important."

"No, he's not. None of them are. But if there was one person here who I'd want to impress, it would be him."

That was good enough for her. She watched him finish the bandaging, trying to learn the technique as he started crossing it over the back of her hand and between her fingers. When he moved on to her left hand, she had learned the process enough to do it herself but let him finish, relishing his touch. He secured the bandage and held her palms.

"There. You're all set."

She didn't see the point of it. Her hands would be mostly healed by dawn, so the bandages were unnecessary. But something about it, about the process and having them on felt *nice*. She looked up at him, wanting to thank him, but he wasn't paying attention anymore. He stared at the courtyard, his eyes unblinking and his brow furrowed.

"What's wrong?"

She heard an unfamiliar voice. He heard it too, and it was apparent he knew it well.

"Aleth, breathe!"

"He's not supposed to be here."

His mouth went dry and his body cold and numb. Every breath was suddenly a struggle.

"No, he can't come back. He's not supposed to be here."

He tore away from the curtains, retreating farther into the room. Tizzy followed him, carefully, cautiously. Things had been wrong before but not like this. She could tell this was different.

"Talk to me. What's happening? You look like you're going to be sick."

His heart was racing. There was both too much to say and nothing to say at all. "I can't do this." He hid his face in his hands and then dug into his scalp. "I can't do this, not now. I can't! He's not supposed to be here. I'm not ready for this shit!"

"*Who?*"

He didn't answer. She pulled his hands away from his face, kissed them, and held them. "You don't want to talk."

He shook his head.

"Okay." She was learning not to push, even though she wanted the answer so badly it burned.

"Tizzy, I can't stay here."

It knocked the wind out of her. "Are you sure? Where are you going to go? And the storm!"

"It'll be okay." He felt like he had left his body, like he was watching them from miles away. "I'll be okay. I just—" he swallowed hard and took a breath, "—I *have* to leave." He leaned down and touched his forehead to hers. "I'm sorry. He wasn't supposed to come back."

"I won't stop you, but I'm coming to find you as soon as this is over. Where will you go?"

"Sheerspine." He squeezed her hands. "If you stay here and wait for me—"

"I'm not spending more time here than I have to. I can find my way to Sheerspine; don't worry about me. Go, and be careful."

He kissed her, and she latched onto him, afraid to let go. Lightning split the sky and he broke away and left, leaving her hollow. Not long ago, she'd felt perfect and complete. It all changed so fast. She came to the curtains, not daring to step onto the balcony beneath the storm, and watched the people coming into view. Contempt flooded her.

Someone had wronged him.

She tried to imagine in what way, and then her mind raced with violent, vengeful thoughts the way it always did. Someone had wronged him, and she was determined to fix it. It made her wonder if she had changed at all since leaving home. Somewhere along the way, between discovering her secrets and being kidnapped and finding the Convent, *somewhere* during her journey, shouldn't she have learned something? Staying level-headed in the face of danger, not jumping to conclusions, diplomacy, even?

She chewed the inside of her lip, wondering what it would be like to take her sword to the person who had hurt Aleth. To slip it deep inside their stomach. Or run it across their throat. Or to hack and hack and hack.

"Maybe I'm worse now."

She *did* feel different. Fear had been her friend, before. Something to make her sick, to shake her insides and keep her alert. Every time she would act despite it, she was told how brave she was, but that was never the case. To act despite it was a dare with herself. A challenge. And now the fear was gone.

There was confidence now, but it was ugly. She stared down below at the people in the courtyard. She felt like she owned them all. Louvita had placed a sense of power in her hands from the very beginning, and she finally felt it running through her.

She was the *Protégé*.

Then there was a knock at the door. Talora and Eidi had come for her.

"Everyone's finally here," Talora said, rubbing her hands together. "Are you ready? Louvita is having everyone meet in the mess hall. She's been preparing for this for weeks!"

"The mess hall? Does Lou have any idea how late it is?"

"She does," Talora said. "But you have to understand that we aren't confined by the societal norms of time. If anything, late like this is when we can be most alive. And we are about to be! Louvita's planned a lavish meal and everything. She's very excited to present you!"

Tizzy scoffed. "Present me?" She shook her head. It didn't matter where she was living; it seemed she would always be stuck attending stupid parties. "Let's get this over with."

CHAPTER 18

SANGUINE SUPPER

Eidi and Talora chatted on the way to the mess hall, but Tizzy didn't hear them. She couldn't focus on anything but Aleth. What could have happened to make him act so strange? She knew his idea of recovering from a problem was to put time and distance between himself and it, but she still felt his leave had been extreme.

But it was fine. It would give her an opportunity to take the problem into her own hands and rip it to shreds.

"Merren and Reshina didn't make it," she heard Eidi say. "That's what Ziaul was saying to Louvita. It's too bad. I was really looking forward to seeing them again."

Talora sighed. "It's hard to believe. They've been here for so long, and they were both so strong. We needed them."

"Ziaul's brought others back, though! Not just the bloodslave! Did you see that Torah was with him?" Eidi was acting excited enough, but Tizzy didn't think her voice matched the movement in her body. Something wasn't right.

"He came back with Torah?" Talora turned her head to look at Eidi, her eyes wide. "Ziaul must have run into him while retrieving the bloodslave."

Tizzy knew the name. It made her feel like fire. Louvita had said it to her. Torah was the one who had ditched Aleth in the woods as a child to be taken by the Hunters.

Tizzy cleared her throat. "So, would it be possible to say that—" she ran her tongue over her teeth, "—he isn't supposed to be here?"

Eidi shrugged. "If by that, you mean we weren't expecting him, then yes. I think you could say that. Torah came with his sister too. I've never met her before. She's really pretty, but she doesn't seem very nice."

They came to the mess hall doors and fussed over Tizzy for a moment before showing her in. Most people knew her to be difficult and suspicious—she relented to the possibility she could even be a bitch—but she couldn't muster up anything so complex for herself at that moment. She felt nothing but growing hot wrath. As she stepped through the doors, she felt a sense of power she'd never experienced before.

Aleth was hers. He was gone, but he was hers. The Convent was hers. Everyone scurrying around her was hers. All of it belonged to her; it was all beneath her thumb, and she was finally going to bend it to the shape she wanted.

Whatever Louvita had planned wasn't ready. Servants were clearing a long table and lighting candles, hastily creating a mood that was intensified by the giant window to the storm outside. Louvita spoke to a tall, dark-skinned man wearing a gold turban. His eyes were sleek and narrow, and they regarded her for only a second.

"Tizena!" Louvita waved her over. Tizzy clenched her jaw.

"*Lou.*"

She should have felt nervous, she knew it, but she didn't. Talora and Eidi let her go and wandered off into conversations of their own. For once, they seemed eager to wash their hands of her.

Louvita's thin, bony arm circled her shoulders. "Ziaul, I am proud to introduce, at last, the Protégé. Tizena Hallenar."

Ziaul brought his hand to his chin as he sized her up. "Hallenar." His voice was deep.

It made her uncomfortable that they *knew*. It was dangerous information that could come back to hurt Allanis whenever they saw fit.

"Please, call me Tizzy." She was not charming or friendly as she said it. She returned the man's unblinking stare.

"Who won?" he asked her. It took her a second to realize he was fixed on her battered face. She decided there was nothing to lie about.

"Lilu."

"Lilu? I was told you were underdeveloped. Yet you take on Lilu?"

"More than once. I'll win one of these days."

She couldn't figure out his expression. Disappointment? Alarm? Or was he possibly impressed? Regardless, he said nothing else. Louvita was more than ready to take over.

"And now, Tizzy, we can introduce you to your bloodslave. This is Amaranth."

She extended her arm, and for the first time, Tizzy noticed a woman at Ziaul's side. Her demeanor was so submissive and patient that she had been all but invisible. She was a plain woman, tall with tan skin and a long face. Her eyes were big, heavy, and brown, cast down at the floor. A veil dappled with beads cascaded down her head and shoulders, but it was the only decorative thing about her.

The woman looked up at her for one long, dour moment and then cast her eyes back down at the ground.

"It is my pleasure, Lady Tizzy."

Tizzy could feel her heart in her throat. This wouldn't do. Not at *all*.

"She will be in your care from now on. Don't let anything happen to her. She is a precious commodity, after all," Louvita said.

Tizzy couldn't find one positive thought. No one had asked her if she wanted a bloodslave, yet here she was with one of her very own to babysit. She didn't have the time to care for some waif.

She gave Amaranth a solemn nod and nothing else.

"Well, it will be a little while yet before everything is ready," Louvita said again. "Feel free to show her around. She hasn't met anyone at the abbey yet."

And she wasn't about to, Tizzy thought. If Amaranth wanted to meet people, she could do it her damn self. She scanned the others in the mess hall, finding Lilu in a corner observing everything with casual disdain. She went to her and stood at her side, neither of them acknowledging the stone-silent bloodslave. Truthfully, Tizzy wasn't even sure if she'd be acknowledged herself, but she preferred Lilu's cold observation to Eidi and Talora's gabbing.

"Where is he?"

Tizzy looked up at her. "He's not coming."

Lilu stared at all the people as if she had something sour in her mouth. "Good."

Even if this mystery person had not been present, Tizzy realized it was better that Aleth hadn't come. The way Louvita referred to him like he was nothing made her gut nauseous with rage. She didn't know how she would keep herself from causing a scene tonight.

She watched the mess hall change as Louvita's servants gave it more attention. A ghastly but gorgeous table runner was rolled out. The fabric was burgundy brocade with a scene stitched throughout. In the candle-light, the thread glittered crimson like bloodlust. She thought she could recognize some of the figures shown as Ancients before they had Ascended or Descended to deities, but each of the depictions somehow seemed off, like there was a secret between them hidden in the stitches. Derivachne, the Goddess of Paranoia; Rosamar, the Goddess of the Earth; Davagni, the God of Divine Wrath; Viaeuro, the Goddess of the Moon. There were others, too, that she knew she should have recognized from her studies, but she never had much interest in the Ancients and their stories.

The gravity of the affair increased as cutlery, and placemats were added to the table. Crystal goblets were carefully placed at each setting, and matching crystal decanters of wine sat down the length of the runner. The mess hall became the last place on Rosamar that Tizzy wanted to be. Thunder boomed after a bolt of lightning lit up the sky.

"Alright everyone, I think we are ready to be seated. A first course will come out momentarily!" Louvita announced. Tizzy had never seen a bigger smile on the woman's face.

She picked a random place to sit. Amaranth sat to her left, and Talora came to her right. Across from her sat a black-haired man she didn't know. He was pale with a roughly trimmed beard and a rugged smile. His wintery blue eyes met everyone else but her. She wasn't surprised—the stare she gave him could've killed him on the spot.

A woman sharing his same attractive features took the seat beside him. Her pillowy lips had a resting scowl as she lowered her hood and combed her fingers through endlessly long black hair. When she inspected Tizzy, she matched Tizzy's deadly expression and said nothing. Tizzy made a personal goal to get along with her as little as possible.

Ziaul sat at the head of the table with Louvita and Lilu sitting on either side of him. He unwrapped his shimmery gold turban, quietly and carefully. Attached to his head were two pythons as thick as his arms, stretching and slinking along until they settled down and hung lazily around his neck and shoulders. Tizzy couldn't believe her eyes. The leader of the Convent was a gorgon.

"It is good to be home." His voice was calm, almost stoic. "Coming back across the Roe River was a challenge. Why is everything east of the Undina Loch so perilous? I'd hate to say our time in the Western Peninsula was easy, but it doesn't compare to the trip home. We lost both Merren and Reshina before we even made it to Suradia."

"It's these *Hunters*," Louvita scowled. "They must be getting closer to finding out who our Protégé is, because their efforts have increased."

Ziaul poured himself a glass of wine. "Then we should take the fight to them before they figure it out."

Briefly, Tizzy's face softened. She noticed he'd been watching her as he said it. Louvita's face was saying she thought the idea was ridiculous, but she couldn't bring herself to say it out loud. Instead, Louvita cleared her throat and turned to the black-haired man.

"Torah! It's wonderful to have you back. How long has it been?"

His smile didn't feel like much. "Almost six months."

Six months, Tizzy noted. Six months ago, he'd done something to her brother, and she'd chisel it into her sarcophagus that she would make him pay for it, whatever it was.

"Well, tell us the story!" Louvita insisted. "How did you come to find your way back to us? And with your sister!"

The woman beside him did not want to be there any more than Tizzy did, but it didn't make her hate her any less. Tizzy watched as the woman filled her goblet to the brim.

"Very well." Torah rubbed the back of his neck. "Initially I returned to Yzen Vale when I left to find Korrena." He gestured to his sister. "I stayed with her until we got it in our heads that we could find a bloodslave for ourselves."

Korrena's eyes went to Amaranth, who refused to break her gaze with her placemat.

"We started the journey to the Western Peninsula. It was painless until we got into a conflict between one of the nomadic tribes and the Riverlands. Korrena is a natural linguist, but I'm afraid I can't speak either language very well, and I may have aggravated an already tense situation. I'm not proud of how we handled it, but the Riverlands are in our debt."

Tizzy glanced over and saw Amaranth fidgeting, her hands under the table. The woman had her skirts in a fierce, white-knuckled hold. Tizzy wasn't sure if the motion was driven by hatred for Torah or real sympathy for Amaranth, but she slid her hand over and into her grasp. They said nothing, but she felt Amaranth squeeze her fingers.

"Oh my." Louvita poured herself a glass of wine. "A whole tribe?"

"Most of them. The Riverlands took a few prisoners, and some others may have escaped," Torah said. "We had to continue our search, and that's when we found Ziaul, Merren, and Reshina in negotiations with the Rrenali of Clan Barsali. We were unable to acquire a bloodslave of our own, but we helped Ziaul secure Amaranth. It was fortunate that word of our battle on the Riverlands hadn't reached them yet."

Korrena cleared her throat. "Clan Barsali and Clan Motshen were amicable, which is rare among the Rrenali." Her voice was deep and sultry, and Tizzy hated it.

"I am sorry to hear your adventure didn't pan out the way you wanted," Louvita said after taking a curious sip. "We're delighted to have you back, though, and Korrena! It's a pleasure to have you with us as well. Ah, look here, our first course! Go on, everyone, enjoy yourselves."

The servants had an individual plate for everyone. When Tizzy was given hers, she thought it looked pointless, like something that Anavelia would serve. There was a slice of toasted bread with a mixture on top of greens and onions and berries. But there was something else. She sniffed at it and recognized the odor immediately.

"Tal." Her voice caught in her throat. "Tal, is this blood?"

"Yes. It's in some of the wines too." She poured them both a glass. "You'd be smart to observe everyone's plates and also *not* be rude. Say what you want about Louvita, but she does put an awful lot of effort into these things."

Talora's plate looked the same, as did Torah and Korrena's. Lilu's toast featured a raw humanoid tongue, and Amaranth's a standard-looking pâté. Louvita's courses were tailored specifically to each species she served.

"Oh, don't be a child. Just *try* it!" Talora hissed. "Most of these are actually quite good." She bit into her toast and perked up. "There must be some mint in here. How interesting!"

Tizzy turned to Amaranth and looked down at her plate with a sigh.

"At least yours looks good. I'd offer to trade plates, but I'm pretty sure this is an acquired taste."

"If mine appears more palatable, my lady, I will offer my plate."

Tizzy regretted trying to lighten the mood at all and looked up at the ceiling to gather her courage. She crunched down into her food. It was unusual to taste blood with something so solid, and she couldn't decide if she liked it. She *did* like the wine.

There was another unfamiliar person at the table with them, but Tizzy wasn't sitting close enough to engage him, and no one spoke to him. She thought she saw a large animal's liver on his plate.

"Who's that?"

Talora shrugged, crunching away. "Don't know. He came in with Ziaul. Must've gotten picked up along the way somewhere."

He didn't look like he belonged, but Tizzy remembered that she too must've seemed plain compared to a purple elf and a man with snakes coming out of his head. He had a soothing face that was absent of the malice that was so prevalent around the table already and a narrow, wiry body. Long silver hair was tied back, and sea-blue eyes caught her staring. He smiled into his wine glass but otherwise paid her no mind.

Halfway into the first course, Ilisha sauntered into the mess hall, nodding to Louvita and sitting across from the silver-haired man. Her expression was flat.

"There you are!" Louvita got up to retrieve the faerie's plate. It looked far more sinister than Tizzy would have imagined. "I wasn't sure if you were going to make it, but I had plates made for you just in case."

Ilisha was polite. "Thank you, Louvita. Your efforts are noted and appreciated." She looked down at the yellow flowers scattered atop a tiny, palpitating heart.

"I left the toast off. I remember you saying you weren't fond of it."

"You are very attentive."

Tizzy noticed Lilu staring at the faerie's plate with envy.

The next course was a soup. Drinking blood by the spoonful was a little better than eating it on toast, but it still made her nauseous. She didn't find basil to be an appropriate pairing. More wine. She needed more wine. She could smell a mouthwatering meaty aroma from the broth in front of the silver-haired man.

Was she smelling his food from all the way down the table? Or was it Amaranth's?

"What's your soup like?"

Amaranth gazed down into the bowl. "It's an onion soup."

Tizzy watched her stir it. It looked like it had barely been touched. "Do you like it?"

"Yes. It's quite good. Would you like to try it?"

She shrugged and took a spoonful, savoring it audibly. "That's really good. Are you just not hungry?"

Amaranth's face turned red. "It's not that, My Lady. I'm certain it was just a simple oversight, but the onions might, ah, it's that the onions, my blood might taste—"

"Oh hell." She tried not to roll her eyes and failed. "That's ridiculous. If you like it and you're hungry, just eat. Don't worry about anything else."

She did not protest and took a delicate sip as she was told. Tizzy ate as much of her own as she could stomach.

Eidi did not get plates like they did, having no way to consume food and no need to either. She sat at the table, full of chatter for everyone—especially Torah—but Tizzy had tuned her out by the time the banshee came around to them. She drank her wine, watching Lilu instead.

"Louvita and Lilu are friends, aren't they?" she whispered to Talora.

"Sure. As much as you can say Lilu is friends with anyone."

"Look. They're not speaking to each other."

She didn't know Lilu to be a social butterfly, but the daemon loved to boast and be condescending whenever possible. Something was different.

"Tizzy, you should stay out of it. You've already got your nose in enough." Talora poured more wine.

"You say that like you're not surprised by this. You know what's going on, don't you?"

"I don't." Talora looked longingly at Tizzy's half-full bowl of soup. "But I'm not as surprised as I should be. Lilu's off somehow. Ever since she found you two out there."

"You really think that changed her?"

Talora only had time to shrug before their plates were taken away in preparation for a third course. There was no time for a third course, Tizzy thought. She had to leave for Sheerspine, and the macabre dinner party in her way was asinine.

The third course was a main dish. She looked down at a petite cut of meat that had barely been seared. The inside was completely raw and was served with a shallow dish of blood. Amaranth was given a small roasted bird. The silver-haired man was given bone marrow.

"This looks delicious!" Talora cooed. "Is this a little more to your liking?"

Tizzy tried to tune her out. She could hear more and more chatter from around the table. Ilisha, with gods knew what on her plate, was speaking to the silver-haired man, but her voice was just low enough to escape Tizzy's comprehension. They *knew* each other. She was about to inform Talora, but she gave up when she looked over and saw her tearing into her steak.

What were they saying? Instead of hearing Ilisha and the unknown man, she heard Torah and Korrena whispering across from her.

"I thought you said there would be someone else."

"Not yet."

Dinner was over after the third course. Louvita offered anyone to stay a little longer for an apertif. Several people accepted, including

Talora. Reluctantly, Torah and Korrena joined too. Tizzy wouldn't be able to corner them, which she knew was a good thing. Before she left, however, she was going to corner *someone*. She searched for the silver-haired man as she walked out of the mess hall and found him in a hallway, observing the stormy courtyard. She approached, sensing Amaranth silent behind her. Tizzy twisted her face in suspicion and annoyance.

"Who are you? You never introduced yourself."

He had a flirtatious smile that she was about to tell him was misplaced. "My name is Canis. And you?"

"Tizzy. *What* are you? Why are you here?"

He was amused instead of offended. "I suppose you couldn't have been any more forward than Louvita, whatever *she* is. I'm merely a shifter, no one important or special, I'm afraid. I'd been living along the Roe River when I came upon Ziaul and his group by chance. The man made me an offer, made me feel powerful and useful. So, here I am."

"Sounds an awful lot like what they sold me," Tizzy said bitterly. "What kind of shifter are you?"

"Direwolf. I'm far less powerful and useful right now in this form. I'm surprised they didn't just feed me dogfood back there."

Her own laughter threw her off guard. It shook her and freed her of her anger for a brief moment. She opened her eyes and recovered, and Canis was smiling wide with his lengthy canines.

"What about you? You're somebody big, aren't you?"

She scoffed with a loud, angry noise. "They sure seem to think so. I'm the *Protégé*. How special. Yeah right, my entire time here has been one big joke."

Why was she still talking to him? Was it the wine? He seemed so harmless that it was charming.

"So *you're* the Protégé. It's refreshing to see you're not as stuffy as I imagined you."

"I'm incredibly stuffy. Just give it time."

It was his turn to laugh now. He seemed like the kind of person who went wherever the wind took him, and she envied it. She sighed and the corner of her mouth turned up into a little smirk.

"Well, it was nice to have met you, Canis." She wondered if she would have stuck around and spoke with him through the rest of the night had she not had more pressing matters. "Have a good rest of your night." With a wave, Tizzy took Amaranth and retired up to her room.

The curtains were blowing wildly about, and the wind had knocked over a vase. Someone had dropped off a small trunk of Amaranth's belongings. At once, Tizzy grabbed her shoulder bag and started packing.

"Lady Tizzy, are we going somewhere?"

"Look." She tore through the clothes in her wardrobe. "I've got to leave. Unfortunately, that means you have to leave with me." She picked the warmest things she could find before searching the room for more useful gear. Holding *Knight of the Red Castle* in her hands, she said, "I know you've barely been here a few hours, and you already had to brave a few storms on the way, but we're going back out there."

"Yes, my lady." Though her face said she was crushed, she didn't dare argue.

"There's another bag in my wardrobe. You should pack it for yourself. Do you have enough clothes?"

"Yes." She opened her trunk and picked through her things.

Ilisha came into the room from the balcony, rain dripping down her soggy wings. Tizzy, startled, stared at her with her bag clutched to her chest.

"Are you here to tell me I'm stupid for this and to convince me to stay?"

Without Aleth around, Ilisha was a much less patient person. "I came to tell you that you're stupid, yes, but if you're going, you'd better find him in one piece. It's unfortunate your bloodslave has barely had a moment's rest. I hope she has more stamina than you."

"So you *do* think I should go."

"Absolutely." She turned to look off the balcony. The rain fell in sheets. "The storm is almost at its apex. If you can bear the wait, you should give it some time. And if you do that, you'd better be careful."

"The atmosphere is that bad?"

Ilisha narrowed her eyes. "How long do you think you can hold out before you say something you regret? Before you say something that goes wrong?"

"Fair point. Is that the only reason you want me to go?"

"No. I want you to go so that you can fucking help your brother stay out of trouble! It's dangerous out there, and, *yes*, the fool should have left, but he shouldn't have done it alone!"

Tizzy's breath hurt in her chest. "Ilisha, he—" she had to force out the words, "—he can handle a storm. I know it's a bad one, but—"

"It's not just the storm."

Her green eyes glowed bright with fear and rage. It was a moment before she could calm herself.

Tizzy spoke with nothing but pure venom. "What did Torah do?"

"That story is not mine to tell, and you know that."

Tizzy suppressed her grumble and crossed her arms. Ilisha turned her attention to the bloodslave.

"Amaranth, is it?"

"Yes."

"Can you do this?"

There was doubt in the bloodslave, so much that it made her tremble. But the longer the silence drew on, the more the doubt melted away into determination.

"I won't falter," she said. "I'll try my hardest not to slow you down, Lady Tizzy."

"Good."

When they finished packing, Ilisha came to Tizzy and stood directly in front of her. She gazed down, so tall and imposing that Tizzy wanted to shrink away.

"Four hours," the faerie said. "If you give it four hours, there will be a break, but a very short one. Start off then, and you will make better time."

"Thank you. I'll keep quiet till then."

"One last thing. I have left you an illumination."

"A what?"

Ilisha cupped her face and bent down just enough to press her lips against her forehead between her rust-brown eyes. Tizzy swatted at her, but then she felt tiny pinpricks crash through her body with a wave of sensation.

"What was that? What did you do?"

"I gave you the eyes to see. Farewell, Tizzy."

***

VAYVEN 6, 1144

The underground corridor going to Suradia sounded as if it were full of ghosts as the wind howled and moaned. Phio knew better. It wasn't really ghosts, but he felt on edge regardless. Centa carried himself fearlessly as per usual, and even Mariette seemed unfazed. If there was anyone who could tell if there was an actual ghost nearby, he knew it was her.

Meeka, however, did not have the same senses about her. The sounds were terrifying her, and it was taking every ounce of courage to keep her wits.

"Does it seem like there's more water down here now?" Centa asked Phio. "I swear it wasn't this deep when we first came down here."

Phio looked down. "There's definitely more." They were walking through six inches of standing water. "The storm out there must really be something."

"Wait, are we gonna get flooded out before we even get there?" Meeka whimpered.

"I doubt the storm is going to get that bad," Centa said, holding Mariette a little tighter. "Relax, Meeka."

"Relax? I can't believe you're asking me to do such a thing! What's going to happen to me anyway when we get to Suradia?"

Centa wasn't sure it was wise to tell her, but he couldn't think of a convincing lie. "We were already on our way to House Hallenar, so we'll be taking you to the queen."

"Wait—the queen?" Meeka stopped. "Why the queen? Just what do you think I've done to deserve that?"

"I don't know. I was hoping you'd be cooperative and tell her that."

Her voice became shrill. "Yeah, is that right? And what if I don't want to cooperate? What's your queen going to do to me then?"

She saw darkness flare up in his eyes when she challenged him, but Phio spoke up before Centa had the chance to make his threat.

"Don't think of it like that, Meeka. Queen Allanis isn't like that, not at all. She's very gracious; you wouldn't be harmed. Not that I condone you giving her a hard time."

She hadn't completely heard him. The look she had seen in Centa's eyes dissolved all the courage she'd been collecting. She walked between them, feeling a hundred miles away from herself as they started talking to each other again.

"I hope the horses are okay," Phio said. "Montague gets spooked by the thunder, but Honua is a good influence."

"In the end, they're beasts, and they'll survive the land like the rest of them."

"Wow, that was incredibly poetic of you, Centa."

"What can I say? I like to read."

Meeka felt the chill rise up her calves. "The water is rising, you guys. *It's rising.* You said it wasn't going to get that bad!"

"How much farther do we have to go, Centa?"

Centa looked behind them and then back ahead. Either way was an endless tunnel of darkness. He'd lost track of how long they had been down there and had no idea what time of day it was.

"We might be half-way."

Phio took a deep breath. "We need to go faster."

"Forget that!" Meeka cried out. "Let's just turn back and stay in that house we found by the bog. We'll never make it out otherwise!"

"We will make it Meeka. We'll be *fine*," Phio told her. "But we can't waste any more time!"

He could see it in her face and in her stance that she was ready to run. She had already made up her mind.

"Meeka, *don't.*"

She took off, and Phio chased after her, having just enough reach to grab her arm and jerk her back. She lost her balance and fell into the rising water.

"Stop it! Just let me go. I'm not dying down here with you assholes, and I'm not going to rot away in a dungeon!"

"You won't!" Phio shouted at her. "We won't let either of those things happen to you. Stop doing this!"

She was nothing if not persistent. She rolled to her feet and charged at him with her bony fists raised. As Phio parried her punches, he felt dread pool in his gut. He balled up his fist and swung.

"Phio!"

Centa watched the girl's body turn with the force of Phio's punch. She careened over, and Phio caught her.

"Out cold." He looked down at her. The dread was crawling up into his throat. "I didn't have a choice. You saw."

"I know. It won't be fun hauling her the rest of the way, though."

Phio heaved her unconscious body onto his back. "She's not that heavy. She can't be that old, either. What do you think? Sixteen? Seventeen?"

"Either is likely." Centa gazed at the ground. The water had risen eleven inches total since they had been there. "Let's move. I bet she's not afraid of being held in Suradia at all. She's probably worried about the Hunters finding out and coming after her."

"Well, as long as we're bypassing the gates, they'll never know."

As they raced down the flooded corridor, he told Centa what the twelve in the forest had said. They both cursed on behalf of Suradia's fate.

***

The storm was at its worst point yet. The wind ripped branches from trees and threw them throughout the Bogwood. Aleth could barely breathe in the torrential downpour. Disoriented, he pulled his cloak tight. It was impossible to recognize his usual landmarks when he could barely see a thing. He needed to find shelter or he would never make it to Sheerspine.

It was miserable, and everything hurt. His body burned from the cold and burned from exhaustion. He'd left as quickly as he could and couldn't remember ever slowing down, his cruel and painful thoughts only driving him harder. Now, he wasn't sure he was even going the right direction. He took a moment and rested beneath an oak tree. Lightning flashed and the thunder immediately followed, roaring into the air.

"Shit." He leaned into the trunk to catch his breath. "It's getting closer." The force of the wind pressed him into the tree, and he wasn't sure he had the strength to break away. He had to keep going. There was no place else to go. Shielding his eyes, he looked ahead. The trees in the distance were taller. No, wait. He looked again. They were *higher*. There was a ridge ahead—he was still going the right way.

The confidence gave him the drive he needed to press on. He'd covered so much ground already, he couldn't give in even though the sound of the rain and wind was mind-numbing. He sloshed through the mud, shutting out all his thoughts.

For hours, he traveled. The storm didn't ease at all and the night grew blacker and bleaker. The corner of the Bogwood he finally came to was thrashed and torn asunder, more than the rest. It was only the storm, he thought. But then the details came into focus. He stared down at one perfectly clear footprint filling with rain.

"Did I circle back?"

He looked around and saw more footprints of different sizes. They weren't his, but that meant there were others out in the storm with him. Nerves bit down and shook him. No one innocent would be out braving the weather. He tried to calm himself and piece through the sounds around him.

The river was close by, rushing violently. The wind screamed and scratched through the trees. Unyielding, the rain fell, its pattering undulating within the gusts. The air above rumbled with pressure and boomed with thunder. And then he singled out one unfamiliar noise. Splashing. People were running, but he couldn't tell if the sound was getting closer or more distant.

Regardless of who they were or what they were doing, he had to keep moving. They would have to do the same. But then there was shouting. They were shouting *at* him. He couldn't make out what they were saying, but he drew Mercy anyway. He wouldn't get caught in an ambush unprepared.

The people confirmed his suspicions. One by one, they surrounded him. At first there were four, and then he thought he counted seven.

"Perfect. Hunters?"

They didn't answer him. Some drew swords, some drew other weapons. The single positive thought he had was that no one was skilled enough with a ranged weapon to dare use it in the storm. The way they looked at each other and waited told him that they had a plan though.

But one person couldn't wait.

One person would make it sloppy. It was a man who held his longsword with both hands, holding it as if he were telling the whole world he was going to lunge and slash upward.

He did, and Aleth opened him up with a single swing. The mud beneath him turned red as he fell face down. None of the others would be making the same mistake.

"Hunters?" he asked again, shouting it into the storm. No one answered. Three came for him this time with a fourth circling and waiting for an opening.

They all seemed to be human, with their unimpressive human strength, but they were trained, and they were fast. Aleth considered them lucky as the ferocity of the wind and rain were leveling the playing field in their favor.

He was fatigued. His arms felt like lead all the way to the tip of his sword. He parried a strike and dodged another. One of the Hunters was a woman with an axe so beautiful and balanced, it cut through the air like a breeze and very nearly cut him the same. She came too close, slipping in the mud, and he slid Mercy into her gut. Before he had pried her off the blade, the other two Hunters attacked him. He swerved around and let one of their attacks catch the woman's body. The other blade *almost* missed him, catching him just across his back.

He let the woman's body fall into the mud and took a second to get everything back into focus. There were now two dead bodies at his feet, two Hunters wildly slicing at him, and a quick glance over his shoulder found one still circling the fight. But there were two more somewhere. Where had they gone? The air felt different.

The swordsmen he was tangled up with were skilled. They fought with the complicated maneuvers and quick, strong movements that came from hundreds and thousands of practice drills. But they were only drills. Neither of them fought with the wild instincts that coursed through a person when they fought for their life. That was a different kind of training, one that, when honed, was deadlier than anything a school could teach. With the fear of their situation finally starting to sink in, the two Hunters fumbled.

One of them thought he had an opening and charged. He was so slow, Aleth thought. Why did everyone move so slow? He sidestepped out of the sword's arc and drove Mercy's pommel into the side of the man's head. There was a crack as his skull split and he stumbled away. Aleth spun around on the second swordsman creeping up behind him and sliced open his throat.

He took a moment to catch his breath, and the wandering Hunter swung a warhammer into his side.

The impact sent Aleth to the ground, and the pain in his ribs paralyzed him. He thought he heard the Hunter laugh, and he cursed to himself. It hurt to talk, to even breathe. His bones were shattered. He looked up, and the man with the hammer was readying a downward swing. Aleth grunted and rolled to his good side and started to rise, the adrenaline barely enough to get him to his feet.

The last time he had broken a rib, it was from falling down the cavern at the Convent. He remembered the pain and the promise he'd made to himself to never be so stupid again. Yet here he was, giving the man with the hammer a death glare. He could taste blood in his mouth—he must have bitten the inside of his cheek on the way down. At least he hoped it was something so harmless.

"I'm surprised you got back up!" the man yelled.

All Aleth could do was shake his head. He was surprised at many things, too many to pick one and make a witty remark about it. He had an awkward grip on Mercy, but there was no other way to hold it that didn't hurt. The man swung at him again, and though he was slow, Aleth felt even slower. He moved out of the arc with as few steps as possible. The next time the man swung, he almost couldn't make it out of the way. He had to figure out how to fight through the pain—he wouldn't be brought down by a man moving at the pace of a glacier.

He sheathed Mercy and braced himself. When the man came at him again, Aleth caught the hammer's neck in his palm. His arms shook, his side exploded in pain, and his muscles ached and tore as he fought the man's strength and momentum. Clenching his jaw through it all, Aleth drove his other fist into the man's stomach. He coughed and released the hammer, and Aleth used it to cave in his skull.

Catching his breath was punishment now. He brought a hand to his side, testing his ribs. The swordsman who'd stumbled away from a hit to the head earlier was lying in the mud on his back, staring up at the sky with lifeless eyes and blood running down his nose. There were two more, Aleth remembered. Where were they? He tried a few steps and gasped. How was he going to keep traveling?

The two finally revealed themselves, and now he knew why the air felt different. A girl held out a silver wand, and a man next to her extended a hand covered in a silver gauntlet.

"Botathorans." Aleth spat out the blood in his mouth.

"Still wondering if we're Hunters?" the girl asked him.

"I'm just thrilled they sent the *real* ones this time," he said. "It's about time I saw what they were hiding up their sleeve."

The man at her side laughed a single snide noise. "I don't know what you are, but I'm guessing you're not a fan of Time Magic."

The Death Goddess, Botathora, gifted her followers magic to manipulate the flow and passage of time, but those weren't the spells Aleth was worried about. A Time Mage's arsenal also included magic to take down the goddess's sworn enemies—all who would cheat death.

Bloodkin made the list. Aleth swallowed hard.

Without warning, the girl sent a crackling bolt of blue Akashic energy his way. It squarely hit the arm opposite his shattered ribs. The pilfered warhammer fell to the ground with a heavy splash and stuck in the mud. The Cold Bolt jarred him, sending a spasm up and down his arm and into his fingers. But it was just a Cold Bolt. He'd been hit by them before, even from Louvita several times. It wasn't a Time Magic spell, it was general magic. Isa's own Cold Bolt would likely have been stronger, he thought.

"Quit toying with him! We've been out here long enough, let's finish this!" the man yelled.

Aleth fumbled for an idea. His right arm still felt numb. Wincing, he decided to draw Mercy with his left. The girl scoffed and fired off another Cold Bolt while something deadlier gathered in the man's gauntlet.

Aleth didn't know what else to do, so he swung his blade into the oncoming bolt. The Akasha bounced off the black metal and dissolved into the air.

"What? What kind of sword is that?"

"Ready your Crux Bolt!" the other mage snapped at her.

Aleth recognized the name of the spell. He'd seen it at the abbey, engraved at the foot of a marble statue of the Goddess of Death.

Wield my Crux Bolt to strike down the enemies of Death and purge them from this world.

At last the girl followed orders, gathering up crackling, steaming gray energy at the tip of her wand. The light from it bounced off the trees and the raindrops, casting vicious shadows that closed in on them.

Aleth wondered how far he could get if he just ran and if it would be far enough. He was slower now; they would catch him. And then what?

The brilliant silver stream of lightning shot off the man's gauntlet with a shriek. There was nothing Aleth could have done. It hit him and knocked him off his feet, sending him sprawling into the mud. Rain stung his eyes. He couldn't move, and his throat was raw from however loud he had roared in agony. He could barely breathe. There was nothing but horrifying, cold pain ripping away his consciousness. With a groan, he rolled to his good side, watching the mages approach him. More magic crackled in their casting tools. The Akashic energy had been so loud, so deafening against the rain and wind, he hadn't heard the heavy stomping until Troll Daughter was already throwing her meaty fist into the man's head.

The girl screamed and fired her bolt but missed. Troll Daughter, spooked, retreated into the trees, and the girl readied another attack.

"Fucking greenkind!" she hollered. "Go back to your cave!" Then she cocked her head, hearing something else. "What is that? Is that a horse?"

Aleth knew exactly what it was, and his heart soared. A black beast reared up from behind an oak, light from the girl's bolt glistening off an onyx horn. The unicorn, bearing an ear-to-ear scar across the back of its neck, charged her and gored her. All seven Hunters, the two Botathorans included, were dead. Troll Daughter came plodding back, making urgent noises and beckoning the unicorn over to where Aleth lay. He was unconscious.

***

Allanis and her Council were tucked far enough into House Hallenar that they could avoid the harshest sounds of the storm. It had kept her up all night despite nestling into Lora's warm embrace. She couldn't quiet her mind then or now, and she worried it would drive her mad. The Council stayed dutifully on task, undeterred by her own inability to focus. Even Athen was deep into the discussion.

The topic had been how to repair the town once the storm had passed and how to prepare for the next one, should the storm season continue the way it was. No one had seen it so bad in years. It sounded like everyone had such great ideas, but they were going in one ear and out the other. Lazarus noticed her distraction.

"Alli, do you approve of more canals?"

"Oh, sure." She knew she should have been embarrassed, but she was too tired for it. "I'm not going to pretend I know what will fix these problems. I'm not an expert. Let's find an expert."

"Where are we going to find an expert?" Athen asked. "Are there experts? On flood prevention?"

Gavin ran his hand across the stubble he was growing—apparently the queen was not the only tired one at the table. "Absolutely," he said to Athen. "The colleges in Saunterton and Yzen Vale teach curriculum on all sorts of subjects, even city planning. An absurdly specific subject, but you'll find the builders and architects in those cities to be the best there are. We can find some of our own builders, though. Carpenters, masons, the lot of them. The ones worth their salt will know how to construct buildings that can divert water in case of mild flooding. Their ideas could potentially be applied to the town at large. Either that or we borrow a planner from one of the other cities."

"There's no time to send someone over and not in this weather." Allanis sighed. "Do we even have any builders here that are worth their salt?"

The comment made Ravina grin. "I can find a few, Your Grace."

Suradia was in good hands whether Allanis was focused that morning or not. Even if Jurdeir had a joke every five seconds. Even if Athen was scribbling little birds and clouds instead of taking notes. Even if Lora was wiping tears of boredom out of the corners of her eyes.

"Well, what else have we got on the agenda?" Allanis asked. "Surely there's more to this meeting than flood prevention and storm walls. What about the open forum? It was tedious as hell, but we got some great ideas from it, didn't we?"

"Your people are certainly *creative* about their problems," Ashbel commented with a yawn. The plum-colored ceramic cup in front of him was drained of its morning tea. "The most distressing matters were a slight letalis problem and the area by the west wall that keeps seeing greenkind. The other issues don't seem half as pressing as those."

Ravina laced her fingers together. "The greenkind would be easier to address if you had an Orcish community in Suradia. But you don't."

Allanis was baffled. "I don't? I thought we did. I could have sworn a few Captive Orcs migrated from Yzen Vale a few years ago."

Gavin rubbed the back of his neck. "They're dead. The last remaining Captive Orc living in the city walls died about a month ago."

Ashbel's frown was flat. "He didn't just die. A handful of your people came for him in the middle of the night and beat him to death. All I had to do was ask one person, and I got the whole story." He sighed. "Allanis, I hate to say it, but many of your people are stupid and terrified. Their ignorance about Captive Orcs led to their violence, and it's probably where half of this greenkind problem is coming from. Captive Orcs were born outside of Orc settlements; they have no ties to the wild greenkind. That being said, their loyalty will still lie with each other over a stupid human population who goes out of their way to kill them.

"There should be new education and laws about the greenkind. Then we'll either have to see about a negotiation with the ones at the west wall or put up extra fortification. If you had an Orcish community here as Ravina suggested, we could appoint an Ambassador. But you don't."

So many steps and such a violent scenario. Then Athen leaned into the table.

"What's letalis?"

"The letalis problem!" Ashbel was grinning. "Yes, let's circle back to that. There aren't as many dealers here as there are in Saunterton, so we aren't seeing it a lot, but we should crack down on it as soon as we can. Letalis leaf is dried and smoked for an extremely addictive high that can give people heart attacks. Sometimes they don't even get the chance to get addicted. Sometimes their heart stops after the first time."

"Gods, and people are really doing that?" Allanis asked. "Here?"

"Yes. I will train the Watch, and we will see to it that the problem doesn't grow."

Once again, so many steps and such a violent scenario. Allanis rubbed her forehead, unable to comment. All she could do was nod. Something stirred with in her, though, a feeling of wanting to go home. But she *was* home. She tried to fight the emotion that threatened to drag her down.

"I can't believe the properties by the Square are so expensive," she mumbled. She thought back to the man Isa had introduced. Gio. "Imagine the growth we'd see if we just halved those costs. It's a blow short-term, but long-term, there's no way it could be worse than what it is now. So many of those buildings are empty. They're doing nothing for us right now." She thought of all the new places she might see on a trip into town and sighed. But it wasn't a happy one or even a dreamy one. "I think I need a recess. Shall we break for a few minutes?"

"Wonderful idea, my queen!" Jurdeir tipped back in his chair. "I know nothing of these matters, anyhow."

Allanis walked out of the room in a daze. Athen watched her go with a frown on his face.

"She doesn't seem like herself lately."

"She's not," Lora said. "She hasn't been sleeping. And how can she when she's stressed about the town, about the Hunters, about Tizzy, and let's not forget that the three of you—" she waved her finger at Gavin, Ashbel, and Lazarus, "—have been working her to death on her stupid Royal Magic!"

Confusion spread over Ashbel's face. "Hunters?"

"Oops."

Lazarus rose. "I'm going to check on Alli. Ash, we'll discuss this later." He was gone a moment later, and silence fell on the Council.

Ashbel recalled the conversation between Allanis and his sister when she had last made her visit to Saunterton. "She said Vandroya was going to—she never said anything about the *Hunters*. I don't understand. Did things change since her visit?"

Ravina folded her arms. "Hunters. After what she told me during my interview, things are starting to add up, and I think it's time the Hallenars started filling in the gaps."

Lora rolled her eyes. "Tizzy and the other brother are ni—"

"*Lora!*" Athen threw his arms out, and she shrugged.

"I'm filling in the gaps. Allanis was going to have to do it sooner or later."

"So let her be the one to do it!"

"When the hell is she going to find the time? Between more open forums, magic lessons, and wrangling this family's problems? When is she supposed to find the time?"

"What's this about another brother?" Ravina asked.

"I'm excusing myself." Jurdeir stood. "This is all so personal, and I am barely listening to anything as it is. Someone fill me in when this is over and it's time for me to teach people how to hit things!"

When he left, Gavin leaned back into his chair and rubbed his brow. "We shouldn't be doing this. Allanis will be very upset."

"She's already upset!" Lora told him. "Now, instead of stressing about how to break the news to the rest of her Council, we can do it for her! Why don't you take it away, Athen?"

"*Fine.*" But it didn't feel right no matter what Lora's reasoning was. He didn't know where to start, anyway. "Ravina, there are eight of us Hallenars."

"I know that. For a time, it was only you, Allanis, and Tizena who remained in Suradia. The others left. Family leaves. It's what they do."

"The first one to leave didn't leave because 'it's what they do.'" He wanted to roll his eyes but didn't. "When he was fourteen, he ran away."

"And why would he run away?" Ravina was suspicious of the story already. "Your family has everything here. You're royalty. What problem could have been bad enough to drive him away from royalty?"

Athen swallowed hard. Out of all the words, which was the right one to use? He was cold.

"Abuse." There, he thought. Someone finally said it. Someone finally called it what it was. "Everyone, but mostly our brother Rhett. It's a long story, okay? One that we don't really understand. It all started because, one day, Tizzy died."

He explained the story the best he could, about Tizzy waking up during the night of her Rite of Crossing, how they'd only known because Adeska and Lazarus had gone out to find Aleth in the middle of the night and found him there.

"When they brought Tizzy and Aleth back, everything was different. They were different. We just felt it, even though we didn't know why or what it meant. It made us mean, like we wanted to push them away. I can't explain it." He told her about some of his own memories and then some of the stories he'd heard whispered between Adeska and Lazarus. "Aleth got the worst of it from Rhett. One day, he'd finally had enough, and he left."

He didn't want to tell any more. That was an ugly enough glimpse into his family, but everyone knew there was more.

"Well, *go on*," Lora hissed. "Get to the point."

He took a deep breath. "Since everything that's happened, we found out—" He chewed on his lip until Lora's stare was too much. "We found out that Tizzy and Aleth are nightwalkers. That's what we felt all those years ago, I guess. It's why we'd been trying to push them away. We just don't know how it—"

"You have siblings that are *bloodkin*?" Ravina's face twisted up in anger.

"We think it happened the night she woke up, but we don't know. They are what they are, and that's as far as we've got it, okay?"

Ashbel shook his head. "But that can't be. Tizzy's been to Lovell Keep with Allanis dozens of times. She couldn't be a—she seemed perfectly fine!"

"She lived with us!" Athen shrugged. "All her life, she's lived with us, and nothing happened. We never had any reason to suspect she could be something like that. I don't even think *she* knew!"

"She didn't." Gavin cleared his throat. "Isa and I found them several days ago. There was a situation, and we came to their aid. When everything was said and done, we had a moment to talk, and she was still trying to find answers herself. That's why she said she left in the first place."

"What about the Hunters?" Ashbel asked. "When did this become about the Hunters?"

"It was always about the Hunters," Athen said. "But I think she told you and Ana it was just Vandroya behind the threat because, back then, we didn't know the nightwalker thing. She didn't want to put all of that on the table without knowing more. But now it makes sense."

Ravina shook her head. "No, it doesn't. There's a detail missing somewhere." She tried to break everything down into simpler pieces, into something linear. "If the Hunters knew that there was a bloodkin in House Hallenar, they would be here. They would have been here a long time ago. So that can't be why they're coming. There's more to the story."

Ashbel blurted out the one thing he'd been trying so hard not to say. "*Sinisia Alvax!*" He clapped his hands over his mouth.

Ravina raised an eyebrow. "Your sister's Master of Dusk? Lord Ashbel—"

"Dammit!" He shook his small fists. "Forget it! I shouldn't have said anything!"

Lora leaned back in her chair and smirked. "This will be good."

"We can't tell Allanis any of it! She can't know; it would destroy her and Ana both, and right now with things the way they are, the mainland *cannot have that*!"

The look of disappointment on Athen's face killed him. The others shared the look, but there was something about Athen's face that hurt him worse. Narrowed rust-brown eyes spoke to years of trust now damaged.

Ashbel took a deep breath. "Ana sent Sinisia to bring Aleth to her. He's the one who has the whole story, who has all the answers, and now, for some stupid reason, my sister thinks she needs to know all of it." He grumbled and mussed his hair. "Jurdeir and I were going to try to sabotage her plan, to prolong the inevitable falling out that would happen once Allanis found out, but we just got so swept up in things here that we haven't found time to track Sinisia at all."

"I thought Ana was Allanis's friend," Athen said. "Why would she do this behind her back?"

"It was probably that asshole *Duke Orin's* idea. If the end of this story gives the Hunters a reason to storm Suradia and House Hallenar, we cannot let anyone get Aleth. In fact, he and Tizzy need to be *here*. This is the safest place for them if we get them here and keep it secret."

Ravina smiled. "What a mess. Thank the gods this job got interesting. Now I finally feel like I have something to do. I never liked Sinisia anyway. Sorry to say it, Lord Ashbel."

Girlish giggling broke the Council's concentration. Isa and Djara danced down the hall together and into the room. Djara carried a decanter of hot mulled cider, and Isa held a tray of pumpkin tarts.

"We heard you were having a recess!" Djara said. "So we came bearing refreshments! Who has an empty cup? Isa and I fancied up the Hallenar cider a bit."

Lora held out her cup in a flash. "To the brim, please."

Isa set her tray down and brought Athen a tart first. He saw her face get rosy, and then he blushed too.

"Here you are," she said. Her smile grew bigger the more she tried to fight it. "You've been working so hard, I thought you might be hungry."

"Thanks, Isa." He had a second to see the pretty hazel color of her eyes before the heat on his cheeks forced his attention to the pastry.

No one noticed Gavin's face filling with rage except Ravina, whose laugh turned into a cackle. She leaned over to him and clapped him on the shoulder.

"She's fifteen." The woman paused for a breath of air. "And by gods, Gavin, she could do a lot worse!"

Isa and Athen had been oblivious to their exchange. She moved down the table to hand everyone else a pumpkin tart, saying good morning to everyone and engaging in her usual pleasantries. Ashbel looked down at his pastry and left it untouched.

Meanwhile, Lazarus had followed Allanis to the kitchen. It was a mess of spices and pumpkin scraps, but it was still the warm and inviting retreat it had always been. The two weren't alone—Adeska wandered the kitchen at a snail's pace, going surface to surface, cleaning up Isa and Djara's mess. The back door was open for a view into the pouring rain outside.

"Adeska?" Allanis came up next to her. "Are you alright?"

She scooped pumpkin guts into her hand and threw them outside. "I guess so. Yeah. I'm just roasting some seeds. I didn't think the girls were going to do anything with them, and I didn't want them to go to waste."

"I see." The chill reached Allanis, and she rubbed the goosebumps forming on her arms. "Are you going to be okay?"

Lazarus stayed by the door, giving them space. He hadn't expected to find Adeska.

"I'm fine." Her voice was flat and tired. She walked to a bucket of water and rinsed the sticky pumpkin off her hands.

"No, you're not." Allanis put a hand on her shoulder. "Are you worried about him?"

"The storm is so bad. I should have waited to tell him. Now he's out there in the middle of all this with our daughter. I hope they're okay."

"They'll make it here alright. Centa's good at this stuff, you know that. But it's normal to feel nervous. Don't forget that, and don't let it destroy you."

She sighed. "I know. I'm scared of what happens when he gets here too. Rori's done so well with Alor all these years. I'm happy to see what they have. I just wish I had never forced her into it in the first place. Things could have been so different. Every time I imagine Centa with a son, with Alor, the way it should have been, gods, Allanis, it hurts so much."

"It's supposed to, Adeska. It's a consequence. It's called guilt, and it's good that you feel it—it means you have a conscience. Just focus on making it right." She rubbed her back and stepped away. "Spend time with Alor. Athen and I will clean up the rest of this mess after the Council meeting is over."

Lazarus put his hands behind his back. "The queen cannot clean her own kitchen."

The sisters turned to see him in the doorway bearing a soft smile. Allanis folded her arms.

"I've been stuck with it plenty of times before."

"You should go get your Council back on task. I'll join you in a moment."

"Isa and Djara ran over there with all the goodies, anyway," Adeska said. "Make sure they save you a tart. I'm sure if they don't, it's an imprisonable offense."

When Allanis left, she smirked and waved the thought away. Lazarus lingered behind with Adeska, staring out into the storm beside her.

"You don't look well," she said. "Have you been sleeping?"

He chuckled. "If only it were something sleep could fix."

"What do you mean?"

He stared down at his hands, covered by sleek brown leather gloves. A bandage peered out from under his left. Adeska breathed in deep when she noticed it.

"What is that?" It was more of an accusation than a question. "You've had it since you came. Lazarus, you told me you wouldn't! That you'd never take it that far! What have you done?"

The guilt in his soul seeped into the room as he took the glove off and unraveled the bandage. Adeska gasped at the gaping maw in the palm of his hand.

"Lazarus, *no!*" She felt her own hands tremble. "You promised me!"

"I know." Rows of its tiny teeth glittered in the low light. "It was the next step. I didn't know how to get out of it."

"And now you can never get out of it! You will be this cursed thing forever now! You said the necromancy was just a means to an end. You swore to me that it wasn't the obsession it looked like!"

"I shouldn't have told you that." He couldn't look at her. "It is an obsession. It always has been."

She looked back outside and then threw her hands up and wailed. "You wanted to be a *doctor*! What happened?"

"The college kicked me out." The maw snapped at the air hungrily. "I never told you. They kicked me out after two months. We were studying a patient, and he just started dying. We scrambled to cure him in time, trying both medicine and Topaz Magic, but neither method worked. The man died. We were supposed to accept that."

"And you couldn't, could you?"

"No. I thought it was ridiculous that we were giving up, that we hadn't done *more*, but they said death was a closed door. It was final, and any attempt to open it again violated every code of Order and Disorder. My curiosity and my drive, the two things that I thought made me an excellent scholar, got me expelled. But before I had even stepped foot off the campus, another professor found me. He praised those traits and said I was exactly the kind of student he'd been looking for."

"He was a necromancer."

"He was. He's dead now."

"*Ironic.*"

"I killed him."

Adeska stared at him, and he continued.

"Believe it or not, I didn't want to learn the things I was learning, not after I'd gotten so far into them. It was gruesome and Forbidden. I didn't think I had the stomach for it, but he wouldn't let me quit. He needed me to learn the advanced material so that I could perform a ritual that would supposedly make him immortal. This stupid, feeble old man *immortal*. He threated to out me if I quit, and I knew it would ruin us. I had no choice."

"But you took Rhett to the Fallarian Isle and learned all the Forbidden things you could get your hands on! You *taught* them. You have a fucking school on Fallarian, Lazarus!"

He brushed his hair back with his gloved hand. The gray at his temples had grown since he'd been in Suradia.

"At first, it was only to have some way to control him. We only wound up there by accident, after all. But there's something about Rhett that just makes you forget."

"Forget what?"

"Humanity. For a while, I actually felt close to him. It felt like we were brothers. I let him pull me into the chaos, deeper and deeper, and I enjoyed it. Did you know Mother communed with daemons when she was carrying him? Father said she had always been haunted by them, but she promised she'd never dabble with them while pregnant. Of course Rhett was the one she slipped up with."

"I always knew there had to be something. He's not like the rest of us. The way *we* are is one thing, but him—" she swallowed hard, "—he's worse."

"He had me fooled for a time. But when I did *this*—" he looked down at his hand again, "—when I received the Anzharian Maw, it was like I came to the surface for air for the first time in years. I became aware of everything I had done. That we had done. It feels awful."

She leaned on his shoulder. "Lazarus, what's wrong with this family?"

"Nobody's perfect."

Truer words had never been spoken, she thought. He would never be able to get rid of the Maw. It was a part of him now, embedded in him, feeding off him for eternity, and would be there even if he amputated.

"The Rot comes next, Lazarus."

"I know."

CHAPTER 19

BONES

N aia looked over her handiwork with satisfaction. She had just finished preparing fresh baskets for rooms ready to be turned over since Sheerspine Spire was dead. The handful of current patrons didn't want to leave in the storm, and there weren't any new patrons braving the weather to check in, either. The lull in business had given her plenty of time to launder and fold towels, refill soap-weed pulp, and reassemble the bath baskets.

Mayriel and Velana came from down the hall to the station that she had set up at the bar counter.

"Wow." Velana wiped sweat off her brow. "Those public baths were disgusting. Aren't we supposed to have someone cleaning those regularly?"

"We did," Naia said, now wiping down the bar counter. "Remember that nice dragonkind man? Grygeth? You could barely tell he was dragonkind except for a few red scales he had on his face that looked like freckles. Well, and the horn on his nose."

"Oh yeah! Good ol' Grygee!" Mayriel stretched all of her arms. "Whatever happened to him?"

"He left! You two don't remember?" Naia handed them baskets to take away. "He said he was off to the Shimara Tail—or was it Siopenne? We had a going away party and everything!"

"We probably don't remember because *all we do is work*," Velana grumbled. The quadramani headed upstairs, leaving Naia to gaze out at the ghostly entry room.

It flowed nicely into the bar and dining area, which currently only seated a couple patrons. The hearth was roaring and crackling, casting a warm glow that reflected off the polished oak tables she had cleaned off. Then she had the fantastic idea to pour herself a drink.

That was when the door burst open. The wind knocked it against the wall as Kenway, drenched in blood and viscera, came in with Troll Daughter. The greenkind carried Aleth in her arms.

"Holy shit! Where'd you guys drag him in from?" Naia leapt over the counter and helped them inside, fighting the wind to get the door shut again.

"It's bad, Naia." Kenway was always serious in some way, but this time was different. She followed them into the kitchen.

"When you said you were taking Troll Daughter out to find something, I didn't think it would be him!"

Kenway cleared off Troll Daughter's main workstation in the middle of the kitchen, and Naia laid down towels. By the time the greenkind set Aleth down, he was starting to stir.

"I don't think that was her intention, either, but he was headed this way. Took down five Hunters before he was brought down."

"Brought down by *what*?"

"The real Hunters. Hit him with a Crux Bolt."

"Gods damn." She stood over him and watched him fade in and out of consciousness. "Hey! Psst, stay with us! Do you know where you are?"

He groaned. "Naia?"

"Wrong. You're at Sheerspine, not at Naia. Good guess though, buddy."

Troll Daughter wandered off, rummaging through drawers and boxes for tools.

"Nai, help me out," Kenway said. "I think she's going to have to open him up." He started pulling at Aleth's shirt, and Aleth swatted at him.

"Stop it, I'm fine!" Naia ignored him and ripped the tunic open. "Hey! What are you doing?"

"Good lords, Aleth. They fucked you up." She stared down at the red and purple splotching along his side from internal bleeding and shook her head. The faint black webbing of an Akashic bruise ran the length of his torso and right arm.

"You ruined the only shirt I have!"

"Focus on the bigger problems at hand!" she barked.

"That's a really big problem!"

Kenway snapped his fingers at him. "Aleth. What were you doing out there? Were you with anyone? Where's your sister?"

"She didn't come with me, she couldn't be out there—*hey*!" He lurched away, then hissed in pain as Naia pressed a cold, wet rag to his side. "Get away from me, all of you!"

Troll Daughter made a loud noise, and Kenway and Naia left. Aleth sighed and lay flat.

"Thanks, Doddie."

She made more sounds. Though she knew the Common tongue as expertly as any scholar born to it, the words that came out of her mouth never matched up with the words in her head no matter how hard she tried. But Aleth had known her long enough to pick up her unique language.

"I'm fine, really," he insisted. "My bones heal just like everything else. I just need time."

"*Peeshes*." She wiggled her fingers around before pressing her weight into a mortar and pestle, grinding up a thick, fleshy plant.

"So there's some bone pieces. They'll dissolve over time. That's how bones work."

"No." It was the only word she could say clearly. She went on to explain that bloodkin bones, his especially, were too strong for the body to break down before they floated around and caused other internal damage.

"And I'll heal from that too."

"*No.*" She said he had a fat chance of doing that if a bone shard found its way to his heart. She worked at the mortar and pestle until there was a pulp at the bottom. After adding a few different oils and a pinch of blue salt to it, she scooped a gob into her hand.

"Doddie, please, do we really have to do this?"

She nodded and applied it to his side. In minutes, it had numbed. She started digging through more jars and made a comment.

"Mipsoo."

"I missed you too."

Her tools were set out beside him, sharp and clean. She was obsessive about the condition of her instruments. It made him nervous the longer she was away.

"Now what are you looking for?"

She came back and shook a jar in his face, watching the salt crystals and herbs dance around inside.

"You don't need to do that," he sputtered. "I can handle this, Doddie, don't knock me out!"

She said he squirmed too much and she was not about to put up with it during a delicate procedure. Somehow, his face managed to get even paler than it was. She tried to reassure him.

"Doddie, I don't want to."

She didn't know how else to comfort him, but she was not going to give in. The only thing she could think to say was, "Please."

He didn't like the dreams he had when Troll Daughter put him under, and he was especially afraid to confront the ones that would surface after all the recent events that had transpired. He took a deep breath and let it out slowly, thankful that he was numb.

"Fine. But wake me up as soon as you're done."

She was delighted and unscrewed the jar. He could smell its contents already and started to feel dizzy, even though he was fighting it as best as he could. She brought the jar up close, and he thought that maybe if he could convince her it wasn't working, she would have no choice but to let him stay awake.

She watched him nod off in record time and screwed the cap back on. It worked every time. She picked up her scalpel and inspected her task at hand.

Naia came in unannounced, and Troll Daughter growled.

"Sorry. Put a sign up or something, gods!"

Troll Daughter grumbled and made her first incision while Naia stared uncomfortably. It was never good news when Aleth made his way back to Sheerspine, she thought.

"Why is he always so filthy when he shows up?" she huffed, scouring through the kitchen for a rag and hot water.

Troll Daughter, exasperated, reminded her that she was trying to concentrate.

"Sorry, Doddie, I just—" She tossed the water and the rag aside and folded her arms tight. "I talk when I'm worried. You know that. Nothing good ever happens to this guy."

As she clamped a pair of forceps on the incision to keep it open, Troll Daughter asked her whose fault she thought that was.

"Whose fault—wait, what are you implying?"

She reminded her of the time they'd kicked him out and told him never to come back. There was far more than a hint of acidity in her voice.

"Look, I know he's your friend, okay? He's our friend too. But he needed to grow the fuck up! Come on!"

Kenway came into the kitchen, cross as ever. "You two could not have picked a less appropriate place to have this discussion. Would it kill you to show him some respect?" He had changed out of his black, gore-drenched traveling clothes and into other black traveling clothes.

"Tell her we made the right call!" Naia shouted at him. "Sometimes we have to make *very* hard decisions, Doddie, and that was one of them! We had to! Tell her, Kenway!"

The man watched Troll Daughter work a crude rib spreader into the incision, suddenly feeling heavy. "All I know is that when he needed me most, I told him to get lost."

She threw her hands in the air in disbelief. "You told him to get lost because he was a wreck! He was destroying our business, destroying himself. He *needed* to get lost!" Naia couldn't believe he had lost his conviction. "This is ridiculous. You saw him this last time he came back. It looked like the time away did him good!"

"I sent him away in anger, Naia. That's the worst way to do anything."

"You had been extremely patient with him up until then."

"I know you're right, okay?" he snapped. "Just let me feel bad! Let me have this brief moment to imagine what things could have been like if I hadn't been an asshole!"

"Fine! Why does there always have to be someone brooding around here?" She left with a loud grunt and slammed the door.

Troll Daughter looked up at Kenway, bloody tweezers in her too-big hands. She asked him to leave, too, and he did. She worked for almost two hours, fighting with an incision that kept trying to heal. When she finished, she had removed nine fragments. She was confident she'd gotten them all and congratulated herself on a job well done.

Sometime after Naia caught Troll Daughter dragging a nice chair from the front room into the kitchen, she came into the scene herself, hands full. Aleth was groggy and awake, sporting fresh bandages and sitting awkwardly in the chair by the hearth. He gazed into the flames, holding a blanket around his shoulders.

"Hey." Naia sauntered up beside him, dragging a stool over with her foot. "How are you?"

He glared at her from the corner of his vision. "Not destroying your business, I hope."

Her stomach turned, and her face went red. "Oh. You heard that."

He bit his lip and sucked in a breath. "Yep."

"None of that meant that I don't like you or that I don't generally enjoy having you around."

He rested his head in the palm of his hand, still watching the fire. "I know." The flames sputtered and crackled. "It just hurt to hear." He let her see a faint smile twist onto his face to kill some of her dread.

"I'm sorry, Aleth. I don't know why I was saying all that stuff. I had no reason to be so upset—"

"It's fine. You were worried. You get riled up when you're worried." He didn't add that he was long since used to it from everyone else, anyway. "If anything, I'm more upset about my shirt."

"About that." She took a muslin-wrapped package out from under her arm and handed it to him. "I come bearing gifts for your recovery." She paused and looked him over. "Doddie really didn't have anything for that Akashic bruise? That thing looks brutal."

He took the package. "Hurts like a bitch. What's this?"

"You'd know if you opened it."

He did, and then he grinned, holding a black tunic up against himself. "Now I match Kenway!" he laughed. "Thanks, Naia. Are you sure this will fit?"

"It's going to fit. May and Vel know what they're doing. They've washed your clothes enough times to know your measurements pretty well."

"That's not why they know my measurements."

She snorted when she laughed. Then she handed him the next gift—a tumbler of red-tinged gold liquor. "Took you long enough to figure that out."

"Don't give me the credit," he said, taking the glass. "Tizzy pointed it out to me." He took a generous gulp and laid his head on the back of the chair. "This is your blood."

She showed off her bandaged wrist. "The best in town."

"And you mixed it with forty-year-old Luna Ridge whiskey."

"I'm impressed. You know your shit."

Grinning, he watched her pour herself a glass. "Naia, this stuff is like—" He paused for thought and then laughed. "It's like five hundred gold a bottle. I *stole* a bottle of this last time I was in Caequin!"

"First glass is on the house. After that, we'll just throw it on your tab next to the surgery."

He took another sip. "Why not? The princess can pay it off when she gets here."

"That's what I like to hear!" She clinked her glass with his. "So, what's the deal with you? How did Kenway and Doddie come across you out there in the storm? Doddie started going crazy about something and took off, so Kenway followed her out. And then they come back with you. Know anything about that?"

"When Tizzy and I found her, she'd been captured by Hunters. And this time, she found her way to Hunters again."

"You think she can sniff them out?"

"Maybe. But how? What is it that she's sniffing out, exactly?"

Naia took a long sip. "We should bring one of the bodies back when the storm clears up. Why'd you leave the Convent? Come on, spit it out. You and your sister have a fight?"

He could feel himself blush. He tried to hide his face, but Naia could see the pink all the way to his collarbone. She slapped her thighs and howled.

"Oh no!" She snorted again.

"I don't know what you're laughing for. It was a really bad fight."

"Oh my gods, and now you're trying to lie." She wiped away a tear. "Why are bloodkin so fucked up? Bless you all." She gasped for air. "Alright, so you left because you and your sister got into a *physical altercation*, is that it?"

He hid his face until it was time to sip from his glass again. "That's not why I left."

"I don't know why you're so red. That's probably the least perverted thing you've done."

"Shut up, Naia."

He didn't want to talk about why he'd left. Any conversation, no matter how embarrassing, would have been preferable to that one, but Naia persisted.

"Either you tell me now or she tells me when she gets here," she said. "It's up to you. I can wait if I have to, but I am going to find out."

"Someone showed up. I didn't want to be around him."

"That's it?" she sipped.

"That's it."

She watched him grow distant, returning his stare to the fire. When he drank, he swallowed hard. There was more to it, she could see that much plainly, but he'd never say it. She moved a lock of hair away from her third eye and looked him over.

"Torah."

He didn't answer her and stared into the glass. He knew his silence would be answer enough.

"I've only met him the one time you two stayed here. If you ask me, he was a little whiny and pretentious." She took another drink. "Like you!"

"I'm not pretentious."

"But you're definitely whiny."

He shot her a glare, but the corners of his mouth turned up. "Maybe a little."

She had glimpsed enough to know he wanted to bury the incident. For a second, she thought to give him his space and leave, but she didn't. She sat with him, and they drank in thoughtful silence.

***

Phio's distress had reached new heights as he slogged through water up to his waist with Meeka unconscious on his back. He thought Centa was better suited to carry her, but their unwritten rule for these scenarios was 'you haul what you drop.' His friend waded along, unhindered by Mariette and the torch.

"Look, we're almost at the end, Phio!"

The never-ending darkness they had been pursuing finally opened up. It was dark, but they could see the outside world, and the sounds of rain were louder than ever. Centa started to run as fast as the rising water would let him, and Phio followed.

The tunnel opened into a deep, rain-gorged canal that cut through the middle of Suradia. Centa stared at it and its depth of water—he had only ever used the tunnel in the summer, when it was dry.

"We're gonna have to swim." Phio couldn't find his breath. "Great. Enclosed, windowless spaces *and* water. This trip has both of the things I'm terrified of."

Mariette, now drenched, finally started crying. Centa held her tight and searched for a way up. "It's gonna be fine, Mari. We're almost there." Farther down the canal, he spotted a bridge and a narrow stairway for maintenance.

"Can you swim with her?" He gestured to Meeka.

"I think so, if I don't have a panic attack and drown first."

"Alright, good. Head for the bridge. Mari, hold on tight!"

He put the girl on his back, and she cried hysterically, wrapping her arms around his neck and holding on for dear life. He stepped into the frigid waters and started to fight the current. He looked back at Phio.

"I'm fine, just go!" he grunted. He struggled to pull Meeka's body with him—he didn't realize how hard he'd hit her—and the water pulled him under sometimes, but he managed. Centa let him be and swam for the bridge.

They made it to the streets of Suradia, and Meeka woke to the nightmare. She shivered violently as the winds hit her cold, wet frame.

The empty town was flooding, trees were toppling, and cobblestones were coming dislodged. Her head burned and throbbed from it all—from the storm, from the punch she'd taken, from the disorientation. All she could do was cry.

Phio put his hands on her shoulders, shielding her from the wind. "We're almost there! You're going to be okay, I promise!"

She hugged him and was overcome with heavy, wracking sobs. They ran. Meeka followed them. She didn't dare find herself where the Hunters could see her, and she needed shelter. At this point, she couldn't fight Centa and Phio anymore. House Hallenar was where she would end up. She'd just have to manage. When it came into view, it was bigger than what the Hunters had described to her in the past. It looked fit for a perfectly humble queen.

Centa banged on the doors as hard as he could, Mariette screaming in his ear. He couldn't be angry with her, not when he was seconds away from joining her. The door opened uncharacteristically fast, and two unfamiliar women stared at him.

"Who are all of you?" Titha asked.

Centa tried to catch his breath. "The queen—we're here to see All—"

"Alright, enough!" Isa waved them in. "Goodness, get inside, all of you! We'll get to the details later!"

Titha agreed and shut and barred the doors after Isa led them in. "I'll stay with them; you should get the queen!"

The girl tore off without another word, scampering down a hallway to do as she'd been told, skirting past Lazarus in the process. Confused, he came to the entry hall.

"What's going on? *Centa!*"

There were very few people Centa wanted to see less right now, but he didn't greet him with any more indifference than usual.

"Lazarus." The adrenaline died down, and he fought to catch his breath as fatigue rattled him. "Adeska?"

"She's fine. Are you?"

Mariette stopped crying. She was left with only sniffles.

Centa set her down and rubbed his face. "We made it. Gods, we fucking made it." He hugged Phio and even clapped Meeka on the shoulder.

Lazarus stared at her, keeping his expression firm. She was quiet and wide-eyed and couldn't stop shivering.

"Friend of yours?"

Centa shrugged. "She's not the worst."

Allanis came striding into the entry hall with Isa at her side, all business in a way Centa had never seen her before. He expected her face to soften when she recognized him, but it didn't.

"You two need to rest."

"I agree," he told her.

"Isa, show Centa and Phio to a room and get Mariette to her mother. Wait, who's that?"

Phio guided the girl to her. "My queen, this is Meeka. She's a Hunter, but she's turning over a new leaf. Isn't that right, Meeka?"

She swallowed hard and nodded. Allanis's powerful gaze went right through her. Phio had never seen this side of her before, and it made him nervous. He told Meeka that she would be okay and that Allanis was pleasant and amicable. Was that still the case?

"Titha, Lazarus, take her down to the cells. See that she has food, new clothes, blankets, whatever she needs. I will be with her later."

And that was all she said. Centa and Phio exchanged worried glances as she left. Isa rushed them away to a spare room, and Titha and Lazarus led Meeka back underground in silence.

Meeka desperately wanted a spark of her old courage, but it was nowhere to be found. The only comfort that she had was that she was under a roof. The walk to House Hallenar's dungeon was cold, musty, and drafty, but it was met by Stormy halfway down. The mutt scampered after them, excited to sniff a newcomer. Meeka let him lick her hand.

"Down, Stormy," Lazarus commanded. The dog obeyed, settling for racing down the corridor in an attempt to lead the way instead. "Do you like dogs, Meeka?"

"The nice ones."

"Stormy is about as nice as they get. You'll have good company."

"Is there no one else down here?"

"You're the first prisoner the queen has ever had."

This was going much worse than she was prepared for. They locked her in a cell and lit a few sconces in the hall. She was brought a bedroll, blankets, a change of warm clothes that were a little too big, hot food, and a cup of cider. She tried to find it in her to be furious, and under normal circumstances she knew she would have been, but there was nothing but exhaustion and relief to be out of the elements. She succumbed to deep slumber that would hold onto her into the next day.

Allanis sat in her study by a dimly flickering candle, her head down on her desk while Lora rubbed her back.

"Speak your mind, Little Bird."

"I'm not ready."

"To speak your mind?"

She groaned. "To deal with Adeska and Centa. And this Meeka girl. What do I do?"

"You interrogate her."

"And then what?"

Lora sighed and sat on the edge of the desk. "Well, you may not have the stomach for that part. But you'll need to. She might not co-operate, and if her intel is valuable enough, you can't let that stop you. When you're done, whether your efforts are fruitful or not, I personally would turn her over to your Master Cobalt. Little brat thinks he's so tough, let's see *his* call."

"Tomorrow, then." Allanis folded her arms on the desk and rested her head. "I'll let her recuperate today. Tomorrow, though, I'm asking questions."

***

Four hours. The best course of action was sleep, Tizzy knew. It would be the only way to stay out of trouble. Besides, Amaranth would do well with a little bit of rest before the hellish journey Tizzy was about to drag her on. The woman took to sleep as soon as Tizzy had told her the plan.

Barely an hour had passed since Ilisha left them. Tizzy crept out of her room and went to the end of the hallway, opposite the stairs leading back down into the Convent. Standing tall was the worn grandfather clock, at least a century old, ticking away. It was built of nightwood, carved with Botathoran motifs of skulls, spools, and needles and thread. Silver inlay was spotted with touches of patina. She expected no less than to find the device in an abbey devoted to the Time Goddess.

Being as old as it was, she wasn't sure if it had an alarm capability, but with a thorough inspection, she found little holes in the hour markings along the clock face. She scoured the compartments until she found a tiny drawer of silver pegs. Without a sound, she slipped one into the clock face three hours ahead and then snuck back into her room and went to sleep.

To her surprise, her Ethereal body was ready to wander. Her ability hadn't worked since the events in the hovel with Rhett and Tryphaena, and she had started to fear that the trauma had stunted it for good. She breathed a sigh of relief as the rain and wind phased through her.

She was still at the Convent, just outside. She had learned to trust where the ability placed her and took one long, sullen look up at the abbey before exploring the grasses and trees around her. She was tired of this. What was she supposed to see? She half expected to be taken down to the Wistwilds to check on Aleth, but no such luck.

The Wistwilds. She decided to make her way down, after all. It didn't seem like there was much for her to see up on the plateau except the carnage caused by the storm, so she headed to the antechamber to descend into the cavern.

At last, she found what she was meant to find. Voices. Korrena and Torah hurried into the antechamber, never even catching sight of her. Tizzy leaned up against the tiny wood and stone room, straining to hear them from outside. Despite all the rainfall and the screaming winds, they were crystal clear. They didn't continue down into the cavern. They closed the door and stayed there in silence until Korrena finally picked their conversation back up.

"Torah, I want to leave."

"We can't, Kor. Not yet." He sighed. "There's eyes and ears everywhere around here, so just relax and keep to yourself awhile if it's that bad."

"You say that like you've told me something important," she scoffed. "You haven't. You haven't told me a single thing, and I'm getting sick of it."

While she may have hated the woman for no good reason, Tizzy was amused that she could relate to her so well.

"Look." He held her shoulders. "I agreed to something and I have to see it through."

"So see it through and let's go."

"It's not that simple. You know that, Kor. You know how these things are. This isn't our first time at one of these places. The next move isn't mine to make."

"You're tense about it. This isn't something dangerous, is it?"

Torah rubbed his arms and leaned against the wall. "Louvita doesn't seem to think so, but she's been wrong before."

"I can't decide if I like that woman or not. She's chatty."

"What did you two talk about earlier?"

A devilish smile grew on Korrena's face. "My abilities."

"And what did you tell her?"

She leaned on the wall next to him and shrugged. "The truth. I don't plan on being here for very long, but during that time, I wouldn't mind being revered."

"She does have endless uses for a nightwalker who can control bloodkin of *lesser blood*."

"That's about how she put it. She said that other than that Protégé bitch, we're the purest lineage here, so I'll have some material to work with. She's got a problem child in mind already." She laughed. "And as soon as she finds him, he's all mine." She watched Torah's face turn into a grimace. "What is it?"

"Would you leave him alone?"

"You know who she's talking about?"

"Yeah," he grumbled. "Louvita's essentially turned him into her scapegoat. Let him off easy, won't you? I still need to talk to him."

Tizzy felt her blood boil as their conversation drew on, but she saw someone approaching. It was Talora. She came to the antechamber, gave Tizzy a wink, and opened the door.

"There you two are!" she announced with a cheerful smile.

"Tal?" Torah wasn't angry like his sister was, but he was not short on suspicion. "What's the matter?"

"Nothing at all, actually! We've got some more wine out, and we were hoping to start a Liar's Game in the study. I'm the reigning champion, you know."

Torah didn't feel like coming up with an excuse not to join her, so he obliged. Scowling, Korrena followed them back into the abbey. The antechamber was clear.

Tizzy woke to gentle chimes from the hallway. *The clock.* She rushed out of her room to remove the peg and stop the alarm. It was time. Amaranth was waking up when she returned.

"Are you feeling well?" Tizzy asked. She searched the woman's face, finding it pallid and twisted in pain.

"I need to let out the blood," she said. "It hurts."

The sigh Tizzy released was both frustrated and nervous. It would be rude to refuse, she thought. The woman was in pain, and feeding from her would help. But it wasn't solely for Amaranth's benefit, Tizzy had to remind herself. It could turn selfish in a second.

"This is my chance to be better," she whispered.

Amaranth put her hand on her chest and looked away. "Yes, that's what Louvita and Ziaul said of my purpose."

"*No.*" Tizzy glared at her. "That's not what I mean. That is absolutely not what I mean." She tapped her foot and let out a breath. It was time to start over. "I mean that this is my chance to be a better *person*. If I can just show myself that I can do right by *somebody*—" she shrugged and shook her head. "I don't know. Forget it. Will your arm be fine for this?"

Amaranth rolled up her sleeve and showed it to her. "Yes, it will be fine, my lady."

She sat beside her on the chaise, taking the woman's arm in her hand. She stared down at the blue vein just beneath her skin.

"This is not because you're my bloodslave. This has *nothing* to do with that," Tizzy told her. "That's not what this is. You're under my care, and I'm only trying to fix some of the pain from your condition. Do you understand?"

"I do, my lady."

With a bit of patience, Tizzy willed her fangs out. "Also, if this hurts, I'm sorry. I don't have much practice."

"I have no doubt it will be more tolerable than the feedings I endured on my way here."

She was hot with rage again. "Torah and Korrena?"

"He wasn't so bad." Amaranth stared at her boots. "He wasn't careful or gentle, but it wasn't half as bad as how *she* was."

"They fed on you on your way here?"

"Ziaul said that as long as I needed to bloodlet, I might as well not have it go to waste."

Tizzy breathed in deep and let it out slow to calm herself before sinking her teeth into the woman's flesh as gingerly as she could. She was waiting to hear one thing about Torah and Korrena that didn't make her hate them. Maybe, if she could hear *just one thing* that she liked, she wouldn't snap.

Supposedly, Torah had taken Aleth under his wing for years. That had been a comfort until the story Louvita had told her. Why would *anyone* be left in that man's care, and what had gone so wrong that Aleth couldn't forgive him? Her brother had the annoying ability to forgive just about anyone for anything. She truly believed that if Rhett ever had a change of heart and apologized, Aleth would grant him complete absolution without a second thought.

But not Torah. Not the man who had ditched him in the woods against a group of Hunters to save his own skin—allegedly. That would have been more than enough to earn an eternal grudge from her. In fact, it already had the second Louvita told her. But that wasn't it. It couldn't be. Something else had happened, and she was dying to find out and do something about it.

"My lady," Amaranth cleared her throat. "I feel better now."

Tizzy broke away from the wound and helped bandage her up. She surveyed the land from the balcony and saw that Ilisha's words had been true. The wind and rain had eased substantially, and the occasional rumble of thunder was a good ten seconds out when there was a flash in the sky.

"This is our chance," Tizzy said. "Are you ready?"

Amaranth belted a purse at her waist and held her shoulder bag close. "I am, my lady."

"Good. I'm probably getting us in over our heads."

The woman smiled, and they left unseen.

CHAPTER 20

HEARKEN MALICE

VAYVEN 7, 1144

Once again, Lazarus hadn't slept. He had never been one to sleep much anyway. There was always too much on his mind, and the voices of the Maw flooded his head constantly. But, for all his questionable choices, he was an incredibly willful creature and wouldn't succumb to insanity so easily.

The Maw didn't appreciate being regarded as a nuisance and snapped at the bandages as Lazarus tried to conceal it. The parasite called the Anzharian Maw was the key to the corpse-raising spells and rituals that necromancy was feared for across the world. He had gone beyond petty boneyard tricks and could siphon the life from the living to create with the dead. It was a pity no one could recognize what a creative art it really was.

He hadn't used the Maw since leaving the Fallarian Isle. The memory of the last life he'd drained, of the husk of a man he'd dumped into the seas at the docks, shook him to the core. The Maw would not let him forget. It was hungry. It wanted life, and it would gnaw away at his until it was fed.

Lazarus stepped out of his room as dawn rolled in. House Hallenar was quieter since the storm had lulled and Centa had arrived safely. Ashbel had a slew of ideas he wanted to present at the next Council meeting, so he expected Allanis to get it started within the next few hours. He had some time to himself to walk the halls and breathe before another chaotic day went into motion.

The routine he'd set for himself every morning thus far consisted of cider in the library with an Akashic Primer for light reading. He was on Primer XI, and it was full of wonderfully fresh information. The thought of applying new techniques was exciting, and his imagination whisked him away.

Until he glimpsed Adeska walking past the doorway. She shuffled down the hall, trying to keep her voice hushed as she guided Alor. Lazarus could feel the dread in his stomach like daggers of ice.

"You're going to meet your father, Alor!"

"I'm scared."

"Why are you scared, baby?"

"You were afraid to have me. You said he was mean."

Had she said that? Her heart ached. The boy may have misunderstood her words the way she had said them, but he understood their hidden meaning too well.

"Don't be afraid of him, Alor. He's not mean, but what I say to him will hurt his feelings, do you understand?" It was going to cut him deep and leave him empty.

"Is it my fault?"

"No. It's *my* fault," she said. "He'll be sad, and he'll be angry, but that's how people feel when someone hurts them."

Her one hope was that Centa would control his explosive emotions around a small child—it worked often enough with Mariette. She squeezed Alor's hand, and they walked the halls until they found Centa alone in a drawing room. Lazarus shadowed them.

Centa stared out a window that opened to a view of the Bogwood beyond the northern wall. The rain fell hard over the fire-colored forest, but the wind had died. A hammering—loud, constant, and even—filled the air. He didn't see Adeska come into the room and stand at the hearth, but he could feel her there.

"I'm so glad you made it," she said.

He turned to face her, and she ran to him. He knew she would tell him something awful. He knew that holding her now might never feel the same again, so he held her tight. He loved her and the four strands of gray he spotted in her golden blonde hair. He loved her and how soft and full she felt in his arms. Maybe nothing would change after all, he thought.

"It was rough."

"I'm so sorry I asked you to come out in that storm. I should have known it was coming."

He pressed his lips to hers to feel the spark for only a second. "It's okay. We made it. We're alright. There's nothing else to worry about."

She swallowed hard. "Centa." She held his hands and squeezed them. She suddenly didn't have the air in her chest to utter the next words.

"Maybe you don't have to tell me."

"No. If you had any idea what it was—" she choked down the tears, "—you wouldn't let me keep it from you anymore."

She stepped away from him to compose herself, feeling faint as she beckoned Alor over and held his hand. When the boy looked up at him, Centa felt the urge to run. Something in him knew he had to run.

"Centa." She wet her lips. "I want you to meet someone. This is Alor." She had to say the next part, but she couldn't. She watched him crouch down to make the boy's acquaintance and look him over.

Alor was terrified of the man. He wanted to go back to Rori's room and look at her books and pet Stormy. He didn't want to be with the people who were his parents, but there was nowhere else to go.

"Adeska." Centa looked up at her after staring into Alor's big brown eyes.

"He's your son."

Even through the confusion, he hurt. How could the boy be his son? How had he never met him before? Why was this happening *now*? He could see so much of himself in Alor's face.

"When?"

Adeska wrung her hands. "When you left to see your family, I was already pregnant. I didn't know until—" A trembling sigh left her. "Until Myentra. I found out after she took us. He'll be four soon."

Alor didn't know if he was supposed to say something. He didn't belong there. He wanted to run to Rori.

Centa stood up, his eyes glassy. "Why didn't you tell me? Where has he been all this time?" With each question, his heart grew hot. "How could you have kept him from me? I don't understand!"

A tear slipped down her cheek. "I gave birth while I was captive. When you and the others came for us, for me and Cato, I got scared." She looked away. "I thought... Centa, I thought you would see us and the baby, and you would think—" She swallowed hard. "I got scared and I gave him to Rori."

"You gave my son to Rori?" He was shaking.

"I'm sorry, Centa."

The sound of nothingness bore into him, a buzzing in his head that he knew wasn't there. He looked down at Alor and the way the boy returned his gaze like a stranger.

"I should have held him that day." He tried to reimagine the day he'd found them and what it might have been like if she had shown him the baby. How could she think he'd be angry? His mock emotions for the scene were a mix of heartbreak, hope, and relief. "I should have been holding him. And playing with him and feeding him and staying up with him at night when he couldn't sleep..."

"You still can! Nothing is over."

"You took all of that away from me, and you gave it to fucking Rori!"

She wanted to tell him to calm down, but what right did she have? He was already calmer than she expected. It made the guilt too much to bear.

When she looked down at Alor, the boy's eyes were shut tight.

"I'm not saying I made the right decision because I didn't." She sniffled. "But I know how you feel about Cato, and I know you know how Cato feels about me. I was afraid you would never trust either of us and you would never be able to see Alor as yours."

Centa's eyes were wet. A tear escaped his glare.

"Is this the part where you tell me the truth about Mariette?"

His voice was dark. This side of him was what she had been waiting for. It was going to happen. She wanted to be strong for it, but she didn't have one good choice to stand on for courage.

"It is," she told him. "Have you known she was his?"

Nothing hurt worse than hearing her admit it. It took the breath out of him. He looked away, fighting bitter tears that were ready to fall. Memories came back to him in flashes, looks from family and friends that he'd ignored, suspicions he'd declined to entertain. Every single time, he had been a joke. He'd been the fool.

"I didn't want to. I kept ignoring how obvious it seemed." Even though she was so much like him in his mannerisms and personality, the cold hard truth was that Mariette looked just like Cato. "I thought it was a coincidence or a strange twist of Akasha that made her look the way she does. I thought all of those things because I *trusted* you."

Adeska wiped her cheek. "I know, sweetheart, I—"

"I trusted you! I trusted both of you and you both fucking betrayed me!"

Lazarus stayed quiet in the hallway, praying that Adeska could temper Centa's rage, no matter how rightful it was. He listened for sounds from the boy, but Alor was still as stone and just as quiet.

"It had nothing to do with betraying you!" she shouted back. "We thought we were going to die! We were devastated and scared and—"

"And on your deathbed, you decided it would be a great comfort to be unfaithful!"

"On my *deathbed,* I just wanted someone to love me, and you weren't there!"

"Oh, but Cato was there," he sneered. "How long do you think he had been waiting for that moment? I bet he thought it was fucking sublime."

"Centa, please, stop it!"

Lazarus steadied his breathing and came into the room. In the beginning, their fight may have been productive, but that was over.

"You two need to take a break from this."

Centa's anger locked onto him lightning fast. "What the hell are you doing here?"

"This is between us!" Adeska hissed. "I had it under control!"

"You had it under control?" Centa snapped. "You can't get yourself under control; how can you possibly think you've got this in your hands?"

"Centa, I'm sorry! Please, I don't know what else I can do!"

"You can't do anything. You're a whore who hid my child from me!"

"That's enough!" Lazarus yelled. He stepped between them and Adeska backed away, sobbing. Centa stared him down.

"Stay out of this, necromancer."

It was barely more than a whisper, yet it contained every threat in his being. Lazarus couldn't walk away, not now. Centa was about to snap. He could see it in the man's eyes.

"I'll leave when you calm down."

Lazarus was so perfectly still about it, it made Centa even angrier. "This is none of your business. Get out! This is the last time I'm going to say it!"

"I'm not going to let you hurt her. Calm down and I'll leave."

He huffed. "Just because you know her, you think you know *us*? You think you know how we work?" He shoved Lazarus back just an inch. "You think you know what's best for us just because you're advising the queen? Now you're going to squeeze yourself into this too?"

Lazarus looked up at him and then back at her.

"Please, you two, stop this. Lazarus, just go!"

If she wanted him to leave, he should leave. That was a sound, rational thought. But the Maw's voice raced through his mind above all reason, and he could feel it snapping every time he looked at Centa.

"I'm not leaving."

"I hate this fucking family!"

The next time Centa shoved him, Lazarus felt his fire ignite and shoved back, but it was not a matched effort. Centa's own ignition was the uncontrollable fury of a wildfire as he balled up his fists and struck Lazarus in the face.

Adeska yelled something, and Alor hid behind her as the men fought. She was supposed to be the one fending him off, she thought. Like usual. She could handle Centa. This was her fight anyway, and as well-meaning as her brother had been, she wasn't going to let him rob her of the responsibility.

But Centa was no longer himself. He saw only red—it was in his body language, the way he moved without thought, with nothing but the pure desire to harm. Lazarus could feel it in every hit he took. The Maw wanted the rawness of it, it wanted the anguish and the rage, and Lazarus knew if he obliged, he could bring the man down.

The fight suddenly changed. Centa pulled a knife from his belt.

"Lazarus, get out!" Adeska pleaded. "You're not going to win when he's like this!"

Centa had nothing to say to either of them anymore. The knife trembled in his white-knuckled grasp. Lazarus stared it down, praying to be somewhere between logic and pure instinct when it came time to avoid the strike. The Maw knew what to do. It knew how to fix this; its hunger was practically screaming in his mind. Just take the glove off, just unwrap the bandage…

"Win? This isn't about winning something, Adeska! This was about protecting you!"

"Don't protect me from this. You weren't there to protect him from the things I've done!"

Centa sliced through the air with a ragged breath. Lazarus juked out of the way—he was getting too old for this. The Maw begged to be exposed. Begged to be fed. Everything could be over in seconds.

"How is what you did comparable to *this*?" he shouted at her.

Centa's voice barely sounded like his own. "You don't know us."

"It's not about all the bullshit we're dealing with now!" She couldn't breathe right. The air felt cold on her skin. The room started to spin. "I'm talking about when *I* get like that. Like him! You really think I'd put up with him if I weren't just as bad?"

The knife came at him again, and Lazarus fought to wrestle it away. Centa was strong and fierce, and the Maw's nagging was growing quieter as fear and rational thought made its way back to the surface.

"Adeska," he growled, struggling with Centa's force. "You couldn't possibly—"

Centa's elbow dug deep into his ribs, and he felt the air leave his lungs. He knew the knife was next.

"Centa, stop this!" She knew he couldn't hear her, but it didn't matter. She was putting an end to this. She rushed forward, thrusting herself between them, forcing them away. They stumbled back, and she spun around to Centa. He looked right through her.

"Centa."

It couldn't have ended any other way, she told herself. She had let it get too far out of hand. Still, she gasped and dug her nails into him when it happened.

"Adeska!"

He looked down and pulled the knife out of her stomach. She cried out, her fingers racing to the wound as the blade slipped out of her and red poured into her hands.

"No! Adeska, no, no, I'm sorry—"

Lazarus shoved him out of the way. "What did you do? What is the matter with you?"

Adeska took a step back, wobbling, and he caught her. She wanted to say something, maybe to tell Centa that she wasn't angry, but it hurt to think about that. She stared at him as Lazarus brought her to the ground and laid her on her back.

"You're going to be okay," he said. He could barely stay calm, himself. "You're going to be fine, okay?"

"Alor."

Both men followed her finger to the doorway as it dripped with blood. The boy stared at them, his eyes wide with horror. The very next second, he ran.

"Go after him!" Lazarus snapped.

"You think he's going to come to me after what I just did? I'm not going to chase him down with his mother's blood literally on my hands!"

"He's your son. Go fucking get him!"

"Stop it, please." Adeska reached out for them, her face ghostly white. "No more of this."

Lazarus swallowed hard as he studied the wound. Warm blood pumped freely onto his fingers as he pulled at the gash. It was deep. The knife had cut something it shouldn't have. "Get out, Centa. Just fucking get out."

"She's my wife. I can't just leave her!"

He glared up at the man, his rust-brown eyes hot and burning with tears. "I don't care. *Get out.*"

There was running in the hallway, and then Rori was in the room with them, screaming and crying and balling up her fists at Centa. She knew. She never even had to ask.

Lazarus pressed down on the wound, but blood still gushed. "Send Isa in here, then go find a Topaz Mage!"

"Wait, where's Alor?"

"Rori, now!"

She didn't hesitate another moment and vanished.

Centa was torn between finding his son and staying at Adeska's side, but neither choice seemed like the right one. He stared down at the red settling into the lines on his hands. Then he left.

***

The gates to Saunterton stood tall and regal in the murky night. Sinisia watched them grow as she neared them, the storm lanterns glowing in the distance. The sweat of anxiety was cold on her skin. She had never been so intimidated by her city before, and she had never failed her queen before, either.

Up until this incident, she had been Anavelia's pride and joy. She had been sent on countless missions, ones much more complicated and dangerous than the one she was on now. How would she explain failure to Anavelia? The guards welcomed her with a curt nod, and the gates closed behind her.

The city was alive at night as much as it was during the day, rain or shine. Storm lanterns lit up the streets, their light reflecting off the puddles and wet cobblestones. Entertainers still found ways to display their talents, and people still watched from the comfort of their hoods and cloaks. People dined on hot foods underneath garish awnings and danced like they hadn't a care in the world.

Sinisia wished they could know what she knew.

Her horse took her up to Lovell Keep and around the back to a small gate along the courtyard wall. It wasn't so late that her queen wouldn't be awake, but she hadn't sent a carrier to prepare her for her arrival. She hoped she wouldn't be interrupting anything important.

She slipped a steel key into the lock, the clinking of the tumblers drowned out by the thumping in her chest. She had most of her story lined up, but few people were as unpredictable as the Lovells, so saying she was ready for her confrontation was impossible. Her queen was easy to manipulate until she wasn't. Then she was sharp and ruthless.

The lock surrendered with a twist, and the gate opened. She left her horse just inside and continued to the Keep. The trail was paved with large stones that glittered with mica in the lantern light. It would take her to the servant quarters and then to the busy halls that would lead her to her queen.

Anavelia had been expecting her for a while now. Though not at that very second. She stood in her room in the glow of candles, staring out into the city through a partially drawn curtain. Orin stood behind her and brought his arm around with a glass of wine.

"My queen?"

"Thank you, my love." She plucked it from his fingers and took a delicate sip. Peppery and sweet.

"What is plaguing my queen this night?"

His warm hands were soothing on her bare shoulders. "Guilt," she told him. "I loved how complicated things were becoming at first. It was such a refreshing twist, and I wanted more and more, but now I'm afraid the novelty has all worn off, and I just feel *bad*."

"Is this about Queen Allanis?"

"That sweet girl is my friend. It would go against her wishes if she knew what I was up to. So shouldn't I stop?"

"My queen, what if the answers you found made you end your friendship with her?"

"You say that like this is some petty schoolyard matter, Orin. We're not children."

"Consider it, please. What if you learned something that changed how you feel about her?"

He had planted the seed. She couldn't stop thinking about it. What secrets could Allanis possibly have? The girl told her everything. She didn't seem like she was even capable of keeping secrets.

"You said her family pushed the brother away. Why? What does Aleth Hallenar know? And what's really happened now that he's come back?" Orin prompted.

He saw the goosebumps on her skin and wrapped his arms around her. She couldn't change her mind about this, not yet, he thought. It was too important.

"Maybe you're right. But what if you're not, and all this goes to hell? What if I betray my friend for nothing?"

"Then what could she really do about it? What would you really lose?"

"Orin, my *brother* is in Suradia. I could lose him. This is a pivotal moment for Allanis. What she's going through is going to change her, and I don't know if it will change her into the kind of person who would hurt him or not. I don't want to take that chance. He is outnumbered and more vulnerable than he realizes."

He couldn't blame her for her concerns. He wanted to ask how she would feel if Ashbel were here instead of there, but he knew better. The question would annoy and anger her. He gave up, for the time being, and let his hands slide down to her hips. He kissed her neck and breathed her in deep, finding the spot where she dabbed her perfume every day. Orange and cloves.

She turned around in his grasp and drew him in for a kiss. She had been advised so many times not to, but she couldn't help it. His lips were so soft, and he was just so *good* at it. She wished she loved him, and she wished he loved her. But she did what she always did— played pretend for a beautiful moment that felt real enough.

He caressed her cheek, and she ran her fingers through his hair and tugged. He started to work down her robe, but there was a knock at the door.

"Ignore it, my queen," he whispered, nibbling her shoulder.

She was very inclined to do so until she heard Sinisia announce herself.

"Your Grace, I have returned."

Orin stopped his conquest and swallowed hard. "I will leave you."

"I'm sorry, Orin."

He composed himself and let himself out, exchanging brief glances with Sinisia before disappearing down the halls.

Anavelia sighed. "Come in, Sinisia. Please report." She straightened out her robe and pulled it up over her shoulders.

Sinisia stepped in and closed the door. "Good evening, Your Grace."

Anavelia took a sip from her glass. "You took much longer than I anticipated."

"I am loathe to report my mission is not yet a success, Your Grace." She watched Anavelia's expression turn sour. "Finding him is not like finding others you've tasked me with. This is different. He knows what he's doing. He knows someone is looking, and he doesn't want to be found."

"I thought you had a lead."

"I did, Your Grace. I found them dead before they could give me the information. I'm sorry, Your Grace."

"They were dead?" Anavelia took another drink, letting the wine dance on her tongue as she thought. Sinisia would not meet her gaze, casting her eyes to the ground instead. Anavelia swallowed. "Are you saying Aleth killed them?"

Images of the torn and bloody bodies flashed in Sinisia's mind. "No, Your Grace. The evidence points to something different. It could still be tied to him, but I can't be sure." She breathed in deep. "It has not been a completely worthless excursion, however."

"Oh?"

"Your Grace, there are people trying very hard to kill him."

Anavelia swirled the wine in her glass. "Why?"

"I don't know. But it is no small matter, Your Grace. People want him dead—powerful people—and he has powerful allies."

Anavelia set the glass down on her dresser and stared back out to the city. "Does he know about you? Has he seen you?"

"No," she lied. "No, Your Grace."

"I'm disappointed in your failure, but this mission is done. I want you to stop pursuing him at once."

"Your Grace?"

"That's an order, Sinisia. I don't care who he is or what he knows. It's not worth it anymore."

"Yes. Of course."

"You are dismissed."

As soon as she left Anavelia's room, a sigh of relief overcame her, and she could breathe again. Her perfect record was tarnished, but she would accept it if it meant she didn't have to tangle with the Hunters' business a second time.

She was on her way to the cellar for a bottle of elvish wine when Orin whisked her into a parlor. She yanked her arm out of his grasp.

"What do you want?" she hissed. "This is over, Orin! Queen's orders!"

"We can't do that, Sinisia; you know that! You know what'll happen if we don't follow through." He waved his finger at her, and she bared her teeth.

"Nothing will happen to you, you ball of *slime*."

"But your father!"

"I'm starting to wonder if your word is worth a damn to King Mabus."

"It's worth more than *your* word, that's for sure. If you want him to set your father free, you can't quit now. Neither of us can!"

"But your idea ruined everything!" She shoved him into a table. "We never should have colluded with the Hunters, with that asshole Rhett Hallenar! Now he's helping them! He's going to give Cyrus all the information they're looking for. We're fucked!"

"What?"

"I was *right there*, Orin. The Hunters had them both, Aleth and Tizena. I was just steps away from them both. I was waiting for the right moment to free him and bring him here, but it was as I told you before. Rhett Hallenar was there. He had some sort of deal with the Hunters."

"That's what you said in your letter. What the hell kind of a deal? How did that even happen?"

"I don't know. I think when I entered the fray, they had been working together to find Aleth. When we found him, Rhett promised to turn him over to the Hunters after he had made his peace. So, I did what you said. I offered to pay Rhett double to have Aleth turned over to me instead. He agreed. The next thing I know, he's trying to kill him! They're brothers, Orin. This makes no sense!"

"He tried to kill him?"

"I don't know what's going on with that fucked-up family, but it's not worth it. Not anymore. I will find another way to free my father."

"No, Sinisia, please! This will work!" He grabbed her hand. "I need your help. I can't do this without you!"

"I don't care!" She snatched her hand away and rubbed her temples. "Orin, I need to think. Alright? I need to think. I cannot work with Rhett again. I don't care what he knows, and trust me, he may not know who the Protégé is, but there are so many other things he could tell us. And I don't care."

"Did you learn anything?"

She sighed and folded her arms. "Maybe. Rhett was with a Poison Mother, and they were working on something to sell to Cyrus. But the whole thing, Orin, the whole thing fell apart when a Greater Daemon showed up to save Aleth and Tizena."

"A *Greater Daemon*? Who are these people?"

"I don't know. You're the one holding so many cards, why don't you tell me? Does it have something to do with this Convent Aleth is in?"

"I thought it was just some stupid offshoot of an Emrin's place, like a, I don't know, a troubled boys' home! I didn't think there would be gods-damned daemons involved!"

"You probably didn't know Rhett Hallenar was a daemonologist, either."

"No, god's fuck! Sinisia, don't you see? This is a terrible time to quit! There is so much more to know!"

She shook her head. "No. Let me think, Orin! This is a bad idea. I can tell it's a bad idea. I don't know if I can handle this."

"But you can handle anything!"

"I used to think so. I'm a little smarter than that now. We're in over our heads, and Mabus and Cyrus probably are too. Give me some time. I need a next move if *forward* is the direction I'm headed."

"Fine. But you can't both serve your queen and free your father. You know it's come to that, don't you?"

"I do. Good night."

***

"You fucking *stabbed her*?"

Allanis's roar carried throughout the Council room. The flames from a row of pillar candles shied away from her. Centa flinched.

"I did. I'm sorry, Allanis. It was an accident."

"An accident!" She threw her hands out. "Yes, an accident, because you originally intended to stab my *brother*!"

He rubbed his face. "I did. I got carried away. I'm sorry."

"Thank the gods you're sorry. That'll help!"

They were in the room alone, but Titha and Jurdeir stood just outside the door. Centa was grateful there was no one else around to see his shame.

"Allanis, what can I do? Please, let me help. I love her; I didn't mean for this to happen."

"You can do nothing." She had never felt more fire behind her eyes in all her life. "Take him away."

Titha and Jurdeir came in, soundlessly, and Jurdeir pressed his hand against Centa's back.

"Take me away? Allanis, what are you doing?"

"You stabbed my sister! What the hell do you think I'm doing?"

"Allanis, please!"

Jurdeir cleared his throat. "Come on, just go. No one wants this to be ugly. Listen to your queen."

Centa shrugged away from his hand but relented and followed them down into the cells. He knew he would have made the exact same call if he had been in Allanis's position. She watched him go, breathing a tense sigh, rubbing her eyes. When she opened them a moment later, Lazarus stood before her.

"And *you*!" She picked up right where she had left off. "Nobody asked you to mediate! What were you thinking?"

He held his hands neatly at his back. "I'm sorry, Alli."

"I am so tired of this. Of that word! You think just because you say it, everything is going to magically get better and I'm going to just, what, absolve you of everything?"

"Certainly not, but I think it's better than if I neglected to say it at all."

"I rely on you, Lazarus!" The tears of frustration hadn't yet come, but they loomed. "I rely on you to be smart, to make good choices that I don't have to worry about. What is going on with you lately? Was I wrong to trust you? Should I have taken your grievous mistake into account in the beginning, after all?"

He knew what she meant by *grievous mistake*. He knew she was referring to his path into the Forbidden. He felt drained and heavy and wondered if the truth would set him free.

"I was afraid for her, Alli. What if I hadn't stepped in? Would it have been worse?"

"I don't know; I'm not Father! I didn't get his gift. None of us did!" She stared into the ceiling. "So, I am not going to play *what if*. The only game I'm going to play is *what happened*, and after what happened, I should dump you in a cell right next to Centa!"

"Alli!"

"Don't you 'Alli' me!" she snapped. "You know Centa can't stand you. You knew what effect you were going to have on the situation!" She breathed in, feeling her eyes water. "Gods, Lazarus, *why*?"

"A lapse in judgment." He swallowed hard. "I'm sorry. Alli, I'm not well."

She stilled. "What do you mean you're not well?"

He didn't know how to explain himself. What would she think if she knew about the Maw and what it was doing to him? He would lose her trust; there was no question about it. But she relied on him. She needed him to be trustworthy.

"Nevermind. Forget I said anything. I'll be fine. This will not happen again."

She watched him leave and hated every part of it. She had just scolded him, reprimanded him like a child. All her life, she had been the one making poor choices and getting lectured for it, often by him. She never thought she would see the day the roles were reversed.

Her next move was to make sure Centa was secure in his cell. Then she would finally have to do something about Meeka. Couldn't it all wait? She just wanted to lock herself in her room for the next three days and see if anything worked itself out.

But she didn't. She sat in silence for a few moments and then started for the cells. She would not be an absent queen. She would handle this situation, just as she would handle the rest of them.

The entrance to the cells did not announce itself. It was nothing more than a heavy wooden door with a short stairwell into darkness.

By the time she had arrived, a small audience waited for her, blocking her descent. Lora, Ravina, and Gavin.

"What is it, now?" Allanis asked with a sigh.

"Nothing at all, Your Grace," Gavin answered. "We are here to take Meeka to your interrogation chamber. You still wanted her questioned, right?"

She couldn't remember having told anyone. Wearily, she nodded. "Yes, take her to the room and have her wait for me. I'll question her alone in a moment."

The others started to move, heading off to the cells as instructed, but they halted at the sound of Ravina's voice.

"Your Grace, I have something to say."

"Not now, Ravina," Gavin whispered, reaching for her arm. "Now is not a good time. Now is a *terrible* time."

Lora narrowed her eyes. Whatever it was they wanted to talk about was news to her. Ravina only shook her head.

"Times will only be worse the longer I wait, Gavin."

"What is it?" Allanis asked, jutting out her jaw.

Ravina took a deep breath. "Your brother Lazarus. I don't think he should be on your Council, and I think you know that."

"My Council is my decision, and I think his advice is perfectly sound, Ravina. We should end this conversation here."

"I want to end it with one last thing." She looked over her shoulder, then turned her stare back on Allanis with something bordering on fear in her wide, dark eyes. "You're the queen. Suradia should come first, not your family. You don't have that luxury. The situation with Tizzy and Aleth is different, and we can't be sure yet of the outcome of our current course. But with Lazarus? Your Grace—"

"He's *fine!*" Allanis yelled. "He's stressed, as am I! Give him some time to rest, and he'll be just as competent as the rest of you! Now take Meeka to the interrogation room, *please*."

"Yes, Your Grace."

She turned and left, posture tight to hide any emotions writhing within. Gavin and Lora followed Ravina into the cells.

"What was that?" Lora hissed. "You're overstepping—"

"I'm trying to pull her focus back where it belongs!" Ravina snapped. "You all know I'm right!"

Down in the cells, Centa hadn't had but a moment to talk to Meeka before she was taken away. The girl was alarmed to see him locked away beside her and started to protest loudly and violently when Ravina tried to subdue her.

"Where's Jurdeir? This isn't in my job description," the woman grunted.

Lora replied with a snort. "At least you *have* a job description."

"Whatever you guys are gonna do—" Meeka sneered, writhing in Ravina's grasp, "—you can do right here! You can torture me and beat me—"

"For gods' sake, Meeka, just go with them!" Centa pleaded. "They're not going to torture you; this isn't that kind of place!"

"You also said your queen was friendly and agreeable, and she threw me in her dungeon the second she met me!"

Gavin cleared his throat. Belligerent teenage girls were in his wheelhouse.

"There's an awful lot happening now, Meeka." She stopped struggling with Ravina and stared at him. "More than the queen is used to. You have to remember that she isn't that much older than you are. She'll reward you with her trust if you cooperate and don't add anything else to her plate right now. That's the best you can hope for."

The girl huffed and gave up, but before they led her down the corridor to the chamber, she glared at Centa.

"If I had known it would turn out this way, I would have made you drop me in that well. I would have made you break my back and split my head open."

Then Centa was alone, alone with the worst of his thoughts. He wanted to see Adeska, to feel her strength in his hand, to whisper to her that she was strong. There was so much to be angry about, so much betrayal that still made it hard to breathe, but he had just validated every reason she had for betraying him in the first place.

"You know I had to do this, Centa."

Allanis stood over him on the other side of the bars.

"I know."

"Did she tell you everything?"

He swallowed hard. "She ruined our family, Allanis. How am I going to forgive her?"

"I'm not here to say that you should."

He looked up at her and was cold. She was not the same person he used to know.

"But I have to if we're ever going to move on from this. If we're ever going to go back home and raise Mariette and Alor when this is over—"

Allanis shook her head slowly, clenching her jaw. "No, Centa. Your vision is far too hopeful for what's transpired."

"What do you mean?"

"Sister?"

Rori came down into the cells with timid steps. Allanis did her best to stay composed, but annoyance was bleeding through her façade. "What is it?"

"It's the Topaz Mage we brought in from the Hesperan Hospice. He can't—well, he says it's not working. He can't heal her wound."

"Why not?"

"He doesn't know. It's just not responding to the magic. He has her stable for now, and Isa and I are making some salves, but it might not be enough."

"Do *you* know anything about this?"

When her gaze turned back to him, he saw nothing but hatred.

"It's why we quit the raids when we took down the Greater Daemon. The curse. When the hellfires were dragging him back into his realm, he cursed her. She would never feel the goddess Hespera's light again. So, after that, we *had* to settle down. The life we lived before was too dangerous, I didn't want her picking up the warrior mantle again, and since she wanted to start a family anyway, it worked out."

"You're saying you might have just killed her."

He closed his eyes. "Don't say that. She's going to be okay."

She turned away from him and headed for the interrogation chamber, wiping away little tears that she couldn't hold in anymore.

"Allanis!" Rori chased after her. "What should I—"

"Go away, Rori."

"But Alor! No one can find him."

She grumbled. "Then tell someone to keep looking! You and Isa stay with Adeska. Find someone to look for Alor. And tell everyone else to leave me alone!"

Rori didn't know what else to say and left her side. Allanis hated that she didn't have the patience enough to care that she'd hurt her sister's feelings. When she reached the iron-barred door to the interrogation chamber, her audience was back. Ravina, Gavin, and Lazarus. Her brother's addition shocked her so soon after hearing Ravina speak out.

"I told you I would speak to her alone," she told them. "You can all leave."

"Would you rather we wait for you in the Council room to discuss your findings?" Gavin asked.

"Oh." She rubbed her face. "Right. Yes, that makes sense. I'm sorry I'm so tense, everyone. I really am."

"Don't be, Your Grace—"

"Gavin, stop calling me that."

"*Allanis*. We can take over any of this if you'd like to rest. That's why you hired us. You don't have to do this alone."

"He's right," Lazarus said. The stare she gave him was dry and tired. "You should rest. I would like to conduct the questioning for you, Alli. That's why I came down here."

"You?" Something didn't feel right. "Are you sure? I get it. You think I don't know what I'm doing. You don't think I can—"

"That's not it." He sighed. "Believe me, you have shown us that you're capable. I don't want to take any credit away from you."

"Then what is this about?"

"You know what it's about."

She rolled her eyes. "Redemption. Of course. If that's what you want, fine. I'll be in the Council room when you're finished. Gather everyone on your way in, and we'll review."

She had been looking forward to talking with Meeka. It would've been a brief escape, to get to know her and what she'd been through. She was more interested in the girl and who she was than what secrets she was keeping. But this way, she might be able to use Lazarus's results to put Ravina at ease. She grumbled, remembering simpler times, and searched for Lora.

Lazarus waited before entering the room. Ravina and Gavin stood on either side of him.

"Are you sure you've got this?" Ravina asked. "This is more up my alley. I can get all the answers out of her without issue. You don't need to prove anything to your sister."

"I will lead the interrogation, Ravina. Everything will be fine. You two should get the others and wait in the Council room like she said."

Gavin met Ravina's eyes for a moment, sharing an uneasy glance. "You don't want us to wait out here for you? You're doing this completely alone? I hope you know what you're doing. We trust you; don't ruin that."

They left him, and he weighed in on the bad decisions he was going to make and prayed the outcome would be worth it. He didn't want to think about what would happen if it wasn't.

He entered the room and closed the door behind him. The space was cramped, telling him the generations of Byland rulers who'd lived in the manor before them did not typically take to torture. Though he did spy a floor grate in the center of the room. In the torchlight, Meeka sat with her hands chained to a desk, patient but with venom in her eyes.

"I thought I would be speaking to the queen!"

"The queen is busy. You will be speaking with me instead."

"I will do no such thing!"

There was a lump in his throat and a knot in his stomach. He could feel the Maw's appetite.

"Not even a little bit? We could talk about anything, Meeka. It doesn't have to be about the Hunters."

"I have been lied to over and over again, ever since I met those two assholes at Barton Hovel! I am done cooperating! Let the Hunters find me and kill me. I don't care!"

He couldn't believe she was so ready to die. "How old are you?"

"I'm ninety-seven, you prick!"

"The truth is in your best interest. The truth might convince me not to do what I'm about to."

"Can't be any worse than Phio wanting to shoot me. He didn't, by the way, but he did punch me! In the face! Can you believe a grown man hitting a sixteen-year-old girl in the face? You people are barbaric."

"You're only sixteen, and you want to die for these Hunters?"

"I would rather they kill me than for them to do what they would if they kept me alive. There's a fate much worse than death."

"You can't even begin to imagine what a fate worse than death is like, Meeka." He pulled off his gloves and stared into the Maw. "Maybe I should give you perspective. At your age, you should have an undying fire for life and a fear for its end."

She could see the needle-like teeth glistening in the light of the torches and her eyes went wide. "What is that?" Her stomach turned and crawled up her throat, and she thought she would be sick.

"Do you know what happens to people like me when we die?" he asked. "Botathora damns our souls, banishes us from rebirth, even from Eternal rest. We stay in the hellish fields of her Underworld, toiling away forever for our sins against life. And that's how it should be."

"You're a—" she panted, "—you're a n—"

"Yes, Meeka."

"A necromancer."

He showed her the Maw, the gaping pit of darkness with its rows of teeth all snapping at her. She backed away as far as the restraints would let her and retched.

"Does the queen know what you are?"

"The queen will have to deal with me in time. This is not about her, though. This is about you."

"I'll tell you everything!"

"I know you will. And you will spare no detail."

He clamped his hand over her mouth, and for a few short moments, she fought for her life. She was wild and thrashing and terrified, then seconds later she convulsed and slumped over. There was no better feeling than to be full of life—Lazarus could feel so much of hers suddenly coursing through him as the Maw twisted and flexed against her mouth. He was young and awake again, the pains of his body all but gone. Color washed away the drabness of his skin, and his muscles trembled with energy. And now he knew where she came from, could see the faces of the people who'd raised her. He saw Vandroya. There was more, but he had to pull himself away.

When he released the Maw, Meeka twitched and shuddered, barely able to sit upright. Several teeth had punctured the skin around her mouth. Blood ran down her lips.

"I took about ten years," he said. "I'm sorry. With food and rest, you'll feel better in a few days. But there are ten years you will never live to see."

He regretted it as soon as he left the room. As soon as he had taken the Maw away from her. Maybe he had regretted it even before that. Allanis would be furious and disappointed when she found out.

And she would find out eventually.

TO BE CONTINUED IN NIGHTWALKER BOOK TWO

ACKNOWLEDGEMENTS

I can't possibly wrap this up without some special acknowledgements! The people in my life have been very instrumental in making my debut novel happen.

Nightwalker is not the first book I've written, but it's definitely the first book I've ever published. Boy has it been a journey! Once I decided to take it seriously, I threw so much of myself into making it happen that the rest of my life kind of fell to the side. If I wasn't working my day job, sleeping, or eating, I was writing. So my first acknowledgement goes out to my husband, Jason. Sorry for neglecting you, but thank you for taking care of life for me while I worked to make this happen. It means the world to me.

But when did I wind up taking my writing *seriously*? My friends all knew I wrote and my co-workers had all seen me in the breakroom before, furiously scribbling away in notebooks. Well, slowly but surely some of these people started to get curious. I have a friend who lived in Germany at the time who I bought handmade candles from, Amanda A., and I remember talking to her about it and she wanted to read what I was working on… so I let her.

She loved it, and the confidence she gave me was really the turning point for Nightwalker. Without her words in the beginning, I probably would have lost interest in this project just like the rest, and would have let it collect dust for another few years before picking it up again.

Then I started letting other friends see it. Nicole and Artie, thank you two so much for your early interest! Artie has actually read more of Nightwalker than anyone. Every week she'd be asking for new chapters, so she's actually already 70,000 words into book two!

I have to give a shoutout to Kaley, too, of course, and to every brunch day spent cackling ideas at a volume only attainable through mimosas. Every time people eavesdrop and look over to us uncomfortably, it fills me with glee! Thank you for sticking it out since high school. You know these characters almost better than I do.

My mother! I cannot forget my mother and George. Absolutely not. The reason this book is available so early in the year at all is because they believed in me so much that they gave me the money to pay my editor, Amanda E. I was able to pay her in one fell swoop instead of in installments, and that got this project *hauling ass*. Mom, George, thank you for trusting me and believing in me.

Thank you Erin for being the early face of Tizzy! You rocked it. Thank you Analie for agreeing to be the early face of Aleth, even if we never made it happen. That's okay. You would have rocked it, too. *One day it will happen*!

And last but not least, to the ladies of the Nightwalker Book Club: Thank you! We only met a few times, but everything you had to say was so helpful. You guys are some of the greatest beta readers I could ask for. I got lucky to have you guys in my life, thank you so much.

ABOUT THE AUTHOR

AJ Gala first started writing in kindergarten when she learned the alphabet could be used to make words. Her first book was written in Crayola marker and featured a princess with *way* too many pets.

As she grew older, her stories matured and became long and epic. The world of Rosamar was born after she fell in love with tabletop roleplaying, and its where most of her half-finished novels take place.

When she isn't writing, she draws or explores Downtown Sacramento for vegetarian restaurants. Currently, she lives in Northern California with her husband, two cats, and an angry turtle.
Follow her on www.facebook.com/ajgalawrites
Instagram.com/aj_gala
www.aj-gala.com

ABOUT THE EDITOR

Amanda Edens is a developmental fiction editor who delights in guiding self-publishing fiction authors to unearthing the unseen potential of their work... and has been doing so since 2014. Amanda earned her Bachelor of Arts in Creative Writing after riding a Greyhound 2,000 miles from home to a school she had never seen and on little more than a childish whim. She brings that sense of adventure (plus all the cool stuff she studied about storytelling) to every project.

Amanda met her one true love in college, a fellow English major, and together they lead a cozy life with their dog Molly. He sells authentic rare books, and she tries not to stalk him at work or drool over all the priceless tomes. Amanda also collects typewriters. No lie.

As an editor, Amanda's goal isn't to intimidate writers, change their style, or make them feel bad about their art; it's to help them produce the best story possible and publish with confidence. If you need a partner in the editing process, visit amandaedens.com for more information.

Amanda also creates free resources for writers, including her podcast Ask Your Editor, a WRITING podcast for WRITERS, which can be found at askyoureditor.com. Visit facebook.com/askyoureditor for more information and access to additional free resources.

Editor's Note
AJ,

Thank you for bringing me along on this journey. I'm honored to have helped you bring your debut novel to print, and I'm excited to see how the rest of this story unfolds.

P.S. Sorry I didn't mention "my cute microwave" in the bio, but at least I included the dog.